Billy Budd & Typee

exhibit the genius of Melville as a writer and social critic, offering added insight into the philosophical and moral concerns revealed most notably in his great epic, *Moby Dick*.

Part memoir and part romance, **Typee** stems from the author's voyage on a whaling ship and his experiences among the natives of the Marquesas Islands. A popular success when it first appeared, it set the pattern for Melville's early series of South Sea adventures, including *Omoo, Redburn,* and *White-Jacket*.

Billy Budd is, on the surface, a simple story of a young sailor conscripted at sea from the *Rights-of-Man* to serve in the Royal Navy at the time of the Nore Mutiny in 1797. One of the greatest short stories of American literature, its central characters—Billy Budd, Captain Vere, John Claggart, master-of-arms, and "the Dansker"— have been acknowledged equal in depth and power to Ishmael and Captain Ahab in *Moby Dick*. A supremely dramatic work, it vigorously portrays Melville's concern for human justice and the morality of modern society.

BILLY BUDD
and
TYPEE

Herman Melville

Introduction by Maxwell Geismar

WASHINGTON SQUARE PRESS, INC. • NEW YORK

BILLY BUDD AND TYPEE

A *Washington Square Press* edition

1st printing.........................April, 1962
8th printing.......................March, 1968

L

Published by
Washington Square Press, Inc., 630 Fifth Avenue, New York, N.Y.

WASHINGTON SQUARE PRESS editions are distributed in the
U.S. by Simon & Schuster, Inc., 630 Fifth Avenue, New
York, N.Y. 10020 and in Canada by Simon & Schuster
of Canada, Ltd., Richmond Hill, Ontario, Canada.

CONTENTS

Billy Budd

AND

Typee

INTRODUCTION

THE PRESENT VOLUME contains the last short story or novel-ette, *Billy Budd*, which Melville wrote during the years 1888–1891, but which was published only in 1924. Melville's first novel, *Typee*, appeared in 1846. Between these two books there is, of course, the famous *Moby Dick*; and between them also is Melville's enigmatic, tormented and tragic career as one of the few great American fiction writers, immensely popular at the outset and gradually condemned to the neglect and oblivion that extended for a quarter of a century after his death.

During this period his books were not reprinted; his name was stricken from that illustrious roster of the New England transcendentalists, which included Thoreau, Emerson and Hawthorne. Melville, who belonged to them in one sense surely, was as mute as Walt Whitman, who had started with Emerson's glowing approval. That is to say, our primary novelist and our prime poet of the period—the writers who formed the real bridge between the two great American liter-ary revivals—were virtually taboo. Why? In Melville's case, at least, it is the purpose of this Introduction to suggest a few possible reasons.

2

Coming from a respectable New York family of Dutch and English stock, but one that the father's bankruptcy and death had brought into poverty and disrepute, Melville went to sea at nineteen. He never forgot this wealth of physical and material experience, which was denied to the more scholarly or reclusive New Englanders. This was in 1838. Three years later he shipped aboard the *Acushnet* for a South Sea whaling cruise that was to last four years. It was during this cruise that, with the "Toby" of *Typee,* he deserted the whaler at Nukuheva in the Marquesas Islands and established his somewhat enforced residence among the "savage" and cannibalistic Typees (or Taipis, in modern usage). From this experience came the first modern novel of the South Seas, immensely popular in its own day and still remarkably fresh, entertaining and acute.

Right here, indeed, occurred Melville's deep and almost traumatic split from the central values of that western European and American "civilization," which just then in the mid-nineteenth century saw itself destined for endless aeons of "progress." How sharply, clearly, definitively *Typee* strikes this note, which becomes the central Melvillian theme of primitive nature *versus society*. For Taipian culture was the original Eden—or the pre-Edenite community of love and friendship and joy—which civilization had remembered, yearned for and could never achieve. For these "frightful savages" had turned out to be the most gentle, considerate, affectionate, happy, natural and satisfying people. Their "social order" was splendidly regulated to afford the minimum of social pressure. There was no law to constrain their behavior; no police force, no crime. There was no real estate, no stress on private property; yet each family had its own home, its own possessions—and there were no thieves and no padlocks in Typee. There was no austere or repressive theology. The Taipis simply scolded—or sometimes abused—their heathen gods when things did not go right, but things always seemed to go right. Each wife had two husbands, of course, or sometimes three; but there was no concept of romantic love, no sexual feuds, no crimes of passion—and no marriage contract. The Taipis worshiped physical beauty and health; they spent much time adorning and anointing their bodies. They were very careful in war (which was mostly sham) not to mutilate themselves; the men were handsome, the women beautiful beyond compare. Their vision of heaven was simply more breadfruit, even more gaiety and pleasure, still more beautiful women—and they were in no hurry to get there. Were they, in short, the most accomplished and urbane race of people in the South Seas—in the whole world perhaps? Still the novel's hero had to leave them. He was branded by the mark of Adam, the knowledge of evil, sin and corruption. He himself was the product and the victim of centuries of civilization. He could not remain, nor could he ever (except in his memory, in his values, in his later judgments) return to Typee.

And meanwhile what happened to Melville himself? *Typee* was part of a whole cluster of early works. *Omoo* (1847), *Redburn* (1849) and *White-Jacket* (1850) all contributed to his early popular fame. *Moby Dick* (1851) was, as we know now, the masterpiece, but in its own time it was attacked and criticized for its uncouth form, its verbosity, its irrelevancies, its extravagant emotions centered around the cruise of an ordinary whaling ship—and perhaps for other things not entirely mentionable to the increasingly staid and proper literary conscience of New England and New York. By this time Melville had married the daughter of an eminent Boston judge; he had settled down to that respectable domestic life that at heart he abhorred. For a time he lived near Pittsfield, Massachusetts, next to his intimate friend and literary idol, Hawthorne, who had both secret and expressed reservations as to Melville and Melville's work. And *Pierre,* in 1852, suddenly completed Melville's downfall.

This was a curious and often distressing romance-fantasy of incest and moral disintegration, in which Melville was nevertheless trying to penetrate his own (or man's) deepest buried nature and hidden, primitive affections—and it received even more critical abuse for its lack of form and for its revelation of things better left unsaid and unknown. During the writing of *Moby Dick*, Melville was filled with premonitions of his own decline and disintegration. Was *Pierre* simply the record of this, or even a deliberate attempt, as it were, at literary suicide? He published, at any rate, one more volume of fine short stories, *The Piazza Tales*, in 1856. The two remaining novels were inferior; his sales were poor; his books were not reprinted; he took to writing indifferent poetry, which he published at his own, or his uncle's, expense. For over thirty years he worked as a customs inspector in New York, as a forgotten and unknown, if not dishonored, man. Until, that is, the three last years of his life when he wrote *Billy Budd*, one of the great short stories of the world. While I was reading it over, I felt that it was just about the best short story ever written.

3

Had Melville, too, insulted God and drowned? which is the prevailing interpretation of the monomaniacal sea captain Ahab in *Moby Dick*. Or had he, in reality, thrown his own species of thunderbolt at New England's puritanical God of wrath, who just then controlled the literary conscience (and press) of the country? Was *Pierre* really the record of a disintegrating personality, brought by its own conflicts to the edge of insanity; or was it another part, ineptly concealed and disguised to the point of absurdity, of Melville's consistent attempts to record the truth of man's nature in a society which increasingly ignored and inhibited the primary and plenary level of existence? And does *Billy Budd* itself record the "truce," the "peace" and the final "reconciliation" of Melville, with both a hostile universe, which is the embodiment of evil, and a hostile God, who is the embodiment of perhaps strange, but necessary, justice?

These are the questions that still prevail among Melville's readers; and this is the usual interpretation of his last story. Yet *Typee* hardly suggests this conclusion, just as *Moby Dick* hardly confirms it. Ahab's real crime is that he is the prophetic embodiment of western or modern man, a mad dictator in a doomed ship (or society of mankind), who imposes his inflamed egotism upon the natural order of things. The white whale upon whom Ahab seeks revenge for his castrated leg is neither good nor evil. These concepts are man-made and like all of man's morality do not explain the real universe. In point of fact, the whales in *Moby Dick* are always viewed as the symbol of life eternal—ancient, beautiful, nourishing and, in their own orbit, even described as playful and affectionate.

Ahab's crime, as the leader of modern society, is that he has attempted to destroy life itself; just as Melville always viewed society as the destroyer of Taipian life. And for *this* Ahab is thrown back into the ancient, anonymous sea of life. Yes, I know there are other parallel or even contrasting interpretations here. Like any major writer Melville wrote on different levels; and in *Moby Dick* Ahab's personal wound and defiance of God-the-Father is the psychological counterpoint, as it were, to the novel's true metaphysical moral. But then suppose that God-the-Father turns out to be a woman— the true matriarchal goddess of Polynesian culture—and that *She* (embodied in the mammal whales, the womblike ocean) is the true, the original, ancient and enduring source of life?

Such, at any rate, appears to me closer to Melville's whole intent as an artist than that specious diabolism or demonism so freely attributed to him by critics of today's more desperate age. Life was not evil to him—generous, abundant and confiding spirit that he was—nor certainly was the nature that he expounded in *Typee*. Nor was evil in his own mind— except as he was typical of the whole mind of western man whose natural playfulness, good nature, curiosity and desire were even in the mid-nineteenth century being throttled down, held under, obliterated by so-called civilization to reappear only as vice and crime and sin, and all sorts of truly savage and barbaric, murderous and frustrated forms of cruelty. And such is the real moral of *Billy Budd*—embodied as it is in a perfect little gem of storytelling.

The late fable is almost a play, where every word, every accent, every gesture has its part in the narrative weight— as if Melville, too, were atoning, by his perfect craft, for his earlier looseness and carelessness of form, but not indeed atoning or repenting for any of his earlier convictions. For just what kind of reconciliation—with God, society or man—

did the story describe? The year 1797, to which the action of *Billy Budd* belonged, had witnessed all the horrors of the French Revolution, and the subsequent Nore Mutiny in the English navy itself. But Billy, the best sailor on a reputable English merchantman, the "jewel" of the crew, the "peace-maker," the handsome boy, still waves good-by to the *Rights-of-Man* (the name of his ship) when he is conscripted on the high seas for service on the H.M.S. *Indomitable*.

Isn't this hero simply Melville's last and farewell portrait of Taipian nature—of the natural man—healthy, open, handsome, good-humored, generous, confiding, close to the animal level of natural functioning, and quite unaware of sin or evil and all other such civilizational concepts. At least Billy, who soon is called "Baby" Budd and is the favorite among even the hard-bitten sailors of a British man-of-war, has all the pre-Adamic and pre-Edenite virtues. He is "a sort of up-right barbarian," an uncorrupted pagan hero. Like the great heroes of myth, too, he is illegitimate and doesn't know his own parents, who are presumably of noble birth. How Melville stresses "these primitive qualities" in "our Handsome Sailor," and how he creates the illusion in the story of an almost improbable innocence—improbable, that is, to our sophistication. Even Billy's stutter, which according to Melville is designed to make him real, which shows Satan's contribution to his angelic constitution—this gift from the "envious Marplot of Eden"—is certainly not to be viewed in the Freudian sense of "repressed hostility." Nonsense! If anything, it is the mark of animal nature, which doesn't really *need* speech to express itself, which has not yet reached the level of speech; or of man's higher intelligence, which has brought down upon him all of his civilizational discontents.

But Billy's story is also the parable of innocence without experience or that "defensive ugliness," which Melville noted as being so necessary after the fall of man; or of natural innocence defeated by evil intellect. And here the story swings into a discursive passage on naval history, on Nelson and Trafalgar and the "iron admirals" of the great sailing ships; on the "proselyting armies" of the French Directory and their impact on the British sailors; on the secret or carefully repressed accounts of the mutinies in the British navy itself; on all the "glories" of naval war—and all the undertones of mass rebellion. These are the two poles of *Billy Budd;* and if this divergence is a literary sin, as Melville said, it has at least "that pleasure which is wickedly said to be in sinning." The narrative prose of this tale is so dense, so beautiful, precisely because it is a mixture of history and myth behind the human drama; not to mention the other levels of radical social criticism, of philosophy or metaphysics, of cultural and religious speculation.

Billy is the victim of this historical climate; just as Captain the Honorable Edward Fairfax Vere is the typical product of such a period. "So it was that for a time on more than one quarterdeck," Melville added, "anxiety did exist." Starry Vere's name, given to him by a favorite kinsman, Lord Denton, comes straight out of a seventeenth-century poem by Andrew Marvell; just as, throughout the tale, the Melvillian wealth of imagery ranges from the pagan myths to Hebrew scripture to the arrival of the Siamese twins in the United States—and more, as you will see. What a tremendous body of knowledge and learning went into this epic of a simple sailor! Now Vere is perhaps one of the best, or most typical, examples of an honorable English aristocrat doing his duty to his King, his country and his ship. His opposition to the French Revolutionary period was not even based on the fact of his belonging to the "privileged classes," but because he believed, quite "disinterestedly," that the theories of those social innovators were "incapable of embodiment in lasting institutions, and at war with the peace of the world and the true welfare of mankind."

Captain Vere is an honorable man of law and order. But the French Revolution had created the same atmosphere of hysteria in the England of that period as the Russian Revolution did in mid-twentieth-century America.

And what shall we say of the third member of this ill-fated male trinity on board the H.M.S. *Indomitable?* Around John Claggart, master-at-arms, Melville brought together another fascinating cluster of sea facts—just as *Moby Dick* gives the whole economic base of the whaling industry and of the floating whale-oil factories. Was Claggart, who is also compared to the Rev. Dr. Titus Oates, a natural villain with something "defective or abnormal in the constitution and blood"? Was he simply the evil principle in nature itself, compared with Billy's primary and absolute goodness? This would please those critics who see Melville as a native American Dostoevsky in the transcendentalist epoch of universal sweetness and light. And Melville was too much of a realist not to acknowledge that evil shapes and forms exist in nature itself. He was actually our first great and primary realist, as well as our first great naturalist (if we ignore the doctrinaire historians of our literary movements). He was the real link between the transcendentalists and Theodore Dreiser, who in turn, oddly enough, was something of a transcendentalist at heart.

Melville indeed describes Claggart's "ferreting genius," his "ingratiating deference," his "austere patriotism," or pretense of patriotism, in terms of that "natural depravity" that was recognized both in the Bible and in Plato. This maritime chief of police is among those who have "a mania in the brain or rabies of the heart." He is the serpent in Billy's Edenite garden of life and a brilliant portrait in the story. The discussion of his evil is a marvelous section again of philosophy, metaphysics, religion, social history and economic conditions. And Melville mentions almost every possible reason for Claggart's "unreasoning" hatred of Billy except the one that is so clearly revealed in the narrative itself. That Claggart "might have been" (or actually is) in love with Billy; that he has repressed this passion, being above all a man of "reason"; and that he is insanely jealous of Billy's good looks, good humor and general popularity. But Claggart's hatred is repressed too. He goes about his secret persecution of the Handsome Sailor altogether logically and "reasonably."

Those are the true madmen, according to Melville, who give every appearance of decency, respectability, sobriety, common sense and calm judgment; their emotions being completely controlled by the mind. Yes, Claggart was "the direct reverse of a saint," but also— "To pass from a normal nature to him one must cross 'the deadly space between.' " Neither did he typify Melville's view that nature itself was evil—far from it. Perhaps it was just *because* he did not permit his own natural functioning, whatever it was, to operate that he became all repression, all intellect, all evil. Claggart's depravity partook nothing "of the sordid or sensual," so Melville added, and for such notable instances of vice, "since these have no vulgar alloy of the brute in them, but invariably are dominated by intellectuality, one must go elsewhere. Civilization, especially if of the austerer sort, is auspicious to it." Now is the argument a little clearer? Claggart is in actuality a later, a final portrait of Ahab and just as monomaniacal or even more dangerous because his madness is held under tighter control. And he is pursuing not a whale but a doe, as it were—and he, in a manner, succeeds. Billy Budd is all innocent life; and Claggart is again Melville's concept, not indeed of natural evil, but of the civilized western man who had been cut off from all the natural impulses, who has now become an actual criminal.

Though space is short, I cannot omit a reference to "the Dansker" in *Billy Budd*—another of the marvelous profiles of seafaring men in the story. There are the meetings of "the young Achilles" and the "sea Chiron," who knows the truth of what is happening, but has reached "that bitter prudence which never interferes in aught and never gives advice." Then there is the dramatic episode that hinges on "a man-of-war's-man's spilled soup," that "greasy fluid" that Claggart believes Billy to have deliberately let drop in his path. "Passion, and passion in its profoundest, is not a thing demanding a palatial stage whereon to play its part," said Melville. "Down among the groundlings, among the beggars and rakers of the garbage, profound passion is enacted. And the circumstances that provoke it, however trivial or mean, are no measure of its power." And wasn't Melville here, quite like Whitman, sounding the manifesto of the new literature of democracy? Wasn't he the other prime poet of this new literature—with his passionate groundlings, his fateful cup of greasy soup—who in fact prophesied the advent of the American realists and naturalists of the twentieth century?

But then the other, the "aristocratic principle" of our native literature, so widely acclaimed in the last decade, is probably confined to only one American fiction-writer—Henry James. There is the confrontation scene in *Billy Budd* where Claggart finally traduces the Handsome Sailor to Captain Vere (the charge is fomenting mutiny and treason) and the skeptical captain orders Billy to face his enemy. Scenting this mysterious danger, Billy has been behaving, Melville says, "like a young horse fresh from the pasture suddenly inhaling a vile whiff from some chemical factory." (And now is it clear where this artist stood as to nature and society, as to animal health and social "progress"?) Billy's seaborne innocence has the fatal lack of the landsman's finesse, we are told in traversing that "oblique, tedious, barren game hardly worth that poor candle burnt out in playing it." There is also the "glittering dental satire" of Claggart's, shortly before he repeats the same false accusation to Billy's face, and the sailor, overcome by anger and despair, unable to speak (his stutter betrays him), strikes Claggart "full upon the forehead" and kills him.

Billy's reaction is instinctive; and he strikes just at that "center of reason" that has condemned his primitive virtue to shame and dishonor. Again Melville repeats this theme when he remarks that the Handsome Sailor, Baby Budd, might have posed for "Adam before the fall." This blow upon the forehead is the response of "betrayed nature," as it were, to the "superior knowledge" of evil. But why does Captain Vere suddenly change (like the moon emerging from eclipse with "another aspect") from a beneficent father-image to the stern law-giver? He knows that Billy is "right," that Claggart is a "dead serpent" who has corrupted Adam with false knowledge; that this is also the "divine judgment on Ananias," who lied not to men but to God, and was struck down by an angel of God. "Yet the angel must hang!"

Why? And which God in fact are we dealing with? Does Vere represent the Hebraic God of justice (also wrath) whose advent signified the taming of pagan nature? Or is it that dour and puritanical figurehead of New England's Calvinism for whom life was *only* sin and depravity? Or is there still another aspect of "God" involved here? Why *does* Vere change so suddenly; and then demand Billy's punishment so intensely, so relentlessly, when he might have waited to present the case to the admirality—when his own subordinate officers are reluctant to accede to his command of hanging the Handsome Sailor?

We realize that this honorable sea captain has in turn become obsessed with the necessity of Billy's death; or that he is the "sudden victim of aberration," as the ship's surgeon thinks about Vere's own quest of vengeance and punishment. Is this the treacherous nature of all fathers, as Melville might have opined, and of all father-Gods too, standing so righteously for law and order and all those repressive institutions of society? For there is no doubt that deep within his own heart, Captain Vere is afraid of incipient mutiny on the H.M.S. *Indomitable*. He too, represents, at base, the anxiety and the hysteria of his age before the rising tide of revolutionary reforms. Billy must be made an example of the warship's relentless discipline—just or not—but immediately, at once, publicly. The ship's crew, as Vere says, must realize this; or else they might think that authority was indecisive, was trembling. According to "natural justice," Billy is "innocent before God," Vere even declares. But *their* allegiance is not to nature, but to the King—and the King has declared a state of Martial Law—the law of the Mutiny Act itself.

Thus Billy is the victim not only of the vicious and "rational" Claggart, but of civilized justice too, which includes, which bends down before, the social pressures of the time. Is this the famous Melvillian acquiescence to God and society —the final submission of this rebellious and purehearted spirit to the forces of law, justice, order and "social reality"? (Isn't there also, in this parable of the pagan sailor subjected to such mysterious persecution and sudden death, some identification with Melville himself, some reflection of his own mysteriously thwarted literary career?) No, the acquiescence, the submission, the resignation of the artist in *Billy Budd* were those only of a Greek tragedy; and if the story's hero goes to his death so stoically, so heroically, to the point of saluting Captain Vere, it is the last mark of Billy's sublime nature, rather than of Melville's approval of Vere's possessed behavior. But Billy, as the embodiment of primary and pagan human nature, *had* to die before the advance of society and the path of civilizational "progress." Just as the beautiful, free, joyous natural society of Typee had to be corrupted and condemned —and finally obliterated—by the combined force of the whaling ships and the missionaries; by the brute force of economics, and the rationalizing facade of religion.

There is the ambiguous false ending of *Billy Budd,* where Melville does seem to accept the sailor's death, as "the way things are." But the real moral of the fable comes after and transcends the pretended moral of mutiny and martial law. (This story is no *Caine Mutiny*; just as *Typee* had a far different conclusion from that in James Michener's *Hawaii.*) There is the sudden ironical reference to the battle lanterns that hang over Billy's chained, imprisoned and doomed body. "Fed with the oil supplied by the war-contractors (whose gains, honest or otherwise, are in every land an anticipated portion of the harvest of death), with flickering splashes of dirty yellow light they pollute the pale moonshine . . ." There is the description of the ship's chaplain endeavoring vainly to convert Billy's pagan soul. "Not that, like children, Billy was incapable of conceiving what death really is. No, but he was wholly without irrational fear of it, a fear more prevalent in highly civilized communities than those so-called barbarous ones which in all respects stand nearer to unadulterate nature."

"A barbarian Billy radically was," Melville affirmed once more at the story's end. And a barbarian, in this sense, Melville remained, without change, without renunciation, without atonement and without compromise, to the end of his own life. Of course Billy, unlike Melville, listened politely to the formal theological doctrine of his period. "And this sailor way of taking clerical discourse is not wholly unlike the way in which the pioneer of Christianity full of transcendent miracles was received long ago on tropic isles by any superior *savage* so called—a Tahitian, say of Captain Cook's time or shortly after that time." Yes, that natural paradise of Typee still bloomed in Melville's memories of life and man. And then, just what is the purpose of a chaplain aboard a man-of-war? "Bluntly put, a chaplain is the minister of the Prince of Peace serving in the host of the god of war—Mars. . . . Why then is he there? Because he indirectly subserves the purpose attested by the cannon; because, too, he lends the sanction of the religion of the meek to that which practically is the abrogation of everything but brute force."

Was *that* the end product of the long centuries of man's heartbreaking struggle for social evolution? Well, at least Melville still thought so toward the close of the nineteenth century; and perhaps even more strongly, if more subtly, in *Billy Budd* than in *Moby Dick*. Nowhere had he changed his earliest, his primary, his deepest convictions as an artist—those radical convictions that made him the great and original American artist that he was. Here was the final protest; but where was that final resignation? Beneath the irony and humor in the marvelous prose texture of the tale, *Billy Budd* is a remarkable example of tragic realism; but it was no example of false resignation to the ways of the world, or of Melville's moral conversion, or his recanting. He was no Claggart, no false informer as to the real conditions of man's life and destiny.

There is that final brilliant touch in *Billy Budd* of the British navy's official account of the Handsome Sailor's death. (So much for the free press.) The royal British blue-jackets had another version of the affair in which Baby Budd was the lamb of God, the scapegoat upon whose beautiful pagan head (and broken neck) were vented all the discontents of civilization, in its martial phase.

A note on method: This "new" or at least different approach, as I believe, to Billy Budd *is based on a fusion of Freudian and Reichian concepts of culture and personality, plus the cultural critique of Otto Rank, as recently projected and developed by our own brilliant young psycho-cultural historian and critic, Jack Jones. That Melville's work contained such psychological and civilizational insights, quite intuitively and altogether prophetically, is nothing new, of course, in the chronicle of major artists.*

—MAXWELL GEISMAR

Billy Budd

BILLY BUDD

THE YEAR 1797, the year of this narrative, belongs to a period which, as every thinker now feels, involved a crisis for Christendom not exceeded in its undetermined momentousness at the time by any other era whereof there is record. The opening proposition made by the Spirit of that Age involved rectification of the Old World's hereditary wrongs. In France, to some extent, this was bloodily effected. But what then? Straightway the Revolution itself became a wrongdoer, one more oppressive than the kings. Under Napoleon it enthroned upstart kings, and initiated that prolonged agony of continual war whose final throe was Waterloo. During those years not the wisest could have foreseen that the outcome of all would be what to some thinkers apparently it has since turned out to be—a political advance along nearly the whole line for Europeans.

Now, as elsewhere hinted, it was something caught from the Revolutionary Spirit that at Spithead emboldened the man-of-war's men to rise against real abuses, long-standing ones, and afterwards at the Nore to make inordinate and aggressive demands—successful resistance to which was confirmed only when the ringleaders were hung for an admonitory spectacle to the anchored fleet. Yet in a way analogous to the operation of the Revolution at large—the Great Mutiny, though by Englishmen naturally deemed monstrous at the time, doubtless gave the first latent prompting to most important reforms in the British navy.

The manuscript title is "Billy Budd / Sailor / (an inside narrative)"; and beneath it appears the following: "Dedicated to Jack Chase, Englishman, wherever that great heart may now be here on earth or harbored in paradise. Captain of the maintop in the year 1843 in the U.S. frigate *United States*."

This Preface appeared in the first publication of this work, under the title *Billy Budd, Foretopman*, in 1924.

3

I

IN THE TIME before steamships, or then more frequently than now, a stroller along the docks of any considerable seaport would occasionally have his attention arrested by a group of bronzed mariners, man-of-war's men or merchant-sailors in holiday attire ashore on liberty. In certain instances they would flank, or, like a bodyguard quite surround some superior figure of their own class, moving along with them like Aldebaran[1] among the lesser lights of his constellation. That signal object was the "Handsome Sailor" of the less prosaic time alike of the military and merchant navies. With no perceptible trace of the vainglorious about him, rather with the off-hand unaffectedness of natural regality, he seemed to accept the spontaneous homage of his shipmates. A somewhat remarkable instance recurs to me. In Liverpool, now half a century ago I saw under the shadow of the great dingy street-wall of Prince's Dock (an obstruction long since removed) a common sailor, so intensely black that he must needs have been a native African of the unadulterate blood of Ham.[2] A symmetric figure much above the average height. The two ends of a gay silk handkerchief thrown loose about the neck danced upon the displayed ebony of his chest; in his ears were big hoops of gold, and a Scotch Highland bonnet with a tartan band set off his shapely head.

It was a hot noon in July; and his face, lustrous with perspiration, beamed with barbaric good humor. In jovial sallies right and left, his white teeth flashing into view, he rollicked

---

1 This large red star was regarded by the ancients as the "eye" of the Bull, the constellation Taurus.

2 In popular superstition, the Negroes, because Noah laid the curse of servitude upon the descendants of his youngest son, Ham, who mocked him; *cf.* Genesis ix: 22–25.

along, the center of a company of his shipmates. These were made up of such an assortment of tribes and complexions as would have well fitted them to be marched up by Anacharsis Cloots[3] before the bar of the first French Assembly as representatives of the human race. At each spontaneous tribute rendered by the wayfarers to this black pagod of a fellow— the tribute of a pause and stare, and less frequent an exclamation—the motley retinue showed that they took that sort of pride in the evoker of it which the Assyrian priests doubtless showed for their grand sculptured bull when the faithful prostrated themselves.

To return.

If in some cases a bit of a nautical Murat[4] in setting forth his person ashore, the handsome sailor of the period in question evinced nothing of the dandified Billy-be-Damn, an amusing character all but extinct now, but occasionally to be encountered, and in a form yet more amusing than the original, at the tiller of the boats on the tempestuous Erie Canal or, more likely, vaporing in the groggeries along the towpath. Invariably a proficient in his perilous calling, he was also more or less of a mighty boxer or wrestler. It was strength and beauty. Tales of his prowess were recited. Ashore he was the champion; afloat the spokesman; on every suitable occasion always foremost. Close-reefing topsails in a gale, there he was, astride the weather yardarm end, foot in the Flemish horse as "stirrup," both hands tugging at the "earring" as at a bridle, in very much the attitude of young Alexander curbing the fiery Bucephalus.[5] A superb figure, tossed up as by the horns of Taurus against the thunderous sky, cheerily hallooing to the strenuous file along the spar.

The moral nature was seldom out of keeping with the physical make. Indeed, except as toned by the former, the

---

3 Carlyle, in his *French Revolution* (1837), popularized Cloots's escapade, as here described, by which he claimed the democratic privileges of the Assembly for this group representing various countries and stations.

4 Joachim Murat (1767?–1815); French military adventurer, and conspirator with Napoleon. As King of Naples he was called "the Dandy King" for his foppishness.

5 The famous war horse of Alexander the Great (356–323 B.C.)

comeliness and power, always attractive in masculine conjunction, hardly could have drawn the sort of honest homage the Handsome Sailor in some examples received from his less gifted associates.

Such a cynosure, at least in aspect, and something such too in nature, though with important variations made apparent as the story proceeds, was welkin-eyed Billy Budd, or Baby Budd as more familiarly under circumstances hereafter to be given he at last came to be called, aged twenty-one, a foretopman of the British fleet toward the close of the last decade of the eighteenth century. It was not very long prior to the time of the narration that follows that he had entered the King's service, having been impressed[6] on the Narrow Seas from a homeward-bound English merchantman into a seventy-four[8] outward-bound, H.M.S. *Indomitable;* which ship, as was not unusual in those hurried days having been obliged to put to sea short of her proper complement of men. Plump upon Billy at first sight in the gangway the boarding officer Lieutenant Ratcliffe pounced, even before the merchantman's crew was formally mustered on the quarterdeck for his deliberate inspection. And him only he elected. For whether it was because the other men when ranged before him showed to ill advantage after Billy, or whether he had some scruples in view of the merchantman being rather shorthanded, however it might be, the officer contented himself with his first spontaneous choice. To the surprise of the ship's company, though much to the lieutenant's satisfaction Billy made no demur. But, indeed, any demur would have been as idle as the protest of a goldfinch popped into a cage.

Noting this uncomplaining acquiescence, all but cheerful one might say, the shipmates turned a surprised glance of silent reproach at the sailor. The shipmaster was one of those worthy mortals found in every vocation even the humbler ones—the sort of person whom everybody agrees in calling

---

6 Laws covering British naval recruitment then permitted commanders to complete their crews by forcing, or "impressing," merchant sailors, on land or sea, into service.

7 *I.e.,* a ship carrying seventy-four guns.

"a respectable man." And—nor so strange to report as it may appear to be—though a ploughman of the troubled waters, life-long contending with the intractable elements, there was nothing this honest soul at heart loved better than simple peace and quiet. For the rest, he was fifty or thereabouts, a little inclined to corpulence, a prepossessing face, unwhiskered, and of an agreeable color—a rather full face, humanely intelligent in expression. On a fair day with a fair wind and all going well, a certain musical chime in his voice seemed to be the veritable unobstructed outcome of the innermost man. He had much prudence, much conscientiousness, and there were occasions when these virtues were the cause of overmuch disquietude in him. On a passage, so long as his craft was in any proximity to land, no sleep for Captain Graveling. He took to heart those serious responsibilities not so heavily borne by some shipmasters.

Now while Billy Budd was down in the forecastle getting his kit together, the *Indomitable's* lieutenant, burly and bluff, nowise disconcerted by Captain Graveling's omitting to proffer the customary hospitalities on an occasion so unwelcome to him, an omission simply caused by preoccupation of thought, unceremoniously invited himself into the cabin, and also to a flask from the spirit locker, a receptacle which his experienced eye instantly discovered. In fact he was one of those sea dogs in whom all the hardship and peril of naval life in the great prolonged wars of his time never impaired the natural instinct for sensuous enjoyment. His duty he always faithfully did; but duty is sometimes a dry obligation, and he was for irrigating its aridity, whensoever possible, with a fertilizing decoction of strong waters. For the cabin's proprietor there was nothing left but to play the part of the enforced host with whatever grace and alacrity were practicable. As necessary adjuncts to the flask, he silently placed tumbler and water jug before the irrepressible guest. But excusing himself from partaking just then, he dismally watched the unembarrassed officer deliberately diluting his grog a little, then tossing it off in three swallows, pushing the empty tumbler away, yet not so far as to be beyond easy reach, at the same time settling himself in his seat and smacking his lips with high satisfaction, looking straight at the host.

These proceedings over, the master broke the silence; and there lurked a rueful reproach in the tone of his voice; "Lieutenant, you are going to take my best man from me, the jewel of 'em."

"Yes, I know," rejoined the other, immediately drawing back the tumbler preliminary to a replenishing; "Yes, I know. Sorry."

"Beg pardon, but you don't understand, Lieutenant. See here now. Before I shipped that young fellow, my forecastle was a rat-pit of quarrels. It was black times, I tell you, aboard the *'Rights'* here. I was worried to that degree my pipe had no comfort for me. But Billy came; and it was like a Catholic priest striking peace in an Irish shindy. Not that he preached to them or did anything in particular; but a virtue went out of him, sugaring the sour ones. They took to him like hornets to treacle; all but the buffer of the gang, the big shaggy chap with the fire-red whiskers. He indeed out of envy, perhaps, of the newcomer, and thinking such a 'sweet and pleasant fellow,' as he mockingly designated him to the others, could hardly have the spirit of a gamecock, must needs bestir himself in trying to get up an ugly row with him. Billy forebore with him and reasoned with him in a pleasant way—he is something like myself, Lieutenant, to whom aught like a quarrel is hateful—but nothing served. So, in the second dogwatch one day the Red Whiskers in presence of the others, under the pretence of showing Billy just whence a sirloin steak was cut—for the fellow had once been a butcher—insultingly gave him a dig under the ribs. Quick as lightning Billy let fly his arm. I dare say he never meant to do quite as much as he did, but anyhow he gave the burly fool a terrible drubbing. It took about half a minute, I should think. And, lord bless you, the lubber was astonished at the celerity. And will you believe it, Lieutenant, the Red Whiskers now really loves Billy—loves him, or is the biggest hypocrite that ever I heard of. But they all love him. Some of 'em do his washing, darn his old trousers for him; the carpenter is at odd times making a pretty little chest of drawers for him. Anybody will do anything for Billy Budd; and it's the happy family here. But now, Lieutenant, if that young fellow goes —I know how it will be aboard the '*Rights*.' Not again very soon shall I, coming up from dinner, lean over the capstan smoking a quiet pipe—no, not very soon again, I think. Ay, Lieutenant, you are going to take away the jewel of 'em; you are going to take away my peacemaker!" And with that the good soul had really some ado in checking a rising sob.

"Well," said the officer who had listened with amused interest to all this, and was now waxing merry with his tipple; "Well, blessed are the peacemakers especially the fighting peacemakers! And such are the seventy-four beauties some of which you see poking their noses out of the portholes of yonder warship lying-to for me" pointing through the cabin window at the *Indomitable*. "But courage! don't look so downhearted, man. Why, I pledge you in advance the royal approbation. Rest assured that His Majesty will be delighted to know that in a time when his hardtack is not sought for by sailors with such avidity as should be; a time also when some shipmasters privily resent the borrowing from them a tar or two for the service; His Majesty, I say, will be delighted to learn that one shipmaster at least cheerfully surrenders to the King, the flower of his flock, a sailor who with equal loyalty makes no dissent— But where's my beauty? Ah," looking through the cabin's open door, "here he comes; and, by Jove —lugging along his chest—Apollo with his portmanteau!— My man," stepping out to him, "you can't take that big box aboard a warship. The boxes there are mostly shot-boxes. Put your duds in a bag, lad. Boot and saddle for the cavalryman, bag and hammock for the man-of-war's man."

The transfer from chest to bag was made. And, after seeing his man into the cutter and then following him down, the lieutenant pushed off from the *Rights-of-Man*. That was the merchant-ship's name; though by her master and crew abbreviated in sailor fashion into *The Rights*. The hardheaded Dundee owner was a staunch admirer of Thomas Paine whose book in rejoinder to Burke's arraignment of the French

Revolution had then been published for some time and had gone everywhere. In christening his vessel after the title of Paine's volume the man of Dundee was something like his contemporary shipowner, Stephen Girard[8] of Philadelphia, whose sympathies, alike with his native land and its liberal philosophers, he evinced by naming his ships after Voltaire, Diderot, and so forth.

But now, when the boat swept under the merchantman's stern and officer and oarsmen were noting—some bitterly and others with a grin—the name emblazoned there; just then it was that the new recruit jumped up from the bow where the coxswain had directed him to sit, and waving his hat to his silent shipmates sorrowfully looking over at him from the taffrail, bade the lads a genial good-by. Then, making a salutation as to the ship herself, "And good-by to you too, old *Rights of Man*."

"Down, sir!" roared the lieutenant, instantly assuming all the rigor of his rank, though with difficulty repressing a smile.

To be sure, Billy's action was a terrible breach of naval decorum. But in that decorum he had never been instructed; in consideration of which the lieutenant would hardly have been so energetic in reproof but for the concluding farewell to the ship. This he rather took as meant to convey a covert sally on the new recruit's part, a sly slur at impressment in general, and that of himself in especial. And yet, more likely, if satire it was in effect, it was hardly so by intention, for Billy though happily endowed with the gayety of high health, youth, and a free heart, was yet by no means of a satirical turn. The will to it and the sinister dexterity were alike wanting. To deal in double meanings and insinuation of any sort was quite foreign to his nature.

As to his enforced enlistment, that he seemed to take pretty much as he was wont to take any vicissitude of weather. Like the animals, though no philosopher, he was, without knowing it, practically a fatalist. And, it may be that he rather liked

---

8 Girard (1750–1831), the great Philadelphia merchant and banker, remained in his native France until he was twenty-seven, and read widely among the liberal authors of that period.

this adventurous turn in his affairs, which promised an opening into novel scenes and martial excitements.

Aboard the *Indomitable* our merchant-sailor was forthwith rated as an able seaman and assigned to the starboard watch of the foretop. He was soon at home in the service, not at all disliked for his unpretentious good looks and a sort of genial happy-go-lucky air. No merrier man in his mess: in marked contrast to certain other individuals included like himself among the impressed portion of the ship's company; for these when not actively employed were sometimes, and more particularly in the last dogwatch when the drawing near of twilight induced revery, apt to fall into a saddish mood which in some partook of sullenness. But they were not so young as our foretopman, and no few of them must have known a hearth of some sort, others may have had wives and children left, too probably, in uncertain circumstances, and hardly any but must have had acknowledged kith and kin, while for Billy, as will shortly be seen, his entire family was practically invested in himself.

II

THOUGH OUR NEW-MADE foretopman was well received in the top and on the gundecks, hardly here was he that cynosure he had previously been among those minor ship's companies of the merchant marine, with which companies only had he hitherto consorted.

He was young; and despite his all but fully developed frame in aspect looked even younger than he really was, owing to a lingering adolescent expression in the as yet smooth face all but feminine in purity of natural complexion but where, thanks to his seagoing, the lily was quite suppressed and the rose had some ado visibly to flush through the tan.

To one essentially such a novice in the complexities of factitious life, the abrupt transition from his former and simpler sphere to the ampler and more knowing world of a great warship; this might well have abashed him had there been any conceit or vanity in his composition. Among her miscellaneous multitude, the *Indomitable* mustered several individuals who however inferior in grade were of no common natural stamp, sailors more signally susceptive of that air which continuous martial discipline and repeated presence in battle can in some degree impart even to the average man. As the *handsome sailor* Billy Budd's position aboard the seventy-four was something analogous to that of a rustic beauty transplanted from the provinces and brought into competition with the highborn dames of the court. But this change of circumstances he scarce noted. As little did he observe that something about him provoked an ambiguous smile in one or two harder faces among the blue-jackets. Nor less unaware was he of the peculiar favorable effect his person and demeanor had upon the more intelligent gentlemen of the quarterdeck. Nor could this well have been otherwise. Cast in a mold peculiar to the finest physical examples of those Englishmen in whom the Saxon strain would seem not at all to partake of any Norman or other admixture, he showed in fact that humane look of reposeful good nature which the Greek sculptor in some instances gave to his heroic strong man, Hercules. But this again was subtly modified by another and pervasive quality. The ear, small and shapely, the arch of the foot, the curve in mouth and nostril, even the indurated hand dyed to the orange-tawny of the toucan's bill, a hand telling alike of the halyards and tar bucket; but, above all, something in the mobile expression, and every chance attitude and movement, something suggestive of a mother eminently favored by Love and the Graces; all this strangely indicated a lineage in direct contradiction to his lot. The mysteriousness here, became less mysterious through a matter-of-fact elicited when Billy at the capstan was being formally mustered into the service. Asked by the officer, a small brisk little gentleman as it chanced among other questions, his place of birth, he replied, "Please, sir, I don't know."

"Don't know where you were born?— Who was your father?"

"God knows, sir."

Struck by the straightforward simplicity of these replies, the officer next asked "Do you know anything about your beginning?"

"No, sir. But I have heard that I was found in a pretty silk-lined basket hanging one morning from the knocker of a good man's door in Bristol."

"*Found* say you? Well," throwing back his head and looking up and down the new recruit; "Well, it turns out to have been a pretty good find. Hope they'll find some more like you, my man; the fleet sadly needs them."

Yes, Billy Budd was a foundling, a presumable bye-blow,[9] and, evidently, no ignoble one. Noble descent was as evident in him as in a blood horse.

For the rest, with little or no sharpness of faculty or any trace of the wisdom of the serpent, nor yet quite a dove, he possessed that kind and degree of intelligence going along with the unconventional rectitude of a sound human creature, one to whom not yet has been proffered the questionable apple of knowledge. He was illiterate; he could not read, but he could sing, and like the illiterate nightingale was sometimes the composer of his own song.

Of self-consciousness he seemed to have little or none, or about as much as we may reasonably impute to a dog of Saint Bernard's breed.

Habitually living with the elements and knowing little more of the land than as a beach, or, rather, that portion of the terraqueous globe providentially set apart for dance-houses' doxies and tapsters, in short what sailors call a "fiddlers' green," his simple nature remained unsophisticated by those moral obliquities which are not in every case incompatible with that manufacturable thing known as respectability. But are sailors, frequenters of "fiddlers' greens," without vices? No; but less often than with landsmen do their vices, so called, partake of crookedness of heart, seeming less to proceed from viciousness than exuberance of vitality after long constraint;

---

9 Usually, "by-blow"—an illegitimate child.

frank manifestations in accordance with natural law. By his original constitution aided by the co-operating influences of his lot, Billy in many respects was little more than a sort of upright barbarian, much such perhaps as Adam presumably might have been ere the urbane serpent wriggled himself into his company.

And here be it submitted that apparently going to corroborate the doctrine of man's fall, a doctrine now popularly ignored, it is observable that where certain virtues pristine and unadulterate peculiarly characterize anybody in the external uniform of civilization, they will upon scrutiny seem not to be derived from custom or convention, but rather to be out of keeping with these, as if indeed exceptionally transmitted from a period prior to Cain's city and citified man. The character marked by such qualities has to an unvitiated taste an untampered-with flavor like that of berries, while the man thoroughly civilized even in a fair specimen of the breed has to the same moral palate a questionable smack as of a compounded wine. To any stray inheritor of these primitive qualities found, like Caspar Hauser,[1] wandering dazed in any Christian capital of our time the good-natured poet's famous invocation, near two thousand years ago, of the good rustic out of his latitude in the Rome of the Caesars, still appropriately holds:

"Honest and poor, faithful in word and thought
    What has thee, Fabian, to the city brought."[2]

Though our Handsome Sailor had as much of masculine beauty as one can expect anywhere to see; nevertheless, like the beautiful woman in one of Hawthorne's minor tales,[3] there was just one thing amiss in him. No visible blemish indeed, as with the lady; no, but an occasional liability to a vocal defect.

---

1 Kaspar Hauser (1812?–1833) mysteriously appeared in 1828 in Nuremberg, Germany. Popularly imagined to be of noble birth, he aroused international attention, and was mysteriously assassinated.

2 Martial, *Epigrams,* Book IV, 5.

3 Apparently "The Birthmark."

Though in the hour of elemental uproar or peril, he was everything that a sailor should be, yet under sudden provocation of strong heart-feeling his voice otherwise singularly musical, as if expressive of the harmony within, was apt to develop an organic hesitancy, in fact more or less of a stutter or even worse. In this particular Billy was a striking instance that the arch interferer, the envious marplot of Eden still has more or less to do with every human consignment to this planet of earth. In every case, one way or another he is sure to slip in his little card, as much as to remind us—I too have a hand here.

The avowal of such an imperfection in the Handsome Sailor should be evidence not alone that he is not presented as a conventional hero, but also that the story in which he is the main figure is no romance.

III

AT THE TIME of Billy Budd's arbitrary enlistment into the *Indomitable* that ship was on her way to join the Mediterranean fleet. No long time elapsed before the junction was effected. As one of that fleet the seventy-four participated in its movements, though at times on account of her superior sailing qualities, in the absence of frigates, dispatched on separate duty as a scout and at times on less temporary service. But with all this the story has little concernment, restricted as it is to the inner life of one particular ship and the career of an individual sailor.

It was the summer of 1797. In the April of that year had occurred the commotion at Spithead followed in May by a second and yet more serious outbreak in the fleet at the Nore. The latter is known, and without exaggeration in the epithet, as the Great Mutiny. It was indeed a demonstration more menacing to England than the contemporary manifestoes and conquering and proselyting armies of the French Directory.

To the British Empire the Nore Mutiny was what a strike in the fire brigade would be to London threatened by general arson. In a crisis when the kingdom might well have anticipated the famous signal that some years later published along the naval line of battle what it was that upon occasion England expected of Englishmen;[4] *that* was the time when at the mastheads of the three-deckers and seventy-fours moored in her own roadstead—a fleet, the right arm of a power then all but the sole free conservative one of the Old World, the blue-jackets, to be numbered by thousands, ran up with huzzas the British colors with the union and cross wiped out; by that cancellation transmuting the flag of founded law and freedom defined, into the enemy's red meteor of unbridled and unbounded revolt. Reasonable discontent growing out of practical grievances in the fleet had been ignited into irrational combustion as by live cinders blown across the Channel from France in flames.

The event converted into irony for a time those spirited strains of Dibdin[5]—as a songwriter no means auxiliary to the English government at the European conjuncture—strains celebrating, among other things, the patriotic devotion of the British tar:

"And as for my life, 'tis the King's!"

Such an episode in the island's grand naval story her naval historians naturally abridge; one of them (G. P. R. James)[6] candidly acknowledging that fain would he pass it over did not "impartiality forbid fastidiousness." And yet his mention is less a narration than a reference, having to do hardly at all with details. Nor are these readily to be found in the libraries. Like some other events in every age befalling states everywhere including America the Great Mutiny was of such character that national pride along with views of policy

---

4 In 1805, in the naval battle against the French and Spanish off Trafalgar, where he was killed, Admiral Nelson ran up the famous signal "England expects every man to do his duty."

5 Charles Dibdin (1745–1814) was an English dramatist, but his enduring fame rests on his sailor songs and chanteys.

6 G. P. R. James (1799–1860), a very popular and prolific British novelist.

would fain shade it off into the historical background. Such events can not be ignored, but there is a considerate way of historically treating them. If a well-constituted individual refrains from blazoning aught amiss or calamitous in his family; a nation in the like circumstance may without reproach be equally discreet.

Though after parleyings between government and the ringleaders, and concessions by the former as to some glaring abuses, the first uprising—that at Spithead—with difficulty was put down, or matters for the time pacified; yet at the Nore the unforeseen renewal of insurrection on a yet larger scale, and emphasized in the conferences that ensued by demands deemed by the authorities not only inadmissible but aggressively insolent, indicated—if the red flag did not sufficiently do so—what was the spirit animating the men. Final suppression, however, there was; but only made possible perhaps by the unswerving loyalty of the marine corps and voluntary resumption of loyalty among influential sections of the crews.

To some extent the Nore Mutiny may be regarded as analogous to the distempering irruption of contagious fever in a frame constitutionally sound, and which anon throws it off.

At all events, of these thousands of mutineers were some of the tars who not so very long afterwards—whether wholly prompted thereto by patriotism, or pugnacious instinct, or by both,—helped to win a coronet for Nelson at the Nile,[7] and the naval crown of crowns for him at Trafalgar. To the mutineers those battles and especially Trafalgar were a plenary absolution and a grand one: for all that goes to make up scenic naval display, heroic magnificence in arms, those battles especially Trafalgar stand unmatched in human annals.

---

7 For his victory at the Nile (1798), Nelson was made a baron; later he became a viscount.

IV

Concerning "The greatest sailor since the world began." Tennyson[8]

IN THIS MATTER of writing, resolve as one may to keep to the main road, some by-paths have an enticement not readily to be withstood. I am going to err into such a by-path. If the reader will keep me company I shall be glad. At the least we can promise ourselves that pleasure which is wickedly said to be in sinning, for a literary sin the divergence will be.

Very likely it is no new remark that the inventions of our time have at last brought about a change in sea warfare in degree corresponding to the revolution in all warfare effected by the original introduction from China into Europe of gunpowder. The first European firearm, a clumsy contrivance, was, as well known, scouted by no few of the knights as a base implement, good enough peradventure for weavers too craven to stand up crossing steel with steel in frank fight. But as ashore knightly valor though shorn of its blazonry did not cease with the knights, neither on the seas though nowadays in encounters there a certain kind of displayed gallantry be fallen out of date as hardly applicable under changed circumstances, did the nobler qualities of such naval magnates as Don John of Austria, Doria, Van Tromp, Jean Bart, the long line of British admirals and the American Decaturs of 1812 become obsolete with their wooden walls.[9]

---

8 The line, which is line 7 in Tennyson's "Ode on the Death of the Duke of Wellington" (1852), reads: "The greatest sailor since our world began."

9 All famous "iron admirals" of the wooden ships. Don John of Austria commanded the fleet of the Holy League in the defeat of the Turks at Lepanto (1571); Andrea Doria (1468–1560), Genoese admiral, was the "Liberator of Genoa" from the Turks; Maarten Tromp (1597–1653) commanded the Dutch fleets in struggles for independence from Spain, Portugal, and Britain; Jean Bart, famous French soldier of fortune, commanded privateers against the Dutch (1686–1697); and the American naval hero Stephen Decatur was renowned for daring exploits against the Tripoli pirates (1803–1804) and for victories over British ships in the War of 1812.

Nevertheless, to anybody who can hold the present at its worth without being inappreciative of the past, it may be forgiven, if to such a one of the solitary old hulk at Portsmouth, Nelson's *Victory*, seems to float there, not alone as the decaying monument of a fame incorruptible, but also as a poetic reproach, softened by its picturesqueness, to the *Monitors*[1] and yet mightier hulls of the European ironclads. And this not altogether because such craft are unsightly, unavoidably lacking the symmetry and grand lines of the old battleships, but equally for other reasons.

There are some, perhaps, who while not altogether inaccessible to that poetic reproach just alluded to, may yet on behalf of the new order, be disposed to parry it; and this to the extent of iconoclasm, if need be. For example, prompted by the sight of the star inserted in the *Victory's* quarterdeck designating the spot where the great sailor fell, these martial utilitarians may suggest considerations implying that Nelson's ornate publication of his person in battle was not only unnecessary, but not military, nay, savored of foolhardiness and vanity. They may add, too, that at Trafalgar it was in effect nothing less than a challenge to death; and death came; and that but for his bravado the victorious Admiral might possibly have survived the battle, and so, instead of having his sagacious dying injunctions overruled by his immediate successor in command he himself when the contest was decided might have brought his shattered fleet to anchor, a proceeding which might have averted the deplorable loss of life by shipwreck in the elemental tempest that followed the martial one.

Well, should we set aside the more disputable point whether for various reasons it was possible to anchor the fleet, then plausibly enough the Benthamites[2] of war may urge the above.

But the *might-have-been* is but boggy ground to build on.

---

1 During the Civil War, the *Monitor's* defeat of the southern *Merrimac* at Hampton Roads (March, 1862) ended the first engagement between ironclad ships.

2 Jeremy Bentham (1748–1832), British jurist and utilitarian philosopher, in *Principles of Morals and Legislation* (1789) propounded his famous dictum that "the greatest happiness of the greatest number is the foundation of morals and legislation."

And, certainly, in foresight as to the larger issue of an encounter, and anxious preparations for it—buoying the deadly way and mapping it out, as at Copenhagen[3]—few commanders have been so painstakingly circumspect as this same reckless declarer of his person in fight.

Personal prudence even when dictated by quite other than selfish considerations surely is no special virtue in a military man; while an excessive love of glory, impassioning a less burning impulse, the honest sense of duty, is the first. If the name *Wellington* is not so much of a trumpet to the blood as the simpler name *Nelson,* the reason for this may perhaps be inferred from the above. Alfred[4] in his funeral ode on the victor of Waterloo ventures not to call him the greatest soldier of all time, though in the same ode he invokes Nelson as "the greatest sailor since the world began."

At Trafalgar Nelson on the brink of opening the fight sat down and wrote his last brief will and testament. If under the presentiment of the most magnificent of all victories to be crowned by his own glorious death, a sort of priestly motive led him to dress his person in the jeweled vouchers of his own shining deeds; if thus to have adorned himself for the altar and the sacrifice were indeed vainglory, then affectation and fustian is each more heroic line in the great epics and dramas, since in such lines the poet but embodies in verse those exaltations of sentiment that a nature like Nelson, the opportunity being given, vitalizes into acts.

V

YES, THE OUTBREAK at the Nore was put down. But not every grievance was redressed. If the contractors, for example, were no longer permitted to ply some practices peculiar to their tribe everywhere, such as providing shoddy cloth, rations not sound, or false in the measure, not the less impressment, for one thing, went on. By custom sanctioned for centuries, and

---

3 Nelson's siege of Copenhagen (1801) became a famous example of strategy.

4 *I.e.,* Tennyson; *cf.* epigraph to this chapter.

judicially maintained by a lord chancellor as late as Mansfield,[5] that mode of manning the fleet, a mode now fallen into a sort of abeyance but never formally renounced, it was not practicable to give up in those years. Its abrogation would have crippled the indispensable fleet, one wholly under canvas, no steam power, its innumerable sails and thousands of cannon, everything in short, worked by muscle alone; a fleet the more insatiate in demand for men, because then multiplying its ships of all grades against contingencies present and to come of the convulsed Continent.

Discontent foreran the two mutinies, and more or less it lurkingly survived them. Hence it was not unreasonable to apprehend some return of trouble sporadic or general. One instance of such apprehensions: In the same year with this story, Nelson, then Vice Admiral Sir Horatio, being with the fleet off the Spanish coast, was directed by the admiral in command to shift his pennant from the *Captain* to the *Theseus;* and for this reason: that the latter ship having newly arrived on the station from home where it had taken part in the Great Mutiny, danger was apprehended from the temper of the men; and it was thought that an officer like Nelson was the one, not indeed to terrorize the crew into base subjection, but to win them, by force of his mere presence back to an allegiance if not as enthusiastic as his own, yet as true. So it was that for a time on more than one quarterdeck anxiety did exist. At sea precautionary vigilance was strained against relapse. At short notice an engagement might come on. When it did, the lieutenants assigned to batteries felt it incumbent on them, in some instances, to stand with drawn swords behind the men working the guns.

VI

BUT ON BOARD the seventy-four in which Billy now swung his hammock, very little in the manner of the men and nothing obvious in the demeanor of the officers would have suggested

---

5 William Murray, Baron Mansfield, British parliamentarian, became lord chief justice in 1756, and was later a cabinet minister (1773–1788).

to an ordinary observer that the Great Mutiny was a recent event. In their general bearing and conduct the commissioned officers of a warship naturally take their tone from the commander, that is if he have that ascendancy of character that ought to be his.

Captain the Honorable Edward Fairfax Vere, to give his full title, was a bachelor of forty or thereabouts, a sailor of distinction even in a time prolific of renowned seamen. Though allied to the higher nobility his advancement had not been altogether owing to influences connected with that circumstance. He had seen much service, been in various engagements, always acquitting himself as an officer mindful of the welfare of his men, but never tolerating an infraction of discipline; thoroughly versed in the science of his profession, and intrepid to the verge of temerity, though never injudiciously so. For his gallantry in the West Indian waters as flag-lieutenant under Rodney in that admiral's crowning victory over De Grasse,[6] he was made a post-captain.

Ashore in the garb of a civilian scarce anyone would have taken him for a sailor, more especially that he never garnished unprofessional talk with nautical terms, and grave in his bearing, evinced little appreciation of mere humor. It was not out of keeping with these traits that on a passage when nothing demanded his paramount action, he was the most undemonstrative of men. Any landsman observing this gentleman not conspicuous by his stature and wearing no pronounced insignia, emerging from his cabin to the open deck, and noting the silent deference of the officers retiring to leeward, might have taken him for the King's guest, a civilian aboard the King's-ship, some highly honorable discreet envoy on his way to an important post. But in fact this unobtrusiveness of demeanor may have proceeded from a certain unaffected modesty of manhood sometimes accompanying a resolute nature, a modesty evinced at all times not calling for

6 The British admiral George Brydges, Baron Rodney (1719–1792) defeated the French admiral De Grasse in a naval engagement off Dominica, in the Leewards, in 1782.

pronounced action, and which shown in any rank of life suggests a virtue aristocratic in kind.

As with some others engaged in various departments of the world's more heroic activities, Captain Vere though practical enough upon occasion would at times betray a certain dreaminess of mood. Standing alone on the weather side of the quarterdeck, one hand holding by the rigging he would absently gaze off at the blank sea. At the presentation to him then of some minor matter interrupting the current of his thoughts he would show more or less irascibility; but instantly he would control it.

In the navy he was popularly known by the appellation— Starry Vere. How such a designation happened to fall upon one who whatever his sturdy qualities was without any brilliant ones was in this wise: A favorite kinsman, Lord Denton, a freehearted fellow, had been the first to meet and congratulate him upon his return to England from his West Indian cruise; and but the day previous turning over a copy of Andrew Marvell's poems had lighted, not for the first time however, upon the lines entitled *Appleton House,* the name of one of the seats of their common ancestor, a hero in the German wars of the seventeenth century, in which poem occur the lines,

> "This 'tis to have been from the first
> In a domestic heaven nursed,
> Under the discipline severe
> Of Fairfax and the starry Vere."

And so, upon embracing his cousin fresh from Rodney's great victory wherein he had played so gallant a part, brimming over with just family pride in the sailor of their house, he exuberantly exclaimed, "Give ye joy, Ed; give ye joy, my starry Vere!" This got currency, and the novel prefix serving in familiar parlance readily to distinguish the *Indomitable's* captain from another Vere his senior, a distant relative an officer of like rank in the navy, it remained permanently attached to the surname.

VII

In view of the part that the commander of the *Indomitable* plays in scenes shortly to follow, it may be well to fill out that sketch of him outlined in the previous chapter.

Aside from his qualities as a sea officer Captain Vere was an exceptional character. Unlike no few of England's renowned sailors, long and arduous service with signal devotion to it, had not resulted in absorbing and *salting* the entire man. He had a marked leaning toward everything intellectual. He loved books, never going to sea without a newly replenished library, compact but of the best. The isolated leisure, in some cases so wearisome, falling at intervals to commanders even during a war cruise, never was tedious to Captain Vere. With nothing of that literary taste which less heeds the thing conveyed than the vehicle, his bias was toward those books to which every serious mind of superior order occupying any active post of authority in the world, naturally inclines: books treating of actual men and events no matter of what era—history, biography and unconventional writers, who, free from cant and convention, like Montaigne, honestly and in the spirit of common sense philosophize upon realities.

In this line of reading he found confirmation of his own more reasoned thoughts—confirmation which he had vainly sought in social converse, so that as touching most fundamental topics, there had got to be established in him some positive convictions, which he fore-felt would abide in him essentially unmodified so long as his intelligent part remained unimpaired. In view of the troubled period in which his lot was cast this was well for him. His settled convictions were as a dyke against those invading waters of novel opinion social political and otherwise, which carried away as in a torrent no few minds in those days, minds by nature not inferior to his own. While other members of that aristocracy to which by birth he belonged were incensed at the innovators mainly because their theories were inimical to the privileged classes, not alone Captain Vere disinterestedly opposed them because they seemed to him incapable of embodiment in lasting institutions, but at war with the peace of the world and the true welfare of mankind.

With minds less stored than his and less earnest, some officers of his rank, with whom at times he would necessarily consort, found him lacking in the companionable quality, a dry and bookish gentleman as they deemed. Upon any chance withdrawal from their company one would be apt to say to another, something like this: "Vere is a noble fellow, Starry Vere. Spite the gazettes, Sir Horatio" meaning him with the lord title[7] "is at bottom scarce a better seaman or fighter. But between you and me now don't you think there is a queer streak of the pedantic running through him? Yes, like the King's yarn in a coil of navy rope?"

Some apparent ground there was for this sort of confidential criticism; since not only did the captain's discourse never fall into the jocosely familiar, but in illustrating of any point touching the stirring personages and events of the time he would be as apt to cite some historic character or incident of antiquity as that he would cite from the moderns. He seemed unmindful of the circumstance that to his bluff company such remote allusions however pertinent they might really be were altogether alien to men whose reading was mainly confined to the journals. But considerateness in such matters is not easy to natures constituted like Captain Vere's. Their honesty prescribes to them directness, sometimes far-reaching like that of a migratory fowl that in its flight never heeds when it crosses a frontier.

VIII

THE LIEUTENANTS and other commissioned gentlemen forming Captain Vere's staff it is not necessary here to particularize, nor needs it to make any mention of any of the warrant-officers. But among the petty-officers was one who having much to do with the story, may as well be forthwith intro-

---

7 *I.e.*, Admiral Horatio Nelson, a viscount.

duced. His portrait I essay, but shall never hit it. This was John Claggart, the master-at-arms. But that sea title may to landsmen seem somewhat equivocal. Originally doubtless that petty-officer's function was the instruction of the men in the use of arms, sword or cutlas. But very long ago, owing to the advance in gunnery making hand-to-hand encounters less frequent and giving to niter and sulphur the pre-eminence over steel, that function ceased; the master-at-arms of a great warship becoming a sort of chief of police charged among other matters with the duty of preserving order on the populous lower gundecks.

Claggart was a man about five and thirty, somewhat spare and tall, yet of no ill figure upon the whole. His hand was too small and shapely to have been accustomed to hard toil. The face was a notable one; the features all except the chin cleanly cut as those on a Greek medallion; yet the chin, beardless as Tecumseh's,[8] had something of strange protuberant heaviness in its make that recalled the prints of the Rev. Dr. Titus Oates, the historic deponent with the clerical drawl in the time of Charles II and the fraud of the alleged Popish Plot.[9] It served Claggart in his office that his eye could cast a tutoring glance. His brow was of the sort phrenologically associated with more than average intellect; silken jet curls partly clustering over it, making a foil to the pallor below, a pallor tinged with a faint shade of amber akin to the hue of time-tinted marbles of old. This complexion, singularly contrasting with the red or deeply bronzed visages of the sailors, and in part the result of his official seclusion from the sunlight, though it was not exactly displeasing, nevertheless seemed to hint of something defective or abnormal in the constitution and blood. But his general aspect and manner were so suggestive of an education and career incongruous with his naval function that when not actively engaged in it he looked like

---

8 Shawnee chieftain (1768?–1813), leader of a western Indian alliance; he joined the British and was killed in the War of 1812.

9 Titus Oates (1649–1705) was fabricator in 1678 of the alleged "Popish Plot" to seize the English crown for Catholicism by assassinating King Charles and terrorizing London.

a man of high quality, social and moral, who for reasons of his own was keeping incog.[1] Nothing was known of his former life. It might be that he was an Englishman; and yet there lurked a bit of accent in his speech suggesting that possibily he was not such by birth, but through naturalization in early childhood. Among certain grizzled sea gossips of the gundecks and forecastle went a rumor perdue that the master-at-arms was a *chevalier* who had volunteered into the King's navy by way of compounding for some mysterious swindle whereof he had been arraigned at the King's Bench. The fact that nobody could substantiate this report was, of course, nothing against its secret currency. Such a rumor once started on the gundecks in reference to almost anyone below the rank of a commissioned officer would, during the period assigned to this narrative, have seemed not altogether wanting in credibility to the tarry old wiseacres of a man-of-war crew. And indeed a man of Claggart's accomplishments, without prior nautical experience entering the navy at mature life, as he did, and necessarily allotted at the start to the lowest grade in it; a man too who never made allusion to his previous life ashore; these were circumstances which in the dearth of exact knowledge as to his true antecedents opened to the invidious a vague field for unfavorable surmise.

But the sailors' dogwatch gossip concerning him derived a vague plausibility from the fact that now for some period the British navy could so little afford to be squeamish in the matter of keeping up the muster rolls, that not only were press gangs notoriously abroad both afloat and ashore, but there was little or no secret about another matter, namely that the London police were at liberty to capture any able-bodied suspect, any questionable fellow at large and summarily ship him to the dockyard or fleet. Furthermore, even among voluntary enlistments there were instances where the motive thereto partook neither of patriotic impulse nor yet of a random desire to experience a bit of sea life and martial adventure. Insolvent debtors of minor grade, together with the promiscuous lame

1 Then a familiar abbreviation for *incognito,* "unrecognized."

ducks of morality found in the navy a convenient and secure refuge. Secure, because once enlisted aboard a King's-ship, they were as much in sanctuary, as the transgressor of the Middle Ages harboring himself under the shadow of the altar. Such sanctioned irregularities, which for obvious reasons the government would hardly think to parade at the time and which consequently, and as affecting the least influential class of mankind, have all but dropped into oblivion, lend color to something for the truth whereof I do not vouch, and hence have some scruple in stating; something I remember having seen in print though the book I cannot recall; but the same thing was personally communicated to me now more than forty years ago by an old pensioner in a cocked hat with whom I had a most interesting talk on the terrace at Greenwich, a Baltimore Negro, a Trafalgar man.[2] It was to this effect: In the case of a warship short of hands whose speedy sailing was imperative, the deficient quota in lack of any other way of making it good, would be eked out by drafts culled direct from the jails. For reasons previously suggested it would not perhaps be easy at the present day directly to prove or disprove the allegation. But allowed as a verity, how significant would it be of England's straits at the time confronted by those wars which like a flight of harpies rose shrieking from the din and dust of the fallen Bastille. That era appears measurably clear to us who look back at it, and but read of it. But to the grandfathers of us graybeards, the more thoughtful of them, the genius of it presented an aspect like that of Camoen's[3] Spirit of the Cape, an eclipsing menace mysterious and prodigious. Not America was exempt from apprehension. At the height of Napoleon's unexampled conquests, there were Americans who had fought at Bunker Hill who looked forward to the possibility that the Atlantic might prove no barrier against the ultimate schemes of this French upstart from the revolutionary chaos who seemed in act of fulfilling judgment prefigured in the Apocalypse.

2 *I.e.*, one who had fought at the Battle of Trafalgar (1805), Nelson's fatal victory.

3 Properly, "Camoens," English spelling for "Camoes," Portuguese poet.

But the less credence was to be given to the gundeck talk touching Claggart, seeing that no man holding his office in a man-of-war can ever hope to be popular with the crew. Besides, in derogatory comments upon anyone against whom they have a grudge, or for any reason or no reason mislike, sailors are much like landsmen, they are apt to exaggerate or romance it.

About as much was really known in the *Indomitable's* tars of the master-at-arms' career before entering the service as an astronomer knows about a comet's travels prior to its first observable appearance in the sky. The verdict of the sea quidnuncs[4] has been cited only by way of showing what sort of moral impression the man made upon rude uncultivated natures whose conceptions of human wickedness were necessarily of the narrowest, limited to ideas of vulgar rascality— a thief among the swinging hammocks during a night watch, or the manbrokers and landsharks of the seaports.

It was no gossip, however, but fact, that though, as before hinted, Claggart upon his entrance into the navy was, as a novice, assigned to the least honorable section of a man-of-war's crew, embracing the drudgery, he did not long remain there.

The superior capacity he immediately evinced, his constitutional sobriety, ingratiating deference to superiors, together with a peculiar ferreting genius manifested on a singular occasion, all this capped by a certain austere patriotism abruptly advanced him to the position of master-at-arms.

Of this maritime chief of police the ship's corporals, so called, were the immediate subordinates, and compliant ones; and this, as is to be noted in some business departments ashore, almost to a degree inconsistent with entire moral volition. His place put various converging wires of underground influence under the chief's control, capable when astutely worked through his understrappers of operating to the mysterious discomfort, if nothing worse, of any of the sea commonalty.

_____
4 Literally, "what now?" Hence, a busybody, a gossip.

IX

LIFE IN THE FORETOP well agreed with Billy Budd. There, when not actually engaged on the yards yet higher aloft, the topmen, who as such had been picked out for youth and activity, constituted an aerial club lounging at ease against the smaller stun'sails rolled up into cushions, spinning yarns like the lazy gods, and frequently amused with what was going on in the busy world of the decks below. No wonder then that a young fellow of Billy's disposition was well content in such society. Giving no cause of offence to anybody, he was always alert at a call. So in the merchant service it had been with him. But now such a punctiliousness in duty was shown that his topmates would sometimes good-naturedly laugh at him for it. This heightened alacrity had its cause, namely, the impression made upon him by the first formal gangway punishment he had ever witnessed, which befell the day following his impressment. It had been incurred by a little fellow, young, a novice, an afterguardsman absent from his assigned post when the ship was being put about; a dereliction resulting in a rather serious hitch to that maneuver, one demanding instantaneous promptitude in letting go and making fast. When Billy saw the culprit's naked back under the scourge gridironed with red welts, and worse; when he marked the dire expression on the liberated man's face as with his woolen shirt flung over him by the executioner he rushed forward from the spot to bury himself in the crowd, Billy was horrified. He resolved that never through remissness would he make himself liable to such a visitation or do or omit aught that might merit even verbal reproof. What then was his surprise and concern when ultimately he found himself getting into petty trouble occasionally about such matters as the stowage of his bag or something amiss in his hammock, matters under the police oversight of the ship's corporals of the lower decks, and which brought down on him a vague threat from one of them.

So heedful in all things as he was, how could this be? He could not understand it, and it more than vexed him. When he spoke to his young topmates about it they were either lightly incredulous or found something comical in his unconcealed anxiety. "Is it your bag, Billy?" said one, "well, sew yourself up in it, bully boy, and then you'll be sure to know if anybody meddles with it."

Now there was a veteran aboard who because his years began to disqualify him for more active work had been recently assigned duty as mainmastman in his watch, looking to the gear belayed at the rail roundabout that great spar near the deck. At off times the foretopman had picked up some acquaintance with him, and now in his trouble it occurred to him that he might be the sort of person to go to for wise counsel. He was an old Dansker long anglicized in the service, of few words, many wrinkles and some honorable scars. His wizened face, time-tinted and weather-stained to the complexion of an antique parchment, was here and there peppered blue by the chance explosion of a gun cartridge in action. He was an *Agamemnon* man; some two years prior to the time of this story having served under Nelson when but Sir Horatio in that ship immortal in naval memory, and which, dismantled and in part broken up to her bare ribs, is seen a grand skeleton in Haydon's[5] etching. As one of a boarding party from the *Agamemnon* he had received a cut slantwise along one temple and cheek leaving a long pale scar like a streak of dawn's light falling athwart the dark visage. It was on account of that scar and the affair in which it was known that he had received it, as well as from his blue-peppered complexion that the Dansker went among the *Indomitable's* crew by the name of "Board-her-in-the-smoke."

Now the first time that his small weasel eyes happened to light on Billy Budd, a certain grim internal merriment set all his ancient wrinkles into antic play. Was it that his eccentric unsentimental old sapience primitive in its kind saw or thought

5 Benjamin Robert Haydon (1786–1846), English historical painter, much praised by contemporary romantic writers.

it saw something which in contrast with the warship's environment looked oddly incongruous in the handsome sailor? But after slyly studying him at intervals, the old Merlin's equivocal merriment was modified; for now when the twain would meet, it would start in his face a quizzing sort of look, but it would be but momentary and sometimes replaced by an expression of speculative query as to what might eventually befall a nature like that, dropped into a world not without some mantraps and against whose subtleties simple courage, lacking experience and address and without any touch of defensive ugliness, is of little avail; and where such innocence as man is capable of does yet in a moral emergency not always sharpen the faculties or enlighten the will.

However it was the Dansker in his ascetic way rather took to Billy. Nor was this only because of a certain philosophic interest in such a character. There was another cause. While the old man's eccentricities, sometimes bordering on the ursine, repelled the juniors, Billy, undeterred thereby, revering him as a salt hero would make advances, never passing the old Agamemnon-man without a salutation marked by that respect which is seldom lost on the aged however crabbed at times or whatever their station in life.

There was a vein of dry humor, or what not, in the mastman; and, whether in freak of patriarchal irony touching Billy's youth and athletic frame, or for some other and more recondite reason, from the first in addressing him he always substituted Baby for Billy. The Dansker in fact being the originator of the name by which the foretopman eventually became known aboard ship.

Well then, in his mysterious little difficulty going in quest of the wrinkled one, Billy found him off duty in a dogwatch ruminating by himself seated on a shot box of the upper gundeck now and then surveying with a somewhat cynical regard certain of the more swaggering promenaders there. Billy recounted his trouble, again wondering how it all happened. The salt seer attentively listened, accompanying the foretopman's recital with queer twitchings of his wrinkles and problematical little sparkles of his small ferret eyes. Making an end of his story, the foretopman asked, "And now, Dansker, do tell me what you think of it."

The old man, shoving up the front of his tarpaulin and deliberately rubbing the long slant scar at the point where it entered the thin hair, laconically said, "Baby Budd, *Jemmy Legs*"[6] (meaning the master-at-arms) "is down on you."

"*Jemmy Legs!*" ejaculated Billy his welkin eyes expanding; "what for? Why he calls me *the sweet and pleasant young fellow,* they tell me."

"Does he so?" grinned the grizzled one; then said "Ay, Baby Lad, a sweet voice has *Jemmy Legs.*"

"No, not always. But to me he has. I seldom pass him but there comes a pleasant word."

"And that's because he's down upon you, Baby Budd."

Such reiteration along with the manner of it, incomprehensible to a novice, disturbed Billy almost as much as the mystery for which he had sought explanation. Something less unpleasingly oracular he tried to extract; but the old sea Chiron[7] thinking perhaps that for the nonce he had sufficiently instructed his young Achilles, pursed his lips, gathered all his wrinkles together and would commit himself to nothing further.

Years, and those experiences which befall certain shrewder men subordinated life-long to the will of superiors, all this had developed in the Dansker the pithy guarded cynicism that was his leading characteristic.

X

THE NEXT DAY an incident served to confirm Billy Budd in his incredulity as to the Dansker's strange summing up of the case submitted. The ship at noon going large before the wind was rolling on her course, and he below at dinner and en-

6 "Jimmy-Legs" is still a term of disparagement for the master-at-arms in the United States Navy.

7 In Greek myth, the wisest of the centaurs, skilled in healing, who befriended Achilles and other heroes.

gaged in some sportful talk with the members of his mess,
chanced in a sudden lurch to spill the entire contents of his
soup pan upon the new scrubbed deck. Claggart, the master-
at-arms, official rattan in hand, happened to be passing along
the battery in a bay of which the mess was lodged, and the
greasy liquid streamed just across his path. Stepping over it,
he was proceeding on his way without comment, since the
matter was nothing to take notice of under the circumstances,
when he happened to observe who it was that had done the
spilling. His countenance changed. Pausing, he was about to
ejaculate something hasty at the sailor, but checked himself,
and pointing down to the streaming soup, playfully tapped him
from behind with his rattan, saying in a low musical voice
peculiar to him at times "Handsomely done, my lad! And
handsome is as handsome did it too!" And with that passed
on. Not noted by Billy as not coming within his view was
the involuntary smile, or rather grimace, that accompanied
Claggart's equivocal words. Aridly it drew down the thin
corners of his shapely mouth. But everybody taking his remark as meant for humorous, and at which therefore as
coming from a superior they were bound to laugh, "with
counterfeited glee"[8] acted accordingly; and Billy tickled, it
may be, by the allusion to his being the handsome sailor,
merrily joined in; then addressing his messmates exclaimed
"There now, who says that Jemmy Legs is down on me!"
"And who said he was, Beauty?" demanded one Donald with
some surprise. Whereat the foretopman looked a little foolish
recalling that it was only one person, Board-her-in-the-smoke,
who had suggested what to him was the smoky idea that this
master-at-arms was in any peculiar way hostile to him. Meantime that functionary resuming his path must have momen-
tarily worn some expression less guarded than that of the
bitter smile, and usurping the face from the heart, some
distorting expression perhaps, for a drummer boy heedlessly
frolicking along from the opposite direction and chancing to

---

8 *Cf.* Oliver Goldsmith, "The Deserted Village," relating to the severe school-
master.

come into light collision with his person was strangely disconcerted by his aspect. Nor was the impression lessened when the official impulsively giving him a sharp cut with the rattan, vehemently exclaimed "Look where you go!"

XI

WHAT WAS THE MATTER with the master-at-arms? And, be the matter what it might, how could it have direct relation to Billy Budd with whom prior to the affair of the spilled soup he had never come into any special contact official or otherwise? What indeed could the trouble have to do with one so little inclined to give offence as the merchant-ship's *peacemaker,* even him who in Claggart's own phrase was "the sweet and pleasant young fellow"? Yes, why should *Jemmy Legs,* to borrow the Dansker's expression, be *down* on the Handsome Sailor? But, at heart and not for nothing, as the late chance encounter may indicate to the discerning, down on him, secretly down on him, he assuredly was.

Now to invent something touching the more private career of Claggart, something involving Billy Budd, of which something the latter should be wholly ignorant, some romantic incident implying that Claggart's knowledge of the young blue-jacket began at some period anterior to catching sight of him on board the seventy-four—all this, not so difficult to do, might avail in a way more or less interesting to account for whatever of enigma may appear to lurk in the case. But in fact there was nothing of the sort. And yet the cause, necessarily to be assumed as the sole one assignable, is in its very realism as much charged with that prime element of Radcliffian[9] romance, *the mysterious,* as any that the ingenuity of the author of the *Mysteries of Udolpho* could devise. For what can more partake of the mysterious than an antipathy spontaneous and profound such as is evoked in certain exceptional mortals by the mere aspect of some other mortal,

---

9 *The Mysteries of Udolpho* (1794), by Ann Radcliffe, was among the most popular of Gothic romances.

however harmless he may be? if not called forth by this very harmlessness itself.

Now there can exist no irritating juxtaposition of dissimilar personalities comparable to that which is possible aboard a great warship fully manned and at sea. There, every day among all ranks almost every man comes into more or less of contact with almost every other man. Wholly there to avoid even the sight of an aggravating object one must needs give it Jonah's toss[1] or jump overboard himself. Imagine how all this might eventually operate on some peculiar human creature the direct reverse of a saint?

But for the adequate comprehending of Claggart by a normal nature these hints are insufficient. To pass from a normal nature to him one must cross "the deadly space between." And this is best done by indirection.

Long ago an honest scholar my senior, said to me in reference to one who like himself is now no more, a man so unimpeachably respectable that against him nothing was ever openly said though among the few something was whispered, "Yes, X—— is a nut not to be cracked by the tap of a lady's fan. You are aware that I am the adherent of no organized religion much less of any philosophy built into a system. Well, for all that, I think that to try and get into X——, enter his labyrinth and get out again, without a clue derived from some source other than what is known as *knowledge of the world*—that were hardly possible, at least for me."

"Why" said I, "X—— however singular a study to some, is yet human, and knowledge of the world assuredly implies the knowledge of human nature, and in most of its varieties."

"Yes, but a superficial knowledge of it, serving ordinary purposes. But for anything deeper, I am not certain whether to know the world and to know human nature be not two distinct branches of knowledge, which while they may coexist in the same heart, yet either may exist with little or nothing of the other. Nay, in an average man of the world, his constant

---

1 In the language of seafaring, the putting overboard of an unlucky person or object.

rubbing with it blunts that fine spiritual insight indispensable to the understanding of the essential in certain exceptional characters, whether evil ones or good. In a matter of some importance I have seen a girl wind an old lawyer about her little finger. Nor was it the dotage of senile love. Nothing of the sort. But he knew law better than he knew the girl's heart. Coke and Blackstone[2] hardly shed so much light into obscure spiritual places as the Hebrew prophets. And who were they? Mostly recluses."

At the time my inexperience was such that I did not quite see the drift of all this. It may be that I see it now. And, indeed, if that lexicon which is based on Holy Writ were any longer popular, one might with less difficulty define and denominate certain phenomenal men. As it is, one must turn to some authority not liable to the charge of being tinctured with the Biblical element.

In a list of definitions included in the authentic translation of Plato, a list attributed to him, occurs this: "Natural Depravity: a depravity according to nature." A definition which though savoring of Calvinism, by no means involves Calvin's dogmas as to total mankind. Evidently its intent makes it applicable but to individuals. Not many are the examples of this depravity which the gallows and jail supply. At any rate for notable instances, since these have no vulgar alloy of the brute in them, but invariably are dominated by intellectuality, one must go elsewhere. Civilization, especially if of the austerer sort, is auspicious to it. It folds itself in the mantle of respectability. It has its certain negative virtues serving as silent auxiliaries. It never allows wine to get within its guard. It is not going too far to say that it is without vices or small sins. There is a phenomenal pride in it that excludes them from anything mercenary or avaricious. In short the depravity here meant partakes nothing of the sordid or sensual. It is serious, but free from acerbity. Though no flatterer of mankind it never speaks ill of it.

---

2 The *Reports* and the *Institutes* of Sir Edward Coke (1552–1634), and the *Commentaries* of Sir William Blackstone (1723–1780) were the foundations of modern British and American jurisprudence.

But the thing which in eminent instances signalizes so exceptional a nature is this: though the man's even temper and discreet bearing would seem to intimate a mind peculiarly subject to the law of reason, not the less in his heart he would seem to riot in complete exemption from that law, having apparently little to do with reason further than to employ it as an ambidexter implement for effecting the irrational. That is to say: Toward the accomplishment of an aim which in wantonness of malignity would seem to partake of the insane, he will direct a cool judgement sagacious and sound.

These men are true madmen, and of the most dangerous sort, for their lunacy is not continuous but occasional, evoked by some special object; it is probably secretive, which is as much to say it is self-contained, so that when, moreover, most active, it is to the average mind not distinguishable from sanity, and for the reason above suggested that whatever its aims may be, and the aim is never declared—the method and the outward proceeding are always perfectly rational.

Now something such an one was Claggart, in whom was the mania of an evil nature, not engendered by vicious training or corrupting books or licentious living, but born with him and innate, in short "a depravity according to nature."

XII

Lawyers, Experts, Clergy
An Episode

By the way, can it be the phenomenon, disowned or at least concealed, that in some criminal cases puzzles the courts? For this cause have our juries at times not only to endure the prolonged contentions of lawyers with their fees, but also the yet more perplexing strife of the medical experts with theirs? —But why leave it to them? why not subpoena as well the clerical proficients? Their vocation bringing them into peculiar contact with so many human beings, and sometimes in their least guarded hour, in interviews very much more confidential than those of physician and patient; this would seem to qualify them to know something about those intricacies involved in the question of moral responsibility; whether in a given case, say, the crime proceeded from mania in the brain or rabies of the heart. As to any differences among themselves these clerical proficients might develop on the stand, these could hardly be greater than the direct contradictions exchanged between the remunerated medical experts.

Dark sayings are these, some will say. But why? Is it because they somewhat savor of Holy Writ in its phrase "mysteries of iniquity"?[3] If they do, such savor was far from being intended for little will it commend these pages to many a reader of today.

The point of the present story turning on the hidden nature of the master-at-arms has necessitated this chapter. With an added hint or two in connection with the incident at the mess, the resumed narrative must be left to vindicate, as it may, its own credibility.

XIII

Pale ire, envy and despair[4]

THAT CLAGGART'S figure was not amiss, and his face, save the chin, well molded, has already been said. Of these favorable points he seemed not insensible, for he was not only neat but careful in his dress. But the form of Billy Budd was heroic; and if his face was without the intellectual look of the pallid Claggart's, not the less was it lit, like his, from within, though from a different source. The bonfire in his heart made luminous the rose-tan in his cheek.

---

3 *Cf.* II Thessalonians, ii: 7: "For the mystery of iniquity doth already work . . ." The words that follow recognize a Satanic and active principle of evil in nature.

4 *Cf.* Milton, *Paradise Lost*, Book IV, 1, 115. Doomed to be man's evil betrayer, the tortured Satan approached Eden, "his face / Thrice changed with pale–ire, envy, and despair."

In view of the marked contrast between the persons of the twain, it is more than probable that when the master-at-arms in the scene last given applied to the sailor the proverb *Handsome is as handsome does;* he there let escape an ironic inkling, not caught by the young sailors who heard it, as to what it was that had first moved him against Billy, namely, his significant personal beauty.

Now envy and antipathy, passions irreconcilable in reason, nevertheless in fact may spring conjoined like Chang and Eng[5] in one birth. Is Envy then such a monster? Well, though many an arraigned mortal has in hopes of mitigated penalty pleaded guilty to horrible actions, did ever anybody seriously confess to envy? Something there is in it universally felt to be more shameful than even felonious crime. And not only does everybody disown it but the better sort are inclined to incredulity when it is in earnest imputed to an intelligent man. But since its lodgment is in the heart not the brain, no degree of intellect supplies a guarantee against it. But Claggart's was no vulgar form of the passion. Nor, as directed toward Billy Budd did it partake of that streak of apprehensive jealousy that marred Saul's visage perturbedly brooding on the comely young David. Claggart's envy struck deeper. If askance he eyed the good looks, cheery health and frank enjoyment of young life in Billy Budd, it was because these went along with a nature that, as Claggart magnetically felt, had in its simplicity never willed malice or experienced the reactionary bite of that serpent. To him, the spirit lodged within Billy, and looking out from his welkins eyes as from windows, that ineffability it was which made the dimple in his dyed cheek, suppled his joints, and dancing in his yellow curls made him pre-eminently the Handsome Sailor. One person excepted the master-at-arms was perhaps the only man in the ship intellectually capable of adequately appreciating the moral phenomenon presented in Billy Budd. And the insight but intensified his passion, which assuming various secret forms

5 The original Siamese twins (1811–1874), first exhibited in the United States in 1829.

within him, at times assumed that of cynic disdain—disdain of innocence—to be nothing more than innocent! Yet in an aesthetic way he saw the charm of it, the courageous free-and-easy temper of it, and fain would have shared it, but he despaired of it.

With no power to annul the elemental evil in him, though readily enough he could hide it; apprehending the good, but powerless to be it; a nature like Claggart's surcharged with energy as such natures almost invariably are, what recourse is left to it but to recoil upon itself and like the scorpion for which the Creator alone is responsible, act out to the end the part allotted it?

XIV

PASSION, AND PASSION in its profoundest, is not a thing demanding a palatial stage whereon to play its part. Down among the groundlings, among the beggars and rakers of the garbage, profound passion is enacted. And the circumstances that provoke it, however trivial or mean, are no measure of its power. In the present instance the stage is a scrubbed gun-deck, and one of the external provocations a man-of-war's-man's spilled soup.

Now when the master-at-arms noticed whence came that greasy fluid streaming before his feet, he must have taken it—to some extent wilfully, perhaps—not for the mere accident it assuredly was, but for the sly escape of a spontaneous feeling on Billy's part more or less answering to the antipathy on his own. In effect a foolish demonstration, he must have thought, and very harmless, like the futile kick of a heifer, which yet were the heifer a shod stallion, would not be so harmless. Even so was it that into the gall of Claggart's envy he infused the vitriol of his contempt. But the incident confirmed to him certain telltale reports purveyed to his ear by *Squeak*, one of his more cunning corporals, a grizzled little man, so nicknamed by the sailors on account of his squeaky voice, and sharp visage ferreting about the dark corners of the lower decks after interlopers, satirically suggesting to them the idea of a rat in a cellar.

From his chief's employing him as an implicit tool in laying little traps for the worriment of the foretopman—for it was from the master-at-arms that the petty persecutions heretofore adverted to had proceeded—the corporal having naturally enough concluded that his master could have no love for the sailor, made it his business, faithful understrapper that he was, to foment the ill blood by perverting to his chief certain innocent frolics of the good-natured foretopman, besides inventing for his mouth sundry contumelious epithets he claimed to have overheard him let fall. The master-at-arms never suspected the veracity of these reports, more especially as to the epithets, for he well knew how secretly unpopular may become a master-at-arms, at least a master-at-arms of those days zealous in his function, and how the blue-jackets shoot at him in private their raillery and wit; the nickname by which he goes among them (*Jemmy Legs*) implying under the form of merriment their cherished disrespect and dislike.

But in view of the greediness of hate for patrolmen it hardly needed a purveyor to feed Claggart's passion. An uncommon prudence is habitual with the subtler depravity, for it has everything to hide. And in case of an injury but suspected, its secretiveness voluntarily cuts it off from enlightenment or disillusion; and, not unreluctantly, action is taken upon surmise as upon certainty. And the retaliation is apt to be in monstrous disproportion to the supposed offence; for when in anybody was revenge in its exactions aught else but an inordinate usurer. But how with Claggart's conscience? For though consciences are unlike as foreheads, every intelligence, not excluding the scriptural devils who "believe and tremble," has one. But Claggart's conscience being but the lawyer to his will, made ogres of trifles, probably arguing that the motive imputed to Billy in spilling the soup just when he did, together with the epithets alleged, these, if nothing more, made a strong case against him; nay, justified animosity into a sort of retributive righteousness. The Pharisee

is the Guy Fawkes[6] prowling in the hid chambers underlying
the Claggarts. And they can really form no conception of an
unreciprocated malice. Probably, the master-at-arms' clandestine persecution of Billy was started to try the temper of the
man; but it had not developed any quality in him that enmity
could make official use of or even pervert into plausible self-
justification; so that the occurrence at the mess, petty if it
were, was a welcome one to that peculiar conscience assigned
to be the private mentor of Claggart; and, for the rest, not
improbably it put him upon new experiments.

XV

NOT MANY DAYS after the last incident narrated something
befell Billy Budd that more graveled him than aught that
had previously occurred.

It was a warm night for the latitude; and the foretopman,
whose watch at the time was properly below, was dozing on
the uppermost deck whither he had ascended from his hot
hammock one of hundreds suspended so closely wedged together over a lower gundeck that there was little or no swing
to them. He lay as in the shadow of a hillside, stretched
under the lee of the booms, a piled ridge of spare spars
amidships between foremast and mainmast and among which
the ship's largest boat, the launch, was stowed. Alongside of
three other slumberers from below, he lay near that end of
the booms which approaches the foremast; his station aloft
on duty as a foretopman being just over the deck station of the
forecastlemen, entitling him according to usage to make himself more or less at home in that neighborhood.

Presently he was stirred into semiconsciousness by somebody, who must have previously sounded the sleep of the
others, touching his shoulder, and then as the foretopman

6 Principal conspirator in the Gunpowder Plot (1604–1605) to blow up the
British Houses of Parliament.

raised his head, breathing into his ear in a quick whisper, "Slip into the lee forechains, Billy; there is something in the wind. Don't speak. Quick, I will meet you there," and disappeared.

Now Billy like sundry other essentially good-natured ones had some of the weaknesses inseparable from essential good nature; and among these was a reluctance, almost an incapacity of plumply saying *no* to an abrupt proposition not obviously absurd, on the face of it, nor obviously unfriendly, nor iniquitous. And being of warm blood he had not the phlegm tacitly to negative any proposition by unresponsive inaction. Like his sense of fear, his apprehension as to aught outside of the honest and natural was seldom very quick. Besides, upon the present occasion, the drowse from his sleep still hung upon him.

However it was, he mechanically rose, and sleepily wondering what could be in the wind, betook himself to the designated place, a narrow platform, one of six, outside of the high bulwarks and screened by the great dead-eyes and multiple columned lanyards of the shrouds and backstays; and, in a great warship of that time, of dimensions commensurate with the hull's magnitude; a tarry balcony in short overhanging the sea, and so secluded that one mariner of the *Indomitable,* a nonconformist old tar of a serious turn, made it even in daytime his private oratory.

In this retired nook the stranger soon joined Billy Budd. There was no moon as yet; a haze obscured the starlight. He could not distinctly see the stranger's face. Yet from something in the outline and carriage, Billy took him to be, and correctly, for one of the afterguard.

"Hist! Billy," said the man in the same quick cautionary whisper as before; "You were impressed, weren't you? Well, so was I"; and he paused, as to mark the effect. But Billy not knowing exactly what to make of this said nothing. Then the other; "We are not the only impressed ones, Billy. There's a gang of us— Couldn't you—help—at a pinch?"

"What do you mean?" demanded Billy here thoroughly shaking off his drowse.

"Hist, hist!" the hurried whisper now growing husky, "see here," and the man held up two small objects faintly twinkling in the nightlight, "see, they are yours, Billy, if you'll only—"

But Billy broke in, and in his resentful eagerness to deliver himself his vocal infirmity somewhat intruded: "D-D-Damme, I don't know what you are d-d-driving at, or what you mean, but you had better g-g-go where you belong!" For the moment the fellow, as confounded, did not stir; and Billy springing to his feet, said, "If you d-don't start I'll t-t-toss you back over the r-rail!" There was no mistaking this and the mysterious emissary decamped, disappearing in the direction of the mainmast in the shadow of the booms.

"Hallo, what's the matter?" here came growling from a forecastleman awakened from his deck doze by Billy's raised voice. And as the foretopman reappeared and was recognized by him; "Ah, Beauty, is it you? Well, something must have been the matter for you st-st-stuttered."

"Oh," rejoined Billy, now mastering the impediment; "I found an afterguardsman in our part of the ship here and I bid him be off where he belongs."

"And is that all you did about it, foretopman?" gruffly demanded another, an irascible old fellow of brick-colored visage and hair, and who was known to his associate forecastlemen as *Red Pepper;* "Such sneaks I should like to marry to the gunner's daughter!" by that expression meaning that he would like to subject them to disciplinary castigation over a gun.

However, Billy's rendering of the matter satisfactorily accounted to these inquiries for the brief commotion, since of all the sections of a ship's company the forecastlemen, veterans for the most part and bigoted in their sea prejudices, are the most jealous in resenting territorial encroachments, especially on the part of any of the afterguard, of whom they have but a sorry opinion, chiefly landsmen, never going aloft except to reef or furl the mainsail, and in no wise competent to handle a marlinspike or turn in a *dead-eye,* say.

XVI

THIS INCIDENT SORELY puzzled Billy Budd. It was an entirely new experience; the first time in his life that he had ever been personally approached in underhand intriguing fashion. Prior to this encounter he had known nothing of the afterguardsman, the two men being stationed wide apart, one forward and aloft during his watch, the other on deck and aft.

What could it mean? And could they really be guineas, those two glittering objects the interloper had held up to his eyes? Where could the fellow get guineas? Why even buttons are not so plentiful at sea. The more he turned the matter over, the more he was nonplussed, and made uneasy and discomforted. In his disgustful recoil from an overture which though he but ill comprehended he instinctively knew must involve evil of some sort, Billy Budd was like a young horse fresh from the pasture suddenly inhaling a vile whiff from some chemical factory and by repeated snortings tries to get it out of his nostrils and lungs. This frame of mind barred all desire of holding further parley with the fellow, even were it but for the purpose of gaining some enlightenment as to his design in approaching him. And yet he was not without natural curiosity to see how such a visitor in the dark would look in broad day.

He espied him the following afternoon in his first dog-watch below, one of the smokers on that forward part of the upper gundeck allotted to the pipe.[7] He recognized him by his general cut and build, more than by his round freckled face and glassy eyes of pale blue, veiled with lashes all but white. And yet Billy was a bit uncertain whether indeed it were he—yonder chap about his own age chatting and laughing in freehearted way, leaning against a gun; a genial young fellow enough to look at, and something of a rattlebrain, to all appearance. Rather chubby too for a sailor, even an after-

---

[7] A portion of the forward gundeck where the sailors were allowed to smoke.

guardsman. In short the last man in the world, one would think, to be overburdened with thoughts, especially those perilous thoughts that must needs belong to a conspirator in any serious project, or even to the underling of such a conspirator.

Although Billy was not aware of it, the fellow, with a sidelong watchful glance had perceived Billy first, and then noting that Billy was looking at him, thereupon nodded a familiar sort of friendly recognition as to an old acquaintance, without interrupting the talk he was engaged in with the group of smokers. A day or two afterwards chancing in the evening promenade on a gundeck, to pass Billy, he offered a flying word of good-fellowship as it were, which by its unexpectedness, and equivocalness under the circumstances so embarrassed Billy that he knew not how to respond to it, and let it go unnoticed.

Billy was now left more at a loss than before. The ineffectual speculation into which he was led was so disturbingly alien to him that he did his best to smother it. It never entered his mind that here was a matter which from its extreme questionableness, it was his duty as a loyal blue-jacket to report in the proper quarter. And, probably, had such a step been suggested to him, he would have been deterred from taking it by the thought, one of novice magnanimity, that it would savor overmuch of the dirty work of a telltale. He kept the thing to himself. Yet upon one occasion, he could not forbear a little disburdening himself to the old Dansker, tempted thereto perhaps by the influence of a balmy night when the ship lay becalmed; the twain, silent for the most part, sitting together on deck, their heads propped against the bulwarks. But it was only a partial and anonymous account that Billy gave, the unfounded scruples above referred to preventing full disclosure to anybody. Upon hearing Billy's version, the sage Dansker seemed to divine more than he was told; and after a little meditation during which his wrinkles were pursed as into a point, quite effacing for the time that quizzing expression his face sometimes wore—"Didn't I say so, Baby Budd?"

"Say what?" demanded Billy.

"Why, *Jemmy Legs* is *down* on you."

"And what" rejoined Billy in amazement, "has *Jemmy Legs* to do with that cracked afterguardsman?"

"Ho, it was an afterguardsman then. A cat's-paw, a cat's-paw!" And with that exclamation, which, whether it had reference to a light puff of air just then coming over the calm sea, or subtler relation to the afterguardsman, there is no telling, the old Merlin gave a twisting wrench with his black teeth at his plug of tobacco, vouchsafing no reply to Billy's impetuous question, though now repeated, for it was his wont to relapse into grim silence when interrogated in skeptical sort as to any of his sententious oracles, not always very clear ones, rather partaking of that obscurity which invests most Delphic deliverances from any quarter.

Long experience had very likely brought this old man to that bitter prudence which never interferes in aught and never gives advice.

XVII

YES, DESPITE THE DANSKER'S pithy insistence as to the master-at-arms being at the bottom of these strange experiences of Billy on board the *Indomitable,* the young sailor was ready to ascribe them to almost anybody but the man who, to use Billy's own expression, "always had a pleasant word for him." This is to be wondered at. Yet not so much to be wondered at. In certain matters, some sailors even in mature life remain unsophisticated enough. But a young seafarer of the disposition of our athletic foretopman, is much of a child-man. And yet a child's utter innocence is but its blank ignorance, and the innocence more or less wanes as intelligence waxes. But in Billy Budd intelligence, such as it was, had advanced, while yet his simple-mindedness remained for the most part unaffected. Experience is a teacher indeed; yet did Billy's years make his experience small. Besides, he had none of that intuitive knowledge of the bad which in natures not good or incompletely so foreruns experience, and therefore may pertain, as in some instances it too clearly does pertain, even to youth.

And what could Billy know of man except of man as a mere sailor? And the old-fashioned sailor, the veritable man-before-the-mast, the sailor from boyhood up, he, though indeed of the same species as a landsman is in some respects singularly distinct from him. The sailor is frankness, the landsman is finesse. Life is not a game with the sailor, demanding the long head; no intricate game of chess where few moves are made in straightforwardness, and ends are attained by indirection; an oblique, tedious, barren game hardly worth that poor candle burnt out in playing it.[8]

Yes, as a class, sailors are in character a juvenile race. Even deviations are marked by juvenility. And this more especially holding true with the sailors of Billy's time. Then, too, certain things which apply to all sailors, do more pointedly operate here and there, upon the junior one. Every sailor, too, is accustomed to obey orders without debating them; his life afloat is externally ruled for him; he is not brought into that promiscuous commerce with mankind where unobstructed free agency on equal terms—equal superficially, at least—soon teaches one that unless upon occasion he exercise a distrust keen in proportion to the fairness of the appearance, some foul turn may be served him. A ruled undemonstrative distrustfulness is so habitual, not with businessmen so much, as with men who know their kind in less shallow relations than business, namely, certain men-of-the-world, that they come at last to employ it all but unconsciously; and some of them would very likely feel real surprise at being charged with it as one of their general characteristics.

---

8 *Cf.* Shakespeare, *Macbeth*, Act V, Scene 5, 11. 15–17.

XVIII

BUT AFTER THE LITTLE matter at the mess Billy Budd no more found himself in strange trouble at times about his hammock or his clothes bag or what not. While, as to that smile that occasionally sunned him, and the pleasant passing word, these were if not more frequent, yet if anything more pronounced than before.

But for all that, there were certain other demonstrations now. When Claggart's unobserved glance happened to light on belted Billy rolling along the upper gundeck in the leisure of the second dogwatch exchanging passing broadsides of fun with other young promenaders in the crowd; that glance would follow the cheerful sea Hyperion[9] with a settled meditative and melancholy expression, his eyes strangely suffused with incipient feverish tears. Then would Claggart look like the man of sorrows. Yes, and sometimes the melancholy expression would have in it a touch of soft yearning, as if Claggart could even have loved Billy but for fate and ban. But this was an evanescence, and quickly repented of, as it were, by an immitigable look, pinching and shriveling the visage into the momentary semblance of a wrinkled walnut. But sometimes catching sight in advance of the foretopman coming in his direction, he would, upon their nearing, step aside a little to let him pass, dwelling upon Billy for the moment with the glittering dental satire of a Guise.[1] But upon any abrupt unforeseen encounter a red light would flash forth from his eye like a spark from an anvil in a dusk smithy. That quick fierce light was a strange one, darted from orbs which in

---

9 In early Greek myth, the Titan Helios, god of the sun; later identified with Apollo, god of manly youth and beauty.

1 The Guises, a powerful ducal family of France in the sixteenth and seventeenth centuries, engaged in violent intrigues attractive to romancers, for example Dumas. As for the "glittering dental satire," cf. Hamlet's discovery "that one may smile . . . and be a villain" (Act I, Scene 5, ll. 103–105).

repose were of a color nearest approaching a deeper violet, the softest of shades.

Though some of these caprices of the pit could not but be observed by their object, yet were they beyond the construing of such a nature. And the *thews* of Billy were hardly compatible with that sort of sensitive spiritual organization which in some cases instinctively conveys to ignorant innocence an admonition of the proximity of the malign. He thought the master-at-arms acted in a manner rather queer at times. That was all. But the occasional frank air and pleasant word went for what they purported to be, the young sailor never having heard as yet of the "too fair-spoken man."

Had the foretopman been conscious of having done or said anything to provoke the ill will of the official, it would have been different with him, and his sight might have been purged if not sharpened. As it was, innocence was his blinder.

So was it with him in yet another matter. Two minor officers—the armorer and captain of the hold, with whom he had never exchanged a word, his position in the ship not bringing him into contact with them; these men now for the first began to cast upon Billy when they chanced to encounter him, that peculiar glance which evidences that the man from whom it comes has been some way tampered with and to the prejudice of him upon whom the glance lights. Never did it occur to Billy as a thing to be noted or a thing suspicious, though he well knew the fact, that the armorer and captain of the hold, with the ship's-yeoman, apothecary, and others of that grade, were by naval usage, messmates of the master-at-arms, men with ears convenient to his confidential tongue.

But the general popularity that our Handsome Sailor's manly forwardness upon occasion, and his irresistible good nature, indicating no mental superiority tending to excite an invidious feeling; this good will on the part of most of his shipmates made him the less to concern himself about such mute aspects toward him as those whereto allusion has just been made.

As to the afterguardsman, though Billy for reasons already given necessarily saw little of him, yet when the two did happen to meet, invariably came the fellow's offhand cheerful recognition, sometimes accompanied by a passing pleasant word or two. Whatever that equivocal young person's original design may really have been, or the design of which he might have been the deputy, certain it was from his manner upon these occasions, that he had wholly dropped it.

It was as if his precocity of crookedness (and every vulgar villain is precocious) had for once deceived him, and the man he had sought to entrap as a simpleton had, through his very simplicity ignorantly baffled him.

But shrewd ones may opine that it was hardly possible for Billy to refrain from going up to the afterguardsman and bluntly demanding to know his purpose in the initial interview, so abruptly closed in the forechains. Shrewd ones may also think it but natural in Billy to set about sounding some of the other impressed men of the ship in order to discover what basis, if any, there was for the emissary's obscure suggestions as to plotting disaffection aboard. Yes, the shrewd may so think. But something more, or rather, something else than mere shrewdness is perhaps needful for the due understanding of such a character as Billy Budd's.

As to Claggart, the monomania in the man—if that indeed it were—as involuntarily disclosed by starts in the manifestations detailed, yet in general covered over by his self-contained and rational demeanor; this, like a subterranean fire, was eating its way deeper and deeper in him. Something decisive must come of it.

XIX

AFTER THE MYSTERIOUS interview in the forechains, the one so abruptly ended there by Billy, nothing especially German[2] to the story occurred until the events now about to be narrated.

Elsewhere it has been said that in the lack of frigates (of course better sailers than line-of-battle ships) in the English squadron up the Straits at that period, the *Indomitable* was

---

2 Cf. "germane," meaning "akin."

occasionally employed not only as an available substitute for a scout, but at times on detached service of more important kind. This was not alone because of her sailing qualities, not common in a ship of her rate, but quite as much, probably, that the character of her commander, it was thought, specially adapted him for any duty where under unforeseen difficulties a prompt initiative might have to be taken in some matter demanding knowledge and ability in addition to those qualities implied in good seamanship. It was on an expedition of the latter sort, a somewhat distant one, and when the *Indomitable* was almost at her furthest remove from the fleet that in the latter part of an afternoon watch she unexpectedly came in sight of a ship of the enemy. It proved to be a frigate. The latter perceiving through the glass that the weight of men and metal would be heavily against her, invoking her light heels crowded sail to get away. After a chase urged almost against hope and lasting until about the middle of the first dogwatch, she signally succeeded in effecting her escape.

Not long after the pursuit had been given up, and ere the excitement incident thereto had altogether waned away, the master-at-arms ascending from his cavernous sphere made his appearance cap in hand by the mainmast respectfully waiting the notice of Captain Vere then solitary walking the weather side of the quarterdeck, doubtless somewhat chafed at the failure of the pursuit. The spot where Claggart stood was the place allotted to men of lesser grades seeking some more particular interview either with the officer-of-the-deck or the captain himself. But from the latter it was not often that a sailor or petty-officer of those days would seek a hearing; only some exceptional cause, would, according to established custom, have warranted that.

Presently, just as the commander absorbed in his reflections was on the point of turning aft in his promenade, he became sensible of Claggart's presence, and saw the doffed cap held in deferential expectancy. Here be it said that Captain Vere's personal knowledge of this petty-officer had only begun at the time of the ship's last sailing from home, Claggart then for the first, in transfer from a ship detained for repairs, supplying on board the *Indomitable* the place of a previous master-at-arms disabled and ashore.

No sooner did the commander observe who it was that now deferentially stood awaiting his notice, than a peculiar expression came over him. It was not unlike that which uncontrollably will flit across the countenance of one at unawares encountering a person who though known to him indeed has hardly been long enough known for thorough knowledge, but something in whose aspect nevertheless now for the first provokes a vaguely repellent distaste. But coming to a stand, and resuming much of his wonted official manner, save that a sort of impatience lurked in the intonation of the opening word, he said "Well? What is it, Master-at-Arms?"

With the air of a subordinate grieved at the necessity of being a messenger of ill tidings, and while conscientiously determined to be frank, yet equally resolved upon shunning overstatement, Claggart at this invitation or rather summons to disburden, spoke up. What he said, conveyed in the language of no uneducated man, was to the effect following if not altogether in these words, namely, that during the chase and preparations for the possible encounter he had seen enough to convince him that at least one sailor aboard was a dangerous character in a ship mustering some who not only had taken a guilty part in the late serious troubles, but others also who, like the man in question, had entered His Majesty's service under another form than enlistment.

At this point Captain Vere with some impatience, interrupted him: "Be direct, man; say impressed men."

Claggart made a gesture of subservience, and proceeded.

Quite lately he (Claggart) had begun to suspect that on the gundecks some sort of movement prompted by the sailor in question was covertly going on, but he had not thought himself warranted in reporting the suspicion so long as it remained indistinct. But from what he had that afternoon observed in the man referred to the suspicion of something clandestine going on had advanced to a point less removed from certainty. He deeply felt, he added, the serious responsibility assumed in making a report involving such possible consequences to the individual mainly concerned, besides tending to augment those natural anxieties which every naval commander must feel in view of extraordinary outbreaks so recent as those which, he sorrowfully said it, it needed not to name.

Now at the first broaching of the matter Captain Vere, taken by surprise, could not wholly dissemble his disquietude. But as Claggart went on, the former's aspect changed into restiveness under something in the witness' manner in giving his testimony. However, he refrained from interrupting him. And Claggart, continuing, concluded with this:

"God forbid, your honor, that the *Indomitable's* should be the experience of the—"

"Never mind that!" here peremptorily broke in the superior, his face altering with anger, instinctively divining the ship that the other was about to name, one in which the Nore Mutiny had assumed a singularly tragical character that for a time jeopardized the life of its commander. Under the circumstances he was indignant at the purposed allusion. When the commissioned officers themselves were on all occasions very heedful how they referred to the recent events, for a petty-officer unnecessarily to allude to them in the presence of his captain, this struck him as a most immodest presumption. Besides, to his quick sense of self-respect, it even looked under the circumstances something like an attempt to alarm him. Nor at first was he without some surprise that one who so far as he had hitherto come under his notice had shown considerable tact in his function should in this particular evince such lack of it.

But these thoughts and kindred dubious ones flitting across his mind were suddenly replaced by an intuitional surmise which though as yet obscure in form served practically to affect his reception of the ill tidings. Certain it is, that long versed in everything pertaining to the complicated gundeck life, which like every other form of life, has its secret mines and dubious side, the side popularly disclaimed, Captain Vere did not permit himself to be unduly disturbed by the general tenor of his subordinate's report. Furthermore, if in view of recent events prompt action should be taken at the first palpable sign of recurring insubordination, for all that, not judicious would it be, he thought, to keep the idea of lingering disaffection alive by undue forwardness in crediting an informer even if his own subordinate and charged among other things with police surveillance of the crew. This feeling would not perhaps have so prevailed with him were it not that upon a prior occasion the patriotic zeal officially evinced by Claggart had somewhat irritated him as appearing rather supersensible and strained. Furthermore, something even in the official's self-possessed and somewhat ostentatious manner in making his specifications strangely reminded him of a bandsman, perjurous witness in a capital case before a court-martial ashore of which, when a lieutenant, he Captain Vere had been a member.

Now the peremptory check given to Claggart in the matter of the arrested allusion was quickly followed up by this: "You say that there is at least one dangerous man aboard. Name him."

"William Budd. A foretopman, your honor—"

"William Budd" repeated Captain Vere with unfeigned astonishment, "and mean you the man that Lieutenant Ratcliffe took from the merchantman not very long ago—the young fellow who seems to be so popular with the men—Billy, the Handsome Sailor, as they call him?"

"The same, your honor; but for all his youth and good looks, a deep one. Not for nothing does he insinuate himself into the good will of his shipmates, since at the least all hands will at a pinch say a good word for him at all hazards. Did Lieutenant Ratcliffe happen to tell your honor of that adroit fling of Budd's, jumping up in the cutter's bow under the merchantman's stern when he was being taken off? It is even masked by that sort of good-humored air that at heart he resents his impressment. You have but noted his fair cheek. A man-trap may be under his ruddy-tipped daisies."

Now the Handsome Sailor as a signal figure among the crew had naturally enough attracted the Captain's attention from the first. Though in general not very demonstrative to his officers, he had congratulated Lieutenant Ratcliffe upon his good fortune in lighting on such a fine specimen of the genus homo, who in the nude might have posed for a statue of young Adam before the Fall.

As to Billy's adieu to the ship *Rights-of-Man,* which the boarding lieutenant had indeed reported to him but in a deferential way more as a good story than aught else, Captain Vere, though mistakenly understanding it as a satiric sally, had but thought so much the better of the impressed man for it; as a military sailor, admiring the spirit that could take an arbitrary enlistment so merrily and sensibly. The foretopman's conduct, too, so far as it had fallen under the captain's notice had confirmed the first happy augury, while the new recruit's qualities as a *sailor-man* seemed to be such that he had thought of recommending him to the executive officer for promotion to a place that would more frequently bring him under his own observation, namely, the captaincy of the mizzen-top, replacing there in the starboard watch a man not so young whom partly for that reason he deemed less fitted for the post. Be it parenthesized here that since the mizzen-top-men having not to handle such breadths of heavy canvas as the lower sails on the mainmast and foremast, a young man if of the right stuff not only seems best adapted to duty there, but in fact is generally selected for the captaincy of that top, and the company under him are light hands and often but striplings. In sum, Captain Vere had from the beginning deemed Billy Budd to be what in the naval parlance of the time was called a *"King's bargain,"* that is to say, for His Britannic Majesty's navy a capital investment at small outlay or none at all.

After a brief pause during which the reminiscences above mentioned passed vividly through his mind and he weighed the import of Claggart's last suggestion conveyed in the phrase "pitfall under the clover,"[3] and the more he weighed it the

---

3 *Cf.* "A man-trap . . . under his . . . daisies," ending the third paragraph above. There Melville had first written, then canceled, "a pitfall under his ruddy clover," the words that Captain Vere remembers here. The discrepancy might have been corrected had Melville seen the manuscript through press.

ess reliance he felt in the informer's good faith. Suddenly he
turned upon him and in a low voice: "Do you come to me,
Master-at-Arms, with so foggy a tale? As to Budd, cite me
an act or spoken word of his confirmatory of what you in
general charge against him. Stay," drawing nearer to him,
"heed what you speak. Just now, and in a case like this, there
is a yardarm end for the false witness."

"Ah, your honor!" sighed Claggart mildly shaking his
shapely head as in sad deprecation of such unmerited severity
of tone. Then, bridling—erecting himself as in virtuous self-
assertion, he circumstantially alleged certain words and acts,
which collectively, if credited, led to presumptions mortally
inculpating Budd. And for some of these averments, he added,
substantiating proof was not far.

With gray eyes impatient and distrustful essaying to fathom
to the bottom Claggart's calm violet ones, Captain Vere again
heard him out; then for the moment stood ruminating. The
mood he evinced, Claggart—himself for the time liberated
from the other's scrutiny—steadily regarded with a look difficult to render—a look curious of the operation of his tactics,
a look such as might have been that of the spokesman of the
envious children of Jacob deceptively imposing upon the
troubled patriarch the blood-dyed coat of young Joseph.

Though something exceptional in the moral quality of Captain Vere made him, in earnest encounter with a fellowman,
a veritable touchstone of that man's essential nature, yet now
as to Claggart and what was really going on in him his feeling
partook less of intuitional conviction than of strong suspicion
clogged by strange dubieties. The perplexity he evinced proceeded less from aught touching the man informed against—
as Claggart doubtless opined—than from considerations how
best to act in regard to the informer. At first indeed he was
naturally for summoning that substantiation of his allegations
which Claggart said was at hand. But such a proceeding would
result in the matter at once getting abroad, which in the
present stage of it, he thought, might undesirably affect the
ship's company. If Claggart was a false witness—that closed
the affair. And therefore before trying the accusation, he

would first practically test the accuser; and he thought this could be done in a quiet undemonstrative way.

The measure he determined upon involved a shifting of the scene, a transfer to a place less exposed to observation than the broad quarterdeck. For although the few gun room officers there at the time had, in due observance of naval etiquette, withdrawn to leeward the moment Captain Vere had begun his promenade on the deck's weather side; and though during the colloquy with Claggart they of course ventured not to diminish the distance; and though throughout the interview Captain Vere's voice was far from high, and Claggart's silvery and low; and the wind in the cordage and the wash of the sea helped the more to put them beyond earshot; nevertheless, the interview's continuance already had attracted observation from some topmen aloft and other sailors in the waist or further forward.

Having determined upon his measures, Captain Vere forthwith took action. Abruptly turning to Claggart he asked, "Master-at-Arms, is it now Budd's watch aloft?"

"No, your honor." Whereupon, "Mr. Wilkes!" summoning the nearest midshipman, "tell Albert to come to me." Albert was the captain's hammock boy, a sort of sea valet in whose discretion and fidelity his master had much confidence. The lad appeared. "You know Budd the foretopman?"

"I do, sir."

"Go find him. It is his watch off. Manage to tell him out of earshot that he is wanted aft. Contrive it that he speaks to nobody. Keep him in talk yourself. And not till you get well aft here, not till then let him know that the place where he is wanted is my cabin. You understand. Go.—Master-at-Arms, show yourself on the decks below, and when you think it time for Albert to be coming with his man, stand by quietly to follow the sailor in."

XX

Now WHEN THE FORETOPMAN found himself closeted there, as it were, in the cabin with the captain and Claggart, he was surprised enough. But it was a surprise unaccompanied by apprehension or distrust. To an immature nature essentially honest and humane, forewarning intimations of subtler danger from one's kind come tardily if at all. The only thing that took shape in the young sailor's mind was this: Yes, the captain, I have always thought, looks kindly upon me. Wonder if he's going to make me his coxswain. I should like that. And maybe now he is going to ask the master-at-arms about me.

"Shut the door there, sentry," said the commander. "Stand without, and let nobody come in.—Now, Master-at-Arms, tell this man to his face what you told of him to me," and stood prepared to scrutinize the mutually confronting visages.

With the measured step and calm collected air of an asylum physician approaching in the public hall some patient beginning to show indications of a coming paroxysm, Claggart deliberately advanced within short range of Billy, and mesmerically looking him in the eye, briefly recapitulated the accusation.

Not at first did Billy take it in. When he did, the rose-tan of his cheek looked struck as by white leprosy. He stood like one impaled and gagged. Meanwhile the accuser's eyes removing not as yet from the blue dilated ones, underwent a phenomenal change, their wonted rich violet color blurring into a muddy purple. Those lights of human intelligence losing human expression, gelidly protruding like the alien eyes of certain uncatalogued creatures of the deep. The first mesmeric glance was one of serpent fascination; the last was as the hungry lurch of the torpedo fish.

"Speak, man!" said Captain Vere to the transfixed one struck by his aspect even more than by Claggart's. "Speak! defend yourself." Which appeal caused but a strange dumb

61

gesturing and gurgling in Billy; amazement at such an accusation so suddenly sprung on inexperienced nonage; this, and, it may be horror of the accuser, serving to bring out his lurking defect and in this instance for the time intensifying it into a convulsed tongue-tie; while the intent head and entire form straining forward in an agony of ineffectual eagerness to obey the injunction to speak and defend himself, gave an expression to the face like that of a condemned vestal priestess in the moment of being buried alive, and in the first struggle against suffocation.

Though at the time Captain Vere was quite ignorant of Billy's liability to vocal impediment, he now immediately divined it, since vividly Billy's aspect recalled to him that of a bright young schoolmate of his whom he had once seen struck by much the same startling impotence in the act of eagerly rising in the class to be foremost in response to a testing question put to it by the master. Going close up to the young sailor, and laying a soothing hand on his shoulder, he said: "There is no hurry, my boy. Take your time, take your time." Contrary to the effect intended, these words so fatherly in tone, doubtless touching Billy's heart to the quick, prompted yet more violent efforts at utterance—efforts ending for the time in confirming the paralysis, and bringing to his face an expression which was as a crucifixion to behold. The next instant, quick as the flame from a discharged cannon at night, his right arm shot out, and Claggart dropped to the deck. Whether intentionally or but owing to the young athlete's superior height, the blow had taken effect full upon the forehead, so shapely and intellectual-looking a feature in the master-at-arms; so that the body fell over lengthwise, like a heavy plank tilted from erectness. A gasp or two, and he lay motionless.

"Fated boy," breathed Captain Vere in tone so low as to be almost a whisper, "what have you done! But here, help me."

The twain raised the felled one from the loins up into a sitting position. The spare form flexibly acquiesced, but inertly. It was like handling a dead snake. They lowered it back. Regaining erectness Captain Vere with one hand covering his

face stood to all appearance as impassive as the object at his
feet. Was he absorbed in taking in all the bearings of the event
and what was best not only now at once to be done, but also
in the sequel? Slowly he uncovered his face; and the effect
was as if the moon emerging from eclipse should reappear
with quite another aspect than that which had gone into hiding. The father in him, manifested toward Billy thus far in
the scene, was replaced by the military disciplinarian. In his
official tone he bade the foretopman retire to a stateroom aft,
(pointing it out) and there remain till thence summoned. This
order Billy in silence mechanically obeyed. Then going to the
cabin door where it opened on the quarterdeck, Captain
Vere said to the sentry without, "Tell somebody to send Albert
here." When the lad appeared his master so contrived it that
he should not catch sight of the prone one. "Albert," he said
to him, "tell the surgeon I wish to see him. You need not
come back till called." When the surgeon entered—a self-
poised character of that grave sense and experience that
hardly anything could take him aback—Captain Vere, advanced to meet him, thus unconsciously intercepting his view
of Claggart and interrupting the other's wonted ceremonious
salutation, and said, "Nay, tell me how it is with yonder
man," directing his attention to the prostrate one.

The surgeon looked, and for all his self-command, somewhat started at the abrupt revelation. On Claggart's always
pallid complexion, thick black blood was now oozing from
nostril and ear. To the gazer's professional eye it was un-
mistakably no living man that he saw.

"Is it so then?" said Captain Vere intently watching him. "I
thought it. But verify it." Whereupon the customary tests
confirmed the surgeon's first glance, who now looking up in
unfeigned concern, cast a look of intense inquisitiveness upon
his superior. But Captain Vere, with one hand to his brow,
was standing motionless. Suddenly, catching the surgeon's arm
convulsively, he exclaimed pointing down to the body—"It is
the divine judgment on Ananias![4] Look!"

4 Having lied, "not . . . unto men, but unto God," Ananias was stricken dead
(Acts v: 1–5).

Disturbed by the excited manner he had never before observed in the *Indomitable's* captain, and as yet wholly ignorant of the affair, the prudent surgeon nevertheless held his peace, only again looking an earnest interrogation as to what it was that had resulted in such a tragedy.

But Captain Vere was now again motionless standing absorbed in thought. But again starting, he vehemently exclaimed—"Struck dead by an angel of God! Yet the angel must hang!"

At these passionate interjections, mere incoherences to the listener as yet unapprised of the antecedents, the surgeon was profoundly discomposed. But now as recollecting himself, Captain Vere in less harsh tone briefly related the circumstances leading up to the event.

"But come; we must dispatch," he added. "Help me to remove him (meaning the body) to yonder compartment," designating one opposite that where the foretopman remained immured. Anew disturbed by a request that as implying a desire for secrecy, seemed unaccountably strange to him, there was nothing for the subordinate to do but comply.

"Go now," said Captain Vere with something of his wonted manner—"Go now. I shall presently call a drum-head court. Tell the lieutenants what has happened, and tell Mr. Mordant," meaning the captain of marines, "and charge them to keep the matter to themselves."

XXI

FULL OF DISQUIETUDE and misgiving the surgeon left the cabin. Was Captain Vere suddenly affected in his mind, or was it but a transient excitement, brought about by so strange and extraordinary a happening? As to the drum-head court, it struck the surgeon as impolitic, if nothing more. The thing to do, he thought, was to place Billy Budd in confinement and in a way dictated by usage, and postpone further action in so extraordinary a case, to such time as they should rejoin the squadron, and then refer it to the admiral. He recalled the unwonted agitation of Captain Vere and his excited exclamations so at variance with his normal manner. Was he unhinged? But assuming that he is, it is not so susceptible of proof. What then can he do? No more trying situation is conceivable than that of an officer subordinate under a captain whom he suspects to be, not mad indeed, but yet not quite unaffected in his intellect. To argue his order to him would be insolence. To resist him would be mutiny.

In obedience to Captain Vere he communicated what had happened to the lieutenants and captain of marines, saying nothing as to the captain's state. They fully shared his own surprise and concern. Like him too they seemed to think that such a matter should be referred to the admiral.

XXII

WHO IN THE RAINBOW can draw the line where the violet tint ends and the orange tint begins? Distinctly we see the difference of the colors, but where exactly does the one first blendingly enter into the other? So with sanity and insanity. In pronounced cases there is no question about them. But in some supposed cases, in various degrees supposedly less pronounced, to draw the exact line of demarkation few will undertake though for a fee some professional experts will. There is nothing namable but that some men will undertake to do it for pay.

Whether Captain Vere, as a surgeon professionally and privately surmised, was really the sudden victim of any degree of aberration, one must determine for himself by such light as this narrative may afford.

That the unhappy event which has been narrated could not have happened at a worse juncture was but too true. For it was close on the heel of the suppressed insurrections, an after-time very critical to naval authority, demanding from every English sea commander two qualities not readily interfusable

—prudence and rigor. Moreover there was something crucial in the case.

In the jugglery of circumstances preceding and attending the event on board the *Indomitable* and in the light of that martial code whereby it was formally to be judged, innocence and guilt personified in Claggart and Budd in effect changed places. In a legal view the apparent victim of the tragedy was he who had sought to victimize a man blameless; and the indisputable deed of the latter, navally regarded, constituted the most heinous of military crimes. Yet more. The essential right and wrong involved in the matter, the clearer that might be, so much the worse for the responsibility of a loyal sea commander inasmuch as he was not authorized to determine the matter on that primitive basis.

Small wonder then that the *Indomitable's* captain though in general a man of rapid decision, felt that circumspectness not less than promptitude was necessary. Until he could decide upon his course, and in each detail; and not only so, but until the concluding measure was upon the point of being enacted, he deemed it advisable, in view of all the circumstances to guard as much as possible against publicity. Here he may or may not have erred. Certain it is however that subsequently in the confidential talk of more than one or two gun rooms and cabins he was not a little criticized by some officers, a fact imputed by his friends and vehemently by his cousin Jack Denton to professional jealousy of Starry Vere. Some imaginative ground for invidious comment there was. The maintenance of secrecy in the matter, the confining all knowledge of it for a time to the place where the homicide occurred, the quarterdeck cabin; in these particulars lurked some resemblance to the policy adopted in those tragedies of the palace which have occurred more than once in the capital founded by Peter the Barbarian.[5]

The case indeed was such that fain would the *Indomitable's* captain have deferred taking any action whatever respecting

5 Peter I, Czar of Russia (1682–1725), called Peter the Great, founded the new Russian capital of St. Petersburg (1703).

it further than to keep the foretopman a close prisoner till the ship rejoined the squadron and then submitting the matter to the judgement of his admiral.

But a true military officer is one particular like a true monk. Not with more of self-abnegation will the latter keep his vows of monastic obedience than the former his vows of allegiance to martial duty.

Feeling that unless quick action was taken on it, the deed of the foretopman, so soon as it should be known on the gun-decks would tend to awaken any slumbering embers of the Nore among the crew, a sense of the urgency of the case over-ruled in Captain Vere every other consideration. But though a conscientious disciplinarian he was no lover of authority for mere authority's sake. Very far was he from embracing op-portunities for monopolizing to himself the perils of moral responsibility, none at least that could properly be referred to an official superior or shared with him by his official equals or even subordinates. So thinking, he was glad it would not be at variance with usage to turn the matter over to a summary court of his own officers, reserving to himself as the one on whom the ultimate accountability would rest, the right of maintaining a supervision of it, or formally or informally interposing at need. Accordingly a drum-head court was summarily convened, he electing the individuals composing it, the first lieutenant, the captain of marines, and the sailing master.

In associating an officer of marines with the sea lieutenants in a case having to do with a sailor the commander perhaps deviated from general custom. He was prompted thereto by the circumstance that he took that soldier to be a judicious person, thoughtful, and not altogether incapable of grappling with a difficult case unprecedented in his prior experience. Yet even as to him he was not without some latent misgiving, for withal he was an extremely good-natured man, an enjoyer of his dinner, a sound sleeper, and inclined to obesity. A man who though he would always maintain his manhood in battle might not prove altogether reliable in a moral dilemma involv-ing aught of the tragic. As to the first lieutenant and the sailing master, Captain Vere could not but be aware that though honest natures, of approved gallantry upon occasion, their intelligence was mostly confined to the matter of active seamanship and the fighting demands of their profession. The court was held in the same cabin where the unfortunate affair had taken place. This cabin, the commander's, embraced the entire area under the poopdeck. Aft, and on either side, was a small stateroom; the one room temporarily a jail and the other a dead-house, and a yet smaller compartment leaving a space between, expanding forward into a goodly oblong of length coinciding with the ship's beam. A skylight of moderate dimension was overhead and at each end of the oblong space were two sashed porthole windows easily convertible back into embrasures for short carronades.

All being quickly in readiness, Billy Budd was arraigned, Captain Vere necessarily appearing as the sole witness in the case, and as such temporarily sinking his rank, though singularly maintaining it in a matter apparently trivial, namely, that he testified from the ship's weather side, with that object having caused the court to sit on the lee side. Concisely he narrated all that had led up to the catastrophe, omitting nothing in Claggart's accusation and deposing as to the manner in which the prisoner had received it. At this testimony the three officers glanced with no little surprise at Billy Budd, the last man they would have suspected either of the mutinous design alleged by Claggart or the undeniable deed he himself had done.

The first lieutenant, taking judicial primacy and turning toward the prisoner, said, "Captain Vere has spoken. Is it or is it not as Captain Vere says?" In response came syllables not so much impeded in the utterance as might have been anticipated. They were these: "Captain Vere tells the truth. It is just as Captain Vere says, but it is not as the master-at-arms said. I have eaten the King's bread and I am true to the King."

"I believe you, my man" said the witness, his voice indicating a suppressed emotion not otherwise betrayed.

"God will bless you for that, Your Honor!" not without stammering said Billy, and all but broke down. But immediately was recalled to self-control by another question, to which with the same emotional difficulty of utterance he said, "No, there was no malice between us. I never bore malice against the master-at-arms. I am sorry that he is dead. I did not mean to kill him. Could I have used my tongue I would not have struck him. But he foully lied to my face and in presence of my captain, and I had to say something, and I could only say it with a blow, God help me!"

In the impulsive above-board manner of the frank one, the court saw confirmed all that was implied in words that just previously had perplexed them, coming as they did from the testifier to the tragedy and promptly following Billy's impassioned disclaimer of mutinous intent—Captain Vere's words, "I believe you, my man."

Next it was asked of him whether he knew of or suspected aught savoring of incipient trouble (meaning mutiny, though the explicit term was avoided) going on in any section of the ship's company.

The reply lingered. This was naturally imputed by the court to the same vocal embarrassment which had retarded or obstructed previous answers. But in main it was otherwise here; the question immediately recalling to Billy's mind the interview with the afterguardsman in the forechains. But an innate repugnance to playing a part at all approaching that of an informer against one's own shipmates—the same erring sense of uninstructed honor which had stood in the way of his reporting the matter at the time though as a loyal man-of-war-man it was incumbent on him, and failure so to do if charged against him and proven, would have subjected him to the heaviest of penalties; this, with the blind feeling now his, that nothing really was being hatched, prevailed with him. When the answer came it was a negative.

"One question more," said the officer of marines now first speaking and with a troubled earnestness. "You tell us that what the master-at-arms said against you was a lie. Now why should he have so lied, so maliciously lied, since you declare there was no malice between you?"

At that question unintentionally touching on a spiritual

sphere wholly obscure to Billy's thoughts, he was nonplussed, evincing a confusion indeed that some observers, such as can readily be imagined, would have construed into involuntary evidence of hidden guilt. Nevertheless he strove some way to answer, but all at once relinquished the vain endeavor, at the same time turning an appealing glance towards Captain Vere as deeming him his best helper and friend. Captain Vere who had been seated for a time rose to his feet, addressing the interrogator. "The question you put to him comes naturally enough. But how can he rightly answer it? or anybody else? unless indeed it be he who lies within there," designating the compartment where lay the corpse. "But the prone one there will not rise to our summons. In effect, though, as it seems to me, the point you make is hardly material. Quite aside from any conceivable motive actuating the master-at-arms, and irrespective of the provocation to the blow, a martial court must needs in the present case confine its attention to the blow's consequence, which consequence justly is to be deemed not otherwise than as the striker's deed."

This utterance the full significance of which it was not at all likely that Billy took in, nevertheless caused him to turn a wistful interrogative look toward the speaker, a look in its dumb expressiveness not unlike that which a dog of generous breed might turn upon his master seeking in his face some elucidation of a precious gesture ambiguous to the canine intelligence. Nor was the same utterance without marked effect upon the three officers, more especially the soldier. Couched in it seemed to them a meaning unanticipated, involving a prejudgment on the speaker's part. It served to augment a mental disturbance previously evident enough.

The soldier once more spoke; in a tone of suggestive dubiety addressing at once his associates and Captain Vere: "Nobody is present—none of the ship's company, I mean, who might shed lateral light, if any is to be had, upon what remains mysterious in this matter."

"That is thoughtfully put," said Captain Vere. "I see your drift. Ay, there is a mystery; but, to use a Scriptural phrase, it is 'a mystery of iniquity,' a matter for psychologic theologians to discuss. But what has a military court to do with it? Not to add that for us any possible investigation of it is cut off by the lasting tongue-tie of—him—in yonder," again designating the mortuary stateroom. "The prisoner's deed,— with that alone we have to do."

To this, and particularly the closing reiteration, the marine soldier knowing not how aptly to reply, sadly abstained from saying aught. The first lieutenant who at the outset had not unnaturally assumed primacy in the court, now overwhelmingly instructed by a glance from Captain Vere, a glance more effective than words, resumed that primacy. Turning to the prisoner, "Budd," he said, and scarce in equable tones, "Budd, if you have aught further to say for yourself, say it now."

Upon this the young sailor turned another quick glance toward Captain Vere; then, as taking a hint from that aspect, a hint confirming his own instinct that silence was now best, replied to the lieutenant "I have said all, sir."

The marine—the same who had been the sentinel without the cabin door at the time that the foretopman followed by the master-at-arms, entered it—he, standing by the sailor throughout these judicial proceedings, was now directed to take him back to the after compartment originally assigned to the prisoner and his custodian. As the twain disappeared from view, the three officers as partially liberated from some inward constraint associated with Billy's mere presence, simultaneously stirred in their seats. They exchanged looks of troubled indecision, yet feeling that decide they must and without long delay. As for Captain Vere, he for the time stood unconsciously with his back toward them, apparently in one of his absent fits, gazing out from a sashed porthole to windward upon the monotonous blank of the twilight sea. But the court's silence continuing, broken only at moments by brief consultations in low earnest tones, this seemed to arm him and energize him. Turning, he to-and-fro paced the cabin athwart; in the returning ascent to windward, climbing the slant deck in the ship's lee roll; without knowing it symbolizing thus in his action a mind resolute to surmount difficulties even if against primitive instincts strong as the wind and the sea. Presently he came to a stand before the three. After scanning their faces he stood less as mustering his thoughts for expression, than as one inly deliberating how best to put them to well-meaning men not intellectually mature, men with whom it was necessary to demonstrate certain principles that were axioms to himself. Similar impatience as to talking is perhaps one reason that deters some minds from addressing any popular assemblies.

When speak he did, something both in the substance of what he said and his manner of saying it showed the influence of unshared studies modifying and tempering the practical training of an active career. This, along with his phraseology now and then was suggestive of the grounds whereon rested that imputation of a certain pedantry socially alleged against him by certain naval men of wholly practical cast, captains who nevertheless would frankly concede that His Majesty's navy mustered no more efficient officer of their grade than Starry Vere.

What he said was to this effect: "Hitherto I have been but the witness, little more; and I should hardly think now to take another tone, that of your coadjutor, for the time, did I not perceive in you,—at the crisis too—a troubled hesitancy, proceeding, I doubt not from the clash of military duty with moral scruple—scruple vitalized by compassion. For the compassion how can I otherwise than share it. But, mindful of paramount obligations I strive against scruples that may tend to enervate decision. Not, gentlemen, that I hide from myself that the case is an exceptional one. Speculatively regarded, it well might be referred to a jury of casuists. But for us here acting not as casuists or moralists, it is a case practical, and under martial law practically to be dealt with.

"But your scruples: do they move as in a dusk? Challenge them. Make them advance and declare themselves. Come now: do they import something like this: If, mindless of palliating circumstances, we are bound to regard the death of the master-at-arms as the prisoner's deed, then does that deed constitute a capital crime whereof the penalty is a mortal one. But in natural justice is nothing but the prisoner's overt act to be considered? How can we adjudge to summary and shameful death a fellow-creature innocent before God, and whom we feel to be so?—Does that state it aright? You sign sad assent. Well, I too feel that, the full force of that. It is Nature. But do these buttons that we wear attest that our allegiance is to Nature? No, to the King. Though the ocean, which is inviolate Nature primeval, though this be the element where we move and have our being as sailors, yet as the King's officers lies our duty in a sphere correspondingly natural? So little is that true, that in receiving our commissions we in the most important regards ceased to be natural free agents. When war is declared are we the commissioned fighters previously consulted? We fight at command. If our judgments approve the war, that is but coincidence. So in other particulars. So now. For suppose condemnation to follow these present proceedings. Would it be so much we ourselves that would condemn as it would be martial law operating through us? For that law and the rigor of it, we are not responsible. Our vowed responsibilty is in this: that however pitilessly that law may operate, we nevertheless adhere to it and administer it.

"But the exceptional in the matter moves the hearts within you. Even so too is mine moved. But let not warm hearts betray heads that should be cool. Ashore in a criminal case will an upright judge allow himself off the bench to be waylaid by some tender kinswoman of the accused seeking to touch him with her tearful plea? Well the heart here denotes the feminine in man is as that piteous woman, and hard though it be, she must here be ruled out."

He paused, earnestly studying them for a moment; then resumed.

"But something in your aspect seems to urge that it is not solely the heart that moves in you, but also the conscience, the private conscience. But tell me whether or not, occupying the position we do, private conscience should not yield to that imperial one formulated in the code under which alone we officially proceed?"

Here the three men moved in their seats, less convinced

than agitated by the course of an argument troubling but the more the spontaneous conflict within.

Perceiving which, the speaker paused for a moment; then abruptly changing his tone, went on.

"To steady us a bit, let us recur to the facts.—In wartime at sea a man-of-war's-man strikes his superior in grade, and the blow kills. Apart from its effect the blow itself is, according to the Articles of War, capital crime. Furthermore—"

"Ay, sir," emotionally broke in the officer of marines, "in one sense it was. But surely Budd purposed neither mutiny nor homicide."

"Surely not, my good man. And before a court less arbitrary and more merciful than a martial one, that plea would largely extenuate. At the Last Assizes[6] it shall acquit. But how here? We proceed under the law of the Mutiny Act. In feature no child can resemble his father more than that Act resembles in spirit the thing from which it derives—War. In His Majesty's service—in this ship indeed—there are Englishmen forced to fight for the King against their will. Against their conscience, for aught we know. Though as their fellow-creatures some of us may appreciate their position, yet as navy officers, what reck we of it? Still less recks the enemy. Our impressed men he would fain cut down in the same swath with our volunteers. As regards the enemy's naval conscripts, some of whom may even share our own abhorrence of the regicidal French Directory,[7] it is the same on our side. War looks but to the frontage, the appearance. And the Mutiny Act, War's child, takes after the father. Budd's intent or nonintent is nothing to the purpose.

"But while, put to it by those anxieties in you which I can not but respect, I only repeat myself—while thus strangely we prolong proceedings that should be summary—the enemy

---

6 Assizes are the highest judicial courts of review of the British counties; here the term refers to the scriptural Judgment Day.

7 The executive council of the French First Republic (1795–1799). This was the enemy against whom the British fleet was engaged in 1797, the year of this story (*cf.* the Preface).

may be sighted and an engagement result. We must do; and one of two things must we do—condemn or let go."

"Can we not convict and yet mitigate the penalty?" asked the junior lieutenant here speaking, and falteringly, for the first.

"Lieutenant, were that clearly lawful for us under the circumstances consider the consequences of such clemency. The people" (meaning the ship's company) "have native-sense; most of them are familiar with our naval usage and traditions; and how would they take it? Even could you explain to them —which our official position forbids—they, long molded by arbitrary discipline have not that kind of intelligent responsiveness that might qualify them to comprehend and discriminate. No, to the people the foretopman's deed however it be worded in the announcement will be plain homicide committed in a flagrant act of mutiny. What penalty for that should follow, they know. But it does not follow. *Why?* they will ruminate. You know what sailors are. Will they not revert to the recent outbreak at the Nore? Ay. They know the well-founded alarm—the panic it struck throughout England. Your clement sentence they would account pusillanimous. They would think that we flinch, that we are afraid of them—afraid of practising a lawful rigor singularly demanded at this juncture lest it should provoke new troubles. What shame to us such a conjecture on their part, and how deadly to discipline. You see then, whither prompted by duty and the law I steadfastly drive. But I beseech you, my friends, do not take me amiss. I feel as you do for this unfortunate boy. But did he know our hearts, I take him to be of that generous nature that he would feel even for us on whom in this military necessity so heavy a compulsion is laid."

With that, crossing the deck he resumed his place by the sashed porthole, tacitly leaving the three to come to a decision. On the cabin's opposite side the troubled court sat silent. Loyal lieges, plain and practical, though at bottom they dissented from some points Captain Vere had put to them, they were without the faculty, hardly had the inclination to gainsay one whom they felt to be an earnest man, one too not less their superior in mind than in naval rank. But it is not improbable that even such of his words as were not without influence over them, less came home to them than his closing appeal to their instinct as sea officers in the forethought he threw out as to the practical consequences to discipline, considering the unconfirmed tone of the fleet at the time, should a man-of-war's-man's violent killing at sea of a superior in grade be allowed to pass for aught else than a capital crime demanding prompt infliction of the penalty.

Not unlikely they were brought to something more or less akin to that harassed frame of mind which in the year 1842 actuated the commander of the U.S. brig-of-war *Somers* to resolve, under the so-called Articles of War, Articles modeled upon the English Mutiny Act, to resolve upon the execution at sea of a midshipman and two petty-officers as mutineers designing the seizure of the brig. Which resolution was carried out though in a time of peace and within not many days sail of home. An act vindicated by a naval court of inquiry subsequently convened ashore. History, and here cited without comment. True, the circumstances on board the *Somers* were different from those on board the *Indomitable*. But the urgency felt, well-warranted or otherwise, was much the same.

Says a writer whom few know, "Forty years after a battle it is easy for a noncombatant to reason about how it ought to have been fought. It is another thing personally and under fire to direct the fighting while involved in the obscuring smoke of it. Much so with respect to other emergencies involving considerations both practical and moral, and when it is imperative promptly to act. The greater the fog the more it imperils the steamer, and speed is put on though at the hazard of running somebody down. Little ween the snug card players in the cabin of the responsibilities of the sleepless man on the bridge."

In brief, Billy Budd was formally convicted and sentenced to be hung at the yardarm in the early morning watch, it being now night. Otherwise, as is customary in such cases, the sentence would forthwith have been carried out. In wartime on the field or in the fleet, a mortal punishment decreed by a drum-head court—on the field sometimes decreed by but a nod from the general—follows without delay on the heel of conviction without appeal.

XXIII

IT WAS CAPTAIN VERE himself who of his own motion communicated the finding of the court to the prisoner; for that purpose going to the compartment where he was in custody and bidding the marine there to withdraw for the time.

Beyond the communication of the sentence what took place at this interview was never known. But in view of the character of the twain briefly closeted in that stateroom, each radically sharing in the rarer qualities of our nature—so rare indeed as to be all but incredible to average minds however much cultivated—some conjectures may be ventured.

It would have been in consonance with the spirit of Captain Vere should he on this occasion have concealed nothing from the condemned one—should he indeed have frankly disclosed to him the part he himself had played in bringing about the decision, at the same time revealing his actuating motives. On Billy's side it is not improbable that such a confession would have been received in much the same spirit that prompted it. Not without a sort of joy indeed he might have appreciated the brave opinion of him implied in his captain making such a confidant of him. Nor, as to the sentence itself could he have been insensible that it was imparted to him as to one not afraid to die. Even more may have been. Captain Vere in the end may have developed the passion sometimes latent under an exterior stoical or indifferent. He was old enough to have been Billy's father. The austere devotee of military duty letting himself melt back into what remains primeval in our formalized humanity may in the end have caught Billy to his heart even as Abraham may have caught young Isaac on the brink of resolutely offering him up in obedience to the exacting behest. But there is no telling the sacrament, seldom if in any case revealed to the gadding world wherever under circumstances at all akin to those here attempted to be set forth two of great Nature's nobler order embrace. There is privacy at the time, inviolable to the survivor, and holy oblivion the sequel to each diviner magnanimity, providentially covers all at last.

The first to encounter Captain Vere in act of leaving the compartment was the senior lieutenant. The face he beheld, for the moment one expressive of the agony of the strong, was to that officer, though a man of fifty, a startling revelation. That the condemned one suffered less than he who mainly had effected the condemnation was apparently indicated by the former's exclamation in the scene soon perforce to be touched upon.

XXIV

OF A SERIES of incidents within a brief term rapidly following each other, the adequate narration may take up a term less brief, especially if explanation or comment here and there seem requisite to the better understanding of such incidents. Between the entrance into the cabin of him who never left it alive, and him who when he did leave it left it as one condemned to die; between this and the closeted interview just given less than an hour and a half had elapsed. It was an interval long enough however to awaken speculation among no few of the ship's company as to what it was that could be detaining in the cabin the master-at-arms and the sailor; for a rumor that both of them had been seen to enter it and neither of them had been seen to emerge, this rumor had got abroad upon the gundecks and in the tops; the people of a great warship being in one respect like villagers taking microscopic note of every outward movement or nonmovement going on. When therefore in weather not at all tempestuous all hands were called in the second dogwatch, a summons under such circumstances not usual in those hours, the crew were not wholly unprepared for some announcement extraordinary, one having connection too with the continued absence of the two men from their wonted haunts.

There was a moderate sea at the time; and the moon, newly risen and near to being at its full, silvered the white spardeck wherever not blotted by the clear-cut shadows horizontally thrown of fixtures and moving men. On either side the quarterdeck the marine guard under arms was drawn up; and Captain Vere standing in his place surrounded by all the wardroom officers, addressed his men. In so doing his manner showed neither more nor less than that property pertaining to his supreme position aboard his own ship. In clear terms and concise he told them what had taken place in the cabin; that the master-at-arms was dead; that he who had killed him had been already tried by a summary court and condemned to death; and that the execution would take place in the early morning watch. The word *mutiny* was not named in what he said. He refrained too from making the occasion an opportunity for any preachment as to the maintenance of discipline, thinking perhaps that under existing circumstances in the navy the consequence of violating discipline should be made to speak for itself.

Their captain's announcement was listened to by the throng of standing sailors in a dumbness like that of a seated congregation of believers in hell listening to the clergyman's announcement of his Calvinistic text.

At the close, however, a confused murmur went up. It began to wax. All but instantly, then, at a sign, it was pierced and suppressed by shrill whistles of the boatswain and his mates piping down one watch.

To be prepared for burial Claggart's body was delivered to certain petty-officers of his mess. And here, not to clog the sequel with lateral matters, it may be added that at a suitable hour, the master-at-arms was committed to the sea with every funeral honor properly belonging to his naval grade.

In this proceeding as in every public one growing out of the tragedy strict adherence to usage was observed. Nor in any point could it have been at all deviated from, either with respect to Claggart or Billy Budd, without begetting undesirable speculations in the ship's company, sailors, and more particularly men-of-war's men, being of all men the greatest sticklers for usage.

For similar cause, all communication between Captain Vere and the condemned one ended with the closeted interview already given, the latter being now surrendered to the ordinary routine preliminary to the end. This transfer under guard from the captain's quarters was effected without unusual precautions—at least no visible ones.

If possible not to let the men so much as surmise that their officers anticipate aught amiss from them is the tacit rule in a military ship. And the more that some sort of trouble should really be apprehended the more do the officers keep that apprehension to themselves; though not the less unostentatious vigilance may be augmented.

In the present instance the sentry placed over the prisoner had strict orders to let no one have communication with him but the chaplain. And certain unobtrusive measures were taken absolutely to insure this point.

XXV

IN A SEVENTY-FOUR of the old order the deck known as the upper gundeck was the one covered over by the spardeck which last though not without its armament was for the most part exposed to the weather. In general it was at all hours free from hammocks; those of the crew swinging on the lower gundeck, and berthdeck, the latter being not only a dormitory but also the place for the stowing of the sailors' bags, and on both sides lined with the large chests or movable pantries of the many messes of the men.

On the starboard side of the *Indomitable's* upper gundeck,

behold Billy Budd under sentry lying prone in irons in one of the bays formed by the regular spacing of the guns comprising the batteries on either side. All these pieces were of the heavier caliber of that period. Mounted on lumbering wooden carriages they were hampered with cumbersome harness of breeching and strong side-tackles for running them out. Guns and carriages, together with the long rammers and shorter lintstocks lodged in loops overhead—all these, as customary, were painted black; and the heavy hempen breechings tarred to the same tint, wore the like livery of the undertakers. In contrast with the funereal hue of these surroundings the prone sailor's exterior apparel, white jumper and white duck trousers, each more or less soiled, dimly glimmered in the obscure light of the bay like a patch of discolored snow in early April lingering at some upland cave's black mouth. In effect he is already in his shroud or the garments that shall serve him in lieu of one. Over him but scarce illuminating him, two battle lanterns swing from two massive beams of the deck above. Fed with the oil supplied by the war-contractors (whose gains, honest or otherwise, are in every land an anticipated portion of the harvest of death) with flickering splashes of dirty yellow light they pollute the pale moonshine, all but ineffectually struggling in obstructed flecks through the open ports from which the tompioned[8] cannon protrude. Other lanterns at intervals serve but to bring out somewhat the obscurer bays which like small confessionals or side-chapels in a cathedral branch from the long dim-vistaed broad aisle between the two batteries of that covered tier.

Such was the deck where now lay the Handsome Sailor. Through the rose-tan of his complexion, no pallor could have shown. It would have taken days of sequestration from the winds and the sun to have brought about the effacement of that. But the skeleton in the cheekbone at the point of its angle was just beginning delicately to be defined under the warm-tinted skin. In fervid hearts self-contained some brief

---

8 Usually, "tampioned"; plugged with a tampion, as the muzzle of a gun not in use.

experiences devour our human tissue as secret fire in a ship's hold consumes cotton in the bale.

But now lying between the two guns, as nipped in the vice of fate, Billy's agony, mainly proceeding from a generous young heart's virgin experience of the diabolical incarnate and effective in some men—the tension of that agony was over now. It survived not the something healing in the closeted interview with Captain Vere. Without movement, he lay as in a trance. That adolescent expression previously noted as his, taking on something akin to the look of a slumbering child in the cradle when the warm hearth-glow of the still chamber at night plays on the dimples that at whiles mysteriously form in the cheek, silently coming and going there. For now and then in the gyved one's trance a serene happy light born of some wandering reminiscence or dream would diffuse itself over his face, and then wane away only anew to return.

The chaplain coming to see him and finding him thus, and perceiving no sign that he was conscious of his presence, attentively regarded him for a space, then slipping aside, withdrew for the time, peradventure feeling that even he the minister of Christ though receiving his stipend from Mars had no consolation to proffer which could result in a peace transcending that which he beheld. But in the small hours he came again. And the prisoner now awake to his surroundings noticed his approach and civilly, all but cheerfully, welcomed him. But it was to little purpose that in the interview following the good man sought to bring Billy Budd to some godly understanding that he must die, and at dawn. True, Billy himself freely referred to his death as a thing close at hand; but it was something in the way that children will refer to death in general, who yet among their other sports will play a funeral with hearse and mourners.

Not that like children Billy was incapable of conceiving what death really is. No, but he was wholly without irrational fear of it, a fear more prevalent in highly civilized communities than those so-called barbarous ones which in all respects stand nearer to unadulterate Nature. And, as elsewhere said,

a barbarian Billy radically was; as much so, for all the costume, as his countrymen the British captives, living trophies,
made to march in the Roman triumph of Germanicus.[9] Quite
as much so as those later barbarians, young men probably,
and picked specimens among the earlier British converts to
Christianity, at least nominally such and taken to Rome (as
today converts from lesser isles of the sea may be taken to
London) of whom the Pope of that time, admiring the
strangeness of their personal beauty so unlike the Italian
stamp, their clear ruddy complexion and curled flaxen locks,
exclaimed, "Angles" (meaning *English* the modern derivative)
"Angles do you call them? And is it because they look so like
angels?" Had it been later in time one would think that the
Pope had in mind Fra Angelico's[1] seraphs some of whom,
plucking apples in gardens of the Hesperides have the faint
rose-bud complexion of the more beautiful English girls.

If in vain the good chaplain sought to impress the young
barbarian with ideas of death akin to those conveyed in the
skull, dial, and crossbones on old tombstones; equally futile
to all appearance were his efforts to bring home to him the
thought of salvation and a Saviour. Billy listened, but less out
of awe or reverence perhaps than from a certain natural
politeness; doubtless at bottom regarding all that in much
the same way that most mariners of his class take any discourse abstract or out of the common tone of the work-a-day
world. And this sailor way of taking clerical discourse is not
wholly unlike the way in which the pioneer of Christianity
full of transcendent miracles was received long ago on tropic
isles by any superior *savage* so called—a Tahitian, say of
Captain Cook's time or shortly after that time.[2] Out of natural
courtesy he received, but did not appropriate. It was like a

9 Germanicus Caesar (15 B.C.–19 A.D.), Roman general and conqueror, whose
triumphs were spectacularly celebrated in Rome in 17 A.D.

1 Italian friar-painter of the fifteenth century, famous for his religious fres-
coes. The Hesperides, in classical myth, were fabulous gardens where grew
golden apples, guarded by a dragon.

2 Captain James Cook (1728–1779), British explorer, made remarkable discoveries in the Pacific, visiting the Marquesas Islands and Tahiti, where Melville adventured in 1842.

gift placed in the palm of an outreached hand upon which the fingers do not close.

But the *Indomitable's* chaplain was a discreet man possessing the good sense of a good heart. So he insisted not in his vocation here. At the instance of Captain Vere, a lieutenant had apprised him of pretty much everything as to Billy; and since he felt that innocence was even a better thing than religion wherewith to go to judgment, he reluctantly withdrew; but in his emotion not without first performing an act strange enough in an Englishman, and under the circumstances yet more so in any regular priest. Stooping over, he kissed on the fair cheek his fellowman, a felon in martial law, one who though on the confines of death he felt he could never convert to a dogma; nor for all that did he fear for his future.

Marvel not that having been made acquainted with the young sailor's essential innocence (an irruption of heretic thought hard to suppress) the worthy man lifted not a finger to avert the doom of such a martyr to martial discipline. So to do would not only have been as idle as invoking the desert, but would also have been an audacious transgression of the bounds of his function, one as exactly prescribed to him by military law as that of the boatswain or any other naval officer. Bluntly put, a chaplain is the minister of the Prince of Peace serving in the host of the god of war—Mars. As such, he is as incongruous as that musket of Blücher etc.[3] at Christmas. Why then is he there? Because he indirectly subserves the purpose attested by the cannon; because, too, he lends the sanction of the religion of the meek to that which practically is the abrogation of everything but brute force.

---

3 The manuscript is illegible; "Blücher etc." is a conjectural reading. Prussian Field Marshal Gebhard von Blücher (1742–1819), who had aided Wellington at Waterloo, was still famous.

XXVI

THE NIGHT SO LUMINOUS on the spardeck but otherwise on
the cavernous ones below, levels so like the tiered galleries in
a coalmine—the luminous night passed away. But, like the
prophet in the chariot disappearing in heaven and dropping
his mantle to Elisha, the withdrawing night transferred its
pale robe to the breaking day. A meek shy light appeared in
the East, where stretched a diaphanous fleece of white furrowed vapor. That light slowly waxed. Suddenly eight bells
was struck aft, responded to by one louder metallic stroke
from forward. It was four o'clock in the morning. Instantly
the silver whistles were heard summoning all hands to witness
punishment. Up through the great hatchways rimmed with
racks of heavy shot, the watch below came pouring over-
spreading with the watch already on deck the space between
the mainmast and foremast including that occupied by the
capacious launch and the black booms tiered on either side
of it, boat and booms making a summit of observation for the
powder boys and younger tars. A different group comprising
one watch of topmen leaned over the rail of that sea balcony,
no small one in a seventy-four, looking down on the crowd
below. Man or boy none spake but in whisper, and few spake
at all. Captain Vere—as before, the central figure among the
assembled commissioned officers—stood nigh the break of
the poopdeck facing forward. Just below him on the quarterdeck the marines in full equipment were drawn up much as
at the scene of the promulgated sentence.

At sea in the old time, the execution by halter of a military
sailor was generally from the foreyard. In the present instance, for special reasons the mainyard was assigned. Under
an arm of that lee yard[4] the prisoner was presently brought

---

[4] Melville wrote both "weather" and "lee" above the word "yard," and
failed to cancel either of these opposites. The lee yard would be more likely,
as being more sheltered.

up, the chaplain attending him. It was noted at the time and remarked upon afterwards that in this final scene the good man evinced little or nothing of the perfunctory. Brief speech indeed he had with the condemned one, but the genuine Gospel was less on his tongue than in his aspect and manner toward him. The final preparations personal to the latter being speedily brought to an end by two boatswain's-mates, the consummation impended. Billy stood facing aft. At the penultimate moment, his words, his only ones, words wholly unobstructed in the utterance were these—"God bless Captain Vere!" Syllables so unanticipated coming from one with the ignominious hemp about his neck—a conventional felon's benediction directed aft towards the quarters of honor; syllables too delivered in the clear melody of a singing bird on the point of launching from the twig, had a phenomenal effect, not unenhanced by the rare personal beauty of the young sailor spiritualized now through late experiences so poignantly profound.

Without volition as it were, as if indeed the ship's populace were but the vehicles of some vocal current electric, with one voice from alow and aloft came a resonant sympathetic echo —"God bless Captain Vere!" And yet at that instant Billy alone must have been in their hearts, even as he was in their eyes.

At the pronounced words and the spontaneous echo that voluminously rebounded them, Captain Vere, either through stoic self-control or a sort of momentary paralysis induced by emotional shock, stood erectly rigid as a musket in the ship armorer's rack.

The hull deliberately recovering from the periodic roll to leeward was just regaining an even keel, when the last signal, a preconcerted dumb one, was given. At the same moment it chanced that the vapory fleece hanging low in the East, was shot through with a soft glory as of the fleece of the Lamb of God seen in mystical vision, and simultaneously therewith, watched by the wedged mass of upturned faces, Billy ascended; and, ascending, took the full rose of the dawn.

In the pinioned figure, arrived at the yard end, to the wonder of all no motion was apparent, none save that created by the ship's motion, in moderate weather so majestic in a great ship ponderously cannoned.

XXVII

A digression

WHEN SOME DAYS afterward in reference to the singularity just mentioned, the purser, a rather ruddy rotund person more accurate as an accountant than profound as a philosopher, said at mess to the surgeon, "What testimony to the force lodged in willpower," the latter—saturnine spare and tall, one in whom a discreet causticity went along with a manner less genial than polite, replied, "Your pardon, Mr. Purser. In a hanging scientifically conducted—and under special orders I myself directed how Budd's was to be effected —any movement following the completed suspension and originating in the body suspended, such movement indicates mechanical spasm in the muscular system. Hence the absence of that is no more attributable to willpower as you call it than to horsepower—begging your pardon."

"But this muscular spasm you speak of, is not that in a degree more or less invariable in these cases?"

"Assuredly so, Mr. Purser."

"How then, my good sir, do you account for its absence in this instance?"

"Mr. Purser, it is clear that your sense of the singularity in this matter equals not mine. You account for it by what you call willpower a term not yet included in the lexicon of science. For me I do not, with my present knowledge pretend to account for it at all. Even should we assume the hypothesis that at the first touch of the halyards the action of Budd's heart, intensified by extraordinary emotion at its

climax, abruptly stopped—much like a watch when in carelessly winding it up you strain at the finish, thus snapping
the chain—even under that hypothesis how account for the
phenomenon that followed?"

"You admit then that the absence of spasmodic movement
was phenomenal."

"It was phenomenal, Mr. Purser, in the sense that it was
an appearance the cause of which is not immediately to be
assigned."

"But tell me, my dear sir," pertinaciously continued the
other, "was the man's death effected by the halter, or was it
a species of euthanasia?"

"*Euthanasia,* Mr. Purser, is something like your *willpower:*
I doubt its authenticity as a scientific term—begging your
pardon again. It is at once imaginative and metaphysical—in
short, Greek. But," abruptly changing his tone, "there is a case
in the sick bay that I do not care to leave to my assistants.
Beg your pardon, but excuse me." And rising from the mess
he formally withdrew.

XXVIII

THE SILENCE AT THE moment of execution and for a moment
or two continuing thereafter, a silence but emphasized by
the regular wash of the sea against the hull or the flutter of
a sail caused by the helmsman's eyes being tempted astray,
this emphasized silence was gradually disturbed by a sound
not easily to be verbally rendered. Whoever has heard the
freshet-wave of a torrent suddenly swelled by pouring showers
in tropical mountains, showers not shared by the plain; whoever has heard the first muffled murmur of its sloping advance
through precipitous woods, may form some conception of
the sound now heard. The seeming remoteness of its source
was because of its murmurous indistinctness since it came
from close-by, even from the men massed on the ship's open

deck. Being inarticulate, it was dubious in significance further than it seemed to indicate some capricious revulsion of thought or feeling such as mobs ashore are liable to, in the present instance possibly implying a sullen revocation on the men's part of their involuntary echoing of Billy's benediction. But ere the murmur had time to wax into clamor it was met by a strategic command, the more telling that it came with abrupt unexpectedness.

"Pipe down the starboard watch, Boatswain, and see that they go."

Shrill as the shriek of the sea hawk the whistles of the boatswain and his mates pierced that ominous low sound, dissipating it; and yielding to the mechanism of discipline the throng was thinned by one half. For the remainder most of them were set to temporary employments connected with trimming the yards and so forth, business readily to be got up to serve occasion by any officer-of-the-deck.

Now each proceeding that follows a mortal sentence pronounced at sea by a drum-head court is characterised by promptitude not perceptibly merging into hurry, though bordering that. The hammock, the one which had been Billy's bed when alive, having already been ballasted with shot and otherwise prepared to serve for his canvas coffin, the last offices of the sea undertakers, the sailmaker's mates, were now speedily completed. When everything was in readiness a second call for all hands made necessary by the strategic movement before mentioned was sounded and now to witness burial.

The details of this closing formality it needs not to give. But when the tilted plank let slide its freight into the sea, a second strange human murmur was heard, blended now with another inarticulate sound proceeding from certain larger sea fowl whose attention having been attracted by the peculiar commotion in the water resulting from the heavy sloped dive of the shotted hammock into the sea, flew screaming to the spot. So near the hull did they come, that the stridor or bony creak of their gaunt double-jointed pinions was audible. As the ship under light airs passed on, leaving the burial spot astern, they still kept circling it low down with the moving shadow of their outstretched wings and the croaked requiem of their cries.

Upon sailors as superstitious as those of the age preceding ours, men-of-war's men too who had just beheld the prodigy of repose in the form suspended in air and now foundering in the deeps; to such mariners the action of the sea fowl though dictated by mere animal greed for prey, was big with no prosaic significance. An uncertain movement began among them, in which some encroachment was made. It was tolerated but for a moment. For suddenly the drumbeat to quarters, which familiar sound happening at least twice every day, had upon the present occasion a signal peremptoriness in it. True martial discipline long continued superinduces in average man a sort of impulse of docility whose operation at the official sound of command much resembles in its promptitude the effect of an instinct.

The drumbeat dissolved the multitude, distributing most of them along the batteries of the two covered gundecks. There, as wont, the guns' crews stood by their respective cannon erect and silent. In due course the first officer, sword under arm and standing in his place on the quarterdeck, formally received the successive reports of the sworded lieutenants commanding the sections of batteries below; the last of which reports being made, the summed report he delivered with the customary salute to the commander. All this occupied time, which in the present case, was the object of beating to quarters at an hour prior to the customary one. That such variance from usage was authorized by an officer like Captain Vere, a martinet as some deemed him, was evidence of the necessity for unusual action implied in what he deemed to be temporarily the mood of his men. "With mankind," he would say, "forms, measured forms are everything; and that is the import couched in the story of Orpheus with his lyre spellbinding the wild denizens of the wood." And this he once applied to the disruption of forms going on across the Channel and the consequences thereof.

At this unwonted muster at quarters, all proceeded as at the regular hour. The band on the quarterdeck played a sacred air. After which the chaplain went through the customary morning service. That done, the drum beat the retreat, and toned by music and religious rites subserving the discipline and purpose of war, the men in their wonted orderly manner, dispersed to the places allotted them when not at the guns.

And now it was full day. The fleece of low-hanging vapor had vanished, licked up by the sun that late had so glorified it. And the circumambient air in the clearness of its serenity was like smooth white marble in the polished block not yet removed from the marble-dealer's yard.

XXIX

THE SYMMETRY OF form attainable in pure fiction can not so readily be achieved in a narration essentially having less to do with fable than with fact. Truth uncompromisingly told will always have its ragged edges; hence the conclusion of such a narration is apt to be less finished than an architectural finial.

How it fared with the Handsome Sailor during the year of the Great Mutiny has been faithfully given. But though properly the story ends with his life, something in way of sequel will not be amiss. Three brief chapters will suffice.

In the general re-christening under the Directory of the craft originally forming the navy of the French monarchy, the *St. Louis* line-of-battle ship was named the *Athéiste.* Such a name, like some other substituted ones in the Revolutionary fleet while proclaiming the infidel audacity of the ruling power was yet, though not so intended to be, the aptest name, if one consider it, ever given to a warship; far more so indeed than the *Devastation,* the *Erebus* (the *Hell*) and similar names bestowed upon fighting ships.

On the return passage to the English fleet from the detached cruise during which occurred the events already recorded, the *Indomitable* fell in with the *Athéiste*. An engagement ensued; during which Captain Vere in the act of putting his ship alongside the enemy with a view of throwing his boarders across her bulwarks, was hit by a musketball from a porthole of the enemy's main cabin. More than disabled he dropped to the deck and was carried below to the same cockpit where some of his men already lay. The senior lieutenant took command. Under him the enemy was finally captured and though much crippled was by rare good fortune successfully taken into Gibraltar, an English port not very distant from the scene of the fight. There, Captain Vere with the rest of the wounded was put ashore. He lingered for some days, but the end came. Unhappily he was cut off too early for the Nile and Trafalgar.[5] The spirit that spite its philosophic austerity may yet have indulged in the most secret of all passions, ambition, never attained to the fullness of fame.

Not long before death while lying under the influence of that magical drug which soothing the physical frame mysteriously operates on the subtler element in man, he was heard to murmur words inexplicable to his attendant—"Billy Budd, Billy Budd." That these were not the accents of remorse, would seem clear from what the attendant said to the *Indomitable's* senior officer of marines who, as the most reluctant to condemn of the members of the drum-head court, too well knew, though here he kept the knowledge to himself, who Billy Budd was.

XXX

SOME FEW WEEKS after the execution, among other matters under the head of *News from the Mediterranean*, there appeared in a naval chronicle of the time, an authorized weekly publication, an account of the affair. It was doubtless for the

---

5 Admiral Nelson destroyed Napoleon's fleet at the Battle of the Nile (1798); at Trafalgar in 1805 he ended the French naval wars with victory, and was himself killed.

most part written in good faith, though the medium, partly rumor, through which the facts must have reached the writer, served to deflect and in part falsify them. The account was as follows:

"On the tenth of the last month a deplorable occurrence took place on board H.M.S. *Indomitable*. John Claggart, the ship's master-at-arms, discovering that some sort of plot was incipient among an inferior section of the ship's company, and that the ringleader was one William Budd; he, Claggart, in the act of arraigning the man before the captain was vindictively stabbed to the heart by the suddenly drawn sheath-knife of Budd.

"The deed and the implement employed, sufficiently suggest that though mustered into the service under an English name the assassin was no Englishman, but one of those aliens adopting English cognomens whom the present extraordinary necessities of the service have caused to be admitted into it in considerable numbers.

"The enormity of the crime and the extreme depravity of the criminal, appear the greater in view of the character of the victim, a middle-aged man respectable and discreet, belonging to that minor official grade, the petty-officers, upon whom, as none know better than the commissioned gentlemen, the efficiency of His Majesty's navy so largely depends. His function was a responsible one; at once onerous and thankless and his fidelity in it the greater because of his strong patriotic impulse. In this instance as in so many other instances in these days, the character of this unfortunate man signally refutes, if refutation were needed, that peevish saying attributed to the late Dr. Johnson, that patriotism is the last refuge of a scoundrel.

"The criminal paid the penalty of his crime. The promptitude of the punishment has proved salutary. Nothing amiss is now apprehended aboard H.M.S. *Indomitable*."

The above, appearing in a publication now long ago superannuated and forgotten, is all that hitherto has stood in human record to attest what manner of men respectively were John Claggart and Billy Budd.

XXXI

EVERYTHING IS FOR A term remarkable in navies. Any tangible object associated with some striking incident of the service is converted into a monument. The spar from which the foretopman was suspended, was for some few years kept trace of by the blue-jackets. Their knowledge followed it from ship to dockyard and again from dockyard to ship, still pursuing it even when at last reduced to a mere dockyard boom. To them a chip of it was as a piece of the cross. Ignorant though they were of the secret facts of the tragedy, and not thinking but that the penalty was somehow unavoidably inflicted from the naval point of view, for all that they instinctively felt that Billy was a sort of man as incapable of mutiny as of willful murder. They recalled the fresh young image of the Handsome Sailor, that face never deformed by a sneer or subtler vile freak of the heart within. Their impression of him was doubtless deepened by the fact that he was gone, and in a measure mysteriously gone. At the time on the gundecks of the *Indomitable* the general estimate of his nature and its unconscious simplicity eventually found rude utterance from another foretopman, one of his own watch; gifted, as some sailors are, with an artless poetic temperament; the tarry hands made some lines which after circulating among the shipboard crew for a while, finally got rudely printed at Portsmouth as a ballad. The title given to it was the sailor's.

Billy in the Darbies[6]

Good of the chaplain to enter Lone Bay
And down on his marrowbones here and pray
For the likes just o' me, Billy Budd.—But look:
Through the port comes the moonshine astray!

---

6 Manacles or irons.

It tips the guard's cutlas and silvers this nook;
But 'twill die in the dawning of Billy's last day.
A jewel block they'll make of me tomorrow,
Pendant pearl from the yardarm end
Like the eardrop I gave to Bristol Molly—
O, 'tis me, not the sentence they'll suspend.
Ay, Ay, all is up; and I must up too
Early in the morning, aloft from alow.
On an empty stomach, now, never it would do.
They'll give me a nibble—bit o' biscuit ere I go.
Sure, a messmate will reach me the last parting cup;
But, turning heads away from the hoist and the belay,
Heaven knows who will have the running of me up!
No pipe to those halyards.—But aren't it all sham?
A blur's in my eyes; it is dreaming that I am.
A hatchet to my hawser? all adrift to go?
The drum roll to grog, and Billy never know?
But Donald he has promised to stand by the plank;
So I'll shake a friendly hand ere I sink.
But—no! It is dead then I'll be, come to think.—
I remember Taff the Welshman when he sank.
And his cheek it was like the budding pink.
But me they'll lash me in hammock, drop me deep.
Fathoms down, fathoms down, how I'll dream fast asleep.
I feel it stealing now. Sentry, are you there?
Just ease this darbies at the wrist, and roll me over fair,
I am sleepy, and the oozy weeds about me twist.

April 19th, 1891

Typee

TYPEE

PREFACE

MORE THAN THREE years have elapsed since the occurrence of
the events recorded in this volume. The interval, with the exception of the last few months, has been chiefly spent by the
author tossing about on the wide ocean. Sailors are the only
class of men who nowadays see anything like stirring adventure; and many things which to fireside people appear strange
and romantic, to them seem as commonplace as a jacket out at
elbows. Yet, notwithstanding the familiarity of sailors with all
sorts of curious adventure, the incidents recorded in the following pages have often served, when 'spun as a yarn,' not
only to relieve the weariness of many a night-watch at sea,
but to excite the warmest sympathies of the author's shipmates. He has been therefore led to think that his story could
scarcely fail to interest those who are less familiar than the
sailor with a life of adventure.

In his account of the singular and interesting people among
whom he was thrown, it will be observed that he chiefly treats
of their more obvious peculiarities; and, in describing their
customs, refrains in most cases from entering into explanations
concerning their origin and purposes. As writers of travels
among barbarous communities are generally very diffuse on
these subjects, he deems it right to advert to what may be
considered a culpable omission. No one can be more sensible than the author of his deficiencies in this and many other
respects; but when the very peculiar circumstances in which
he was placed are understood, he feels assured that all these
omissions will be excused.

In very many published narratives no little degree of attention is bestowed upon dates; but, as the author lost all knowledge of the days of the week, during the occurrence of the

scenes herein related, he hopes that the reader will charitably pass over his shortcomings in this particular.

In the Polynesian words used in this volume—except in those cases where the spelling has been previously determined by others—that form of orthography has been employed, which might be supposed most easily to convey their sound to a stranger. In several works descriptive of the islands in the Pacific, many of the most beautiful combinations of vocal sounds have been altogether lost to the ear of the reader by an overattention to the ordinary rules of spelling.

There are a few passages in the ensuing chapters which may be thought to bear rather hard upon a reverend order of men, the account of whose proceedings in different quarters of the globe—transmitted to us through their own hands—very generally, and often very deservedly, receives high commendation. Such passages will be found, however, to be based upon facts admitting of no contradiction, and which have come immediately under the writer's cognizance. The conclusions deduced from these facts are unavoidable, and in stating them the author has been influenced by no feeling of animosity, either to the individuals themselves or to that glorious cause which had not always been served by the proceedings of some of its advocates.

The great interest with which the important events lately occurring at the Sandwich, Marquesa, and Society Islands, have been regarded in America and England, and indeed throughout the world, will, he trusts, justify a few otherwise unwarrantable digressions.

There are some things related in the narrative which will be sure to appear strange, or perhaps entirely incomprehensible, to the reader; but they cannot appear more so to him than they did to the author at the time. He has stated such matters just as they occurred, and leaves every one to form his own opinion concerning them; trusting that his anxious desire to speak the unvarnished truth will gain for him the confidence of his readers.

I

The sea—longings for shore—a landsick ship—destination of the voyagers—the Marquesas—adventure of a missionary's wife among the savages—characteristic anecdote of the Queen of Nukuheva.

SIX MONTHS AT SEA! Yes, reader, as I live, six months out of sight of land; cruising after the sperm whale beneath the scorching sun of the Line, and tossed on the billows of the wide-rolling Pacific—the sky above, the sea around, and nothing else! Weeks and weeks ago our fresh provisions were all exhausted. There is not a sweet potato left; not a single yam. Those glorious bunches of bananas which once decorated our stern and quarterdeck have, alas, disappeared! and the delicious oranges which hung suspended from our tops and stays—they, too, are gone! Yes, they are all departed, and there is nothing left us but salt horse and sea biscuit. Oh! ye state-room sailors, who make so much ado about a fourteen-days' passage across the Atlantic; who so pathetically relate the privations and hardships of the sea, where, after a day of breakfasting, lunching, dining off five courses, chatting, playing whist, and drinking champagne punch, it was your hard lot to be shut up in little cabinets of mahogany and maple, and sleep for ten hours, with nothing to disturb you but 'those good-for-nothing tars, shouting and tramping overhead,'—what would ye say to our six months out of sight of land?

Oh! for a refreshing glimpse of one blade of grass—for a snuff at the fragrance of a handful of the loamy earth! Is there nothing fresh around us? Is there no green thing to be seen? Yes, the inside of our bulwarks is painted green; but what a vile and sickly hue it is, as if nothing bearing even the semblance of verdure could flourish this weary way from land. Even the bark that once clung to the wood we use for fuel has been gnawed off and devoured by the captain's pig; and so long ago, too, that the pig himself has in turn been devoured.

There is but one solitary tenant in the chicken coop, once a gay and dapper young cock, bearing him so bravely among the coy hens. But look at him now; there he stands, moping all the day long on that everlasting one leg of his. He turns with disgust from the moldy corn before him and the brackish water in his little trough. He mourns no doubt his lost companions, literally snatched from him one by one, and never seen again. But his days of mourning will be few; for Mungo, our black cook, told me yesterday that the word had at last gone forth, and poor Pedro's fate was sealed. His attenuated body will be laid out upon the captain's table next Sunday, and long before night will be buried with all the usual ceremonies beneath that worthy individual's vest. Who would believe that there could be any one so cruel as to long for the decapitation of the luckless Pedro; yet the sailors pray every minute, selfish fellows, that the miserable fowl may be brought to his end. They say the captain will never point the ship for the land so long as he has in anticipation a mess of fresh meat. This unhappy bird can alone furnish it; and when he is once devoured, the captain will come to his senses. I wish thee no harm, Peter; but as thou are doomed, sooner or later, to meet the fate of all thy race; and if putting a period to thy existence is to be the signal for our deliverance, why—truth to speak—I wish thy throat cut this very moment; for, oh! how I wish to see the living earth again! The old ship herself longs to look out upon the land from her hawse-holes once more, and Jack Lewis said right the other day when the captain found fault with his steering.

'Why, d'ye see, Captain Vangs,' says bold Jack, 'I'm as good a helmsman as ever put hand to spoke; but none of us can steer the old lady now. We can't keep her full and bye, sir: watch her ever so close, she will fall off; and then, sir, when I put the helm down so gently, and try like to coax her to the work, she won't take it kindly, but will fall round off again; and it's all because she knows the land is under the lee, sir, and she won't go any more to windward.' Aye, and why should she, Jack? Didn't every one of her stout timbers grow on shore, and hasn't she sensibilities as well as we?

Poor old ship! Her very looks denote her desires: how deplorably she appears! The paint on her sides, burnt up by the scorching sun, is puffed out and cracked. See the weeds she trails along with her, and what an unsightly bunch of those horrid barnacles has formed about her stern piece; and every time she rises on a sea, she shows her copper torn away, or hanging in jagged strips.

Poor old ship! I say again: for six months she has been rolling and pitching about, never for one moment at rest. But courage, old lass, I hope to see thee soon within a biscuit's toss of the merry land, riding snugly at anchor in some green cove, and sheltered from the boisterous winds.

'Hurra, my lads! It's a settled thing; next week we shape our course to the Marquesas!' The Marquesas! What strange visions of outlandish things does the very name spirit up! Naked houris—cannibal banquets—groves of coconut—coral-reefs—tattooed chiefs—and bamboo temples; sunny valleys planted with breadfruit trees—carved canoes dancing on the flashing blue waters—savage woodlands guarded by horrible idols—*heathenish rites and human sacrifices*.

Such were the strangely jumbled anticipations that haunted me during our passage from the cruising ground. I felt an irresistible curiosity to see those islands which the olden voyagers had so glowingly described.

The group for which we were now steering (although among the earliest of European discoveries in the South Seas, having been first visited in the year 1595) still continues to be tenanted by beings as strange and barbarous as ever. The missionaries, sent on a heavenly errand, had sailed by their lovely shores, and had abandoned them to their idols of wood and stone. How interesting the circumstances under which they were discovered! In the watery path of Mendanna, cruising in quest of some region of gold, these isles had sprung up like a scene of enchantment, and for a moment the Spaniard believed his bright dream was realized. In honor of the Marquess de Mendoza, then viceroy of Peru—under whose auspices the navigator sailed—he bestowed upon them the name which denoted the rank of his patron, and gave to the world on his return a vague and magnificent account of their beauty. But these islands, undisturbed for years, relapsed into their previous obscurity; and it is only recently that anything has been known concerning them. Once in the course of a half century, to be sure, some adventurous rover would break in upon their peaceful repose, and, astonished at the unusual scene, would be almost tempted to claim the merit of a new discovery.

Of this interesting group, but little account has ever been given, if we except the slight mention made of them in the sketches of South Sea voyages. Cook, in his repeated circumnavigations of the globe, barely touched at their shores; and all that we know about them is from a few general narratives. Among these, there are two that claim particular notice. Porter's *Journal of the Cruise of the U.S. frigate 'Essex,' in the Pacific, during the late War,* is said to contain some interesting particulars concerning the islanders. This is a work, however, which I have never happened to meet with; and Stewart, the captain of the American sloop-of-war *Vincennes,* has likewise devoted a portion of his book, entitled *A Visit to the South Seas,* to the same subject.

Within the last few years American and English vessels engaged in the extensive whale fisheries of the Pacific have occasionally, when short of provisions, put into the commodious harbor which there is in one of the islands; but a fear of the natives, founded on a recollection of the dreadful fate which many white men have received at their hands, has deterred their crews from intermixing with the population sufficiently to gain any insight into their peculiar customs and manners.

The Protestant Missions appear to have despaired of reclaiming these islands from heathenism. The usage they in every case received from the natives has been such as to intimidate the boldest of their number. Ellis, in his *Polynesian Researches,* gives some interesting accounts of the abortive attempts made by the Tahiti Mission to establish a branch Mission upon certain islands of the group. A short time before my visit to the Marquesas, a somewhat amusing incident took place in connection with these efforts, which I cannot avoid relating.

An intrepid missionary, undaunted by the ill-success that had attended all previous endeavors to conciliate the savages, and believing much in the efficiency of female influence, introduced among them his young and beautiful wife, the first white woman who had ever visited their shores. The islanders at first gazed in mute admiration at so unusual a prodigy, and seemed inclined to regard it as some new divinity. But after a short time, becoming familiar with its charming aspect, and jealous of the folds which encircled its form, they sought to pierce the sacred veil of calico in which it was enshrined, and in the gratification of their curiosity so far overstepped the limits of good breeding as deeply to offend the lady's sense of decorum. Her sex once ascertained, their idolatry was changed into contempt; and there was no end to the contumely showered upon her by the savages, who were exasperated at the deception which they conceived had been practiced upon them. To the horror of her affectionate spouse, she was stripped of her garments, and given to understand that she could no longer carry on her deceits with impunity. The gentle dame was not sufficiently evangelized to endure this, and, fearful of further improprieties, she forced her husband to relinquish his undertaking, and together they returned to Tahiti.

Not thus shy of exhibiting her charms was the Island Queen, herself, the beauteous wife of Mowanna, the King of Nukuheva. Between two and three years after the adventures recorded in this volume, I chanced, while aboard of a man-of-war, to touch at these islands. The French had then held possession of the Marquesas some time, and already prided themselves upon the beneficial effects of their jurisdiction, as discernible in the deportment of the natives. To be sure, in one of their efforts at reform they had slaughtered about a hundred and fifty of them at Whitihoo—but let that pass. At the time I mention, the French squadron was rendezvousing in the bay of Nukuheva, and, during an interview between one of their captains and our worthy Commodore, it was suggested by the former that we, as the flag ship of the American squadron, should receive, in state, a visit from the royal pair. The French officer likewise represented, with evident satisfaction, that under their tuition the King and Queen had imbibed proper notions of their elevated station, and on all ceremonious occasions conducted themselves with suitable dignity. Accordingly, preparations were made to give Their Majesties a reception on board in a style corresponding with their rank.

One bright afternoon, a gig, gaily bedizened with streamers, was observed to shove off from the side of one of the French frigates, and pull directly for our gangway. In the stern sheets reclined Mowanna and his consort. As they approached, we paid them all the honors due to royalty—manning our yards, firing a salute, and making a prodigious hubbub.

They ascended the accommodation ladder, were greeted by the Commodore, hat in hand, and passing along the quarterdeck, the marine guard presented arms, while the band struck up "The King of the Cannibal Islands." So far all went well. The French officers grimaced and smiled in exceedingly high spirits, wonderfully pleased with the discreet manner in which these distinguished personages behaved themselves.

Their appearance was certainly calculated to produce an effect. His Majesty was arrayed in a magnificent military uniform, stiff with gold lace and embroidery, while his shaven crown was concealed by a huge *chapeau bras,* waving with ostrich plumes. There was one slight blemish, however, in his appearance. A broad patch of tattooing stretched completely across his face, in a line with his eyes, making him look as if he wore a huge pair of goggles, and royalty in goggles suggested some ludicrous ideas. But it was in the adornment of the fair person of his dark-complexioned spouse that the tailors of the fleet had evinced the gaiety of their national taste. She was habited in a gaudy tissue of scarlet cloth, trimmed with yellow silk, which, descending a little below the knees, exposed to view her bare legs, embellished with spiral tattooing, and somewhat resembling two miniature Trajan's columns. Upon her head was a fanciful turban of purple velvet, figured with silver sprigs, and surmounted by a tuft of variegated feathers.

The ship's company, crowding into the gangway to view the sight, soon arrested Her Majesty's attention. She singled out from their number an old salt, whose bare arms and feet and exposed breast were covered with as many inscriptions in India ink as the lid of an Egyptian sarcophagus. Notwithstanding all the sly hints and remonstrances of the French officers, she immediately approached the man, and pulling further open the bosom of his duck frock, and rolling up the leg of his wide trousers, she gazed with admiration at the bright blue and vermilion pricking, thus disclosed to view. She hung over the fellow, caressing him, and expressing her delight in a variety of wild exclamations and gestures. The embarrassment of the polite Gauls at such an unlooked-for occurrence may be easily imagined; but picture their consternation, when all at once the royal lady, eager to display the hieroglyphics on her own sweet form, bent forward for a moment, and turning sharply round, threw up the skirts of her mantle, and revealed a sight from which the aghast Frenchmen retreated precipitately, and, tumbling into their boat, fled the scene of so shocking a catastrophe.

II

Passage from the cruising ground to the Marquesas
—sleepy times aboard ship—South Sea scenery—
land ho!—the French squadron discovered at anchor
in the bay of Nukuheva—strange pilot—escort of
canoes—a flotilla of coconuts—swimming visitors—
the *Dolly* boarded by them—state of
affairs that ensue.

I CAN NEVER forget the eighteen or twenty days during which
the light trade-winds were silently sweeping us toward the
islands. In pursuit of the sperm whale, we had been cruising
on the Line some twenty degrees to the westward of the
Gallipagos; and all that we had to do, when our course was
determined on, was to square in the yards and keep the vessel
before the breeze, and then the good ship and the steady gale
did the rest between them. The man at the wheel never vexed
the old lady with any superfluous steering, but, comfortably
adjusting his limbs at the tiller, would doze away by the hour.
True to her work, the *Dolly* headed to her course, and, like
one of those characters who always do best when let alone,
she jogged on her way like a veteran old sea pacer—as she
was.

What a delightful, lazy, languid time we had whilst we were
thus gliding along! There was nothing to be done; a circumstance that happily suited our disinclination to do anything.
We abandoned the forepeak altogether, and spreading an
awning over the forecastle, slept, ate, and lounged under it
the livelong day. Every one seemed to be under the influence
of some narcotic. Even the officers aft, whose duty required
them never to be seated whilst keeping a deck watch, vainly
endeavored to keep on their pins; and were obliged invariably to compromise the matter by leaning up against the bulwarks and gazing abstractedly over the side. Reading was out

of the question; take a book in your hand, and you were asleep in an instant.

Although I could not avoid yielding in a great measure to the general languor, still at times I contrived to shake off the spell, and to appreciate the beauty of the scene around me. The sky presented a clear expanse of the most delicate blue, except along the skirts of the horizon, where you might see a thin drapery of pale clouds which never varied their form or color. The long, measured, dirgelike swell of the Pacific came rolling along, with its surface broken by little tiny waves, sparkling in the sunshine. Every now and then a shoal of flying fish, scared from the water under the bows, would leap into the air, and fall the next moment like a shower of silver into the sea. Then you would see the superb albacore, with his glittering sides, sailing aloft, and, often describing an arc in his descent, disappear on the surface of the water. Far off, the lofty jet of the whale might be seen, and nearer at hand the prowling shark, that villainous footpad of the seas, would come skulking along, and, at a wary distance, regard us with his evil eye. At times some shapeless monster of the deep, floating on the surface, would, as we approached, sink slowly into the blue waters, and fade away from the sight. But the most impressive feature of the scene was the almost unbroken silence that reigned over sky and water. Scarcely a sound could be heard but the occasional breathing of the grampus and the rippling at the cutwater.

As we drew nearer the land, I hailed with delight the appearance of innumerable seafowl. Screaming and whirling in spiral tracks, they would accompany the vessel, and at times alight on our yards and stays. That piratical-looking fellow, appropriately named the man-of-war's hawk, with his blood-red bill and raven plumage, would come sweeping round us in gradually diminishing circles, till you could distinctly mark the strange flashings of his eye; and then, as if satisfied with his observation, would sail up into the air and disappear from the view. Soon, other evidences of our vicinity to the land were apparent, and it was not long before the glad announcement of its being in sight was heard from aloft—given with that peculiar prolongation of sound that a sailor loves—'Land ho!'

The captain, darting on deck from the cabin, bawled lustily for his spyglass; the mate in still louder accents hailed the masthead with a tremendous 'Where-away?' The black cook thrust his woolly head from the galley, and Boatswain, the dog, leaped up between the knightheads, and barked most furiously. Land ho! Aye, there it was. A hardly perceptible blue irregular outline, indicating the bold contour of the lofty heights of Nukuheva.

This island, although generally called one of the Marquesas, is by some navigators considered as forming one of a distinct cluster, comprising the islands of Ruhooka, Ropo, and Nukuheva; upon which three the appellation of the Washington Group has been bestowed. They form a triangle, and lie within the parallels of 8° 38' and 9° 32' South latitude, and 139° 20' and 140° 10' West longitude from Greenwich. With how little propriety they are to be regarded as forming a separate group will be at once apparent, when it is considered that they lie in the immediate vicinity of the other islands, that is to say, less than a degree to the northwest of them, that their inhabitants speak the Marquesan dialect, and that their laws, religion, and general customs are identical. The only reason why they were ever thus arbitrarily distinguished may be attributed to the singular fact that their existence was altogether unknown to the world until the year 1791, when they were discovered by Captain Ingraham, of Boston, Massachusetts, nearly two centuries after the discovery of the adjacent islands by the agent of the Spanish Viceroy. Notwithstanding this, I shall follow the example of most voyagers, and treat of them as forming part and parcel of the Marquesas.

Nukuheva is the most important of these islands, being the only one at which ships are much in the habit of touching, and is celebrated as being the place where the adventurous Captain Porter refitted his ships during the late war between England and the United States, and whence he sallied out upon the large whaling fleet then sailing under the enemy's flag in the surrounding seas. This island is about twenty miles in length and nearly as many in breadth. It has three good harbors on its coast; the largest and best of which is called by the people living in its vicinity Tyohee, and by Captain Porter was denominated Massachusetts Bay. Among the adverse tribes dwelling about the shores of the other bays, and by all voyagers, it is generally known by the name bestowed upon the island itself—Nukuheva. Its inhabitants have become somewhat corrupted owing to their recent commerce with Europeans; but so far as regards their peculiar customs and general mode of life, they retain their original primitive character, remaining very nearly in the same state of nature in which they were first beheld by white men. The hostile clans, residing in the more remote sections of the island, and very seldom holding any communication with foreigners, are in every respect unchanged from their earliest known condition.

In the bay of Nukuheva was the anchorage we desired to reach. We had perceived the loom of the mountains about sunset; so that after running all night with a very light breeze, we found ourselves close in with the island the next morning, but as the bay we sought lay on its farther side, we were obliged to sail some distance along the shore, catching, as we proceeded, short glimpses of blooming valleys, deep glens, waterfalls, and waving groves, hidden here and there by projecting and rocky headlands, every moment opening to the view some new and startling scene of beauty.

Those who for the first time visit the South Seas, generally are surprised at the appearance of the islands when beheld from the sea. From the vague accounts we sometimes have of their beauty, many people are apt to picture to themselves enameled and softly swelling plains, shaded over with delicious groves, and watered by purling brooks, and the entire country but little elevated above the surrounding ocean. The reality is very different; bold rockbound coasts, with the surf beating high against the lofty cliffs, and broken here and there into deep inlets, which open to the view thickly wooded valleys, separated by the spurs of mountains clothed with tufted grass, and sweeping down toward the sea from an elevated and furrowed interior, form the principal features of these islands.

Toward noon we drew abreast the entrance to the harbor, and at last we slowly swept by the intervening promontory, and entered the bay of Nukuheva. No description can do justice to its beauty; but that beauty was lost to me then, and I saw nothing but the tri-colored flag of France trailing over the stern of six vessels, whose black hulls and bristling broadsides proclaimed their warlike character. There they were, floating in that lovely bay, the green eminences of the shore looking down so tranquilly upon them, as if rebuking the sternness of their aspect. To my eye nothing could be more out of keeping than the presence of these vessels; but we soon learned what brought them there. The whole group of islands had just been taken possession of by Rear-Admiral Du Petit Thouars, in the name of the invincible French nation.

This item of information was imparted to us by a most extraordinary individual, a genuine South-Sea vagabond, who came alongside of us in a whaleboat as soon as we entered the bay, and, by the aid of some benevolent persons at the gangway, was assisted on board, for our visitor was in that interesting stage of intoxication when a man is amiable and helpless. Although he was utterly unable to stand erect or to navigate his body across the deck, he still magnanimously proffered his services to pilot the ship to a good and secure anchorage. Our captain, however, rather distrusted his ability in this respect, and refused to recognize his claim to the character he assumed; but our gentleman was determined to play his part, for by dint of much scrambling he succeeded in getting into the weather-quarter boat, where he steadied himself by holding on to a shroud, and then commenced issuing his commands with amazing volubility and very peculiar gestures. Of course no one obeyed his orders; but as it was impossible to quiet him, we swept by the ships of the squadron with this strange fellow performing his antics in full view of all the French officers.

We afterward learned that our eccentric friend had been a lieutenant in the English navy; but, having disgraced his flag by some criminal conduct in one of the principal ports on the main, he had deserted his ship, and spent many years wandering among the islands of the Pacific, until accidentally being at Nukuheva when the French took possession of the place, he had been appointed pilot of the harbor by the newly constituted authorities.

As we slowly advanced up the bay, numerous canoes pushed off from the surrounding shores, and we were soon in the midst of quite a flotilla of them, their savage occupants struggling to get aboard of us, and jostling one another in their ineffectual attempts. Occasionally the projecting outriggers of their slight shallops, running foul of one another, would become entangled beneath the water, threatening to capsize the canoes, when a scene of confusion would ensue that baffles description. Such strange outcries and passionate gesticulations I never certainly heard or saw before. You would have thought the islanders were on the point of flying at one another's throats, whereas they were only amicably engaged in disentangling their boats.

Scattered here and there among the canoes might be seen numbers of coconuts floating closely together in circular groups, and bobbing up and down with every wave. By some inexplicable means these coconuts were all steadily approaching towards the ship. As I leaned curiously over the side endeavoring to solve their mysterious movements, one mass far in advance of the rest attracted my attention. In its center was something I could take for nothing else than a coconut, but which I certainly considered one of the most extraordinary specimens of the fruit I had ever seen. It kept twirling and dancing about among the rest in the most singular manner, and as it drew nearer I thought it bore a remarkable resemblance to the brown shaven skull of one of the savages. Presently it betrayed a pair of eyes, and soon I became aware that what I had supposed to have been one of the fruit was nothing else than the head of an islander, who had adopted this singular method of bringing his produce to market. The coconuts were all attached to one another by strips of the husk, partly torn from the shell and rudely fastened together.

Their proprietor, inserting his head into the midst of them, impelled his necklace of coconuts through the water by striking out beneath the surface with his feet.

I was somewhat astonished to perceive that among the number of natives that surrounded us not a single female was to be seen. At that time I was ignorant of the fact that by the operation of the taboo the use of canoes in all parts of the island is rigorously prohibited to the entire sex, for whom it is death even to be seen entering one when hauled on shore; consequently, whenever a Marquesan lady voyages by water, she puts in requisition the paddles of her own fair body.

We had approached within a mile and a half perhaps of the foot of the bay, when some of the islanders, who by this time had managed to scramble aboard of us at the risk of swamping their canoes, directed our attention to a singular commotion in the water ahead of the vessel. At first I imagined it to be produced by a shoal of fish sporting on the surface, but our savage friends assured us that it was caused by a shoal of *whinhenies* (young girls), who in this manner were coming off from the shore to welcome us. As they drew nearer, and I watched the rising and sinking of their forms, and beheld the uplifted right arm bearing above the water the girdle of tappa, and their long dark hair trailing beside them as they swam, I almost fancied they could be nothing else than so many mermaids—and very like mermaids they behaved too.

We were still some distance from the beach, and under slow headway, when we sailed right into the midst of these swimming nymphs, and they boarded us at every quarter; many seizing hold of the chain plates and springing into the chains; others, at the peril of being run over by the vessel in her course, catching at the bobstays, and wreathing their slender forms about the ropes, hung suspended in the air. All of them at length succeeded in getting up the ship's side, where they clung dripping with the brine and glowing from the bath, their jet-black tresses streaming over their shoulders, and half enveloping their otherwise naked forms. There they hung, sparkling with savage vivacity, laughing gaily at one another, and chattering away with infinite glee. Nor were they idle the while, for each one performed the simple offices of the toilet for the other. Their luxuriant locks, wound up and twisted into the smallest possible compass, were freed from the briny element; the whole person carefully dried and, from a little round shell that passed from hand to hand, anointed with a fragrant oil: their adornments were completed by passing a few loose folds of white tappa, in a modest cincture, around the waist. Thus arrayed they no longer hesitated, but flung themselves lightly over the bulwarks, and were quickly frolicking about the decks. Many of them went forward, perching upon the headrails or running out upon the bowsprit, while others seated themselves upon the taffrail, or reclined at full length upon the boats. What a sight for us bachelor sailors! how avoid so dire a temptation? For who could think of tumbling these artless creatures overboard, when they had swam miles to welcome us?

Their appearance perfectly amazed me; their extreme youth, the light clear brown of their complexions, their delicate features, and inexpressibly graceful figures, their softly molded limbs, and free unstudied action, seemed as strange as beautiful.

The *Dolly* was fairly captured; and never I will say was vessel carried before by such a dashing and irresistible party of boarders! The ship taken, we could not do otherwise than yield ourselves prisoners, and, for the whole period that she remained in the bay, the *Dolly,* as well as her crew, were completely in the hands of the mermaids.

In the evening after we had come to an anchor the deck was illuminated with lanterns, and this picturesque band of sylphs, tricked out with flowers, and dressed in robes of variegated tappa, got up a ball in great style. These females are passionately fond of dancing, and in the wild grace and spirit of their style excel everything that I have ever seen. The varied dances of the Marquesan girls are beautiful in the extreme, but there is an abandoned voluptuousness in their character which I dare not attempt to describe.

Our ship was now wholly given up to every species of riot

and debauchery. Not the feeblest barrier was interposed between the unholy passions of the crew and their unlimited gratification. The grossest licentiousness and the most shameful inebriety prevailed, with occasional and but short-lived interruptions, through the whole period of her stay. Alas for the poor savages when exposed to the influence of these polluting examples! Unsophisticated and confiding, they are easily led into every vice, and humanity weeps over the ruin thus remorselessly inflicted upon them by their European civilizers. Thrice happy are they who, inhabiting some yet undiscovered island in the midst of the ocean, have never been brought into contaminating contact with the white man.

III

Some account of the late operations of the French at the Marquesas—prudent conduct of the Admiral —sensation produced by the arrival of the strangers —the first horse seen by the islanders—reflections —miserable subterfuge of the French—digression concerning Tahiti—seizure of the island by the Admiral—spirited conduct of an English lady.

IT WAS IN the summer of 1842 that we arrived at the islands; the French had then held possession of them for several weeks. During this time they had disembarked at various points about five hundred troops. These were employed in constructing works of defense, and otherwise providing against the attacks of the natives, who at any moment might be expected to break out in open hostility. The islanders looked upon the people who made this cavalier appropriation of their shores with mingled feelings of fear and detestation. They cordially hated them; but the impulses of their resentment were neutralized by their dread of the floating batteries, which lay with their fatal tubes ostentatiously pointed, not at fortifications and redoubts, but at a handful of bamboo sheds, sheltered in a grove of coconuts! A valiant warrior doubtless, but a prudent one too, was this same Rear-Admiral Du Petit Thouars. Four heavy, double-banked frigates and three corvettes to frighten a parcel of naked heathen into subjection! Sixty eight-pounders to demolish huts of coconut boughs, and Congreve rockets to set on fire a few canoe sheds!

At Nukuheva, there were about one hundred soldiers ashore. They were encamped in tents constructed of the old sails and spare spars of the squadron, within the limits of a redoubt mounted with a few nine-pounders, and surrounded with a fosse. Every other day, these troops were marched out in martial array, to a level piece of ground in the vicinity, and there for hours went through all sorts of military evolutions, surrounded by flocks of the natives, who looked on with savage admiration at the show, and as savage a hatred of the actors. A regiment of the Old Guard, reviewed on a summer's day in the Champs Elysées, could not have made a more critically correct appearance. The officers' regimentals, resplendent with gold lace and embroidery, as if purposely calculated to dazzle the islanders, looked as if just unpacked from their Parisian cases.

The sensation produced by the presence of the strangers had not in the least subsided at the period of our arrival at the islands. The natives still flocked in numbers about the encampment, and watched with the liveliest curiosity everything that was going forward. A blacksmith's forge, which had been set up in the shelter of a grove near the beach, attracted so great a crowd that it required the utmost efforts of the sentries posted around to keep the inquisitive multitude at a sufficient distance to allow the workmen to ply their vocation. But nothing gained so large a share of admiration as a horse, which had been brought from Valparaiso by the *Achille*, one of the vessels of the squadron. The animal, a remarkably fine one, had been taken ashore and stabled in a hut of coconut boughs within the fortified enclosure. Occasionally it was brought out, and, being gaily caparisoned, was ridden by one of the officers at full speed over the hard sand beach. This performance was sure to be hailed with loud plaudits, and the *puarkee nuee* (big hog) was unanimously pronounced by the islanders to be the most extraordinary specimen of zoology that had ever come under their observation.

The expedition for the occupation of the Marquesas had sailed from Brest in the spring of 1842, and the secret of its destination was solely in the possession of its commander. No wonder that those who contemplated such a signal infraction of the rights of humanity should have sought to veil the enormity from the eyes of the world. And yet, notwithstanding their iniquitous conduct in this and in other matters, the French have ever plumed themselves upon being the most humane and polished of nations. A high degree of refinement, however, does not seem to subdue our wicked propensities so much after all; and were civilization itself to be estimated by some of its results, it would seem perhaps better for what we call the barbarous part of the world to remain unchanged.

One example of the shameless subterfuges under which the French stand prepared to defend whatever cruelties they may hereafter think fit to commit in bringing the Marquesan natives into subjection is well worthy of being recorded. On some flimsy pretext or other Mowanna, the King of Nukuheva, whom the invaders by extravagant presents have cajoled over to their interests, and move about like a mere puppet, has been set up as the rightful sovereign of the entire island—the alleged ruler by prescription of various clans who for ages perhaps have treated with each other as separate nations. To reinstate this much-injured prince in the assumed dignities of his ancestors, the disinterested strangers have come all the way from France: they are determined that his title shall be acknowledged. If any tribe shall refuse to recognize the authority of the French, by bowing down to the laced chapeau of Mowanna, let them abide the consequences of their obstinacy. Under cover of a similar pretence, have the outrages and massacres at Tahiti the beautiful, the queen of the South Seas, been perpetrated.

On this buccaneering expedition, Rear-Admiral Du Petit Thouars, leaving the rest of his squadron at the Marquesas—

which had then been occupied by his forces about five months—set sail for the doomed island in the *Reine Blanche* frigate. On his arrival, as an indemnity for alleged insults offered to the flag of his country, he demanded some twenty or thirty thousand dollars to be placed in his hands forthwith, and, in default of payment, threatened to land and take possession of the place.

The frigate, immediately upon coming to an anchor, got springs on her cables, and with her guns cast loose and her men at their quarters, lay in the circular basin of Papeete, with her broadside bearing upon the devoted town; while her numerous cutters, hauled in order alongside, were ready to effect a landing, under cover of her batteries. She maintained this belligerent attitude for several days, during which time a series of informal negotiations were pending, and wide alarm spread over the island. Many of the Tahitians were at first disposed to resort to arms, and drive the invaders from their shores; but more pacific and feebler councils ultimately prevailed. The unfortunate queen, Pomare, incapable of averting the impending calamity, terrified at the arrogance of the insolent Frenchman, and driven at last to despair, fled by night in a canoe to Emio.

During the continuance of the panic there occurred an instance of feminine heroism that I cannot omit to record.

In the grounds of the famous missionary consul, Pritchard, then absent in London, the consular flag of Britain waved as usual during the day, from a lofty staff planted within a few yards of the beach, and in full view of the frigate. One morning an officer, at the head of a party of men, presented himself at the verandah of Mr. Pritchard's house, and inquired in broken English for the lady his wife. The matron soon made her appearance; and the polite Frenchman making one of his best bows, and playing gracefully with the aiguillettes that danced upon his breast, proceeded in courteous accents to deliver his mission. 'The admiral desired the flag to be hauled down—hoped it would be perfectly agreeable—and his men stood ready to perform the duty.' 'Tell the pirate your master,' replied the spirited Englishwoman, pointing to the staff, 'that

if he wishes to strike those colors, he must come and perform
the act himself; I will suffer no one else to do it.' The lady
then bowed haughtily and withdrew into the house. As the
discomfited officer slowly walked away, he looked up to the
flag, and perceived that the cord by which it was elevated to
its place, led from the top of the staff, across the lawn, to an
open upper window of the mansion, where sat the lady, from
whom he had just parted, tranquilly engaged in knitting. Was
that flag hauled down? Mrs. Pritchard thinks not; and Rear-
Admiral Du Petit Thouars is believed to be of the same
opinion.

IV

State of affairs aboard the ship—contents of her
larder—length of South Seamen's voyages—account
of a flying whaleman—determination to leave the
vessel—the bay of Nukuheva—the Typees—invasion of their valley by Porter—reflections—glen
of Tior—interview between the old King
and the French Admiral.

OUR SHIP had not been many days in the harbor of Nukuheva,
before I came to the determination of leaving her. That
my reasons for resolving to take this step were numerous
and weighty, may be inferred from the fact that I chose rather
to risk my fortunes among the savages of the island than to
endure another voyage on board the *Dolly*. To use the concise,
point-blank phrase of the sailors, I had made up my mind to
'run away.' Now as a meaning is generally attached to these
two words no way flattering to the individual to whom they
are applied, it behooves me, for the sake of my own character,
to offer some explanation of my conduct.

When I entered on board the *Dolly,* I signed as a matter
of course the ship's articles, thereby voluntarily engaging and

legally binding myself to serve in a certain capacity for the period of the voyage; and, special considerations apart, I was of course bound to fulfill the agreement. But in all contracts, if one party fail to perform his share of the compact, is not the other virtually absolved from his liability? Who is there who will not answer in the affirmative?

Having settled the principle, then, let me apply it to the particular case in question. In numberless instances had not only the implied but the specified conditions of the articles been violated on the part of the ship in which I served. The usage on board of her was tyrannical; the sick had been inhumanly neglected; the provisions had been doled out in scanty allowance; and her cruises were unreasonably protracted. The captain was the author of these abuses; it was in vain to think that he would either remedy them, or alter his conduct, which was arbitrary and violent in the extreme. His prompt reply to all complaints and remonstrances was—the butt end of a handspike, so convincingly administered as effectually to silence the aggrieved party.

To whom could we apply for redress? We had left both law and equity on the other side of the Cape; and unfortunately, with a very few exceptions, our crew was composed of a parcel of dastardly and mean-spirited wretches, divided among themselves, and only united in enduring without resistance the unmitigated tyranny of the captain. It would have been mere madness for any two or three of the number, unassisted by the rest, to attempt making a stand against his illusage. They would only have called down upon themselves the particular vengeance of this 'Lord of the Plank,' and subjected their shipmates to additional hardships.

But, after all, these things could have been endured awhile, had we entertained the hope of being speedily delivered from them by the due completion of the term of our servitude. But what a dismal prospect awaited us in this quarter! The longevity of Cape Horn whaling voyages is proverbial, frequently extending over a period of four or five years.

Some long-haired bare-necked youths who, forced by the united influences of Captain Marryat and hard times, embark at Nantucket for a pleasure excursion to the Pacific, and whose anxious mothers provide them with bottled milk for the occasion, oftentimes return very respectable middle-aged gentlemen.

The very preparations made for one of these expeditions are enough to frighten one. As the vessel carries out no cargo, her hold is filled with provisions for her own consumption. The owners, who officiate as caterers for the voyage, supply the larder with an abundance of dainties. Delicate morsels of beef and pork, cut on scientific principles from every part of the animal, and of all conceivable shapes and sizes, are carefully packed in salt, and stored away in barrels; affording a never-ending variety in their different degrees of toughness, and in the peculiarities of their saline properties. Choice old water, too, decanted into stout six-barrel casks, and two pints of which are allowed every day to each soul on board; together with ample store of sea bread, previously reduced to a state of petrifaction with a view to preserve it either from decay or consumption in the ordinary mode, are likewise provided for the nourishment and gastronomic enjoyment of the crew.

But not to speak of the quality of these articles of sailors' fare the abundance in which they are put on board a whaling vessel is almost incredible. Oftentimes when we had occasion to break out in the hold, and I beheld the successive tiers of casks and barrels, whose contents were all destined to be consumed in due course by the ship's company, my heart has sunk within me.

Although, as a general case, a ship unlucky in falling in with whales continues to cruise after them until she has barely sufficient provisions remaining to take her home, turning round then quietly and making the best of her way to her friends; yet there are instances when even this natural obstacle to the further prosecution of the voyage is overcome by headstrong captains, who, bartering the fruits of their hard-earned toils for a new supply of provisions in some of the ports of Chili or Peru, begin the voyage afresh with unabated zeal and perseverance. It is in vain that the owners write urgent letters to him to sail for home, and for their sake to bring back the ship, since it appears he can put nothing in her. Not he. He has registered a vow: he will fill his vessel with good sperm oil, or, failing to do so, never again strike Yankee soundings.

I heard of one whaler, which after many years' absence was given up for lost. The last that had been heard of her was a shadowy report of her having touched at some of those unstable islands in the far Pacific, whose eccentric wanderings are carefully noted in each new edition of the South-Sea charts. After a long interval, however, *The Perseverance*—for that was her name—was spoken somewhere in the vicinity of the ends of the earth, cruising along as leisurely as ever, her sails all bepatched and bequilted with rope yarns, her spars fished with old pipe staves, and her rigging knotted and spliced in every possible direction. Her crew was composed of some twenty venerable Greenwich-pensioner-looking old salts, who just managed to hobble about deck. The ends of all the running ropes, with the exception of the signal halyards and poop-down haul, were rove through snatch blocks, and led to the capstan or windlass, so that not a yard was braced or a sail set without the assistance of machinery.

Her hull was incrusted with barnacles, which completely encased her. Three pet sharks followed in her wake and every day came alongside to regale themselves from the contents of the cook's bucket, which were pitched over to them. A vast shoal of bonetas and albacores always kept her company.

Such was the account I heard of this vessel, and the remembrance of it always haunted me; what eventually became of her I never learned; at any rate she never reached home, and I suppose she is still regularly tacking twice in the twenty-four hours somewhere off Buggerry Island, or the Devil's-Tail Peak.

Having said thus much touching the usual length of these voyages, when I inform the reader that ours had as it were just commenced, we being only fifteen months out, and even at that time hailed as a late arrival, and boarded for news, he will readily perceive that there was little to encourage one in looking forward to the future, especially as I had always had a presentiment that we should make an unfortunate voyage, and our experience so far had justified the expectation.

I may here state, and on my faith as an honest man, that though more than three years have elapsed since I left this same identical vessel, she still continues in the Pacific, and but a few days since I saw her reported in the papers as having touched at the Sandwich Islands previous to going on the coast of Japan.

But to return to my narrative. Placed in these circumstances then, with no prospect of matters mending if I remained aboard the *Dolly*, I at once made up my mind to leave her: to be sure it was rather an inglorious thing to steal away privily from those at whose hands I had received wrongs and outrages that I could not resent; but how was such a course to be avoided when it was the only alternative left me? Having made up my mind, I proceeded to acquire all the information I could obtain relating to the island and its inhabitants, with a view of shaping my plans of escape accordingly. The result of these inquiries I will now state, in order that the ensuing narrative may be the better understood.

The bay of Nukuheva in which we were then lying is an expanse of water not unlike in figure the space included within the limits of a horseshoe. It is, perhaps, nine miles in circumference. You approach it from the sea by a narrow entrance, flanked on either side by two small twin islets which soar conically to the height of some five hundred feet. From these the shore recedes on both hands, and describes a deep semicircle.

From the verge of the water the land rises uniformly on all sides, with green and sloping acclivities, until from gently rolling hillsides and moderate elevations it sensibly swells into lofty and majestic heights, whose blue outlines, ranged all around, close in the view. The beautiful aspect of the shore is heightened by deep and romantic glens, which come down to it at almost equal distances, all apparently radiating from a common centre, and the upper extremities of which are lost to the eye beneath the shadow of the mountains. Down each of these little valleys flows a clear stream, here and there assuming the form of a slender cascade, then stealing invisibly along until it burst upon the sight again in larger and more noisy waterfalls, and at last demurely wanders along to the sea.

The houses of the natives, constructed of the yellow bamboo, tastefully twisted together in a kind of wickerwork, and thatched with the long tapering leaves of the palmetto, are scattered irregularly along these valleys beneath the shady branches of the coconut trees.

Nothing can exceed the imposing scenery of this bay. Viewed from our ship as she lay at anchor in the middle of the harbor, it presented the appearance of a vast natural amphitheatre in decay, and overgrown with vines, the deep glens that furrowed its sides appearing like enormous fissures caused by the ravages of time. Very often when lost in admiration at its beauty, I have experienced a pang of regret that a scene so enchanting should be hidden from the world in these remote seas, and seldom meet the eyes of devoted lovers of nature.

Besides this bay the shores of the island are indented by several other extensive inlets, into which descend broad and verdant valleys. These are inhabited by as many distinct tribes of savages, who, although speaking kindred dialects of a common language, and having the same religion and laws, have from time immemorial waged hereditary warfare against each other. The intervening mountains, generally two or three thousand feet above the level of the sea, geographically define the territories of each of these hostile tribes, who never cross them, save on some expedition of war or plunder. Immediately adjacent to Nukuheva, and only separated from it by the mountains seen from the harbor, lies the lovely valley of Happar, whose inmates cherish the most friendly relations with the inhabitants of Nukuheva. On the other side of Happar, and closely adjoining it, is the magnificent valley of the dreaded Typees, the unappeasable enemies of both these tribes.

These celebrated warriors appear to inspire the other islanders with unspeakable terrors. Their very name is a frightful one; for the word 'Typee' in the Marquesan dialect signifies a lover of human flesh. It is rather singular that the title should have been bestowed upon them exclusively, inasmuch as the natives of all this group are irreclaimable cannibals. The name may, perhaps, have been given to denote the peculiar ferocity of this clan, and to convey a special stigma along with it.

These same Typees enjoy a prodigious notoriety all over the islands. The natives of Nukuheva would frequently recount in pantomine to our ship's company their terrible feats, and would show the marks of wounds they had received in desperate encounters with them. When ashore they would try to frighten us by pointing to one of their own number, and calling him a Typee, manifesting no little surprise that we did not take to our heels at so terrible an announcement. It was quite amusing, too, to see with what earnestness they disclaimed all cannibal propensities on their own part while they denounced their enemies—the Typees—as inveterate gormandizers of human flesh; but this is a peculiarity to which I shall hereafter have occasion to allude.

Although I was convinced that the inhabitants of our bay were as arrant cannibals as any of the other tribes on the island, still I could not but feel a particular and most unqualified repugnance to the aforesaid Typees. Even before visiting the Marquesas, I had heard from men who had touched at the group on former voyages some revolting stories in connection with these savages; and fresh in my remembrance was the adventure of the master of the *Katherine,* who, only a few months previous, imprudently venturing into this bay in an armed boat for the purpose of barter, was seized by the natives, carried back a little distance into their valley, and was only saved from a cruel death by the intervention of a young girl, who facilitated his escape by night along the beach to Nukuheva.

I had heard too of an English vessel that many years ago, after a weary cruise, sought to enter the bay of Nukuheva, and, arriving within two or three miles of the land, was met by a large canoe filled with natives, who offered to lead the way to the place of their destination. The captain, unacquainted with the localities of the island, joyfully acceded to the proposition—the canoe paddled on and the ship followed. She was soon conducted to a beautiful inlet, and dropped her anchor in its waters beneath the shadows of the lofty shore. That same night the perfidious Typees, who had thus inveigled her into their fatal bay, flocked aboard the doomed vessel by hundreds, and at a given signal murdered every soul on board.

I shall never forget the observation of one of our crew as we were passing slowly by the entrance of this bay in our way to Nukuheva. As we stood gazing over the side at the verdant headlines, Ned, pointing with his hand in the direction of the treacherous valley exclaimed, 'There—there's Typee. Oh, the bloody cannibals, what a meal they'd make of us if we were to take it into our heads to land! but they say they don't like sailor's flesh, it's too salt. I say, matey, how should you like to be shoved ashore there, eh?' I little thought, as I shuddered at the question, that in the space of a few weeks I should actually be a captive in that selfsame valley.

The French, although they had gone through the ceremony of hoisting their colors for a few hours at all the principal places of the group, had not as yet visited the bay of Typee, anticipating a fierce resistance on the part of the savages there, which for the present at least they wished to avoid. Perhaps they were not a little influenced in the adoption of this unusual policy from a recollection of the warlike reception given by the Typees to the forces of Captain Porter, about the year 1814, when that brave and accomplished officer endeavored to subjugate the clan to gratify the mortal hatred of his allies the Nukuhevas and Happars.

On that occasion I have been told that a considerable detachment of sailors and marines from the frigate *Essex*, accompanied by at least two thousand warriors of Happar and Nukuheva, landed in boats and canoes at the head of the bay, and, after penetrating a little distance into the valley, met with the stoutest resistance from its inmates. Valiantly, although with much loss, the Typees disputed every inch of ground, and after some hard fighting obliged their assailants to retreat and abandon their design of conquest.

The invaders, on their march back to the sea, consoled themselves for their repulse by setting fire to every house and temple in their route; and a long line of smoking ruins defaced the once-smiling bosom of the valley, and proclaimed to its pagan inhabitants the spirit that reigned in the breasts of Christian soldiers. Who can wonder at the deadly hatred of the Typees to all foreigners after such unprovoked atrocities?

Thus it is that they whom we denominate 'savages' are made to deserve the title. When the inhabitants of some sequestered island first descry the 'big canoe' of the European rolling through the blue waters towards their shores, they rush down to the beach in crowds, and with open arms stand ready to embrace the strangers. Fatal embrace! They fold to their bosoms the vipers whose sting is destined to poison all their joys; and the instinctive feeling of love within their breasts is soon converted into the bitterest hate.

The enormities perpetrated in the South Seas upon some of the inoffensive islanders well nigh pass belief. These things are seldom proclaimed at home; they happen at the very ends of the earth; they are done in a corner, and there are none to reveal them. But there is, nevertheless, many a petty trader that has navigated the Pacific whose course from island to island might be traced by a series of cold-blooded robberies, kidnappings, and murders, the iniquity of which might be considered almost sufficient to sink her guilty timbers to the bottom of the sea.

Sometimes vague accounts of such things reach our firesides and we coolly censure them as wrong, impolitic, needlessly severe, and dangerous to the crews of other vessels. How different is our tone when we read the highly wrought description of the massacre of the crew of the *Hobomak* by the Feejees; how we sympathize for the unhappy victims, and with what horror do we regard the diabolical heathens, who, after all, have but avenged the unprovoked injuries which they have received. We breathe nothing but vengeance, and equip armed vessels to traverse thousands of miles of ocean in order to execute summary punishment upon the offenders. On arriving at their destination, they burn, slaughter, and destroy, according to the tenor of written instructions, and sailing away from the scene of devastation call upon all Christendom to applaud their courage and their justice.

How often is the term 'savages' incorrectly applied! None really deserving of it were ever yet discovered by voyagers or by travelers. They have discovered heathens and barbarians, whom by horrible cruelties they have exasperated into savages. It may be asserted without fear of contradiction, that in all the cases of outrages committed by Polynesians, Europeans have at some time or other been the aggressors, and that the cruel and bloodthirsty disposition of some of the islanders is mainly to be ascribed to the influence of such examples.

But to return. Owing to the mutual hostilities of the different tribes I have mentioned, the mountainous tracts which separate their respective territories remain altogether uninhabited; the natives invariably dwelling in the depths of the valleys, with a view of securing themselves from the predatory incursions of their enemies, who often lurk along their borders, ready to cut off any imprudent straggler, or make a descent upon the inmates of some sequestered habitation. I several times met with very aged men, who from this cause had never passed the confines of their native vale, some of them having never even ascended midway up the mountains in the whole course of their lives, and who, accordingly, had little idea of the appearance of any other part of the island, the whole of which is not perhaps more than sixty miles in circuit. The little space in which some of these clans pass away their days would seem almost incredible.

The glen of Tior will furnish a curious illustration of this. The inhabited part is not more than four miles in length, and varies in breadth from half a mile to less than a quarter. The rocky vine-clad cliffs on one side tower almost perpendicularly from their base to the height of at least fifteen hundred feet; while across the vale—in striking contrast to the scenery opposite—grass-grown elevations rise one above another in blooming terraces. Hemmed in by these stupendous barriers, the valley would be altogether shut out from the rest of the world, were it not that it is accessible from the sea at one end, and by a narrow defile at the other.

The impression produced upon my mind, when I first visited this beautiful glen, will never be obliterated.

I had come from Nukuheva by water in the ship's boat, and when we entered the bay of Tior it was high noon. The heat had been intense, as we had been floating upon the long smooth swell of the ocean, for there was but little wind. The sun's rays had expended all their fury upon us; and to add to our discomfort, we had omitted to supply ourselves with water previous to starting. What with heat and thirst together, I became so impatient to get ashore that, when at last we glided toward it, I stood up in the bow of the boat ready for a spring. As she shot two-thirds of her length high upon the beach, propelled by three or four strong strokes of the oars, I leaped among a parcel of juvenile savages, who stood prepared to give us a kind reception, and with them at my heels, yelling like so many imps, I rushed forward across the open ground in the vicinity of the sea, and plunged, diver fashion, into the recesses of the first grove that offered.

What a delightful sensation did I experience! I felt as if floating in some new element, while all sorts of gurgling, trickling, liquid sounds fell upon my ear. People may say what they will about the refreshing influences of a cold-water bath, but commend me when in a perspiration to the shade baths of Tior, beneath the coconut trees, and amidst the cool delightful atmosphere which surrounds them.

How shall I describe the scenery that met my eye, as I looked out from this verdant recess! The narrow valley, with its steep and close-adjoining sides draperied with vines, and arched overhead with a fretwork of interlacing boughs, nearly hidden from view by masses of leafy verdure, seemed from where I stood like an immense arbor disclosing its vista to the eye, whilst as I advanced it insensibly widened into the loveliest vale eye ever beheld.

It so happened that the very day I was in Tior the French admiral, attended by all the boats of his squadron, came down in state from Nukuheva to take formal possession of the place. He remained in the valley about two hours, during which time he had a ceremonious interview with the king.

The patriarch-sovereign of Tior was a man very far advanced in years; but though age had bowed his form and rendered him almost decrepit, his gigantic frame retained all its original magnitude and grandeur of appearance. He advanced, slowly and with evident pain, assisting his tottering steps with the heavy warspear he held in his hand, and attended by a group of grey-bearded chiefs, on one of whom he occasionally leaned for support. The Admiral came forward with head uncovered and extended hand, while the old king saluted him by a stately flourish of his weapon. The next moment they stood side by side, these two extremes of the social scale—the polished, splendid Frenchman, and the poor tattooed savage. They were both tall and noble-looking men; but in other respects how strikingly contrasted! Du Petit Thouars exhibited upon his person all the paraphernalia of his naval rank. He wore a richly decorated admiral's frock coat, a laced *chapeau bras,* and upon his breast were a variety of ribbons and orders; while the simple islander, with the exception of a slight cincture about his loins, appeared in all the nakedness of nature.

At what an immeasurable distance, thought I, are these two beings removed from each other. In the one is shown the result of long centuries of progressive civilization and refinement, which have gradually converted the mere creature into the semblance of all that is elevated and grand; while the other, after the lapse of the same period, has not advanced one step in the career of improvement. 'Yet, after all,' quoth I to myself, 'insensible as he is to a thousand wants, and removed from harassing cares, may not the savage be the happier man of the two?' Such were the thoughts that arose in my mind as I gazed upon the novel spectacle before me. In truth it was an impressive one, and little likely to be effaced. I can recall even now with vivid distinctiveness every feature of the scene. The umbrageous shades where the interview took place—the glorious tropical vegetation around—the picturesque grouping of the mingled throng of soldiery and natives —and even the golden-hued bunch of bananas that I held in my hand at the time, and of which I occasionally partook while making the aforesaid philosophical reflections.

V

Thoughts previous to attempting an escape—Toby, a fellow sailor, agrees to share the adventure—last night aboard the ship.

HAVING FULLY RESOLVED to leave the vessel clandestinely, and having acquired all the knowledge concerning the bay that I could obtain under the circumstances in which I was placed, I now deliberately turned over in my mind every plan of escape that suggested itself, being determined to act with all possible prudence in an attempt where failure would be attended with so many disagreeable consequences. The idea of being taken and brought back ignominiously to the ship was so inexpressibly repulsive to me that I was determined by no hasty and imprudent measures to render such an event probable.

I knew that our worthy captain, who felt such a paternal solicitude for the welfare of his crew, would not willingly consent that one of his best hands should encounter the perils of a sojourn among the natives of a barbarous island; and I was certain that in the event of my disappearance, his fatherly anxiety would prompt him to offer, by way of a reward, yard upon yard of gaily printed calico for my apprehension. He might even have appreciated my services at the value of a musket, in which case I felt perfectly certain that the whole population of the bay would be immediately upon my track, incited by the prospect of so magnificent a bounty.

Having ascertained the fact before alluded to, that the islanders, from motives of precaution, dwelt altogether in the depths of the valleys, and avoided wandering about the more elevated portions of the shore, unless bound on some expedition of war or plunder, I concluded that if I could effect unperceived a passage to the mountains, I might easily remain among them, supporting myself by such fruits as came in my way until the sailing of the ship, an event of which I could not fail to be immediately apprised, as from my lofty position I should command a view of the entire harbor.

The idea pleased me greatly. It seemed to combine a great deal of practicability with no inconsiderable enjoyment in a quiet way; for how delightful it would be to look down upon the detested old vessel from the height of some thousand feet, and contrast the verdant scenery about me with the recollection of her narrow decks and gloomy forecastle! Why, it was really refreshing even to think of it; and so I straightway fell to picturing myself seated beneath a coconut tree on the brow of the mountain, with a cluster of plantains within easy reach, criticizing her nautical evolutions as she was working her way out of the harbor.

To be sure here was one rather unpleasant drawback to these agreeable anticipations—the possibility of falling in with a foraging part of these same bloody-minded Typees, whose appetites, edged perhaps by the air of so elevated a region, might prompt them to devour one. This, I must confess, was a most disagreeable view of the matter.

Just to think of a party of these unnatural gormands taking it into their heads to make a convivial meal of a poor devil, who would have no means of escape or defense; however, there was no help for it. I was willing to encounter some risks in order to accomplish my object, and counted much upon my ability to elude these prowling cannibals amongst the many coverts which the mountains afforded. Besides, the chances were ten to one in my favor that they would none of them quit their own fastnesses.

I had determined not to communicate my design of withdrawing from the vessel to any of my shipmates, and least of all to solicit any one to accompany me in my flight. But it so happened one night that being upon deck, revolving over in my mind various plans of escape, I perceived one of the ship's company leaning over the bulwarks, apparently plunged in a profound reverie. He was a young fellow about my own age, for whom I had all along entertained a great regard, and

Toby, such was the name by which he went among us, for his real name he would never tell us, was every way worthy of it. He was active, ready, and obliging, of dauntless courage, and singularly open and fearless in the expression of his feelings. I had on more than one occasion got him out of scrapes into which this had led him; and I know not whether it was from this cause, or a certain congeniality of sentiment between us, that he had always shown a partiality for my society. We had battled out many a long watch together, beguiling the weary hours with chat, song, and story, mingled with a good many imprecations upon the hard destiny it seemed our common fortune to encounter.

Toby, like myself, had evidently moved in a different sphere of life, and his conversation at times betrayed this, although he was anxious to conceal it. He was one of that class of rovers you sometimes meet at sea, who never reveal their origin, never allude to home, and go rambling over the world as if pursued by some mysterious fate they cannot possibly elude.

There was much even in the appearance of Toby calculated to draw me toward him, for while the greater part of the crew were as coarse in person as in mind, Toby was endowed with a remarkably prepossessing exterior. Arrayed in his blue frock and duck trousers, he was as smart a looking sailor as ever stepped upon a deck; he was singularly small and slightly made, with great flexibility of limb. His naturally dark complexion had been deepened by exposure to the tropical sun, and a mass of jetty locks clustered about his temples and threw a darker shade into his large black eyes. He was a strange, wayward being, moody, fitful, and melancholy—at times almost morose. He had a quick and fiery temper too, which, when thoroughly roused, transported him into a state bordering on delirium.

It is strange the power that a mind of deep passion has over feebler natures. I have seen a brawny fellow, with no lack of ordinary courage, fairly quail before this slender stripling, when in one of his furious fits. But these paroxysms seldom occurred, and in them my bighearted shipmate vented the bile which more calm-tempered individuals get rid of by a continual pettishness at trivial annoyances.

No one ever saw Toby laugh; I mean in the hearty abandonment of broad-mouthed mirth. He did smile sometimes, it is true; and there was a good deal of dry sarcastic humor about him, which told the more from the imperturbable gravity of his tone and manner.

Latterly I had observed that Toby's melancholy had greatly increased, and I had frequently seen him since our arrival at the island gazing wistfully upon the shore, when the remainder of the crew would be rioting below. I was aware that he entertained a cordial detestation of the ship, and believed that, should a fair chance of escape present itself, he would embrace it willingly. But the attempt was so perilous in the place where we then lay, that I supposed myself the only individual on board the ship who was sufficiently reckless to think of it. In this, however, I was mistaken.

When I perceived Toby leaning, as I have mentioned, against the bulwarks and buried in thought, it struck me at once that the subject of his meditations might be the same as my own. And if it be so, thought I, is he not the very one of all my shipmates whom I would choose for the partner of my adventure? and why should I not have some comrade with me to divide its dangers and alleviate its hardships? Perhaps I might be obliged to lie concealed among the mountains for weeks. In such an event what a solace would a companion be.

These thoughts passed rapidly through my mind, and I wondered why I had not before considered the matter in this light. But it was not too late. A tap upon the shoulder served to rouse Toby from his reverie; I found him ripe for the enterprise, and a very few words sufficed for a mutual understanding between us. In an hour's time we had arranged all the preliminaries, and decided upon our plan of action. We then ratified our engagement with an affectionate wedding of palms, and to elude suspicion repaired each to his hammock, to spend the last night on board the *Dolly*.

The next day the starboard watch, to which we both belonged, was to be sent ashore on liberty; and, availing ourselves of this opportunity, we determined, as soon after landing as possible, to separate ourselves from the rest of the men without exciting their suspicions, and strike back at once for the mountains. Seen from the ship, their summits appeared inaccessible, but here and there sloping spurs extended from them almost into the sea, buttressing the lofty elevations with which they were connected, and forming those radiating valleys I have before described. One of these ridges, which appeared more practicable than the rest, we determined to climb. Accordingly, we carefully observed its bearings and locality from the ship, so that when ashore we should run no chance of missing it.

In all this the leading object we had in view was to seclude ourselves from sight until the departure of the vessel; then to take our chance as to the reception the Nukuheva natives might give us; and, after remaining upon the island as long as we found our stay agreeable, to leave it the first favorable opportunity that offered.

VI

A specimen of nautical oratory—criticisms of the sailors—the starboard watch are given a holiday— the escape to the mountains.

EARLY THE NEXT morning the starboard watch were mustered upon the quarterdeck, and our worthy captain, standing in the cabin gangway, harangued us as follows:—

'Now, men, as we are just off a six months' cruise, and have got through most all our work in port here, I suppose you want to go ashore. Well, I mean to give your watch liberty today, so you may get ready as soon as you please, and go; but understand this, I am going to give you liberty because

I suppose you would growl like so many old quarter gunners if I didn't; at the same time, if you'll take my advice, every mother's son of you will stay aboard, and keep out of the way of the bloody cannibals altogether. Ten to one, men, if you go ashore, you will get into some infernal row, and that will be the end of you; for if those tattooed scoundrels get you a little ways back into their valleys, they'll nab you— that you may be certain of. Plenty of white men have gone ashore here and never been seen any more. There was the old *Dido,* she put in here about two years ago, and sent one watch off on liberty; they never were heard of again for a week—the natives swore they didn't know where they were— and only three of them ever got back to the ship again, and one with his face damaged for life, for the cursed heathens tattooed a broad patch clean across his figurehead. But it will be no use talking to you, for go you will, that I see plainly; so all I have to say is, that you need not blame me if the islanders make a meal of you. You may stand some chance of escaping them though, if you keep close about the French encampment, and are back to the ship again before sunset. Keep that much in your mind, if you forget all the rest I've been saying to you. There, go forward; bear a hand and rig yourselves, and stand by for a call. At two bells the boat will be manned to take you off, and the Lord have mercy on you!'

Various were the emotions depicted upon the countenances of the starboard watch whilst listening to this address; but on its conclusion there was a general move toward the forecastle, and we soon were all busily engaged in getting ready for the holiday so auspiciously announced by the skipper. During these preparations his harangue was commented upon in no very measured terms; and one of the party, after denouncing him as a lying old son of a sea cook who begrudged a fellow a few hours' liberty, exclaimed with an oath, 'But you don't bounce me out of my liberty, old chap, for all your yarns; for I would go ashore if every pebble on the beach was a live coal, and every stick a gridiron, and the cannibals stood ready to broil me on landing.'

The spirit of this sentiment was responded to by all hands,

and we resolved that in spite of the captain's croakings we would make a glorious day of it.

But Toby and I had our own game to play, and we availed ourselves of the confusion which always reigns among a ship's company preparatory to going ashore, to confer together and complete our arrangements. As our object was to effect as rapid a flight as possible to the mountains, we determined not to encumber ourselves with any superfluous apparel; and, accordingly, while the rest were rigging themselves out with some idea of making a display, we were content to put on new stout duck trousers, serviceable pumps, and heavy Havre frocks which, with a Payta hat, completed our equipment.

When our shipmates wondered at this, Toby exclaimed in his odd grave way that the rest might do as they liked, but that he for one preserved his go-ashore traps for the Spanish main, where the tie of a sailor's neckerchief might make some difference; but as for a parcel of unbreeched heathen, he wouldn't go to the bottom of his chest for any of them, and was half disposed to appear among them in buff himself. The men laughed at what they thought was one of his strange conceits, and so we escaped suspicion.

It may appear singular that we should have been thus on our guard with our own shipmates; but there were some among us who, had they possessed the least inkling of our project, would, for a paltry hope of reward, have immediately communicated it to the captain.

As soon as two bells were struck, the word was passed for the libertymen to get into the boat. I lingered behind in the forecastle a moment to take a parting glance at its familiar features, and just as I was about to ascend to the deck my eye happened to light on the bread barge and beef kid, which contained the remnants of our hasty meal. Although I had never before thought of providing anything in the way of food for our expedition, as I fully relied upon the fruits of the island to sustain us wherever we might wander, yet I could not resist the inclination I felt to provide luncheon from the relics before me. Accordingly I took a double handful of these small, broken, flinty bits of biscuit which generally go by the name of 'midshipmen's nuts,' and thrust them into the bosom of my frock; in which same ample receptacle I had previously stowed away several pounds of tobacco and a few yards of cotton cloth—articles with which I intended to purchase the good will of the natives as soon as we should appear among them after the departure of our vessel.

This last addition to my stock caused a considerable protuberance in front, which I abated in a measure by shaking the bits of bread around my waist, and distributing the plugs of tobacco among the folds of the garment.

Hardly had I completed these arrangements when my name was sung out by a dozen voices, and I sprung upon the deck, where I found all the party in the boat, and impatient to shove off. I dropped over the side and seated myself with the rest of the watch in the stern sheets, while the poor larborders shipped their oars, and commenced pulling us ashore.

This happened to be the rainy season at the islands, and the heavens had nearly the whole morning betokened one of those heavy showers which during this period so frequently occur. The large drops fell bubbling into the water shortly after our leaving the ship, and by the time we had effected a landing it poured down in torrents. We fled for shelter under cover of an immense canoe house which stood hard by the beach, and waited for the first fury of the storm to pass.

It continued, however, without cessation; and the monotonous beating of the rain overhead began to exert a drowsy influence upon the men, who, throwing themselves here and there upon the large war canoes, after chatting awhile, all fell asleep.

This was the opportunity we desired, and Toby and I availed ourselves of it at once by stealing out of the canoe house and plunging into the depths of an extensive grove that was in its rear. After ten minutes' rapid progress we gained an open space from which we could just descry the ridge we intended to mount looming dimly through the mists of the tropical shower, and distant from us, as we estimated, something more than a mile. Our direct course toward it lay through a rather populous part of the bay; but desirous as we were of evading the natives, and securing an unmolested retreat to the mountains, we determined, by taking a circuit through some extensive thickets, to avoid their vicinity altogether.

The heavy rain that still continued to fall without intermission favoured our enterprise, as it drove the islanders into their houses, and prevented any casual meeting with them. Our heavy frocks soon became completely saturated with water, and by their weight, and that of the articles we had concealed beneath them, not a little impeded our progress. But it was no time to pause when at any moment we might be surprised by a body of the savages, and forced at the very outset to relinquish our undertaking.

Since leaving the canoe house we had scarcely exchanged a single syllable with one another; but when we entered a second narrow opening in the wood, and again caught sight of the ridge before us, I took Toby by the arm and, pointing along its sloping outline to the lofty heights at its extremity, said in a low tone, 'Now, Toby, not a word, nor a glance backward, till we stand on the summit of yonder mountain— so no more lingering, but let us shove ahead while we can, and in a few hours' time we may laugh aloud. You are the lightest and the nimblest, so lead on, and I will follow.'

'All right, brother,' said Toby, 'quick's our play; only let's keep close together, that's all;' and so saying, with a bound like a young roe, he cleared a brook which ran across our path, and rushed forward with a quick step.

When we arrived within a short distance of the ridge, we were stopped by a mass of tall yellow reeds, growing together as thickly as they could stand, and as tough and stubborn as so many rods of steel; and we perceived, to our chagrin, that they extended midway up the elevation we purposed to ascend.

For a moment we gazed about us in quest of a more practicable route; it was, however, at once apparent that there was no resource but to pierce this thicket of canes at all hazards. We now reversed our order of march, I, being the heaviest, taking the lead, with a view of breaking a path through the obstruction, while Toby fell into the rear.

Two or three times I endeavoured to insinuate myself between the canes and by dint of coaxing and bending them to make some progress; but a bullfrog might as well have tried to work a passage through the teeth of a comb, and I gave up the attempt in despair.

Half wild with meeting an obstacle we had so little anticipated, I threw myself desperately against it, crushing to the ground the canes with which I came in contact; and, rising to my feet again, repeated the action with like effect. Twenty minutes of this violent exercise almost exhausted me, but it carried us some way into the thicket; when Toby, who had been reaping the benefit of my labors by following close at my heels, proposed to become pioneer in turn, and accordingly passed ahead with a view of affording me a respite from my exertions. As however with his slight frame he made but bad work of it, I was soon obliged to resume my old place again.

On we toiled, the perspiration starting from our bodies in floods, our limbs torn and lacerated with the splintered fragments of the broken canes, until we had proceeded perhaps as far as the middle of the brake, when suddenly it ceased raining, and the atmosphere around us became close and sultry beyond expression. The elasticity of the reeds, quickly recovering from the temporary pressure of our bodies, caused them to spring back to their original position; so that they closed in upon us as we advanced, and prevented the circulation of the little air which might otherwise have reached us. Besides this, their great height completely shut us out from the view of surrounding objects, and we were not certain but what we might have been going all the time in a wrong direction.

Fatigued with my long-continued efforts, and panting for breath, I felt myself completely incapacitated for any further exertion. I rolled up the sleeve of my frock, and squeezed the moisture it contained into my parched mouth. But the few drops I managed to obtain gave me little relief, and I sank down for a moment with a sort of dogged apathy, from which I was aroused by Toby, who had devised a plan to free us from the net in which we had become entangled.

He was laying about him lustily with his sheath knife, lopping the canes right and left, like a reaper, and soon made quite a clearing around us. This sight reanimated me, and seizing my own knife, I hacked and hewed away without mercy. But alas! the farther we advanced, the thicker and taller, and apparently the more interminable, the reeds became.

I began to think we were fairly snared, and had almost made up my mind that without a pair of wings we should never be able to escape from the toils, when all at once I discerned a peep of daylight through the canes on my right, and, communicating the joyful tidings to Toby, we both fell to with fresh spirit, and speedily opening a passage towards it we found ourselves clear of perplexities, and in the near vicinity of the ridge.

After resting for a few moments we began the ascent, and after a little vigorous climbing found ourselves close to its summit. Instead however of walking along its ridge, where we should have been in full view of the natives in the vales beneath, and at a point where they could easily intercept us were they so inclined, we cautiously advanced on one side, crawling on our hands and knees, and screened from observation by the grass through which we glided, much in the fashion of a couple of serpents. After an hour employed in this unpleasant kind of locomotion, we started to our feet again and pursued our way boldly along the crest of the ridge.

This salient spur of the lofty elevations that encompassed the bay rose with a sharp angle from the valleys at its base, and presented, with the exception of a few steep acclivities, the appearance of a vast inclined plane, sweeping down toward the sea from the heights in the distance. We had ascended it near the place of its termination and at its lowest point, and now saw our route to the mountains distinctly defined along its narrow crest, which was covered with a soft carpet of verdure, and was in many parts only a few feet wide.

Elated with the success which had so far attended our enterprise, and invigorated by the refreshing atmosphere we now inhaled, Toby and I in high spirits were making our way rapidly along the ridge when suddenly from the valleys below which lay on either side of us we heard the distant shouts of the natives, who had just descried us, and to whom our figures, brought in bold relief against the sky, were plainly revealed.

Glancing our eyes into these valleys, we perceived their savage inhabitants hurrying to and fro, seemingly under the influence of some sudden alarm, and appearing to the eye scarcely bigger than so many pigmies; while their white-thatched dwellings dwarfed by the distance, looked like baby houses. As we looked down upon the islanders from our lofty elevation, we experienced a sense of security; feeling confident that, should they undertake a pursuit, it would, from the start we now had, prove entirely fruitless, unless they followed us into the mountains, where we knew they cared not to venture.

However, we thought it as well to make the most of our time; and accordingly, where the ground would admit of it, we ran swiftly along the summit of the ridge, until we were brought to a stand by a steep cliff, which at first seemed to interpose an effectual barrier to our further advance. By dint of much hard scrambling however, and at some risk to our necks, we at last surmounted it, and continued our flight with unabated celerity.

We had left the beach early in the morning, and after an uninterrupted, though at times difficult and dangerous ascent, during which we had never once turned our faces to the sea, we found ourselves, about three hours before sunset, standing on the top of what seemed to be the highest land on the island, an immense overhanging cliff composed of basaltic rocks, hung round with parasitical plants. We must have been more than three thousand feet above the level of the sea, and the scenery viewed from this height was magnificent.

The lonely bay of Nukuheva, dotted here and there with the black hulls of the vessels composing the French squadron, lay reposing at the base of a circular range of elevations, whose verdant sides, perforated with deep glens or diversified with smiling valleys, formed altogether the loveliest view I ever beheld, and were I to live a hundred years, I should never forget the feeling of admiration which I then experienced.

VII

The other side of the mountain—disappointment— inventory of articles brought from the ship—division of the stock of bread—appearance of the interior of the island—a discovery—a ravine and waterfalls —a sleepless night—further discoveries—my illness —a Marquesan landscape.

MY CURIOSITY HAD BEEN not a little raised with regard to the description of country we should meet on the other side of the mountains; and I had supposed, with Toby, that immediately on gaining the heights we should be enabled to view the large bays of Happar and Typee reposing at our feet on one side, in the same way that Nukuheva lay spread out below on the other. But here we were disappointed. Instead of finding the mountain we had ascended sweeping down in the opposite direction into broad and capacious valleys, the land appeared to retain its general elevation, only broken into a series of ridges and inter-vales, which as far as the eye could reach stretched away from us, with their precipitous sides covered with the brightest verdure, and waving here and there with the foliage of clumps of woodland; among which, however, we perceived none of those trees upon whose fruit we had relied with such certainty.

This was a most unlooked-for discovery, and one that promised to defeat our plans altogether, for we could not think of descending the mountain on the Nukuheva side in quest of food. Should we for this purpose be induced to retrace our steps, we should run no small chance of encountering the natives, who in that case, if they did nothing worse to us, would be certain to convey us back to the ship for the sake of the reward in calico and trinkets, which we had no doubt our skipper would hold out to them as an inducement to our capture.

What was to be done? The *Dolly* would not sail perhaps for ten days and how were we to sustain life during this period? I bitterly repented our improvidence in not providing ourselves, as we easily might have done, with a supply of biscuit. With a rueful visage I now bethought me of the scanty handful of bread I had stuffed into the bosom of my frock, and felt somewhat desirous to ascertain what part of it had weathered the rather rough usage it had experienced in ascending the mountain. I accordingly proposed to Toby that we should enter into a joint examination of the various articles we had brought from the ship. With this intent we seated ourselves upon the grass; and a little curious to see with what kind of judgment my companion had filled his frock—which I remarked seemed about as well lined as my own—I requested him to commence operations by spreading out its contents.

Thrusting his hand, then, into the bosom of this capacious receptacle, he first brought to light about a pound of tobacco, whose component parts still adhered together, the whole outside being covered with soft particles of sea bread. Wet and dripping, it had the appearance of having been just recovered from the bottom of the sea. But I paid slight attention to a substance of so little value to us in our present situation, as soon I perceived the indications it gave of Toby's foresight in laying in a supply of food for the expedition.

I eagerly inquired what quantity he had brought with him, when, rummaging once more beneath his garment, he produced a small handful of something so soft, pulpy, and discoloured, that for a few moments he was as much puzzled as myself to tell by what possible instrumentality such a villainous compound had become engendered in his bosom. I can only describe it as a hash of soaked bread and bits of tobacco, brought to a doughy consistency by the united agency of perspiration and rain. But repulsive as it might otherwise have been, I now regarded it as an invaluable treasure, and proceeded with great care to transfer this pastelike mass to a large leaf which I had plucked from a bush beside me. Toby informed me that in the morning he had placed two whole biscuits in his bosom, with a view of munching them, should he feel so inclined, during our flight. These were now reduced to the equivocal substance which I had just placed on the leaf.

Another dive into the frock brought to view some four or five yards of calico print, whose tasteful pattern was rather disfigured by the yellow stains of the tobacco with which it had been brought in contact. In drawing this calico slowly from his bosom inch by inch, Toby reminded me of a juggler performing the feat of the endless ribbon. The next cast was a small one, being a sailor's little ditty bag, containing needles, thread, and other sewing utensils; then came a razor case, followed by two or three separate plugs of Negro head, which were fished up from the bottom of the now empty receptacle. These various matters being inspected, I produced the few things that I had myself brought.

As might have been anticipated from the state of my companion's edible supplies, I found my own in a deplorable condition, and diminished to a quantity that would have formed half a dozen mouthfuls for a hungry man who was partial enough to tobacco not to mind swallowing it. A few morsels of bread, with a fathom or two of white cotton cloth, and several pounds of choice pigtail, composed the extent of my possessions.

Our joint stock of miscellaneous articles was now made up into a compact bundle, which it was agreed we should carry alternately. But the sorry remains of the biscuit were not to be disposed of so summarily: the precarious circumstances in which we were placed made us regard them as something on which very probably depended the fate of our adventure.

After a brief discussion in which we both of us expressed our resolution of not descending into the bay until the ship's departure, I suggested to my companion that little of it as there was, we should divide the bread into six equal portions, each of which should be a day's allowance for both of us. This proposition he assented to; so I took the silk kerchief from my neck, and, cutting it with my knife into half a dozen equal pieces, proceeded to make an exact division.

At first, Toby, with a degree of fastidiousness that seemed to me ill-timed, was for picking out the minute particles of tobacco with which the spongy mass was mixed; but against this proceeding I protested, as by such an operation we must have greatly diminished its quantity.

When the division was accomplished, we found that a day's allowance for the two was not a great deal more than what a tablespoon might hold. Each separate portion we immediately rolled up in the bit of silk prepared for it, and joining them altogether into a small package, I committed them, with solemn injunctions of fidelity, to the custody of Toby. For the remainder of that day we resolved to fast, as we had been fortified by a breakfast in the morning; and now starting again to our feet, we looked about us for a shelter during the night, which, from the appearance of the heavens, promised to be a dark and tempestuous one.

There was no place near us which would in any way answer our purpose; so turning our backs upon Nukuheva, we commenced exploring the unknown regions which lay upon the other side of the mountain.

In this direction, as far as our vision extended, not a sign of life, nor anything that denoted even the transient residence of man, could be seen. The whole landscape seemed one unbroken solitude, the interior of the island having apparently been untenanted since the morning of the creation; and as we advanced through this wilderness, our voices sounded strangely in our ears, as though human accents had never before disturbed the fearful silence of the place, interrupted only by the low murmurings of distant waterfalls.

Our disappointment, however, in not finding the various

fruits with which we had intended to regale ourselves during our stay in these wilds, was a good deal lessened by the consideration that from this very circumstance we should be much less exposed to a casual meeting with the savage tribes about us, who we knew always dwelt beneath the shadows of those trees which supplied them with food.

We wandered along, casting eager glances into every bush we passed, until just as we had succeeded in mounting one of the many ridges that intersected the ground, I saw in the grass before me something like an indistinctly traced footpath, which appeared to lead along the top of the ridge, and to descend with it into a deep ravine about half a mile in advance of us.

Robinson Crusoe could not have been more startled at the footprint in the sand than we were at this unwelcome discovery. My first impulse was to make as rapid a retreat as possible, and bend our steps in some other direction; but our curiosity to see whither this path might lead, prompted us to pursue it. So on we went, the track becoming more and more visible the farther we proceeded, until it conducted us to the verge of the ravine, where it abruptly terminated.

'And so,' said Toby, peering down into the chasm, 'every one that travels this path takes a jump here, eh?'

'Not so,' said I, 'for I think they might manage to descend without it; what say you—shall we attempt the feat?'

'And what, in the name of caves and coal holes, do you expect to find at the bottom of that gulf but a broken neck—why it looks blacker than our ship's hold, and the roar of those waterfalls down there would batter one's brains to pieces.'

'Oh, no, Toby,' I exclaimed, laughing; 'but there's something to be seen here, that's plain, or there would have been no path, and I am resolved to find out what it is.'

'*I* will tell you what, my pleasant fellow,' rejoined Toby quickly, 'if you are going to pry into everything you meet with here that excites your curiosity, you will marvelously soon get knocked on the head; to a dead certainty you will come bang upon a party of these savages in the midst of your discovery-makings, and I doubt whether such an event would particularly delight you. Just take my advice for once, and let us 'bout ship and steer in some other direction; besides, it's getting late, and we ought to be mooring ourselves for the night.'

'That is just the thing I have been driving at,' replied I; 'and I am thinking that this ravine will exactly answer our purpose, for it is roomy, secluded, well watered, and may shelter us from the weather.'

'Aye, and from sleep too, and by the same token will give us sore throats and rheumatisms into the bargain,' cried Toby with evident dislike at the idea.

'Oh, very well then, my lad," said I, 'since you will not accompany me, here I go alone. You will see me in the morning;' and advancing to the edge of the cliff upon which we had been standing, I proceeded to lower myself down by the tangled roots which clustered about all the crevices of the rock. As I had anticipated, Toby, in spite of his previous remonstrances, followed my example, and dropping himself with the activity of a squirrel from point to point, he quickly outstripped me, and effected a landing at the bottom before I had accomplished two-thirds of the descent.

The sight that now greeted us was one that will ever be vividly impressed upon my mind. Five foaming streams, rushing through as many gorges, and swelled and turbid by the recent rains, united together in one mad plunge of nearly eighty feet, and fell with wild uproar into a deep black pool scooped out of the gloomy-looking rocks that lay piled around, and thence in one collected body dashed down a narrow sloping channel which seemed to penetrate into the very bowels of the earth. Overhead, vast roots of trees hung down from the sides of the ravine, dripping with moisture, and trembling with the concussions produced by the fall. It was now sunset, and the feeble uncertain light that found its way into these caverns and woody depths heightened their strange appearance, and reminded us that in a short time we should find ourselves in utter darkness.

As soon as I had satisfied my curiosity by gazing at this

scene, I fell to wondering how it was that what we had taken for a path should have conducted us to so singular a place, and began to suspect that after all I might have been deceived in supposing it to have been a track formed by the islanders. This was rather an agreeable reflection than otherwise, for it diminished our dread of accidentally meeting with any of them, and I came to the conclusion that perhaps we could not have selected a more secure hiding place than this very spot we had so accidentally hit upon. Toby agreed with me in this view of the matter, and we immediately began gathering together the limbs of trees which lay scattered about, with the view of constructing a temporary hut for the night. This we were obliged to build close to the foot of the cataract, for the current of water extended very nearly to the sides of the gorge. The few moments of light that remained we employed in covering our hut with a species of broad-bladed grass that grew in every fissure of the ravine. Our hut, if it deserved to be called one, consisted of six or eight of the straightest branches we could find laid obliquely against the steep wall of rock, with their lower ends within a foot of the stream. Into the space thus covered over we managed to crawl, and dispose our wearied bodies as best we could.

Shall I ever forget that horrid night? As for poor Toby, I could scarcely get a word out of him. It would have been some consolation to have heard his voice, but he lay shivering the livelong night like a man with the palsy, with his knees drawn up to his head, while his back was supported against the dripping side of the rock. During this wretched night there seemed nothing wanting to complete the perfect misery of our condition. The rain descended in such torrents that our poor shelter proved a mere mockery. In vain did I try to elude the incessant streams that poured upon me; by protecting one part I only exposed another, and the water was continually finding some new opening through which to drench us.

I have had many a ducking in the course of my life, and in general cared little about it; but the accumulated horrors of that night, the deathlike coldness of the place, the appalling darkness and the dismal sense of our forlorn condition, almost unmanned me.

It will not be doubted that the next morning we were early risers, and as soon as I could catch the faintest glimpse of anything like daylight I shook my companion by the arm, and told him it was sunrise. Poor Toby lifted up his head, and after a moment's pause said in a husky voice, 'Then, shipmate, my toplights have gone out, for it appears darker now with my eyes open than it did when they were shut.'

'Nonsense!' exclaimed I, 'you are not awake yet.'

'Awake!' roared Toby in a rage, 'awake! You mean to insinuate I've been asleep, do you? It is an insult to a man to suppose he could sleep in such an infernal place as this.'

By the time I had apologized to my friend for having misconstrued his silence, it had become somewhat more light, and we crawled out of our lair. The rain had ceased, but everything around us was dripping with moisture. We stripped off our saturated garments, and wrung them as dry as we could. We contrived to make the blood circulate in our benumbed limbs by rubbing them vigorously with our hands; and after performing our ablutions in the stream, and putting on our still wet clothes, we began to think it advisable to break our long fast, it being now twenty-four hours since we had tasted food.

Accordingly our day's ration was brought out, and seating ourselves on a detached fragment of rock, we proceeded to discuss it. First we divided it into two equal portions, and, carefully rolling one of them up for our evening's repast, divided the remainder again as equally as possible, and then drew lots for the first choice. I could have placed the morsel that fell to my share upon the tip of my finger; but notwithstanding this I took care that it should be full ten minutes before I had swallowed the last crumb. What a true saying it is that 'appetite furnishes the best sauce.' There was a flavour and a relish to this small particle of food that under other circumstances it would have been impossible for the most delicate viands to have imparted. A copious draught of the pure water which flowed at our feet served to complete the meal, and after it we rose sensibly refreshed, and prepared for whatever might befall us.

We now carefully examined the chasm in which we had passed the night. We crossed the stream, and gaining the farther side of the pool I have mentioned, discovered proofs that the spot must have been visited by some one but a short time previous to our arrival. Further observation convinced us that it had been regularly frequented, and, as we afterward conjectured from particular indications, for the purpose of obtaining a certain root, from which the natives obtain a kind of ointment.

These discoveries immediately determined us to abandon a place which had presented no inducement for us to remain, except the promise of security; and as we looked about us for the means of ascending again into the upper regions, we at last found a practicable part of the rock, and half an hour's toil carried us to the summit of the same cliff from which the preceding evening we had descended.

I now proposed to Toby that instead of rambling about the island, exposing ourselves to discovery at every turn, we should select some place as our fixed abode for as long a period as our food should hold out, build ourselves a comfortable hut, and be as prudent and circumspect as possible. To all this my companion assented, and we at once set about carrying the plan into execution.

With this view, after exploring without success a little glen near us, we crossed several of the ridges of which I have before spoken; and about noon found ourselves ascending a long and gradually rising slope, but still without having discovered any place adapted to our purpose. Low and heavy clouds betokened an approaching storm, and we hurried on to gain a covert in a clump of thick bushes which appeared to terminate the long ascent. We threw ourselves under the lee of these bushes, and pulling up the long grass that grew around, covered ourselves completely with it, and awaited the shower.

But it did not come as soon as we had expected, and before many minutes my companion was fast asleep, and I was rapidly falling into the same state of happy forgetfulness. Just at this juncture, however, down came the rain with a violence that put all thoughts of slumber to flight. Although in some measure sheltered, our clothes soon became as wet as ever: this, after all the trouble we had taken to dry them, was provoking enough: but there was no help for it; and I recommend all adventurous youths who abandon vessels in romantic islands during the rainy season to provide themselves with umbrellas.

After an hour or so the shower passed away. My companion slept through it all, or at least appeared so to do; and now that it was over I had not the heart to awaken him. As I lay on my back completely shrouded with verdure, the leafy branches drooping over me, and my limbs buried in grass, I could not avoid comparing our situation with that of the interesting babes in the wood. Poor little sufferers!—no wonder their constitutions broke down under the hardships to which they were exposed.

During the hour or two spent under the shelter of these bushes, I began to feel symptoms which I at once attributed to the exposure of the preceding night. Cold shiverings and a burning fever succeeded one another at intervals, while one of my legs was swelled to such a degree, and pained me so acutely, that I half suspected I had been bitten by some venomous reptile, the congenial inhabitant of the chasm from which we had lately emerged. I may here remark by the way —what I subsequently learned—that all the islands of Polynesia enjoy the reputation, in common with the Hibernian isle, of being free from the presence of any vipers; though whether Saint Patrick ever visited them, is a question I shall not attempt to decide.

As the feverish sensation increased upon me, I tossed about, still unwilling to disturb my slumbering companion, from whose side I removed two or three yards. I chanced to push aside a branch, and by so doing suddenly disclosed to my view a scene which even now I can recall with all the vividness of the first impression. Had a glimpse of the gardens of

Paradise been revealed to me I could scarcely have been more ravished with the sight.

From the spot where I lay transfixed with surprise and delight, I looked straight down into the bosom of a valley, which swept away in long wavy undulations to the blue waters in the distance. Midway toward the sea, and peering here and there amidst the foliage, might be seen the palmetto-thatched houses of its inhabitants glistening in the sun that had bleached them to a dazzling whiteness. The vale was more than three leagues in length, and about a mile across at its greatest width.

On either side it appeared hemmed in by steep and green acclivities, which, uniting near the spot where I lay, formed an abrupt and semicircular termination of grassy cliffs and precipices hundreds of feet in height, over which flowed numberless small cascades. But the crowning beauty of the prospect was its universal verdure; and in this indeed consists, I believe, the peculiar charm of every Polynesian landscape. Everywhere below me, from the base of the precipice upon whose very verge I had been unconsciously reposing, the surface of the vale presented a mass of foliage, spread with such rich profusion that it was impossible to determine of what description of trees it consisted.

But perhaps there was nothing about the scenery I beheld more impressive than those silent cascades, whose slender threads of water, after leaping down the steep cliffs, were lost amidst the rich herbage of the valley.

Over all the landscape there reigned the most hushed repose, which I almost feared to break, lest, like the enchanted gardens in the fairy tale, a single syllable might dissolve the spell. For a long time, forgetful alike of my own situation and the vicinity of my still slumbering companion, I remained gazing around me, hardly able to comprehend by what means I had thus suddenly been made a spectator of such a scene.

VIII

The important question, Typee or Happar?—a wild-
goose chase—my sufferings—disheartening situation
—a night in a ravine—morning meal—happy idea
of Toby—journey toward the valley.

RECOVERING FROM my astonishment at the beautiful scene
before me, I quickly awakened Toby, and informed him of
the discovery I had made. Together we now repaired to the
border of the precipice, and my companion's admiration was
equal to my own. A little reflection, however, abated our surprise at coming so unexpectedly upon this valley, since the
large vales of Happar and Typee, lying upon this side of
Nukuheva, and extending a considerable distance from the
sea towards the interior, must necessarily terminate somewhere
about this point.

The question now was as to which of those two places we
were looking down upon. Toby insisted that it was the abode
of the Happars, and I that it was tenanted by their enemies
the ferocious Typees. To be sure I was not entirely convinced
by my own arguments, but Toby's proposition to descend at
once into the valley, and partake of the hospitality of its inmates, seemed to me to be risking so much upon the strength
of a mere supposition, that I resolved to oppose it until we
had more evidence to proceed upon.

The point was one of vital importance, as the natives of
Happar were not only at peace with Nukuheva, but cultivated
with its inhabitants the most friendly relations, and enjoyed
beside a reputation for gentleness and humanity which led us
to expect from them, if not a cordial reception, at least a
shelter during the short period we should remain in their
territory.

On the other hand, the very name of Typee struck a panic
into my heart which I did not attempt to disguise. The

thought of voluntarily throwing ourselves into the hands of these cruel savages, seemed to me an act of mere madness; and almost equally so the idea of venturing into the valley, uncertain by which of these two tribes it was inhabited. That the vale at our feet was tenanted by one of them, was a point that appeared to us past all doubt, since we knew that they resided in this quarter, although our information did not enlighten us further.

My companion, however, incapable of resisting the tempting prospect which the place held out of an abundant supply of food and other means of enjoyment, still clung to his own inconsiderate view of the subject, nor could all my reasoning shake it. When I reminded him that it was impossible for either of us to know anything with certainty, and when I dwelt upon the horrible fate we should encounter were we rashly to descend into the valley, and discover too late the error we had committed, he replied by detailing all the evils of our present condition, and the sufferings we must undergo should we continue to remain where we then were.

Anxious to draw him away from the subject, if possible—for I saw that it would be in vain to attempt changing his mind—I directed his attention to a long bright unwooded tract of land which, sweeping down from the elevations in the interior, descended into the valley before us. I then suggested to him that beyond this ridge might lie a capacious and untenanted valley, abounding with all manner of delicious fruits; for I had heard that there were several such upon the island, and proposed that we should endeavor to reach it, and if we found our expectations realized we should at once take refuge in it and remain there as long as we pleased.

He acquiesced in the suggestion; and we immediately, therefore, began surveying the country lying before us, with a view of determining upon the best route for us to pursue; but it presented little choice, the whole interval being broken into steep ridges, divided by dark ravines, extending in parallel lines at right angles to our direct course. All these we would be obliged to cross before we could hope to arrive at our destination.

A weary journey! But we decided to undertake it, though, for my own part, I felt little prepared to encounter its fatigues, shivering and burning by turns with the ague and fever; for I know not how else to describe the alternate sensations I experienced, and suffering not a little from the lameness which afflicted me. Added to this was the faintness consequent on our meagre diet—a calamity in which Toby participated to the same extent as myself.

These circumstances, however, only augmented my anxiety to reach a place which promised us plenty and repose, before I should be reduced to a state which would render me altogether unable to perform the journey. Accordingly we now commenced it by descending the almost perpendicular side of a steep and narrow gorge, bristling with a thick growth of reeds. Here there was but one mode for us to adopt. We seated ourselves upon the ground, and guided our descent by catching at the canes in our path. The velocity with which we thus slid down the side of the ravine soon brought us to a point where we could use our feet, and in a short time we arrived at the edge of the torrent, which rolled impetuously along the bed of the chasm.

After taking a refreshing draught from the water of the stream, we addressed ourselves to a much more difficult undertaking than the last. Every foot of our late descent had to be regained in ascending the opposite side of the gorge—an operation rendered the less agreeable from the consideration that in these perpendicular episodes we did not progress a hundred yards on our journey. But, ungrateful as the task was, we set about it with exemplary patience, and, after a snail-like progress of an hour or more, had scaled perhaps one half of the distance, when the fever which had left me for awhile returned with such violence, and accompanied by so raging a thirst, that it required all the entreaties of Toby to prevent me from losing all the fruits of my late exertion, by precipitating myself madly down the cliffs we had just climbed in quest of the water which flowed so temptingly at their base. At the moment all my hopes and fears appeared to be merged in this one desire, careless of the consequences that might result from its gratification. I am aware of no feeling, either of pleasure or of pain, that so completely deprives one of all power to resist its impulses as this same raging thirst.

Toby earnestly conjured me to continue the ascent, assuring me that a little more exertion would bring us to the summit, and that then in less than five minutes we should find ourselves at the brink of the stream, which must necessarily flow on the other side of the ridge.

'Do not,' he exclaimed, 'turn back, now that we have proceeded thus far; for I tell you that neither of us will have the courage to repeat the attempt, if once more we find ourselves looking up to where we now are from the bottom of these rocks!'

I was not yet so perfectly beside myself as to be heedless of these representations, and therefore toiled on, ineffectually endeavoring to appease the thirst which consumed me, by thinking that in a short time I should be able to gratify it to my heart's content.

At last we gained the top of the second elevation, the loftiest of those I have described as extending in parallel lines between us and the valley we desired to reach. It commanded a view of the whole intervening distance; and, discouraged as I was by other circumstances, this prospect plunged me into the very depths of despair. Nothing but dark and fearful chasms, separated by sharp-crested and perpendicular ridges as far as the eye could reach. Could we have stepped from summit to summit of these steep but narrow elevations we could easily have accomplished the distance; but we must penetrate to the bottom of every yawning gulf, and scale in succession every one of the eminences before us. Even Toby, although not suffering as I did, was not proof against the disheartening influences of the sight.

But we did not long stand to contemplate it, impatient as I was to reach the waters of the torrent which flowed beneath us. With an insensibility to danger which I cannot call to mind without shuddering, we threw ourselves down the depths of the ravine, startling its savage solitudes with the echoes produced by the falling fragments of rock we every moment dislodged from their places, careless of the insecurity of our footing, and reckless whether the slight roots and twigs we clutched at sustained us for the while, or treacherously yielded to our grasp. For my own part I scarcely knew whether I was helplessly falling from the heights above, or whether the fearful rapidity with which I descended was an act of my own volition.

In a few minutes we reached the foot of the gorge, and, kneeling upon a small ledge of dripping rocks, I bent over to the stream. What a delicious sensation was I now to experience! I paused for a second to concentrate all my capabilities of enjoyment, and then immerged my lips in the clear element before me. Had the apples of Sodom turned to ashes in my mouth, I could not have felt a more startling revulsion. A single drop of the cold fluid seemed to freeze every drop of blood in my body; the fever that had been burning in my veins gave place on the instant to deathlike chills, which shook me one after another like so many shocks of electricity, while the perspiration produced by my late violent exertions congealed in icy beads upon my forehead. My thirst was gone, and I fairly loathed the water. Starting to my feet, the sight of those dank rocks, oozing forth moisture at every crevice, and the dark stream shooting along its dismal channel, sent fresh chills through my shivering frame, and I felt as uncontrollable a desire to climb up towards the genial sunlight as I before had to descend the ravine.

After two hours' perilous exertions we stood upon the summit of another ridge, and it was with difficulty I could bring myself to believe that we had ever penetrated the black and yawning chasm which then gaped at our feet. Again we gazed upon the prospect which the height commanded, but it was just as depressing as the one which had before met our eyes. I now felt that in our present situation it was in vain for us to think of ever overcoming the obstacles in our way, and I gave up all thoughts of reaching the vale which lay beyond this series of impediments; while at the same time I could not devise any scheme to extricate ourselves from the difficulties in which we were involved.

The remotest idea of returning to Nukuheva, unless assured of our vessel's departure, never once entered my mind, and indeed it was questionable whether we could have succeeded in reaching it, divided as we were from the bay by a distance we could not compute, and perplexed too in our remembrance of localities by our recent wanderings. Besides, it was unendurable the thought of retracing our steps and rendering all our painful exertions of no avail.

There is scarcely anything when a man is in difficulties that he is more disposed to look upon with abhorrence than a right-about retrograde movement—a systematic going over of the already trodden ground; and, especially if he has a love of adventure, such a course appears indescribably repulsive, so long as there remains the least hope to be derived from braving untried difficulties.

It was this feeling that prompted us to descend the opposite side of the elevation we had just scaled, although with what definite object in view it would have been impossible for either of us to tell.

Without exchanging a syllable upon the subject, Toby and myself simultaneously renounced the design which had lured us thus far—perceiving in each other's countenances that desponding expression which speaks more eloquently than words.

Together we stood toward the close of this weary day in the cavity of the third gorge we had entered, wholly incapacitated for any further exertion, until restored to some degree of strength by food and repose.

We seated ourselves upon the least uncomfortable spot we could select, and Toby produced from the bosom of his frock the sacred package. In silence we partook of the small morsel of refreshment that had been left from the morning's repast, and, without once proposing to violate the sanctity of our engagement with respect to the remainder, we rose to our feet and proceeded to construct some sort of shelter under which we might obtain the sleep we so greatly needed.

Fortunately the spot was better adapted to our purpose than

the one in which we had passed the last wretched night. We cleared away the tall reeds from a small but almost level bit of ground, and twisted them into a low basketlike hut, which we covered with a profusion of long thick leaves, gathered from a tree near at hand. We disposed them thickly all around, reserving only a slight opening that barely permitted us to crawl under the shelter we had thus obtained.

These deep recesses, though protected from the winds that assail the summits of their lofty sides, are damp and chill to a degree that one would hardly anticipate in such a climate; and being unprovided with anything but our woollen frocks and thin duck trousers to resist the cold of the place, we were the more solicitous to render our habitation for the night as comfortable as we could. Accordingly, in addition to what we had already done, we plucked down all the leaves within our reach and threw them in a heap over our little hut, into which we now crept, raking after us a reserved supply to form our couch.

That night nothing but the pain I suffered prevented me from sleeping most refreshingly. As it was, I caught two or three naps, while Toby slept away at my side as soundly as though he had been sandwiched between two Holland sheets. Luckily it did not rain, and we were preserved from the misery which a heavy shower would have occasioned us.

In the morning I was awakened by the sonorous voice of my companion ringing in my ears and bidding me rise. I crawled out from our heap of leaves and was astonished at the change which a good night's rest had wrought in his appearance. He was as blithe and joyous as a young bird, and was staying the keenness of his morning's appetite by chewing the soft bark of a delicate branch he held in his hand, and he recommended the like to me as an admirable antidote against the gnawings of hunger.

For my own part, though feeling materially better than I had done the preceding evening, I could not look at the limb that had pained me so violently at intervals during the last twenty-four hours without experiencing a sense of alarm that I strove in vain to shake off. Unwilling to disturb the flow of my comrade's spirits, I managed to stifle the complaints to which I might otherwise have given vent, and calling upon him good-humoredly to speed our banquet, I prepared myself for it by washing in the stream. This operation concluded, we swallowed, or rather absorbed, by a peculiar kind of slow sucking process, our respective morsels of nourishment, and then entered into a discussion as to the steps it was necessary for us to pursue.

'What's to be done now?' inquired I, rather dolefully.

'Descend into that same valley we descried yesterday,' rejoined Toby, with a rapidity and loudness of utterance that almost led me to suspect he had been slyly devouring the broadside of an ox in some of the adjoining thickets. 'What else,' he continued, 'remains for us to do but that, to be sure? Why, we shall both starve to a certainty if we remain here; and as to your fears of those Typees—depend upon it, it is all nonsense.

'It is impossible that the inhabitants of such a lovely place as we saw can be anything else but good fellows; and if you choose rather to perish with hunger in one of these soppy caverns, I for one prefer to chance a bold descent into the valley, and risk the consequences.'

'And who is to pilot us thither,' I asked, 'even if we should decide upon the measure you propose? Are we to go again up and down those precipices that we crossed yesterday, until we reach the place we started from, and then take a flying leap from the cliffs to the valley?'

' 'Faith, I didn't think of that,' said Toby; 'sure enough both sides of the valley appeared to be hemmed in by precipices, didn't they?'

'Yes,' answered I, 'as steep as the sides of a line-of-battle ship, and about a hundred times as high.' My companion sank his head upon his breast and remained for a while in deep thought. Suddenly he sprang to his feet, while his eyes lighted up with that gleam of intelligence that marks the presence of some bright idea.

'Yes, yes,' he exclaimed; 'the streams all run in the same direction, and must necessarily flow into the valley before they reach the sea; all we have to do is just to follow this stream, and sooner or later it will lead us into the vale.'

'You are right, Toby,' I exclaimed, 'you are right; it must conduct us thither, and quickly too; for see with what a steep inclination the water descends.'

'It does, indeed,' burst forth my companion, overjoyed at my verification of his theory, 'it does indeed; why, it is as plain as a pikestaff. Let us proceed at once; come, throw away all those stupid ideas about the Typees, and hurrah for the lovely valley of the Happars!'

'You will have it to be Happar, I see, my dear fellow; pray Heaven you many not find yourself deceived,' observed I, with a shake of my head.

'Amen to all that, and much more,' shouted Toby, rushing forward; 'but Happar it is, for nothing else than Happar can it be. So glorious a valley—such forests of breadfruit trees—such groves of coconut—such wildernesses of guava bushes! Ah, shipmate! don't linger behind: in the name of all delightful fruits, I am dying to be at them. Come on, come on; shove ahead, there's a lively lad; never mind the rocks; kick them out of the way, as I do; and tomorrow, old fellow, take my word for it, we shall be in clover. Come on!' and so saying, he dashed along the ravine like a madman, forgetting my inability to keep up with him. In a few minutes, however, the exuberance of his spirits abated, and, pausing for a while, he permitted me to overtake him.

IX

Perilous passage of the ravine—
descent into the valley.

THE FEARLESS CONFIDENCE of Toby was contagious, and I began to adopt the Happar side of the question. I could not, however, overcome a certain feeling of trepidation as we made our way along these gloomy solitudes. Our progress, at first comparatively easy, became more and more difficult. The bed of the watercourse was covered with fragments of broken rocks, which had fallen from above, offering so many obstructions to the course of the rapid stream, which vexed and fretted about them—forming at intervals small waterfalls, pouring over into deep basins, or splashing wildly upon heaps of stones.

From the narrowness of the gorge, and the steepness of its sides, there was no mode of advancing but by wading through the water; stumbling every moment over the impediments which lay hidden under its surface, or tripping against the huge roots of trees. But the most annoying hindrance we encountered was from a multitude of crooked boughs, which, shooting out almost horizontally from the sides of the chasm, twisted themselves together in fantastic masses almost to the surface of the stream, affording us no passage except under the low arches which they formed. Under these we were obliged to crawl on our hands and feet, sliding along the oozy surface of the rocks, or slipping into the deep pools, and with scarce light enough to guide us. Occasionally we would strike our heads against some projecting limb of a tree; and while imprudently engaged in rubbing the injured part, would fall sprawling amongst flinty fragments, cutting and bruising ourselves, whilst the unpitying waters flowed over our prostrate bodies. Belzoni, worming himself through the subterranean passages of the Egyptian catacombs, could not have met with greater impediments than those we here encountered. But we struggled against them manfully, well knowing our only hope lay in advancing.

Toward sunset we halted at a spot where we made preparations for passing the night. Here we constructed a hut, in much the same way as before, and crawling into it, endeavored to forget our sufferings. My companion, I believe, slept pretty soundly; but at daybreak, when we rolled out of our dwelling, I felt nearly disqualified for any further efforts. Toby prescribed as a remedy for my illness the contents of one of our little silk packages, to be taken at once in a single dose. To this species of medical treatment, however, I would by no means accede, much as he insisted upon it; and so we partook of our usual morsel, and silently resumed our journey. It was now the fourth day since we left Nukuheva, and the gnawings of hunger became painfully acute. We were fain to pacify them by chewing the tender bark of roots and twigs, which, if they did not afford us nourishment, were at least sweet and pleasant to the taste.

Our progress along the steep watercourse was necessarily slow, and by noon we had not advanced more than a mile. It was somewhere near this part of the day that the noise of falling waters, which we had faintly caught in the early morning, became more distinct; and it was not long before we were arrested by a rocky precipice of nearly a hundred feet in depth, that extended all across the channel, and over which the wild stream poured in an unbroken leap. On either hand the walls of the ravine presented their overhanging sides both above and below the fall, affording no means whatever of avoiding the cataract by taking a circuit round it.

'What's to be done now, Toby?' said I.

'Why,' rejoined he, 'as we cannot retreat, I suppose we must keep shoving along.'

'Very true, my dear Toby; but how do you purpose accomplishing that desirable object?'

'By jumping from the top of the fall, if there be no other way,' unhesitatingly replied my companion: 'it will be much the quickest way of descent; but as you are not quite as active as I am, we will try some other way.'

And, so saying, he crept cautiously along and peered over into the abyss, while I remained wondering by what possible means we could overcome this apparently insuperable obstruction. As soon as my companion had completed his survey, I eagerly inquired the result.

'The result of my observations you wish to know, do you?' began Toby, deliberately, with one of his odd looks: 'well, my lad, the result of my observations is very quickly imparted. It is at present uncertain which of our two necks will have the honor to be broken first; but about a hundred to one would be a fair bet in favor of the man who takes the first jump.'

'Then it is an impossible thing, is it?' inquired I, gloomily.

'No, shipmate; on the contrary, it is the easiest thing in life: the only awkward point is the sort of usage which our unhappy limbs may receive when we arrive at the bottom and what sort of traveling trim we shall be in afterward. But follow me now, and I will show you the only chance we have.'

With this he conducted me to the verge of the cataract, and pointed along the side of the ravine to a number of curious-looking roots, some three or four inches in thickness, and several feet long, which after twisting among the fissures of the rock, shot perpendicularly from it and ran tapering to a point in the air, hanging over the gulf like so many dark icicles. They covered nearly the entire surface of one side of the gorge, the lowest of them reaching even to the water. Many were moss grown and decayed, with their extremities snapped short off, and those in the immediate vicinity of the fall were slippery with moisture.

Toby's scheme, and it was a desperate one, was to entrust ourselves to these treacherous-looking roots, and by slipping down from one to another to gain the bottom.

'Are you ready to venture it?' asked Toby, looking at me earnestly, but without saying a word as to the practicability of the plan.

'I am,' was my reply; for I saw it was our only resource if we wished to advance, and as for retreating, all thought of that sort had been long abandoned.

After I had signified my assent, Toby, without uttering a single word, crawled along the dripping ledge until he gained a point from whence he could just reach one of the largest of the pendant roots; he shook it—it quivered in his grasp, and when he let it go it twanged in the air like a strong wire sharply struck. Satisfied by his scrutiny, my light-limbed companion swung himself nimbly upon it, and twisting his legs round it in sailor fashion, slipped down eight or ten feet, where his weight gave it a motion not unlike that of a pendulum. He could not venture to descend any further; so holding on with one hand, he with the other shook one by one all the slender roots around him, and at last, finding one which he thought trustworthy, shifted himself to it and continued his downward progress.

So far so well; but I could not avoid comparing my heavier frame and disabled condition with his light figure and remarkable activity; but there was no help for it, and in less than a minute's time I was swinging directly over his head. As soon as his upturned eyes caught a glimpse of me, he exclaimed in his usual dry tone, for the danger did not seem to daunt him in the least, 'Mate, do me the kindness not to fall until I get out of your way'; and then swinging himself more on one side, he continued his descent. In the meantime I cautiously transferred myself from the limb down which I had been slipping to a couple of others that were near it, deeming two strings to my bow better than one, and taking care to test their strength before I trusted my weight to them.

On arriving toward the end of the second stage in this vertical journey, and shaking the long roots which were round me, to my consternation they snapped off one after another like so many pipe stems, and fell in fragments against the side of the gulf, splashing at last into the waters beneath.

As one after another the treacherous roots yielded to my grasp, and fell into the torrent, my heart sunk within me. The branches on which I was suspended over the yawning chasm swung to and fro in the air, and I expected them every moment to snap in twain. Appalled at the dreadful fate that menaced me, I clutched at the only large root which remained near me, but in vain; I could not reach it, though my fingers were within a few inches of it. Again and again I tried to reach it, until at length, maddened with the thought of my situation, I swayed myself violently by striking my foot against the side of the rock, and at the instant that I approached the large root caught desperately at it, and transferred myself to it. It vibrated violently under the sudden weight, but fortunately did not give way.

My brain grew dizzy with the idea of the frightful risk

I had just run, and I involuntarily closed my eyes to shut out the view of the depth beneath me. For the instant I was safe, and I uttered a devout ejaculation of thanksgiving for my escape.

'Pretty well done,' shouted Toby underneath me; 'you are nimbler than I thought you to be—hopping about up there from root to root like any young squirrel. As soon as you have diverted yourself sufficiently, I would advise you to proceed.'

'Aye, aye, Toby, all in good time: two or three more such famous roots as this, and I shall be with you.'

The residue of my downward progress was comparatively easy; the roots were in greater abundance, and in one or two places jutting out points of rock assisted me greatly. In a few moments I was standing by the side of my companion.

Substituting a stout stick for the one I had thrown aside at the top of the precipice, we now continued our course along the bed of the ravine. Soon we were saluted by a sound in advance, that grew by degrees louder and louder, as the noise of the cataract we were leaving behind gradually died on our ears.

'Another precipice for us, Toby.'

'Very good; we can descend them, you know—come on.'

Nothing indeed appeared to depress or intimidate this intrepid fellow. Typees or Niagaras, he was as ready to engage one as the other, and I could not avoid a thousand times congratulating myself upon having such a companion in an enterprise like the present.

After an hour's painful progress, we reached the verge of another fall, still loftier than the preceding and flanked both above and below with the same steep masses of rock, presenting, however, here and there narrow irregular ledges, supporting a shallow soil, on which grew a variety of bushes and trees, whose bright verdure contrasted beautifully with the foamy waters that flowed between them.

Toby, who invariably acted as pioneer, now proceeded to reconnoitre. On his return, he reported that the shelves of rock on our right would enable us to gain with little risk the bottom of the cataract. Accordingly, leaving the bed of the stream at the very point where it thundered down, we began crawling along one of these sloping ledges until it carried us to within a few feet of another that inclined downward at a still sharper angle, and upon which, by assisting each other, we managed to alight in safety. We warily crept along this, steadying ourselves by the naked roots of the shrubs that clung to every fissure. As we proceeded, the narrow path became still more contracted, rendering it difficult for us to maintain our footing, until suddenly, as we reached an angle of the wall of rock where we had expected it to widen, we perceived to our consternation that a yard or two farther on it abruptly terminated at a place we could not possibly hope to pass.

Toby as usual led the van, and in silence I waited to learn from him how he proposed to extricate us from this new difficulty.

'Well, my boy,' I exclaimed, after the expiration of several minutes, during which time my companion had not uttered a word; 'what's to be done now?'

He replied in a tranquil tone, that probably the best thing we could do in our present strait was to get out of it as soon as possible.

'Yes, my dear Toby, but tell me *how* we are to get out of it.'

'Something in this sort of style,' he replied; and at the same moment to my horror he slipped sideways off the rock, and, as I then thought, by good fortune merely, alighted among the spreading branches of a species of palm tree, that, shooting its hardy roots along a ledge below, curved its trunk upward into the air, and presented a thick mass of foliage about twenty feet below the spot where we had thus suddenly been brought to a standstill. I involuntarily held my breath, expecting to see the form of my companion, after being sustained for a moment by the branches of the tree, sink through their frail support, and fall headlong to the bottom. To my surprise and joy, however, he recovered himself, and disentangled his limbs from the fractured branches, he peered out from his leafy bed, and shouted lustily, 'Come on, my hearty, there is no other alternative!' and with this he ducked beneath the foliage and slipping down the trunk, stood in a moment at least fifty feet beneath me, upon the broad shelf of rock from which sprung the tree he had descended.

What would I not have given at that moment to have been by his side! The feat he had just accomplished seemed little less than miraculous, and I could hardly credit the evidence of my senses when I saw the wide distance that a single daring act had so suddenly placed between us.

Toby's animating 'come on!' again sounded in my ears, and dreading to lose all confidence in myself if I remained meditating upon the step, I once more gazed down to assure myself of the relative bearing of the tree and my own position, and then, closing my eyes and uttering one comprehensive ejaculation of prayer, I inclined myself over toward the abyss, and after one breathless instant fell with a crash into the tree, the branches snapping and crackling with my weight, as I sunk lower and lower among them, until I was stopped by coming in contact with a sturdy limb.

In a few moments I was standing at the foot of the tree, manipulating myself all over with a view of ascertaining the extent of the injuries I had received. To my surprise the only effects of my feat were a few slight contusions too trifling to care about. The rest of our descent was easily accomplished, and in half an hour after regaining the ravine we had partaken of our evening morsel, built our hut as usual, and crawled under its shelter.

The next morning, in spite of our debility and the agony of hunger under which we were now suffering, though neither of us confessed to the fact, we struggled along our dismal and still difficult and dangerous path, cheered by the hope of soon catching a glimpse of the valley before us, and toward evening the voice of a cataract which had for some time sounded like a low deep bass to the music of the smaller waterfalls, broke upon our ears in still louder tones, and assured us that we were approaching its vicinity.

That evening we stood on the brink of a precipice, over

which the dark stream bounded in one final leap of full 300 feet. The sheer descent terminated in the region we so long had sought. On either side of the fall, two lofty and perpendicular bluffs buttressed the sides of the enormous cliff, and projected into the sea of verdure with which the valley waved, and a range of similar projecting eminences stood disposed in a half circle about the head of the vale. A thick canopy of trees hung over the very verge of the fall, leaving an arched aperture for the passage of the waters, which imparted a strange picturesqueness to the scene.

The valley was now before us; but instead of being conducted into its smiling bosom by the gradual descent of the deep watercourse we had thus far pursued, all our labors now appeared to have been rendered futile by its abrupt termination. But, bitterly disappointed, we did not entirely despair.

As it was now near sunset we determined to pass the night where we were, and on the morrow, refreshed by sleep and by eating at one meal all our stock of food, to accomplish a descent into the valley, or perish in the attempt.

We laid ourselves down that night on a spot, the recollection of which still makes me shudder. A small table of rock which projected over the precipice on one side of the stream, and was drenched by the spray of the fall, sustained a huge trunk of a tree which must have been deposited there by some heavy freshet. It lay obliquely, with one end resting on the rock and the other supported by the side of the ravine. Against it we placed in a sloping direction a number of the half-decayed boughs that were strewn about, and covering the whole with twigs and leaves, awaited the morning's light beneath such shelter as it afforded.

During the whole of this night the continual roaring of the cataract—the dismal moaning of the gale through the trees—the pattering of the rain—and the profound darkness, affected my spirits to a degree which nothing had ever before produced. Wet, half famished, and chilled to the heart with the dampness of the place, and nearly wild with the pain I endured, I fairly cowered down to the earth under this multipli-

cation of hardships, and abandoned myself to frightful anticipations of evil; and my companion, whose spirit at last was a
good deal broken, scarcely uttered a word during the whole
night.

At length the day dawned upon us, and, rising from our
miserable pallet, we stretched our stiffened joints, and after
eating all that remained of our bread, prepared for the last
stage of our journey.

I will not recount every hairbreadth escape, and every fearful difficulty that occurred before we succeeded in reaching
the bosom of the valley. As I have already described similar
scenes, it will be sufficient to say that at length, after great
toil and great dangers, we both stood with no limbs broken at
the head of that magnificent vale which five days before had
so suddenly burst upon my sight, and almost beneath the
shadows of those very cliffs from whose summits we had
gazed upon the prospect.

X

The head of the valley—cautious advance—a path
—fruit—discovery of two of the natives—their
singular conduct—approach toward the inhabited
parts of the vale—sensation produced by our appearance—reception at the house of one
of the natives.

How TO OBTAIN the fruit which we felt convinced must grow
near at hand was our first thought.

Typee or Happar? A frightful death at the hands of the
fiercest of cannibals, or a kindly reception from a gentler race
of savages? Which? But it was too late now to discuss a question which would so soon be answered.

The part of the valley in which we found ourselves appeared to be altogether uninhabited. An almost impenetrable

thicket extended from side to side, without presenting a single plant affording the nourishment we had confidently calculated upon; and with this object, we followed the course of the stream, casting quick glances as we proceeded into the thick jungles on either hand.

My companion—to whose solicitations I had yielded in descending into the valley—now that the step was taken, began to manifest a degree of caution I had little expected from him. He proposed that, in the event of our finding an adequate supply of fruit, we should remain in this unfrequented portion of the country—where we should run little chance of being surprised by its occupants, whoever they might be—until sufficiently recruited to resume our journey; when laying in a store of food equal to our wants, we might easily regain the bay of Nukuheva, after the lapse of a sufficient interval to ensure the departure of our vessel.

I objected strongly to this proposition, plausible as it was, as the difficulties of the route would be almost insurmountable, unacquainted as we were with the general bearings of the country, and I reminded my companion of the hardships which we had already encountered in our uncertain wanderings; in a word, I said that since we had deemed it abvisable to enter the valley, we ought manfully to face the consequences, whatever they might be; the more especially as I was convinced there was no alternative left us but to fall in with the natives at once, and boldly risk the reception they might give us; and that, as to myself, I felt the necessity of rest and shelter, and that until I had obtained them I should be wholly unable to encounter such suffering as we had lately passed through. To the justice of these observations Toby somewhat reluctantly assented.

We were surprised that, after moving as far as we had along the valley, we should still meet with the same impervious thickets; and thinking that although the borders of the stream might be lined for some distance with them, yet beyond there might be more open ground, I requested Toby to keep a bright lookout upon one side, while I did the same on the other, in order to discover some opening in the bushes, and especially to watch for the slightest appearance of a path or anything else that might indicate the vicinity of the islanders.

What furtive and anxious glances we cast into those dim-looking shades! With what apprehensions we proceeded, ignorant at what moment we might be greeted by the javelin of some ambushed savage! At last my companion paused, and directed my attention to a narrow opening in the foliage. We struck into it and it soon brought us by an indistinctly traced path to a comparatively clear space, at the further end of which we descried a number of the trees, the native name of which is *annuee,* and which bear a most delicious fruit.

What a race! I hobbling over the ground like some decrepit wretch, and Toby leaping forward like a greyhound. He quickly cleared one of the trees on which there were two or three of the fruit, but to our chagrin they proved to be much decayed; the rinds partly opened by the birds, and their hearts half devoured. However, we quickly dispatched them, and no ambrosia could have been more delicious.

We looked about us uncertain whither to direct our steps, since the path we had so far followed appeared to be lost in the open space around us. At last we resolved to enter a grove near at hand, and had advanced a few rods when, just upon its skirts, I picked up a slender breadfruit shoot perfectly green, and with the tender bark freshly stripped from it. It was still slippery with moisture, and appeared as if it had been but that moment thrown aside. I said nothing, but merely held it up to Toby, who started at this undeniable evidence of the vicinity of the savages.

The plot was now thickening. A short distance further lay a little faggot of the same shoots bound together with a strip of bark. Could it have been thrown down by some solitary native who, alarmed at seeing us, had hurried forward to carry the tidings of our approach to his countrymen?—Typee or Happar?—But it was too late to recede, so we moved on slowly, my companion in advance casting eager glances under the trees on either side, until all at once I saw him recoil as if stung by an adder. Sinking on his knee, he waved me off with one hand, while with the other he held aside some intervening leaves and gazed intently at some object.

Disregarding his injunction, I quickly approached him and caught a glimpse of two figures partly hidden by the dense foliage; they were standing close together, and were perfectly motionless. They must have previously perceived us, and withdrawn into the depths of the wood to elude our observation.

My mind was at once made up. Dropping my staff, and tearing open the package of things we had brought from the ship, I unrolled the cotton cloth, and holding it in one hand plucked with the other a twig from the bushes beside me, and, telling Toby to follow my example, I broke through the covert and advanced, waving the branch in token of peace toward the shrinking forms before me.

They were a boy and girl, slender and graceful, and completely naked, with the exception of a slight girdle of bark, from which depended at opposite points two of the russet leaves of the breadfruit tree. An arm of the boy, half screened from sight by her wild tresses, was thrown about the neck of the girl, while with the other he held one of her hands in his; and thus they stood together, their heads inclined forward, catching the faint noise we made in our progress, and with one foot in advance, as if half inclined to fly from our presence.

As we drew near, their alarm evidently increased. Apprehensive that they might fly from us altogether, I stopped short and motioned them to advance and receive the gift I extended toward them, but they would not; I then uttered a few words of their language with which I was acquainted, scarcely expecting that they would understand me, but to show that we had not dropped from the clouds upon them. This appeared to give them a little confidence, so I approached nearer, presenting the cloth with one hand and holding the bough with the other, while they slowly retreated. At last they suffered us to approach so near to them that we were enabled to throw the cotton cloth across their shoulders, giving them to understand that it was theirs, and by a variety of gestures endeavoring to make them understand that we entertained the highest possible regard for them.

The frightened pair now stood still, whilst we endeavored to make them comprehend the nature of our wants. In doing this Toby went through with a complete series of pantomimic illustrations—opening his mouth from ear to ear, and thrusting his fingers down his throat, gnashing his teeth and rolling his eyes about, till I verily believe the poor creatures took us for a couple of white cannibals who were about to make a meal of them. When, however, they understood us, they showed no inclination to relieve our wants. At this juncture it began to rain violently, and we motioned them to lead us to some place of shelter. With this request they appeared willing to comply, but nothing could evince more strongly the apprehension with which they regarded us, than the way in which, whilst walking before us, they kept their eyes constantly turned back to watch every movement we made, and even our very looks.

'Typee or Happar, Toby?' asked I as we walked after them.

'Of course Happar,' he replied with a show of confidence which was intended to disguise his doubts.

'We shall soon know,' I exclaimed; and at the same moment I stepped forward toward our guides, and pronouncing the two names interrogatively and pointing to the lowest part of the valley, endeavored to come to the point at once. They repeated the words after me again and again, but without giving any peculiar emphasis to either, so that I was completely at a loss to understand them; for a couple of wilier young things than we afterward found them to have been on this particular occasion never probably fell in any traveler's way.

More and more curious to ascertain our fate, I now threw together in the form of a question the words 'Happar' and *'mortarkee,'* the latter being equivalent to the word 'good.' The two natives interchanged glances of peculiar meaning with one another at this, and manifested no little surprise; but on the repetition of the question, after some consultation together, to the great joy of Toby, they answered in the affirmative. Toby was now in ecstasies, especially as the young savages continued to reiterate their answer with great energy, as though desirous of impressing us with the idea that being among the Happars, we ought to consider ourselves prefectly secure.

Although I had some lingering doubts, I feigned great delight with Toby at this announcement, while my companion broke out into a pantomimic abhorrence of Typee, and immeasurable love for the particular valley in which we were; our guides all the while gazing uneasily at one another as if at a loss to account for our conduct.

They hurried on, and we followed them; until suddenly they set up a strange halloo, which was answered from beyond the grove through which we were passing, and the next moment we entered upon some open ground, at the extremity of which we descried a long, low hut and in front of it were several young girls. As soon as they perceived us they fled with wild screams into the adjoining thickets, like so many startled fawns. A few moments after the whole valley resounded with savage outcries, and the natives came running toward us from every direction.

Had an army of invaders made an irruption into their territory they could not have evinced greater excitement. We were soon completely encircled by a dense throng, and in their eager desire to behold us they almost arrested our progress; an equal number surrounding our youthful guides, who with amazing volubility appeared to be detailing the circumstances which had attended their meeting with us. Every item of intelligence appeared to redouble the astonishment of the islanders, and they gazed at us with inquiring looks.

At last we reached a large and handsome building of bamboos, and were by signs told to enter it, the natives opening a lane for us through which to pass; on entering without ceremony, we threw our exhausted frames upon the mats that covered the floor. In a moment the slight tenement was completely full of people, whilst those who were unable to obtain admittance gazed at us through its open canework.

It was now evening, and by the dim light we could just discern the savage countenances around us, gleaming with wild curiosity and wonder; the naked forms and tattooed limbs of brawny warriors with here and there the slighter figures of young girls, all engaged in a perfect storm of conversation, of which we were of course the one only theme, whilst our recent guides were fully occupied in answering the innumerable questions which every one put to them. Nothing can exceed the fierce gesticulation of these people when animated in conversation, and on this occasion they gave loose to all their natural vivacity, shouting and dancing about in a manner that well-nigh intimidated us.

Close to where we lay, squatting upon their haunches, were some eight or ten noble-looking chiefs—for such they subsequently proved to be—who, more reserved than the rest, regarded us with a fixed and stern attention, which not a little discomposed our equanimity. One of them in particular, who appeared to be the highest in rank, placed himself directly facing me; looking at me with a rigidity of aspect under which I absolutely quailed. He never once opened his lips, but maintained his severe expression of countenance, without turning his face aside for a single moment. Never before had I been subjected to so strange and steady a glance; it revealed nothing of the mind of the savage, but it appeared to be reading my own.

After undergoing this scrutiny till I grew absolutely nervous, with a view of diverting it if possible, and conciliating the good opinion of the warrior, I took some tobacco from the bosom of my frock and offered it to him. He quietly rejected the proffered gift, and without speaking, motioned me to return it to its place.

In my previous intercourse with the natives of Nukuheva and Tior, I had found that the present of a small piece of tobacco would have rendered any of them devoted to my service. Was this act of the chief a token of his enmity? Typee or Happar? I asked within myself. I started, for at the same moment this identical question was asked by the strange being before me. I turned to Toby; the flickering light of a native taper showed me his countenance pale with trepidation at this fatal question. I paused for a second, and I know not by what impulse it was that I answered 'Typee.' The piece of dusky statuary nodded in approval, and then murmured *'Mortarkee!'* *'Mortarkee,'* said I, without further hesitation—*'Typee mortarkee.'*

What a transition! The dark figures around us leaped to their feet, clapped their hands in transport, and shouted again and again the talismanic syllables, the utterance of which appeared to have settled everything.

When this commotion had a little subsided, the principal chief squatted once more before me, and throwing himself into a sudden rage, poured forth a string of philippics, which I was at no loss to understand, from the frequent recurrence of the word Happar, as being directed against the natives of the adjoining valley. In all these denunciations my companion and I acquiesced while we extolled the character of the warlike Typees. To be sure our panegyrics were somewhat laconic, consisting in the repetition of that name, united with the potent adjective *mortarkee*. But this was sufficient, and served to conciliate the goodwill of the natives with whom our congeniality of sentiment on this point did more toward inspiring a friendly feeling than anything else that could have happened.

At last the wrath of the chief evaporated, and in a few moments he was as placid as ever. Laying his hand upon his breast, he now gave me to understand that his name was Mehevi, and that, in return, he wished me to communicate my appellation. I hesitated for an instant, thinking that it might be difficult for him to pronounce my real name, and then with the most praiseworthy intentions intimated that I was known as Tom. But I could not have made a worse selection; the chief could not master it: 'Tommo,' 'Tomma,' 'Tommee,' everything but plain 'Tom.' As he persisted in garnishing the word with an additional syllable, I compromised the matter with him at the word 'Tommo;' and by that name I went during the entire period of my stay in the valley. The same proceeding was gone through with Toby whose mellifluous appellation was more easily caught.

An exchange of names is equivalent to a ratification of

goodwill and amity among these simple people; and as we were aware of this fact, we were delighted that it had taken place on the present occasion.

Reclining upon our mats, we now held a kind of levee, giving audience to successive troops of the natives, who introduced themselves to us by pronouncing their respective names, and retired in high good humor on receiving ours in return. During this ceremony the greatest merriment prevailed, nearly every announcement on the part of the islanders being followed by a fresh sally of gaiety which induced me to believe that some of them at least were innocently diverting the company at our expense, by bestowing upon themselves a string of absurd titles of the humor of which we were of course entirely ignorant.

All this occupied about an hour, when the throng having a little diminished, I turned to Mehevi and gave him to understand that we were in need of food and sleep. Immediately the attentive chief addressed a few words to one of the crowd who disappeared and returned in a few moments with a calabash of *poee-poee,* and two or three young coconuts stripped of their husks, and with their shells partly broken. We both of us forthwith placed one of these natural goblets to our lips, and drained it in a moment of the refreshing draught it contained. The *poee-poee* was then placed before us, and even famished as I was, I paused to consider in what manner to convey it to my mouth.

This staple article of food among the Marquesan islanders is manufactured from the produce of the breadfruit tree. It somewhat resembles in its plastic nature our bookbinder's paste, is of a yellow color, and somewhat tart to the taste.

Such was the dish, the merits of which I was now eager to discuss. I eyed it wistfully for a moment, and then unable any longer to stand on ceremony, plunged my hand into the yielding mass, and to the boisterous mirth of the natives drew it forth laden with the *poee-poee,* which adhered in lengthy strings to every finger. So stubborn was its consistency, that in conveying my heavily freighted hand to my mouth, the connecting links almost raised the calabash from the mats on which it had been placed. This display of awkwardness—in which, by the by, Toby kept me company—convulsed the by-standers with uncontrollable laughter.

As soon as their merriment had somewhat subsided Mehevi, motioning us to be attentive, dipped the forefinger of his right hand in the dish, and giving it a rapid and scientific twirl, drew it out coated smoothly with the preparation. With a second peculiar flourish he prevented the *poee-poee* from dropping to the ground as he raised it to his mouth, into which the finger was inserted and drawn forth perfectly free from any adhesive matter. This performance was evidently intended for our instruction; so I again essayed the feat on the principles inculcated, but with very ill success.

A starving man, however, little heeds conventional pro-prieties, especially on a South Sea island, and accordingly Toby and I partook of the dish after our own clumsy fashion, beplastering our faces all over with the glutinous compound, and daubing our hands nearly to the wrist. This kind of food is by no means disagreeable to the palate of a European, though at first the mode of eating it may be. For my own part, after the lapse of a few days I became accustomed to its singu-lar flavor, and grew remarkably fond of it.

So much for the first course; several other dishes followed it, some of which were positively delicious. We concluded our banquet by tossing off the contents of two more young coco-nuts, after which we regaled ourselves with the soothing fumes of tobacco, inhaled from a quaintly carved pipe which passed round the circle.

During the repast, the natives eyed us with intense curiosity, observing our minutest motions, and appearing to discover abundant matter for comment in the most trifling occurrences. Their surprise mounted the highest, when we began to remove our uncomfortable garments, which were saturated with rain. They scanned the whiteness of our limbs, and seemed utterly unable to account for the contrast they presented to the swarthy hue of our faces, embrowned from a six months' ex-posure to the scorching sun of the Line. They felt our skin, much in the same way that a silk mercer would handle a remarkably fine piece of satin; and some of them went so far in their investigation as to apply the olfactory organ.

Their singular behavior almost led me to imagine that they never before had beheld a white man; but a few moments' reflection convinced me that this could not have been the case; and a more satisfactory reason for their conduct has since suggested itself to my mind.

Deterred by the frightful stories related of its inhabitants, ships never enter this bay, while their hostile relations with the tribes in the adjoining valleys prevent the Typees from visiting that section of the island where vessels occasionally lie. At long intervals, however, some intrepid captain will touch on the skirts of the bay, with two or three armed boats' crews, and accompanied by an interpreter. The natives who live near the sea descry the strangers long before they reach their waters, and aware of the purpose for which they come, proclaim loudly the news of their approach. By a species of vocal telegraph the intelligence reaches the inmost recesses of the vale in an inconceivably short space of time, drawing nearly its whole population down to the beach laden with every variety of fruit. The interpreter, who is invariably a tabooed Kannaka,[1] leaps ashore with the goods intended for barter, while the boats, with their oars shipped, and every man on his thwart, lie just outside the surf, heading off from the shore, in readiness at the first untoward event to escape to the open sea. As soon as the traffic is concluded, one of the boats pulls in under cover of the muskets of the others, the fruit is quickly thrown into her, and the transient visitors precipitately retire from what they justly consider so dangerous a vicinity.

The intercourse occurring with Europeans being so restricted, no wonder that the inhabitants of the valley mani-

[1] The word 'Kannaka' is at the present day universally used in the South Seas by Europeans to designate the islanders. In the various dialects of the principal groups it is simply a sexual designation applied to the males; but it is now used by the natives in their intercourse with foreigners in the same sense in which the latter employ it.

A 'tabooed Kannaka' is an islander whose person has been made to a certain extent sacred by the operation of a singular custom hereafter to be explained.

fested so much curiosity with regard to us, appearing as we did among them under such singular circumstances. I have no doubt that we were the first white men who ever penetrated thus far back into their territories, or at least the first who had ever descended from the head of the vale. What had brought us thither must have appeared a complete mystery to them, and from our ignorance of the language it was impossible for us to enlighten them. In answer to inquiries which the eloquence of their gestures enabled us to comprehend, all that we could reply was, that we had come from Nukuheva, a place, be it remembered, with which they were at open war. This intelligence appeared to affect them with the most lively emotions. *'Nukuheva mortarkee?'* they asked. Of course we replied most energetically in the negative.

They then plied us with a thousand questions, of which we could understand nothing more than that they had reference to the recent movements of the French, against whom they seemed to cherish the most fierce hatred. So eager were they to obtain information on this point, that they still continued to propound their queries long after we had shown that we were utterly unable to answer them. Occasionally we caught some indistinct idea of their meaning, when we would endeavor by every method in our power to communicate the desired intelligence. At such times their gratification was boundless, and they would redouble their efforts to make us comprehend them more perfectly. But all in vain; and in the end they looked at us despairing, as if we were the receptacles of invaluable information, but how to come at it they knew not.

After a while the group around us gradually dispersed, and we were left about midnight (as we conjectured) with those who appeared to be permanent residents of the house. These individuals now provided us with fresh mats to lie upon, covered us with several folds of tappa, and then, extinguishing the tapers that had been burning, threw themselves down beside us, and after a little desultory conversation were soon sound asleep.

XI

Midnight reflections—morning visitors—a warrior
in costume—a savage AEsculapius—practice of the
healing art—body servant—a dwelling house of the
valley described—portraits of its inmates.

VARIOUS AND CONFLICTING were the thoughts which oppressed
me during the silent hours that followed the events related in
the preceding chapter. Toby, wearied with the fatigues of the
day, slumbered heavily by my side; but the pain under which
I was suffering effectually prevented my sleeping, and I remained distressingly alive to all the fearful circumstances of
our present situation. Was it possible that, after all our vicissitudes, we were really in the terrible valley of Typee, and at
the mercy of its inmates, a fierce and unrelenting tribe of
savages?

Typee or Happar? I shuddered when I reflected that there
was no longer any room for doubt; and that beyond all hope
of escape, we were now placed in those very circumstances
from the bare thought of which I had recoiled with such abhorrence but a few days before. What might not be our fearful destiny? To be sure, as yet we had been treated with no
violence; nay, had been even kindly and hospitably entertained. But what dependence could be placed upon the fickle
passions which sway the bosom of a savage? His inconstancy
and treachery are proverbial. Might it not be that beneath
these fair appearances the islanders covered some perfidious
design, and that their friendly reception of us might only
precede some horrible catastrophe? How strongly did these
forebodings spring up in my mind as I lay restlessly upon a
couch of mats, surrounded by the dimly revealed forms of
those whom I so greatly dreaded.

From the excitement of these fearful thoughts I sank toward
morning into an uneasy slumber; and on awaking, with a start,

in the midst of an appalling dream, looked up into the eager countenances of a number of the natives, who were bending over me.

It was broad day; and the house was nearly filled with young females, fancifully decorated with flowers, who gazed upon me as I rose with faces in which childish delight and curiosity were vividly portrayed. After waking Toby, they seated themselves round us on the mats, and gave full play to that prying inquisitiveness which time out of mind has been attributed to the adorable sex.

As these unsophisticated young creatures were attended by no jealous duennas, their proceedings were altogether informal, and void of artificial restraint. Long and minute was the investigation with which they honored us, and so uproarious their mirth, that I felt infinitely sheepish; and Toby was immeasurably outraged at their familiarity.

These lively young ladies were at the same time wonderfully polite and humane; fanning aside the insects that occasionally lighted on our brows; presenting us with food; and compassionately regarding me in the midst of my afflictions. But in spite of all their blandishments, my feelings of propriety were exceedingly shocked, for I could not but consider them as having overstepped the due limits of female decorum.

Having diverted themselves to their heart's content, our young visitants now withdrew, and gave place to successive troops of the other sex, who continued flocking toward the house until near noon; by which time I have no doubt that the greater part of the inhabitants of the valley had bathed themselves in the light of our benignant countenances.

At last, when their numbers began to diminish, a superb-looking warrior stooped the towering plumes of his headdress beneath the low portal, and entered the house. I saw at once that he was some distinguished personage, the natives regarding him with the utmost deference, and making room for him as he approached. His aspect was imposing. The splendid long drooping tailfeathers of the tropical bird, thickly interspersed with the gaudy plumage of the cock, were disposed in an immense upright semicircle upon his head, their lower extremities being fixed in a crescent of guinea beads which spanned the forehead. Around his neck were several enormous necklaces of boars' tusks, polished like ivory, and disposed in such a manner as that the longest and largest were upon his capacious chest. Thrust forward through the large apertures in his ears were two small and finely shaped sperm-whale teeth, presenting their cavities in front, stuffed with freshly plucked leaves, and curiously wrought at the other end into strange little images and devices. These barbaric trinkets, garnished in this manner at their open extremities, and tapering and curving round to a point behind the ear, resembled not a little a pair of cornucopias.

The loins of the warrior were girt about with heavy folds of a dark-colored tappa, hanging before and behind in clusters of braided tassels, while anklets and bracelets of curling human hair completed his unique costume. In his right hand he grasped a beautifully carved paddle spear, nearly fifteen feet in length, made of the bright koar wood, one end sharply pointed, and the other flattened like an oar blade. Hanging obliquely from his girdle by a loop of sinnate, was a richly decorated pipe; the slender reed forming its stem was colored with a red pigment, and round it, as well as the idol bowl, fluttered little streamers of the thinnest tappa.

But that which was most remarkable in the appearance of the splendid islander was the elaborated tattooing displayed on every noble limb. All imaginable lines and curves and figures were delineated over his whole body, and in their grotesque variety and infinite profusion I could only compare them to the crowded groupings of quaint patterns we sometimes see in costly pieces of lacework. The most simple and remarkable of all these ornaments was that which decorated the countenance of the chief. Two broad strips of tattooing, diverging from the center of his shaven crown, obliquely crossed both eyes—staining the lids—to a little below either ear, where they united with another stripe which swept in a straight line along the lips and formed the base of the triangle. The warrior, from the excellence of his physical proportions, might certainly have been regarded as one of Nature's noblemen, and the lines drawn upon his face may possibly have denoted his exalted rank.

This warlike personage upon entering the house seated himself at some distance from the spot where Toby and myself reposed, while the rest of the savages looked alternately from us to him, as if in expectation of something they were disappointed in not perceiving. Regarding the chief attentively, I thought his lineaments appeared familiar to me. As soon as his full face was turned upon me and I again beheld its extraordinary embellishment, and met the strange gaze to which I had been subjected the preceding night, I immediately, in spite of the alteration in his appearance, recognized the noble Mehevi. On addressing him, he advanced at once in the most cordial manner, and, greeting me warmly, seemed to enjoy not a little the effect his barbaric costume had produced upon me.

I forthwith determined to secure, if possible, the goodwill of this individual, as I easily perceived he was a man of great authority in his tribe, and one who might exert a powerful influence upon our subsequent fate. In the endeavor I was not repulsed; for nothing could surpass the friendliness he manifested toward both my companion and myself. He extended his sturdy limbs by our side, and endeavored to make us comprehend the full extent of the kindly feelings by which he was actuated. The almost insuperable difficulty in communicating to one another our ideas affected the chief with no little mortification. He evinced a great desire to be enlightened with regard to the customs and peculiarities of the far-off country we had left behind us, and to which under the name of Maneeka he frequently alluded.

But that which more than any other subject engaged his attention was the late proceedings of the 'Franee,' as he called the French, in the neighboring bay of Nukuheva. This seemed a never-ending theme with him, and one concerning which he was never weary of interrogating us. All the information we succeeded in imparting to him on this subject was little more than that we had seen six men-of-war lying in the hostile bay at the time we had left it. When he received this intelligence, Mehevi, by the aid of his fingers, went through a long numerical calculation, as if estimating the number of Frenchmen the squadron might contain.

It was just after employing his faculties in this way that he happened to notice the swelling in my limb. He immediately examined it with the utmost attention, and after doing so despatched a boy who happened to be standing by with some message.

After the lapse of a few moments the stripling re-entered the house with an aged islander who might have been taken for old Hippocrates himself. His head was as bald as the polished surface of a coconut shell, which article it precisely resembled in smoothness and color, while a long silvery beard swept almost to his girdle of bark. Encircling his temples was a bandeau of the twisted leaves of the Omoo tree, pressed closely over the brows to shield his feeble vision from the glare of the sun. His tottering steps were supported by a long slim staff, resembling the wand with which a theatrical magician appears on the stage, and in one hand he carried a freshly plaited fan of the green leaflets of the coconut tree. A flowing robe of tappa, knotted over the shoulder, hung loosely round his stooping form, and heightened the venerableness of his aspect.

Mehevi, saluting this old gentleman, motioned him to a seat between us, and then uncovering my limb, desired him to examine it. The leech gazed intently from me to Toby, and then proceeded to business. After diligently observing the ailing member, he commenced manipulating it; and on the supposition probably that the complaint had deprived the leg of all sensation, began to pinch and hammer it in such a manner that I absolutely roared with the pain. Thinking that I was as capable of making an application of thumps and pinches to the part as anyone else, I endeavored to resist this species of medical treatment. But it was not so easy a matter to get out of the clutches of the old wizard; he fastened on the unfortunate limb as if it were something for which he had been long seeking, and muttering some kind of incantation continued his discipline, pounding it after a fashion that set me wellnigh crazy; while Mehevi, upon the same principle which prompts an affectionate mother to hold a struggling child in a dentist's chair, restrained me in his powerful grasp, and actually encouraged the wretch in his infliction of torture.

Almost frantic with rage and pain, I yelled like a Bedlamite; while Toby, throwing himself into all the attitudes of a posture-master, vainly endeavored to expostulate with the natives by signs and gestures. To have looked at my companion, as, sympathizing with my sufferings, he strove to put an end to them, one would have thought that he was the deaf and dumb alphabet incarnated. Whether my tormentor yielded to Toby's entreaties, or paused from sheer exhaustion, I do not know; but all at once he ceased his operations, and at the same time the chief relinquishing his hold upon me, I fell back, faint and breathless with the agony I had endured.

My unfortunate limb was now left much in the same condition as a rump steak after undergoing the castigating process which precedes cooking. My physician, having recovered from the fatigues of his exertions, as if anxious to make amends for the pain to which he had subjected me, now took some herbs out of a little wallet that was suspended from his waist, and moistening them in water, applied them to the inflamed part, stooping over it at the same time, and either whispering a spell, or having a little confidential chat with some imaginary demon located in the calf of my leg. My limb was now swathed in leafy bandages, and, grateful to Providence for the cessation of hostilities, I was suffered to rest.

Mehevi shortly after rose to depart; but before he went he spoke authoritatively to one of the natives whom he addressed as Kory-Kory; and from the little I could understand of what took place, pointed him out to me as a man whose peculiar business thenceforth would be to attend upon my person. I am not certain that I comprehended as much as this at the time, but the subsequent conduct of my trusty body servant fully assured me that such must have been the case.

I could not but be amused at the manner in which the chief addressed me upon this occasion, talking to me for at least fifteen or twenty minutes as calmly as if I could understand every word that he said. I remarked this peculiarity very often afterward in many other of the islanders.

Mehevi having now departed, and the family physician having likewise made his exit, we were left about sunset with the ten or twelve natives, who by this time I had ascertained composed the household of which Toby and I were members. As the dwelling to which we had been first introduced was the place of my permanent abode while I remained in the valley, and as I was necessarily placed upon the most intimate footing with its occupants, I may as well here enter into a little description of it and its inhabitants. This description will apply also to nearly all the other dwelling places in the vale, and will furnish some idea of the generality of the natives.

Near one side of the valley, and about midway up the ascent of a rather abrupt rise of ground waving with the richest verdure, a number of large stones were laid in successive courses, to the height of nearly eight feet, and disposed in such a manner that their level surface corresponded in shape with the habitation which was perched upon it. A narrow space, however, was reserved in front of the dwelling, upon the summit of this pile of stones (called by the natives a *pi-pi*), which being enclosed by a little picket of canes, gave it somewhat the appearance of a veranda. The frame of the house was constructed of large bamboos planted uprightly, and secured together at intervals by transverse stalks of the light wood of the hibiscus, lashed with thongs of bark. The rear of the tenement—built up with successive ranges of coconut boughs bound one upon another, with their leaflets cunningly woven together—inclined a little from the vertical, and extended from the extreme edge of the *pi-pi* to about twenty feet from its surface; whence the shelving roof—thatched with the long tapering leaves of the palmetto—sloped steeply off to within about five feet of the floor; leaving the eaves drooping with tassel-like appendages over the front of the habitation. This was constructed of light and elegant canes, in a kind of open screen work, tastefully adorned with bindings of variegated sinnate, which served to hold together its various parts. The sides of the house were similarly built; thus presenting three quarters for the circulation of the air, while the whole was impervious to the rain.

In length this picturesque building was perhaps twelve yards, while in breadth it could not have exceeded as many feet. So much for the exterior; which, with its wirelike reed-twisted sides, not a little reminded me of an immense aviary.

Stooping a little, you passed through a narrow aperture in its front; and facing you, on entering, lay two long, perfectly straight, and well-polished trunks of the coconut tree, extending the full length of the dwelling; one of them placed closely against the rear, and the other lying parallel with it some two yards distant, the interval between them being spread with a multitude of gaily worked mats, nearly all of a different pattern. This space formed the common couch and lounging place of the natives, answering the purpose of a divan in Oriental countries. Here would they slumber through the hours of the night, and recline luxuriously during the greater part of the day. The remainder of the floor presented only the cool shining surfaces of the large stones of which the *pi-pi* was composed.

From the ridgepole of the house hung suspended a number of large packages enveloped in coarse tappa; some of which contained festival dresses, and various other matters of the wardrobe, held in high estimation. These were easily accessible by means of a line, which, passing over the ridgepole, had one end attached to a bundle, while with the other, which led to the side of the dwelling and was there secured, the package could be lowered or elevated at pleasure.

Against the farther wall of the house were arranged in tasteful figures a variety of spears and javelins, and other implements of savage warfare. Outside of the habitation, and built upon the piazzalike area in its front, was a little shed used as a sort of larder or pantry, and in which were stored various articles of domestic use and convenience. A few yards from the *pi-pi* was a large shed built of coconut boughs, where the process of preparing the *poee-poee* was carried on, and all culinary operations attended to.

Thus much for the house, and its appurtenances; and it will

be readily acknowledged that a more commodious and appropriate dwelling for the climate and the people could not possibly be devised. It was cool, free to admit the air, scrupulously clean, and elevated above the dampness and impurities of the ground.

But now to sketch the inmates; and here I claim for my tried servitor and faithful valet Kory-Kory the precedence of a first description. As his character will be gradually unfolded in the course of my narrative, I shall for the present content myself with delineating his personal appearance. Kory-Kory, though the most devoted and best-natured servingman in the world, was, alas! a hideous object to look upon. He was some twenty-five years of age, and about six feet in height, robust and well made, and of the most extraordinary aspect. His head was carefully shaven, with the exception of two circular spots, about the size of a dollar, near the top of the cranium, where the hair, permitted to grow of an amazing length, was twisted up in two prominent knots, that gave him the appearance of being decorated with a pair of horns. His beard, plucked out by the roots from every other part of his face, was suffered to droop in hairy pendants, two of which garnished his upper lip, and an equal number hung from the extremity of his chin.

Kory-Kory, with a view of improving the handiwork of nature, and perhaps prompted by a desire to add to the engaging expression of his countenance, had seen fit to embelish his face with three broad longitudinal stripes of tattooing, which, like those country roads that go straight forward in defiance of all obstacles, crossed his nasal organ, descended into the hollow of his eyes, and even skirted the borders of his mouth. Each completely spanned his physiognomy; one extending in a line with his eyes, another crossing the face in the vicinity of the nose, and the third sweeping along his lips from ear to ear. His countenance thus triply hooped, as it were, with tattooing, always reminded me of those unhappy wretches whom I have sometimes observed gazing out sentimentally from behind the grated bars of a prison window; whilst the entire body of my savage valet, covered all over with representations of birds and fishes, and a variety of most unaccountable-looking creatures, suggested to me the idea of a pictorial museum of natural history, or an illustrated copy of Goldsmith's *Animated Nature.*

But it seems really heartless in me to write thus of the poor islander, when I owe perhaps to his unremitting attentions the very existence I now enjoy. Kory-Kory, I mean thee no harm in what I say in regard to thy outward adornings; but they were a little curious to my unaccustomed sight, and therefore I dilate upon them. But to underrate or forget thy faithful services is something I could never be guilty of, even in the giddiest moment of my life.

The father of my attached follower was a native of gigantic frame, and had once possessed prodigious physical powers; but the lofty form was now yielding to the inroads of time, though the hand of disease seemed never to have been laid upon the aged warrior. Marheyo—for such was his name—appeared to have retired from all active participation in the affairs of the valley, seldom or never accompanying the natives in their various expeditions; and employing the greater part of his time in throwing up a little shed just outside the house, upon which he was engaged to my certain knowledge for four months, without appearing to make any sensible advance. I suppose the old gentleman was in his dotage, for he manifested in various ways the characteristics which mark this particular stage of life.

I remember in particular his having a choice pair of ear-ornaments, fabricated from the teeth of some sea monster. These he would alternately wear and take off at least fifty times in the course of the day, going and coming from his little hut on each occasion with all the tranquillity imaginable. Sometimes slipping them through the slits in his ears, he would seize his spear—which in length and slightness resembled a fishing pole—and go stalking beneath the shadows of the neighboring groves, as if about to give a hostile meeting to some cannibal knight. But he would soon return again, and hiding his weapon under the projecting eaves of the house, and rolling his clumsy trinkets carefully in a piece of tappa, would resume his more pacific operations as quietly as if he had never interrupted them.

But despite his eccentricities, Marheyo was a most paternal and warmhearted old fellow, and in this particular not a little resembled his son Kory-Kory. The mother of the latter was the mistress of the family, and a notable housewife, and a most industrious old lady she was. If she did not understand the art of making jellies, jams, custards, tea cakes, and such-like trashy affairs, she was profoundly skilled in the mysteries of preparing *amar, poee-poee,* and *kokoo,* with other substantial matters. She was a genuine busybody; bustling about the house like a country landlady at an unexpected arrival; forever giving the young girls tasks to perform, which the little hussies as often neglected; poking into every corner, and rummaging over bundles of old tappa, or making a prodigious clatter among the calabashes. Sometimes she might have been seen squatting upon her haunches in front of a huge wooden basin, and kneading *poee-poee* with terrific vehemence, dashing the stone pestle about as if she would shiver the vessel into fragments; on other occasions, galloping about the valley in search of a particular kind of leaf used in some of her recondite operations, and returning home, toiling and sweating, with a bundle of it, under which most women would have sunk.

To tell the truth, Kory-Kory's mother was the only industrious person in all the valley of Typee; and she could not have employed herself more actively had she been left an exceedingly muscular and destitute widow, with an inordinate supply of young children in the bleakest part of the civilized world. There was not the slightest necessity for the greater portion of the labor performed by the old lady: but she seemed to work from some irresistible impulse; her limbs continually swaying to and fro, as if there were some indefatigable engine concealed within her body which kept her in perpetual motion.

Never suppose that she was a termagant or a shrew for all this: she had the kindliest heart in the world, and acted toward me in particular in a truly maternal manner, occasionally putting some little morsel of choice food into my hand, some outlandish kind of savage sweetmeat or pastry, like a doting mother petting a sickly urchin with tarts and sugarplums. Warm indeed are my remembrances of the dear, good, affectionate old Tinor!

Besides the individuals I have mentioned, there belonged to the household three young men, dissipated, good-for-nothing, roystering blades of savages, who were either employed in prosecuting love affairs with the maidens of the tribe, or grew boozy on *arva* and tobacco in the company of congenial spirits, the scapegraces of the valley.

Among the permanent inmates of the house were likewise several lovely damsels, who instead of thrumming pianos and reading novels, like more enlightened young ladies, substituted for these employments the manufacture of a fine species of tappa; but for the greater portion of the time were skipping from house to house, gadding and gossiping with their acquaintances.

From the rest of these, however, I must except the beauteous nymph Fayaway, who was my peculiar favorite. Her free, pliant figure was the very perfection of female grace and beauty. Her complexion was a rich and mantling olive, and when watching the glow upon her cheeks I could almost swear that beneath the transparent medium there lurked the blushes of a faint vermilion. The face of this girl was a rounded oval, and each feature as perfectly formed as the heart or imagination of man could desire. Her full lips, when parted with a smile, disclosed teeth of a dazzling whiteness; and when her rosy mouth opened with a burst of merriment, they looked like the milk-white seeds of the *arta,* a fruit of the valley, which, when cleft in twain, shows them reposing in rows on either side, imbedded in the rich and juicy pulp. Her hair of the deepest brown, parted irregularly in the middle, flowed in natural ringlets over her shoulders, and whenever she chanced to stoop, fell over and hid from view her lovely bosom. Gazing into the depths of her strange blue eyes, when she was in a contemplative mood, they seemed most placid yet unfathomable; but when illuminated by some lively emotion, they beamed upon the beholder like stars. The hands of Fayaway were as soft and delicate as those of any countess; for an entire exemption from rude labor marks the girlhood and even prime of a Typee woman's life. Her feet, though wholly exposed, were as diminutive and fairly shaped as those which peep from beneath the skirts of a Lima lady's dress. The skin of this young creature, from continual ablutions and the use of mollifying ointments, was inconceivably smooth and soft.

I may succeed, perhaps, in particularizing some of the individual features of Fayaway's beauty, but that general loveliness of appearance which they all contributed to produce I will not attempt to describe. The easy unstudied graces of a child of nature like this, breathing from infancy an atmosphere of perpetual summer, and nurtured by the simple fruits of the earth; enjoying a perfect freedom from care and anxiety, and removed effectually from all injurious tendencies, strike the eye in a manner which cannot be portrayed. This picture is no fancy sketch; it is drawn from the most vivid recollections of the person delineated.

Were I asked if the beauteous form of Fayaway was altogether free from the hideous blemish of tattooing, I should be constrained to answer that it was not. But the practitioners of the barbarous art, so remorseless in their inflictions upon the brawny limbs of the warriors of the tribe, seem to be conscious that it needs not the resources of their profession to augment the charms of the maidens of the vale.

The females are very little embellished in this way, and Fayaway, with all the other young girls of her age, was even less so than those of her sex more advanced in years. The reason of this peculiarity will be alluded to hereafter. All the tattooing that the nymph in question exhibited upon her person may be easily described. Three minute dots, no bigger than pinheads, decorated either lip, and at a little distance were not at all discernible. Just upon the fall of the shoulder were drawn two parallel lines half an inch apart, and perhaps three inches in length, the interval being filled with delicately executed figures. These narrow bands of tattooing, thus placed, always reminded me of those stripes of gold lace worn by officers in undress, and which are in lieu of epaulets to denote their rank.

Thus much was Fayaway tattooed—the audacious hand which had gone so far in its desecrating work stopping short, apparently wanting the heart to proceed.

But I have omitted to describe the dress worn by this nymph of the valley.

Fayaway—I must avow the fact—for the most part clung to the primitive and summer garb of Eden. But how becoming the costume! It showed her fine figure to the best possible advantage; and nothing could have been better adapted to her peculiar style of beauty. On ordinary occasions she was habited precisely as I have described the two youthful savages whom we had met on first entering the valley. At other times, when rambling among the groves, or visiting at the houses of her acquaintances, she wore a tunic of white tappa, reaching from her waist to a little below the knees; and when exposed for any length of time to the sun, she invariably protected herself from its rays by a floating mantle of the same material, loosely gathered about the person. Her gala dress will be described hereafter.

As the beauties of our own land delight in bedecking themselves with fanciful articles of jewelry, suspending them from their ears, hanging them about their necks, and clasping them around their wrists, so Fayaway and her companions were in the habit of ornamenting themselves with similar appendages.

Flora was their jeweler. Sometimes they wore necklaces of small carnation flowers, strung like rubies upon a fibre of tappa, or displayed in their ears a single white bud, the stem thrust backward through the aperture, and showing in front the delicate petals folded together in a beautiful sphere, and looking like a drop of the purest pearl. Chaplets too, resembling in their arrangement the strawberry coronal worn by an English peeress, and composed of intertwined leaves and blossoms, often crowned their temples; and bracelets and anklets of the same tasteful pattern were frequently to be seen. Indeed, the maidens of the island were passionately fond of flowers, and never wearied of decorating their persons with them; a lovely trait in their character, and one that ere long will be more fully alluded to.

Though, in my eyes at least, Fayaway was indisputably the loveliest female I saw in Typee, yet the description I have given of her will in some measure apply to nearly all the youthful portion of her sex in the valley. Judge ye then, reader, what beautiful creatures they must have been.

XII

Officiousness of Kory-Kory—his devotion—a bath in the stream—want of refinement of the Typee damsels—stroll with Mehevi—a Typee highway— the Taboo Groves—the Hoolah-Hoolah ground— the Ti—timeworn savages—hospitality of Mehevi— midnight misgivings—adventure in the dark—dis- tinguished honors paid to the visitors—strange pro- cession and return to the house of Marheyo.

WHEN MEHEVI had departed from the house, as related in the preceding chapter, Kory-Kory commenced the functions of the post assigned him. He brought us various kinds of food; and, as if I were an infant, insisted upon feeding me with his own hands. To this procedure I, of course, most earnestly objected, but in vain; and having laid a calabash of *kokoo* before me, he washed his fingers in a vessel of water, and then putting his hand into the dish and rolling the food into little balls, put them one after another into my mouth. All my remonstrances against this measure only provoked so great a clamor on his part, that I was obliged to acquiesce; and the operation of feeding being thus faciliated, the meal was quickly dispatched. As for Toby, he was allowed to help himself after his own fashion.

The repast over, my attendant arranged the mats for repose, and, bidding me lie down, covered me with a large robe of tappa, at the same time looking approvingly upon me, and exclaiming, '*Ki-Ki, muee muee, ah! moee moee mortarkee*' (eat plenty, ah! sleep very good). The philosophy of this sentiment I did not pretend to question; for deprived of sleep for several preceding nights, and the pain in my limb having much abated, I now felt inclined to avail myself of the opportunity afforded me.

The next morning, on waking, I found Kory-Kory stretched out on one side of me, while my companion lay upon the other. I felt sensibly refreshed after a night of sound repose, and immediately agreed to the proposition of my valet that I should repair to the water and wash, although dreading the suffering that the exertion might produce. From this apprehension, however, I was quickly relieved; for Kory-Kory, leaping from the *pi-pi,* and then backing himself up against it, like a porter in readiness to shoulder a trunk, with loud vociferations and a superabundance of gestures, gave me to understand that I was to mount upon his back and be thus transported to the stream, which flowed perhaps two hundred yards from the house.

Our appearance upon the veranda in front of the habitation drew together quite a crowd, who stood looking on and conversing with one another in the most animated manner. They reminded one of a group of idlers gathered about the door of a village tavern when the equipage of some distinguished traveller is brought round previous to his departure. As soon as I clasped my arms about the neck of the devoted fellow, and he jogged off with me, the crowd—composed chiefly of young girls and boys—followed after, shouting and capering with infinite glee, and accompanied us to the banks of the stream.

On gaining it, Kory-Kory, wading up to his hips in the water, carried me halfway across, and deposited me on a smooth black stone which rose a few inches above the surface. The amphibious rabble at our heels plunged in after us, and, climbing to the summit of the grass-grown rocks with which the bed of the brook was here and there broken, waited curiously to witness our morning ablutions.

Somewhat embarrassed by the presence of the female portion of the company, and feeling my cheeks burning with bashful timidity, I formed a primitive basin by joining my hands together, and cooled my blushes in the water it contained; then removing my frock bent over and washed myself down to my waist in the stream. As soon as Kory-Kory comprehended from my motions that this was to be the extent of my performance, he appeared perfectly aghast with astonishment, and rushing towards me, poured out a torrent of words in eager deprecation of so limited an operation, enjoining me by unmistakable signs to immerse my whole body. To this I was forced to consent; and the honest fellow, regarding me as a froward, inexperienced child, whom it was his duty to serve at the risk of offending, lifted me from the rock, and tenderly bathed my limbs. This over, and resuming my seat, I could not avoid bursting into admiration of the scene around me.

From the verdant surfaces of the large stones that lay scattered about, the natives were now sliding off into the water, diving and ducking beneath the surface in all directions—the young girls springing buoyantly into the air, and revealing their naked forms to the waist, with their long tresses dancing about their shoulders, their eyes sparkling like drops of dew in the sun, and their gay laughter pealing worth at every frolicsome incident.

On the afternoon of the day that I took my first bath in the valley, we received another visit from Mehevi. The noble savage seemed to be in the same pleasant mood, and was quite as cordial in his manner as before. After remaining about an hour, he rose from the mats, and motioning to leave the house, invited Toby and myself to accompany him. I pointed to my leg; but Mehevi in his turn pointed to Kory-Kory, and removed that objection; so, mounting upon the faithful fellow's shoulders again—like the old man of the sea astride of Sinbad—I followed after the chief.

The nature of the route we now pursued struck me more

forcibly than anything I had yet seen, as illustrating the indolent disposition of the islanders. The path was obviously the
most beaten one in the valley, several others leading from
either side into it, and perhaps for successive generations it
had formed the principal avenue of the place. And yet, until
I grew more familiar with its impediments, it seemed as
difficult to travel as the recesses of a wilderness. Part of it
was broken by frequent inequalities, and thickly strewn with
projecting masses of rocks, whose summits were often hidden
from view by the drooping foliage of the luxuriant vegetation. Sometimes directly over, sometimes evading these obstacles with a wide circuit, the path wound along;—one moment
climbing over a sudden eminence smooth with continued
wear, then descending on the other side into a steep glen, and
crossing the flinty channel of a brook. Here it pursued the
depths of a glade, occasionally obliging you to stoop beneath
vast horizontal branches; and now you stepped over huge
trunks and boughs that lay rotting across the track.

Such was the grand thoroughfare of Typee. After proceeding a little distance along it—Kory-Kory panting and blowing
with the weight of his burden—I dismounted from his back,
and grasping the long spear of Mehevi in my hand, assisted
my steps over the numerous obstacles of the road; preferring
this mode of advance to one which, from the difficulties of
the way, was equally painful to myself and my wearied
servitor.

Our journey was soon at an end; for, scaling a sudden
height, we came abruptly upon the place of our destination.
I wish that it were possible to sketch in words this spot as
vividly as I recollect it.

Here were situated the Taboo Groves of the valley—the
scene of many a prolonged feast, of many a horrid rite. Beneath the dark shadows of the consecrated breadfruit trees
there reigned a solemn twilight—a cathedral-like gloom. The
frightful genius of pagan worship seemed to brood in silence
over the place, breathing its spell upon every object around.
Here and there, in the depths of these awful shades, half
screened from sight by masses of overhanging foliage, rose

the idolatrous altars of the savages, built of enormous blocks of black and polished stone, placed one upon another, without cement, to the height of twelve or fifteen feet, and surmounted by a rustic open temple, enclosed with a low picket of canes, within which might be seen, in various stages of decay, offerings of breadfruit and coconuts, and the putrefying relics of some recent sacrifice.

In the midst of the wood was the hallowed Hoolah-Hoolah ground—set apart for the celebration of the fantastic religious ritual of these people—comprising an extensive oblong *pi-pi*, terminating at either end in a lofty terraced altar, guarded by ranks of hideous wooden idols, and with the two remaining sides flanked by ranges of bamboo sheds, opening toward the interior of the quadrangle thus formed. Vast trees, standing in the middle of this space, and throwing over it an umbrageous shade, had their massive trunks built round with slight stages, elevated a few feet above the ground, and railed in with canes, forming so many rustic pulpits, from which the priests harangued their devotees.

This holiest of spots was defended from profanation by the strictest edicts of the all-pervading taboo, which condemned to instant death the sacrilegious female who should enter or touch its sacred precincts, or even so much as press with her feet the ground made holy by the shadows that it cast.

Access was had to the enclosure through an embowered entrance on one side, facing a number of towering coconut trees, planted at intervals along a level area of a hundred yards. At the further extremity of this space was to be seen a building of considerable size, reserved for the habitation of the priests and religious attendants of the groves.

In its vicinity was another remarkable edifice, built as usual upon the summit of a *pi-pi*, and at least two hundred feet in length, though not more than twenty in breadth. The whole front of this latter structure was completely open, and from one end to the other ran a narrow veranda, fenced in on the edge of the *pi-pi* with a picket of canes. Its interior presented the appearance of an immense lounging place, the entire floor being strewn with successive layers of mats, lying between parallel trunks of coconut trees, selected for the purpose from the straightest and most symmetrical the vale afforded.

To this building, denominated in the language of the natives the Ti, Mehevi now conducted us. Thus far we had been accompanied by a troop of the natives of both sexes; but as soon as we approached its vicinity, the females gradually separated themselves from the crowd, and standing aloof, permitted us to pass on. The merciless prohibitions of the taboo extended likewise to this edifice, and were enforced by the same dreadful penalty that secured the Hoolah-Hoolah ground from the imaginary pollution of a woman's presence.

On entering the house, I was surprised to see six muskets ranged against the bamboo on one side, from the barrels of which depended as many small canvas pouches, partly filled with powder. Disposed about these muskets, like the cutlasses that decorate the bulkhead of a man-of-war's cabin, were a great variety of rude spears and paddles, javelins, and war clubs. This then, said I to Toby, must be the armory of the tribe.

As we advanced further along the building, we were struck with the aspect of four or five hideous old wretches, on whose decrepit forms time and tattooing seemed to have obliterated every trace of humanity. Owing to the continued operation of this latter process, which only terminates among the warriors of the island after all the figures stretched upon their limbs in youth have been blended together—an effect, however, produced only in cases of extreme longevity—the bodies of these men were of a uniform dull green color—the hue which the tattooing gradually assumes as the individual advances in age. Their skin had a frightful scaly appearance, which, united with its singular color, made their limbs not a little resemble dusty specimens of verde-antique. Their flesh, in parts, hung upon them in huge folds, like the overlapping plaits to the flank of a rhinoceros. Their heads were completely bald, whilst their faces were puckered into a thousand wrinkles, and they presented no vestige of a beard. But the most remarkable peculiarity about them was the appearance of their feet; the toes, like the radiating lines of the mariner's compass, pointed to every quarter of the horizon. This was doubtless attributable to the fact, that during nearly a hundred years of existence the said toes never had been subjected to any artificial confinement, and in their old age, being averse to close neighborhood, bid one another keep open order.

These repulsive-looking creatures appeared to have lost the use of their lower limbs altogether; sitting upon the floor cross-legged in a state of torpor. They never heeded us in the least, scarcely looking conscious of our presence, while Mehevi seated us upon the mats, and Kory-Kory gave utterance to some unintelligible gibberish.

In a few moments a boy entered with a wooden trencher of *poee-poee;* and in regaling myself with its contents I was obliged again to submit to the officious intervention of my indefatigable servitor. Various other dishes followed, the chief manifesting the most hospitable importunity in pressing us to partake, and to remove all bashfulness on our part, set us no despicable example in his own person.

The repast concluded, a pipe was lighted, which passed from mouth to mouth, and yielding to its soporific influence, the quiet of the place, and the deepening shadows of approaching night, my companion and I sank into a kind of drowsy repose, while the chief and Kory-Kory seemed to be slumbering beside us.

I awoke from an uneasy nap, about midnight, as I supposed; and, raising myself partly from the mat, became sensible that we were enveloped in utter darkness. Toby lay still asleep, but our late companion had disappeared. The only sound that interrupted the silence of the place was the asthmatic breathing of the old men I have mentioned, who reposed at a little distance from us. Beside them, as well as I could judge, there was no one else in the house.

Apprehensive of some evil, I roused my comrade, and we were engaged in a whispered conference concerning the unexpected withdrawal of the natives when all at once, from the depths of the grove, in full view of us where we lay, shoots of flame were seen to rise, and in a few moments illuminated the surrounding trees, casting, by contrast, into still deeper gloom the darkness around us.

While we continued gazing at this sight, dark figures appeared moving to and fro before the flames; while others, dancing and capering about, looked like so many demons.

Regarding this new phenomenon with no small degree of trepidation, I said to my companion, 'What can all this mean, Toby?'

'Oh, nothing,' replied he; 'getting the fire ready, I suppose.'

'Fire!' exclaimed I, while my heart took to beating like a trip hammer, 'what fire?'

'Why, the fire to cook us, to be sure; what else would the cannibals be kicking up such a row about if it were not for that?'

'Oh, Toby! have done with your jokes; this is no time for them; something is about to happen, I feel confident.'

'Jokes, indeed!' exclaimed Toby, indignantly. 'Did you ever hear me joke? Why, for what do you suppose the devils have been feeding us up in this kind of style during the last three days, unless it were for something that you are too much frightened at to talk about? Look at that Kory-Kory there!— has he not been stuffing you with his confounded mushes, just in the way they treat swine before they kill them? Depend upon it, we will be eaten this blessed night, and there is the fire we shall be roasted by.'

This view of the matter was not at all calculated to allay my apprehensions, and I shuddered when I reflected that we were indeed at the mercy of a tribe of cannibals, and that the dreadful contingency to which Toby had alluded was by no means removed beyond the bounds of possibility.

'There! I told you so! they are coming for us!' exclaimed my companion the next moment, as the forms of four of the islanders were seen in bold relief against the illuminated background, mounting the *pi-pi* and approaching toward us.

They came on noiselessly, nay stealthily, and glided along through the gloom that surrounded us as if about to spring upon some object they were fearful of disturbing before they should make sure of it.—Gracious heaven! the horrible reflections which crowded upon me that moment.—A cold sweat stood upon my brow, and spellbound with terror I awaited my fate!

Suddenly the silence was broken by the well-remembered tones of Mehevi, and at the kindly accents of his voice my fears were immediately dissipated. '*Tommo, Toby, ki ki!*" (eat).—He had waited to address us until he had assured himself that we were both awake, at which he seemed somewhat surprised.

'*Ki ki!* it is?' said Toby in his gruff tones. 'Well, cook us first, will you?—but what's this?' he added, as another savage appeared, bearing before him a large trencher of wood, containing some kind of steaming meat, as appeared from the odors it diffused, and which he deposited at the feet of Mehevi. 'A baked baby, I dare say! but I will have none of it, never mind what it is.—A pretty fool I should make of myself, indeed, waked up here in the middle of the night, stuffing and guzzling, and all to make a fat meal for a parcel of bloody-minded cannibals one of these mornings!—No, I see what they are at very plainly, so I am resolved to starve myself into a bunch of bones and gristle, and then, if they serve me up, they are welcome! But I say, Tommo, you are not going to eat any of that mess there, in the dark, are you? Why, how can you tell what it is?'

'By tasting it, to be sure,' said I, masticating a morsel that Kory-Kory had just put in my mouth; 'and excellently good it is too, very much like veal.'

'A baked baby, by the soul of Captain Cook!' burst forth Toby, with amazing vehemence; 'Veal! why there never was a calf on the island till you landed. I tell you you are bolting down mouthfuls from a dead Happar's carcass, as sure as you live, and no mistake!'

Emetics and lukewarm water! What a sensation in the abdominal regions! Sure enough, where could the fiends incarnate have obtained meat? But I resolved to satisfy myself at all hazards; and, turning to Mehevi, I soon made the ready chief understand that I wished a light to be brought. When the taper came, I gazed eagerly into the vessel, and recognized the mutilated remains of a juvenile porker! '*Puarkee!*' exclaimed Kory-Kory, looking complacently at the dish; and from that day to this I have never forgotten that such is the designation of a pig in the Typee lingo.

The next morning, after being again abundantly feasted by the hospitable Mehevi, Toby and myself arose to depart. But the chief requested us to postpone our intention. '*Abo, abo*' (Wait, wait), he said, and accordingly we resumed our seats, while, assisted by the zealous Kory-Kory, he appeared to be engaged in giving directions to a number of the natives outside, who were busily employed in making arrangements, the nature of which we could not comprehend. But we were not left long in our ignorance, for a few moments only had elapsed when the chief beckoned us to approach, and we perceived that he had been marshalling a kind of guard of honor to escort us on our return to the house of Marheyo.

The procession was led off by two venerable-looking savages, each provided with a spear, from the end of which streamed a pennon of milk-white tappa. After them went several youths, bearing aloft calabashes of *poee-poee;* and followed in their turn by four stalwart fellows, sustaining long bamboos, from the tops of which hung suspended, at least twenty feet from the ground, large baskets of green breadfruit. Then came a troop of boys, carrying bunches of ripe bananas, and baskets made of the woven leaflets of coconut boughs, filled with the young fruit of the tree, the naked shells stripped of their husks peeping forth from the verdant wickerwork that surrounded them. Last of all came a burly islander, holding over his head a wooden trencher, in which lay disposed the remnants of our midnight feast, hidden from view, however, by a covering of breadfruit leaves.

Astonished as I was at this exhibition, I could not avoid smiling at its grotesque appearance, and the associations it naturally called up. Mehevi, it seemed, was bent on replenishing old Marheyo's larder, fearful perhaps that without this precaution his guests might not fare as well as they could desire.

As soon as I descended from the *pi-pi*, the procession formed anew, enclosing us in its center; where I remained part of the time, carried by Kory-Kory, and occasionally relieving him from his burden by limping along with a spear. When we moved off in this order, the natives struck up a musical recitative, which, with various alternations, they continued until we arrived at the place of our destination.

As we proceeded on our way, bands of young girls, darting from the surrounding groves, hung upon our skirts, and accompanied us with shouts of merriment and delight, which almost drowned the deep notes of the recitative. On approaching old Marheyo's domicile, its inmates rushed out to receive us; and while the gifts of Mehevi were being disposed of, the superannuated warrior did the honors of his mansion with all the warmth of hospitality evinced by an English squire when he regales his friends at some fine old patrimonial mansion.

XIII

Attempt to procure relief from Nukuheva—perilous adventure of Toby in the Happar Mountains— eloquence of Kory-Kory.

AMIDST THESE NOVEL scenes a week passed away almost imperceptibly. The natives, actuated by some mysterious impulse, day after day redoubled their attentions to us. Their manner toward us was unaccountable. Surely, thought I, they would not act thus if they meant us any harm. But why this excess of deferential kindness, or what equivalent can they imagine us capable of rendering them for it?

We were fairly puzzled. But despite the apprehensions I

could not dispel, the horrible character imputed to these Typees appeared to me wholly undeserved.

'Why, they are cannibals!' said Toby on one occasion when I eulogized the tribe. 'Granted,' I replied, 'but a more humane, gentlemanly, and amiable set of epicures do not probably exist in the Pacific.'

But, notwithstanding the kind treatment we received, I was too familiar with the fickle disposition of savages not to feel anxious to withdraw from the valley, and put myself beyond the reach of that fearful death which, under all these smiling appearances, might yet menace us. But here there was an obstacle in the way of doing so. It was idle for me to think of moving from the place until I should have recovered from the severe lameness that afflicted me; indeed my malady began seriously to alarm me; for, despite the herbal remedies of the natives, it continued to grow worse and worse. Their mild applications, though they soothed the pain, did not remove the disorder, and I felt convinced that without better aid I might anticipate long and acute suffering.

But how was this aid to be procured? From the surgeons of the French fleet, which probably still lay in the bay of Nukuheva, it might easily have been obtained, could I have made my case known to them. But how could that be effected?

At last, in the exigency to which I was reduced, I proposed to Toby that he should endeavor to go round to Nukuheva, and if he could not succeed in returning to the valley by water, in one of the boats of the squadron, and taking me off, he might at least procure me some proper medicines, and effect his return overland.

My companion listened to me in silence, and at first did not appear to relish the idea. The truth was he felt impatient to escape from the place, and wished to avail himself of our present high favor with the natives to make good our retreat, before we should experience some sudden alteration in their behavior. As he could not think of leaving me in my helpless condition, he implored me to be of good cheer, assured me that I should soon be better and enabled in a few days to return with him to Nukuheva.

Added to this, he could not bear the idea of again returning to this dangerous place; and as for the expectation of persuading the Frenchmen to detach a boat's crew for the purpose of rescuing me from the Typees, he looked upon it as idle; and, with arguments that I could not answer, urged the improbability of their provoking the hostilities of the clan by any such measure; especially as, for the purpose of quieting its apprehensions, they had as yet refrained from making any visit to the bay. 'And even should they consent,' said Toby, 'they would only produce a commotion in the valley, in which we might both be sacrificed by these ferocious islanders.' This was unanswerable; but still I clung to the belief that he might succeed in accomplishing the other part of my plan; and at last I overcame his scruples, and he agreed to make the attempt.

As soon as we succeeded in making the natives understand our intention, they broke out into the most vehement opposition to the measure, and for a while I almost despaired of obtaining their consent. At the bare thought of one of us leaving them, they manifested the most lively concern. The grief and consternation of Kory-Kory, in particular, was unbounded; he threw himself into a perfect paroxysm of gestures, which were intended to convey to us not only his abhorrence of Nukuheva and its uncivilized inhabitants, but also his astonishment that after becoming acquainted with the enlightened Typees, we should evince the least desire to withdraw, even for a time, from their agreeable society.

However, I overbore his objections by appealing to my lameness; from which I assured the natives I should speedily recover, if Toby were permitted to obtain the supplies I needed.

It was agreed that on the following morning my companion should depart, accompanied by some one or two of the household, who should point out to him an easy route, by which the bay might be reached before sunset.

At early dawn of the next day, our habitation was astir. One of the young men mounted into an adjoining coconut tree, and threw down a number of the young fruit, which old Marheyo quickly stripped of the green husks, and strung together upon a short pole. These were intended to refresh Toby on his route.

The preparations being completed, with no little emotion I bade my companion adieu. He promised to return in three days at farthest; and, bidding me keep up my spirits in the interval, turned round the corner of the *pi-pi*, and, under the guidance of the venerable Marheyo, was soon out of sight. His departure oppressed me with melancholy, and, re-entering the dwelling, I threw myself almost in despair upon the matting of the floor.

In two hours' time the old warrior returned, and gave me to understand that, after accompanying my companion a little distance, and showing him the route, he had left him journeying on his way.

It was about noon of this same day, a season which these people are wont to pass in sleep, that I lay in the house, surrounded by its slumbering inmates, and painfully affected by the strange silence which prevailed. All at once I thought I heard a faint shout, as if proceeding from some persons in the depth of the grove which extended in front of our habitation.

The sounds grew louder and nearer, and gradually the whole valley rang with wild outcries. The sleepers around me started to their feet in alarm, and hurried outside to discover the cause of the commotion. Kory-Kory, who had been the first to spring up, soon returned almost breathless and nearly frantic with the excitement under which he seemed to be laboring. All that I could understand from him was that some accident had happened to Toby. Apprehensive of some dreadful calamity, I rushed out of the house, and caught sight of a tumultuous crowd, who, with shrieks and lamentations, were just emerging from the grove bearing in their arms some object, the sight of which produced all this transport of sorrow. As they drew near, the men redoubled their cries, while the girls, tossing their bare arms in the air, exclaimed plaintively, '*Awha! awha! Toby muckee moee!*'— Alas! alas! Toby is killed!

In a moment that crowd opened, and disclosed the apparently lifeless body of my companion borne between two men, the head hanging heavily against the breast of the foremost. The whole face, neck, and bosom were covered with blood, which still trickled slowly from a wound behind the temple. In the midst of the greatest uproar and confusion the body was carried into the house and laid on a mat. Waving the natives off to give room and air, I bent eagerly over Toby, and, laying my hand upon the breast, ascertained that the heart still beat. Overjoyed at this, I seized a calabash of water, and dashed its contents upon his face, then wiping away the blood, anxiously examined the wound. It was about three inches long, and on removing the clotted hair from about it, showed the skull laid completely bare. Immediately with my knife I cut away the heavy locks, and bathed the part repeatedly in water.

In a few moments Toby revived, and opening his eyes for a second, closed them again without speaking. Kory-Kory, who had been kneeling beside me, now chafed his limbs gently with the palms of his hands, while a young girl at his head kept fanning him, and still continued to moisten his lips and brow. Soon my poor comrade showed signs of animation, and I succeeded in making him swallow from a coconut shell a few mouthfuls of water.

Old Tinor now appeared, holding in her hand some simples she had gathered, the juice of which she by signs besought me to squeeze into the wound. Having done so, I thought it best to leave Toby undisturbed until he should have had time to rally his faculties. Several times he opened his lips, but fearful for his safety I enjoined silence. In the course of two or three hours, however, he sat up, and was sufficiently recovered to tell me what had occurred.

'After leaving the house with Marheyo,' said Toby, 'we struck across the valley, and ascended the opposite heights. Just beyond them, my guide informed me, lay the valley of Happar, while along their summits, and skirting the head of the vale, was my route to Nukuheva. After mounting a little way up the elevation my guide paused, and gave me to understand that he could not accompany me any farther, and by various signs intimated that he was afraid to approach any nearer the territories of the enemies of his tribe. He, however, pointed out my path, which now lay clearly before me, and bidding me farewell hastily descended the mountain.

'Quite elated at being so near the Happars, I pushed up the acclivity, and soon gained its summit. It tapered up to a sharp ridge, from whence I beheld both the hostile valleys. Here I sat down and rested for a moment, refreshing myself with my coconuts. I was soon again pursuing my way along the height, when suddenly I saw three of the islanders, who must have just come out of Happar valley, standing in the path ahead of me. They were each armed with a heavy spear, and one from his appearance I took to be a chief. They sung out something, I could not understand what, and beckoned me to come on.

'Without the least hesitation I advanced toward them, and had approached within about a yard of the foremost, when, pointing angrily into the Typee valley, and uttering some savage exclamation, he wheeled round his weapon like lightning, and struck me in a moment to the ground. The blow inflicted this wound, and took away my senses. As soon as I came to myself, I perceived the three islanders standing a little distance off, and apparently engaged in some violent altercation respecting me.

'My first impulse was to run for it; but, in endeavoring to rise, I fell back, and rolled down a little grassy precipice. The shock seemed to rally my faculties; so, starting to my feet, I fled down the path I had just ascended. I had no need to look behind me, for, from the yells I heard, I knew that my enemies were in full pursuit. Urged on by their fearful outcries, and heedless of the injury I had received—though the blood flowing from the wound trickled over into my eyes and almost blinded me—I rushed down the mountain side with the speed of the wind. In a short time I had descended nearly a third of the distance, and the savages had ceased their cries, when suddenly a terrific howl burst upon my ear, and at the same moment a heavy javelin darted past me as I fled, and stuck quivering in a tree close to me. Another yell followed, and a second spear and a third shot through the air within a few feet of my body, both of them piercing the ground obliquely in advance of me. The fellows gave a roar of rage and disappointment; but they were afraid, I suppose, of coming down further into the Typee valley, and so abandoned the chase. I saw them recover their weapons and turn back; and I continued my descent as fast as I could.

'What could have caused this ferocious attack on the part of these Happars I could not imagine, unless it were that they had seen me ascending the mountain with Marheyo, and that the mere fact of coming from the Typee valley was sufficient to provoke them.

'As long as I was in danger I scarcely felt the wound I had received; but when the chase was over I began to suffer from it. I had lost my hat in my flight, and the sun scorched my bare head. I felt faint and giddy; but, fearful of falling to the ground beyond the reach of assistance, I staggered on as well as I could, and at last gained the level of the valley and then down I sunk; and I knew nothing more until I found myself lying upon these mats, and you stooping over me with the calabash of water.'

Such was Toby's account of this sad affair. I afterward learned that fortunately he had fallen close to a spot where the natives go for fuel. A party of them caught sight of him as he fell, and sounding the alarm, had lifted him up; and, after ineffectually endeavoring to restore him at the brook, had hurried forward with him to the house.

This incident threw a dark cloud over our prospects. It reminded us that we were hemmed in by hostile tribes, whose territories we could not hope to pass, on our route to Nukuheva, without encountering the effects of their savage resentment. There appeared to be no avenue opened to our escape but the sea, which washed the lower extremity of the vale.

Our Typee friends availed themselves of the recent disaster of Toby to exhort us to a due appreciation of the blessings we enjoyed among them; contrasting their own generous reception of us with the animosity of their neighbors. They likewise dwelt upon the cannibal propensities of the Happars, a subject which they were perfectly aware could not fail to alarm us; while at the same time they earnestly disclaimed all participation in so horrid a custom. Nor did they omit to call upon us to admire the natural loveliness of their own abode, and the lavish abundance with which it produced all manner of luxuriant fruits; exalting it in this particular above any of the surrounding valleys.

Kory-Kory seemed to experience so heartfelt a desire to infuse into our minds proper views on these subjects, that, assisted in his endeavors by the little knowledge of the language we had acquired, he actually succeeded in making us comprehend a considerable part of what he said. To facilitate our correct apprehension of his meaning, he at first condensed his ideas into the smallest possible compass.

'Happar keekeeno nuee,' he exclaimed; *'nuee, nuee, ki ki kannaka!—ah! owle mortarkee!'* which signifies, 'Terrible fellows those Happars!—devour an amazing quantity of men! —ah, shocking bad!' Thus far he explained himself by a variety of gestures, during the performance of which he would dart out of the house, and point abhorrently towards the Happar valley; running in to us again with a rapidity that showed he was fearful we would lose one part of his meaning before he could complete the other; and continuing his illustrations by seizing the fleshy part of my arm in his teeth, intimating by the operation that the people who lived over in that direction would like nothing better than to treat me in that manner.

Having assured himself that we were fully enlightened on this point, he proceeded to another branch of his subject. *'Ah! Typee mortarkee!—nuee, nuee mioree—nuee, nuee wai—nuee, nuee poee-poee—nuee, nuee kokoo—ah! nuee, nuee ki ki—ah! nuee, nuee, nuee!'* Which, literally interpreted as before, would imply, 'Ah, Typee! isn't it a fine place though! —no danger of starving here, I tell you!—plenty of bread-fruit—plenty of water—plenty of pudding—ah! plenty of everything!—ah! heaps, heaps, heaps!' All this was accompanied by a running commentary of signs and gestures which it was impossible not to comprehend.

As he continued his harangue, however, Kory-Kory, in emulation of our more polished orators, began to launch out rather diffusely into other branches of his subject, enlarging, probably, upon the moral reflections it suggested; and proceeded in such a strain of unintelligible and stunning gibberish, that he actually gave me the headache for the rest of the day.

XIV

A great event happens in the valley—the island telegraph—something befalls Toby—Fayaway displays a tender heart—melancholy reflections— mysterious conduct of the islanders—devotion of Kory-Kory—a rural couch—a luxury—Kory-Kory strikes a light *à la* Typee.

IN THE COURSE of a few days Toby had recovered from the effects of his adventure with the Happar warriors; the wound on his head rapidly healing under the vegetable treatment of the good Tinor. Less fortunate than my companion, however, I still continued to languish under a complaint the origin and nature of which were still a mystery. Cut off as I was from all intercourse with the civilized world, and feeling the inefficiency of anything the natives could do to relieve me; knowing too, that so long as I remained in my present condition, it would be impossible for me to leave the valley, whatever opportunity might present itself; and apprehensive that ere long we might be exposed to some caprice on the part of the islanders, I now gave up all hopes of recovery, and became a prey to the most gloomy thoughts. A deep dejection fell upon me, which neither the friendly remonstrances of my companion, the devoted attentions of Kory-Kory, nor all the soothing influences of Fayaway could remove.

One morning as I lay on the mats in the house, plunged

in melancholy reverie, and regardless of everything around me, Toby, who had left me about an hour, returned in haste, and with great glee told me to cheer up and be of good heart; for he believed from what was going on among the natives, that there were boats approaching the bay.

These tidings operated upon me like magic. The hour of our deliverance was at hand, and starting up, I was soon convinced that something unusual was about to occur. The word *'botee! botee!'* was vociferated in all directions; and shouts were heard in the distance, at first feebly and faintly: but growing louder and nearer at each successive repetition, until they were caught up by a fellow in a coconut tree a few yards off, who sounding them in turn, they were reiterated from a neighboring grove, and so died away gradually from point to point, as the intelligence penetrated into the farthest recesses of the valley. This was the vocal telegraph of the islanders; by means of which condensed items of information could be carried in a very few minutes from the sea to their remotest habitation, a distance of at least eight or nine miles. On the present occasion it was in active operation; one piece of information following another with inconceivable rapidity.

The greatest commotion now appeared to prevail. At every fresh item of intelligence the natives betrayed the liveliest interest, and redoubled the energy with which they employed themselves in collecting fruit to sell to the expected visitors. Some were tearing off the husks from coconuts; some perched in the trees were throwing down breadfruit to their companions, who gathered them into heaps as they fell; while others were plying their fingers rapidly in weaving leafen baskets in which to carry the fruit.

There were other matters too going on at the same time. Here you would see a stout warrior polishing his spear with a bit of old tappa, or adjusting the folds of the girdle about his waist; and there you might decry a young damsel decorating herself with flowers, as if having in her eye some maidenly conquest; while, as in all cases of hurry and confusion in every part of the world, a number of individuals kept hurrying to

and fro, with amazing vigor and perseverance, doing nothing themselves, and hindering others.

Never before had we seen the islanders in such a state of
bustle and excitement; and the scene furnished abundant evidence of the fact—that it was only at long intervals any such
events occur.

When I thought of the length of time that might intervene
before a similar chance of escape would be presented, I bitterly lamented that I had not the power of availing myself
effectually of the present opportunity.

From all that we could gather, it appeared that the natives
were fearful of arriving too late upon the beach, unless they
made extraordinary exertions. Sick and lame as I was, I would
have started with Toby at once, had not Kory-Kory not only
refused to carry me, but manifested the most invincible repugnance to our leaving the neighborhood of the house. The
rest of the savages were equally opposed to our wishes, and
seemed grieved and astonished at the earnestness of my solicitations. I clearly perceived that while my attendant avoided all
appearance of constraining my movements, he was nevertheless determined to thwart my wish. He seemed to me on this
particular occasion, as well as often afterward, to be execut-
ing the orders of some other person with regard to me,
though at the same time feeling toward me the most lively
affection.

Toby, who had made up his mind to accompany the islanders if possible, as soon as they were in readiness to depart, and who for that reason had refrained from showing
the same anxiety that I had done, now represented to me that
it was idle for me to entertain the hope of reaching the
beach in time to profit by any opportunity that might then
be presented.

'Do you not see,' said he, 'the savages themselves are fearful of being too late, and I should hurry forward myself at
once did I not think that if I showed too much eagerness I
should destroy all our hopes of reaping any benefit from this
fortunate event. If you will only endeavor to appear tranquil
or unconcerned, you will quiet their suspicions, and I have no

doubt they will then let me go with them to the beach, supposing that I merely go out of curiosity. Should I succeed in getting down to the boats, I will make known the condition in which I have left you, and measures may then be taken to secure our escape.'

In the expediency of this I could not but acquiesce; and as the natives had now completed their preparations, I watched with the liveliest interest the reception that Toby's application might meet with. As soon as they understood from my companion that I intended to remain, they appeared to make no objection to his proposition, and even hailed it with pleasure. Their singular conduct on this occasion not a little puzzled me at the time, and imparted to subsequent events an additional mystery.

The islanders were now to be seen hurrying along the path which led to the sea. I shook Toby warmly by the hand, and gave him my Payta hat to shield his wounded head from the sun, as he had lost his own. He cordially returned the pressure of my hand, and solemnly promising to return as soon as the boats should leave the shore, sprang from my side, and the next minute disappeared in a turn of the grove.

In spite of the unpleasant reflections that crowded upon my mind, I could not but be entertained by the novel and animated sight which now met my view. One after another the natives crowded along the narrow path, laden with every variety of fruit. Here, you might have seen one, who, after ineffectually endeavoring to persuade a surly porker to be conducted in leading strings, was obliged at last to seize the perverse animal in his arms, and carry him struggling against his naked breast, and squealing without intermission. There went two, who at a little distance might have been taken for the Hebrew spies, on their return to Moses with the goodly bunch of grapes. One trotted before the other at a distance of a couple of yards, while between them, from a pole resting on their shoulders, was suspended a huge cluster of bananas, which swayed to and fro with the rocking gait at which they proceeded. Here ran another, perspiring with his exertions, and bearing before him a quantity of coconuts, who, fearful of being too late, heeded not the fruit that dropped from his basket, and appeared solely intent upon reaching his destination, careless how many of his coconuts kept company with him.

In a short time the last straggler was seen hurrying on his way, and the faint shouts of those in advance died insensibly upon the ear. Our part of the valley now appeared nearly deserted by its inhabitants, Kory-Kory, his aged father, and a few decrepit old people being all that were left.

Toward sunset the islanders in small parties began to return from the beach, and among them, as they drew near to the house, I sought to descry the form of my companion. But one after another they passed the dwelling, and I caught no glimpse of him. Supposing, however, that he would soon appear with some of the members of the household, I quieted my apprehensions and waited patiently to see him advancing in company with the beautiful Fayaway. At last, I perceived Tinor coming forward, followed by the girls and young men who usually resided in the house of Marheyo; but with them came not my comrade, and, filled with a thousand alarms, I eagerly sought to discover the cause of his delay.

My earnest questions appeared to embarrass the natives greatly. All their accounts were contradictory: one giving me to understand that Toby would be with me in a very short time; another that he did not know where he was; while a third, violently inveighing against him, assured me that he had stolen away, and would never come back. It appeared to me, at the time, that in making these various statements they endeavored to conceal from me some terrible disaster, lest the knowledge of it should overpower me.

Fearful lest some fatal calamity had overtaken him, I sought out young Fayaway, and endeavored to learn from her, if possible, the truth.

This gentle being had early attracted my regard, not only from her extraordinary beauty, but from the attractive cast of her countenance, singularly expressive of intelligence and humanity. Of all the natives she alone seemed to appreciate the effect which the peculiarity of the circumstances in which we were placed had produced upon the minds of my companion and myself. In addressing me—especially when I lay reclining upon the mats suffering from pain—there was a tenderness in her manner which it was impossible to misunderstand or resist. Whenever she entered the house, the expression of her face indicated the liveliest sympathy for me; and moving toward the place where I lay, with one arm slightly elevated in a gesture of pity, and her large glistening eyes gazing intently into mine, she would murmur plaintively, '*Awha! awha! Tommo,*' and seat herself mournfully beside me.

Her manner convinced me that she deeply compassionated my situation, as being removed from my country and friends, and placed beyond the reach of all relief. Indeed, at times I was almost led to believe that her mind was swayed by gentle impulses hardly to be anticipated from one in her condition; that she appeared to be conscious there were ties rudely severed, which had once bound us to our homes; that there were sisters and brothers anxiously looking forward to our return, who were, perhaps, never more to behold us.

In this amiable light did Fayaway appear in my eyes; and reposing full confidence in her candor and intelligence, I now had recourse to her, in the midst of my alarm, with regard to my companion.

My questions evidently distressed her. She looked round from one to another of the bystanders, as if hardly knowing what answer to give me. At last, yielding to my importunities, she overcame her scruples, and gave me to understand that Toby had gone away with the boats which had visited the bay, but had promised to return at the expiration of three days. At first I accused him of perfidiously deserting me; but as I grew more composed, I upbraided myself for imputing so cowardly an action to him, and tranquilized myself with the belief that he had availed himself of the opportunity to go round to Nukuheva, in order to make some arrangement by which I could be removed from the valley. At any rate, thought I, he will return with the medicines I require, and then, as soon as I recover, there will be no difficulty in the way of our departure.

Consoling myself with these reflections, I lay down that night in a happier frame of mind than I had done for some time. The next day passed without any allusion to Toby on the part of the natives, who seemed desirous of avoiding all reference to the subject. This raised some apprehensions in my breast; but when night came, I congratulated myself that the second day had now gone by and that on the morrow Toby would again be with me. But the morrow came and went, and my companion did not appear. Ah! thought I, he reckons three days from the morning of his departure—tomorrow he will arrive. But that weary day also closed upon me, without his return. Even yet I could not despair; I thought that something detained him—that he was waiting for the sailing of a boat, at Nukuheva, and that in a day or two at farthest I should see him again. But day after day of renewed disappointment passed by; at last hope deserted me, and I fell a victim to despair.

Yes, thought I, gloomily, he has secured his own escape, and cares not what calamity may befall his unfortunate comrade. Fool that I was to suppose any one would willingly encounter the perils of this valley, after having once got beyond its limits; He had gone, and has left me to combat alone all the dangers by which I am surrounded. Thus would I sometimes seek to derive a desperate consolation from dwelling upon the perfidy of Toby: whilst at other times I sunk under the bitter remorse which I felt as having by my own imprudence brought upon myself the fate which I was sure awaited me.

At other times I thought that perhaps after all these treacherous savages had made away with him, and thence the confusion into which they were thrown by my questions, and their contradictory answers, or he might be a captive in some other part of the valley; or, more dreadful still, might have met with that fate at which my very soul shuddered. But all these speculations were vain; no tidings of Toby ever reached me; he had gone never to return.

The conduct of the islanders appeared inexplicable. All reference to my lost comrade was carefully evaded, and if at any time they were forced to make some reply to my frequent inquiries on the subject, they would uniformly denounce him as an ungrateful runaway, who had deserted his friend, and taken himself off to that vile and detestable place Nukuheva.

But whatever might have been his fate, now that he was gone, the natives multiplied their acts of kindness and attention toward myself, treating me with a degree of deference which could hardly have been surpassed had I been some celestial visitant. Kory-Kory never for one moment left my side, unless it were to execute my wishes. The faithful fellow, twice every day, in the cool of the morning and in the evening, insisted upon carrying me to the stream, and bathing me in its refreshing water.

Frequently in the afternoon he would carry me to a particular part of the stream, where the beauty of the scene produced a soothing influence upon my mind. At this place the waters flowed between grassy banks, planted with enormous breadfruit trees, whose vast branches, interlacing overhead, formed a leafy canopy; near the stream were several smooth black rocks. One of these, projecting several feet above the surface of the water, had upon its summit a shallow cavity, which, filled with freshly gathered leaves, formed a delightful couch.

Here I often lay for hours, covered with a gauzelike veil of tappa, while Fayaway, seated beside me, and holding in her hand a fan woven from the leaflets of a young coconut bough, brushed aside the insects that occasionally lighted on my face, and Kory-Kory, with a view of chasing away my melancholy, performed a thousand antics in the water before us.

As my eye wandered along this romantic stream, it would fall upon the half-immersed figure of a beautiful girl, standing in the transparent water, and catching in a little net a species of diminutive shellfish, of which these people are extravagantly fond. Sometimes a chattering group would be seated upon the edge of a low rock in the midst of the brook, busily engaged in thinning and polishing the shells of coconuts, by rubbing them briskly with a small stone in the water, an operation which soon converts them into a light and elegant drinking vessel, somewhat resembling goblets made of tortoiseshell.

But the tranquilizing influences of beautiful scenery, and the exhibition of human life under so novel and charming an aspect, were not my only sources of consolation.

Every evening the girls of the house gathered about me on the mats, and after chasing away Kory-Kory from my side—who, nevertheless, retired only to a little distance and watched their proceedings with the most jealous attention—would anoint my whole body with a fragrant oil, squeezed from a yellow root, previously pounded between a couple of stones, and which in their language is denominated *aka*. And most refreshing and agreeable are the juices of the *aka*, when applied to one's limbs by the soft palms of sweet nymphs, whose bright eyes are beaming upon you with kindness; and I used to hail with delight the daily recurrence of this luxurious operation, in which I forgot all my troubles, and buried for the time every feeling of sorrow.

Sometimes in the cool of the evening my devoted servitor would lead me out upon the *pi-pi* in front of the house, and seating me near its edge, protect my body from the annoyances of the insects which occasionally hovered in the air, by wrapping me round with a large roll of tappa. He then bustled about, and employed himself at least twenty minutes in adjusting everything to secure my personal comfort.

Having perfected his arrangements, he would get my pipe, and, lighting it, would hand it to me. Often he was obliged to strike a light for the occasion, and as the mode he adopted was entirely different from what I had ever seen or heard of before, I will describe it.

A straight, dry, and partly decayed stick of the habiscus, about six feet in length, and half as many inches in diameter, with a smaller bit of wood not more than a foot long, and scarcely an inch wide, is as invariably to be met with in every house in Typee as a box of lucifer matches in the corner of a kitchen cupboard at home.

The islander, placing the larger stick obliquely against some object, with one end elevated at an angle of forty-five degrees, mounts astride of it like an urchin about to gallop off upon a cane, and then, grasping the smaller one firmly in both hands, he rubs its pointed end slowly up and down the extent of a few inches on the principal stick, until at last he makes a narrow grove in the wood, with an abrupt termination at the point furthest from him, where all the dusty articles which the friction creates are accumulated in a little heap.

At first Kory-Kory goes to work quite leisurely, but gradually quickens his pace, and waxing warm in the employment, drives the stick furiously along the smoking channel, plying his hands to and fro with amazing rapidity, the perspiration starting from every pore. As he approaches the climax of his effort, he pants and gasps for breath, and his eyes almost start from their sockets with the violence of his exertions. This is the critical stage of the operation; all his previous labors are vain if he cannot sustain the rapidity of the movement until the reluctant spark is produced. Suddenly he stops, becomes perfectly motionless. His hands still retain their hold of the smaller stick, which is pressed convulsively against the further end of the channel among the fine powder there accumulated, as if he had just pierced through and through some little viper that was wriggling and struggling to escape from his clutches. The next moment a delicate wreath of smoke curls spirally into the air, the heap of dusty particles glows with fire, and Kory-Kory almost breathless, dismounts from his steed.

This operation appeared to me to be the most laborious species of work performed in Typee; and had I possessed a sufficient intimacy with the language to have conveyed my ideas upon the subject, I should certainly have suggested to the most influential of the natives the expediency of establishing a college of vestals to be centrally located in the valley, for the purpose of keeping alive the indispensable article of fire; so as to supersede the necessity of such a vast outlay of strength and good temper, as were usually squandered on these occasions. There might, however, be special difficulties in carrying this plan into execution.

What a striking evidence does this operation furnish of the wide difference between the extreme of savage and civilized life. A gentleman of Typee can bring up a numerous family of children and give them all a highly respectable cannibal education, with infinitely less toil and anxiety than he expends in the simple process of striking a light; whilst a poor European artisan, who through the instrumentality of a lucifer performs the same operation in one second, is put to his wits' end to provide for his starving offspring that food which the children of a Polynesian father, without troubling their parent, pluck from the branches of every tree around them.

XV

Kindness of Marheyo and the rest of the islanders —a full description of the breadfruit tree—different modes of preparing the fruit.

ALL THE INHABITANTS of the valley treated me with great kindness; but as to the household of Marheyo, with whom I was now permanently domiciled, nothing could surpass their efforts to minister to my comfort. To the gratification of my palate they paid the most unwearied attention. They continually invited me to partake of food, and when after eating heartily I declined the viands they continued to offer me, they seemed to think that my appetite stood in need of some piquant stimulant to excite its activity.

In pursuance of this idea, old Marheyo himself would hie him away to the seashore by the break of day, for the purpose of collecting various species of rare seaweed; some of which among these people are considered a great luxury. After a whole day spent in this employment, he would return about nightfall with several coconut shells filled with different descriptions of kemp. In preparing these for us he manifested all the ostentation of a professed cook, although the chief mystery of the affair appeared to consist in pouring water in judicious quantities upon the slimy contents of his coconut shells.

The first time he submitted one of these saline salads to my critical attention I naturally thought that anything collected at such pains must possess peculiar merits; but one mouthful was a complete dose; and great was the consternation of the old warrior at the rapidity with which I ejected his epicurean treat.

How true it is, that the rarity of any particular article enhances its value amazingly. In some part of the valley—I know not where, but probably in the neighborhood of the sea —the girls were sometimes in the habit of procuring small quantities of salt, a thimbleful or so being the result of the united labors of a party of five or six employed for the greater part of the day. This precious commodity they brought to the house, enveloped in multitudinous folds of leaves; and as a special mark of the esteem in which they held me, would spread an immense leaf on the ground, and dropping one by one a few minute particles of the salt upon it, invite me to taste them.

From the extravagant value placed upon the article I verily believe, that with a bushel of common Liverpool salt all the real estate in Typee might have been purchased. With a small pinch of it in one hand, and a quarter section of a breadfruit in the other, the greatest chief in the valley would have laughed at all the luxuries of a Parisian table.

The celebrity of the breadfruit tree, and the conspicuous place it occupies in a Typee bill of fare, induces me to give at some length a general description of the tree, and the various modes in which the fruit is prepared.

The breadfruit tree, in its glorious prime, is a grand and towering object, forming the same feature in a Marquesan landscape that the patriarchal elm does in New England scenery. The latter tree it not a little resembles in height, in the wide spread of its stalwart branches, and in its venerable and imposing aspect.

The leaves of the breadfruit are of great size, and their edges are cut and scolloped as fantastically as those of a lady's collar. As they annually tend toward decay, they almost rival in the brilliant variety of their gradually changing hues the fleeting shades of the expiring dolphin. The autumnal tints of our American forests, glorious as they are, sink into nothing in comparison with this tree.

The leaf, in one particular stage, when nearly all the prismatic colors are blended on its surface, is often converted by the natives into a superb and striking headdress. The principal fibre traversing its length being split open a convenient distance, and the elastic sides of the aperture pressed apart, the head is inserted between them, the leaf drooping on one side, with its forward half turned jauntily up on the brows, and the remaining part spreading laterally behind the ears.

The fruit somewhat resembles in magnitude and general appearance one of our citron melons of ordinary size; but, unlike the citron, it has no sectional lines drawn along the outside. Its surface is dotted all over with little conical prominences, looking not unlike the knobs on an antiquated church door. The rind is perhaps an eighth of an inch in thickness; and denuded of this, at the time when it is in the greatest perfection, the fruit presents a beautiful globe of white pulp, the whole of which may be eaten, with the exception of a slender core, which is easily removed.

The breadfruit, however, is never used, and is indeed altogether unfit to be eaten, until submitted in one form or other to the action of fire.

The most simple manner in which this operation is performed, and, I think, the best, consists in placing any number of the freshly plucked fruit, when in a particular stage of greenness, among the embers of a fire, in the same way that you would roast a potato. After the lapse of ten or fifteen minutes, the green rind embrowns and cracks, showing through the fissures in its sides the milk-white interior. As soon as it cools, the rind drops off, and you then have the soft round pulp in its purest and most delicious state. Thus eaten, it has a mild and pleasing flavor.

Sometimes, after having been roasted in the fire, the natives snatch it briskly from the embers, and permitting it to slip out of the yielding rind into a vessel of cold water, stir up the mixture, which they call *bo-a-sho*. I never could endure this compound, and indeed the preparation is not greatly in vogue among the more polite Typees.

There is one form, however, in which the fruit is occasionally served, that renders it a dish fit for a king. As soon as it is taken from the fire the exterior is removed, the core extracted, and the remaining part is placed in a sort of shallow stone mortar, and briskly worked with a pestle of the same substance. While one person is performing this operation, another takes a ripe coconut, and breaking it in half, which they also do very cleverly, proceeds to grate the juicy meat into fine particles. This is done by means of a piece of mother-of-pearl shell, lashed firmly to the extreme end of a heavy stick, with its straight side accurately notched like a saw. The stick is sometimes a grotesquely formed limb of a tree, with three or four branches twisting from its body like so many shapeless legs, and sustaining it two or three feet from the ground.

The native, first placing a calabash beneath the nose, as it were, of his curious-looking log steed, for the purpose of receiving the grated fragments as they fall, mounts astride of it as if it were a hobbyhorse, and twirling the inside of one of his hemispheres of coconut around the sharp teeth of the mother-of-pearl shell, the pure white meat falls in snowy showers into the receptacle provided. Having obtained a quantity sufficient for his purpose, he places it in a bag made of the netlike fibrous substance attached to all coconut trees, and compressing it over the breadfruit, which, being now sufficiently pounded, is put into a wooden bowl—extracts a thick creamy milk. The delicious liquid soon bubbles round the fruit, and leaves it at last just peeping above its surface.

This preparation is called *kokoo*, and a most luscious preparation it is. The hobbyhorse and the pestle and mortar were in great requisition during the time I remained in the house of Marheyo, and Kory-Kory had frequent occasion to show his skill in their use.

But the great staple articles of food into which the breadfruit is converted by these natives are known respectively by the names of *amar* and *poee-poee.*

At a certain season of the year, when the fruit of the hundred groves of the valley has reached its maturity, and hangs in golden spheres from every branch, the islanders assemble in harvest groups, and garner in the abundance which surrounds them. The trees are stripped of their nodding burdens, which, easily freed from the rind and core, are gathered together in capacious wooden vessels, where the pulpy fruit is soon worked by a stone pestle, vigorously applied, into a blended mass of a doughy consistency, called by the natives *tutao.* This is then divided into separate parcels, which, after being made up into stout packages, enveloped in successive folds of leaves, and bound round with thongs of bark, are stored away in large receptacles hollowed in the earth, from whence they are drawn as occasion may require.

In this condition the *tutao* sometimes remains for years, and even is thought to improve by age. Before it is fit to be eaten, however, it has to undergo an additional process. A primitive oven is scooped in the ground, and its bottom being loosely covered with stones, a large fire is kindled within it. As soon as the requisite degree of heat is attained, the embers are removed, and the surface of the stones being covered with thick layers of leaves, one of the larger packages of *tutao* is deposited upon them, and overspread with another layer of leaves. The whole is then quickly heaped up with earth, and forms a sloping mound.

The *tutao* thus baked is called *amar;* the action of the oven having converted it into an amber-colored caky substance, a little tart, but not at all disagreeable to the taste.

By another and final process the *amar* is changed into *poee-poee.* This transition is rapidly effected. The *amar* is placed in a vessel, and mixed with water until it gains a proper puddinglike consistency, when, without further preparation, it is in readiness for use. This is the form in which the *tutao* is generally consumed. The singular mode of eating it I have already described.

Were it not that the breadfruit is thus capable of being preserved for a length of time, the natives might be reduced to a state of starvation; for owing to some unknown cause the trees sometimes fail to bear fruit; and on such occasions the islanders chiefly depend upon the supplies they have been enabled to store away.

This stately tree, which is rarely met with upon the Sandwich Islands, and then only of a very inferior quality, and at Tahiti, does not abound to a degree that renders its fruit the principal article of food, attains its greatest excellence in the genial climate of the Marquesan group, where it grows to an enormous magnitude, and flourishes in the utmost abundance.

XVI

Melancholy condition—occurrence at the Ti—anecdote of Marheyo—shaving the head of a warrior.

IN LOOKING BACK to this period, and calling to remembrance the numberless proofs of kindness and respect which I received from the natives of the valley, I can scarcely understand how it was that, in the midst of so many consolatory circumstances, my mind should still have been consumed by the most dismal forebodings, and have remained a prey to the profoundest melancholy. It is true that the suspicious circumstances which had attended the disappearance of Toby were enough of themselves to excite distrust with regard to the savages, in whose power I felt myself to be entirely placed, especially when it was combined with the knowledge that these very men, kind and respectful as they were to me, were, after all, nothing better than a set of cannibals.

But my chief source of anxiety, and that which poisoned

every temporary enjoyment, was the mysterious disease in my leg, which still remained unabated. All the herbal applications of Tinor, united with the severer discipline of the old leech, and the affectionate nursing of Kory-Kory, had failed to relieve me. I was almost a cripple, and the pain I endured at intervals was agonizing. The unaccountable malady showed no signs of amendment; on the contrary, its violence increased day by day, and threatened the most fatal results, unless some powerful means were employed to counteract it. It seemed as if I were destined to sink under this grievous affliction, or at least that it would hinder me from availing myself of any opportunity of escaping from the valley.

An incident which occurred as nearly as I can estimate about three weeks after the disappearance of Toby, convinced me that the natives, from some reason or other, would interpose every possible obstacle to my leaving them.

One morning there was no little excitement evinced by the people near my abode, and which I soon discovered proceeded from a vague report that boats had been seen at a great distance approaching the bay. Immediately all was bustle and animation. It so happened that day that the pain I suffered having somewhat abated, and feeling in much better spirits than usual, I had complied with Kory-Kory's invitation to visit the chief Mehevi at the place called the Ti, which I have before described as being situated within the precincts of the Taboo Groves. These sacred recesses were at no great distance from Marheyo's habitation, and lay between it and the sea; the path that conducted to the beach passing directly in front of the Ti, and thence skirting along the border of the groves.

I was reposing upon the mats, within the sacred building, in company with Mehevi and several other chiefs, when the announcement was first made. It sent a thrill of joy through my whole frame;—perhaps Toby was about to return. I rose at once to my feet, and my instinctive impulse was to hurry down to the beach, equally regardless of the distance that separated me from it and of my disabled condition. As soon as Mehevi noticed the effect the intelligence had produced upon me, and the impatience I betrayed to reach the sea, his countenance assumed that inflexible rigidity of expression which had so awed me on the afternoon of our arrival at the house of Marheyo. As I was proceeding to leave the Ti, he laid his hand upon my shoulder, and said gravely, *'abo, abo'* (wait, wait). Solely intent upon the one thought that occupied my mind, and heedless of his request, I was brushing past him, when suddenly he assumed a tone of authority, and told me to *moee* (sit down). Though struck by the alteration in his demeanor, the excitement under which I labored was too strong to permit me to obey the unexpected command, and I was still limping toward the edge of the *pi-pi* with Kory-Kory clinging to one arm in his efforts to restrain me, when the natives around starting to their feet, ranged themselves along the open front of the building, while Mehevi looked at me scowlingly, and reiterated his commands still more sternly.

It was at this moment, when fifty savage countenances were glaring upon me, that I first truly experienced I was indeed a captive in the valley. The conviction rushed upon me with staggering force, and I was overwhelmed by this confirmation of my worst fears. I saw at once that it was useless for me to resist, and sick at heart, I reseated myself upon the mats, and for the moment abandoned myself to despair.

I now perceived the natives one after the other hurrying past the Ti and pursuing the route that conducted to the sea. These savages, thought I, will soon be holding communication with some of my own countrymen perhaps, who with ease could restore me to liberty did they know of the situation I was in. No language can describe the wretchedness which I felt; and in the bitterness of my soul I imprecated a thousand curses on the perfidious Toby, who had thus abandoned me to destruction. It was in vain that Kory-Kory tempted me with food, or lighted my pipe, or sought to attract my attention by performing the uncouth antics that had sometimes diverted me. I was fairly knocked down by this last misfortune, which, much as I had feared it, I had never before had the courage calmly to contemplate.

Regardless of every thing but my own sorrow, I remained

in the Ti for several hours, until shouts proceeding at intervals from the groves beyond the house proclaimed the return of the natives from the beach.

Whether any boats visited the bay that morning or not, I never could ascertain. The savages assured me that there had not—but I was inclined to believe that by deceiving me in this particular they sought to allay the violence of my grief. However that might be, this incident showed plainly that the Typees intended to hold me a prisoner. As they still treated me with the same sedulous attention as before, I was utterly at a loss how to account for their singular conduct. Had I been in a situation to instruct them in any of the rudiments of the mechanic arts, or had I manifested a disposition to render myself in any way useful among them, their conduct might have been attributed to some adequate motive, but as it was, the matter seemed to me inexplicable.

During my whole stay on the island there occurred but two or three instances where the natives applied to me with the view of availing themselves of my superior information. And these now appear so ludicrous that I cannot forbear relating them.

The few things we had brought from Nukuheva had been done up into a small bundle which we had carried with us in our descent to the valley. This bundle, the first night of our arrival, I had used as a pillow, but on the succeeding morning, opening it for the inspection of the natives, they gazed upon the miscellaneous contents as though I had just revealed to them a casket of diamonds, and they insisted that so precious a treasure should be properly secured. A line was accordingly attached to it, and the other end being passed over the ridge-pole of the house, it was hoisted up to the apex of the roof, where it hung suspended directly over the mats where I usually reclined. When I desired anything from it I merely raised my finger to a bamboo beside me, and taking hold of the string which was there fastened, lowered the package. This was exceedingly handy, and I took care to let the natives understand how much I applauded the invention. Of this package the chief contents were a razor with its case, a supply of needles and thread, a pound or two of tobacco, and a few yards of a bright-colored calico.

I should have mentioned that shortly after Toby's disappearance, perceiving the uncertainty of the time I might be obliged to remain in the valley—if, indeed, I ever should escape from it—and considering that my whole wardrobe consisted of a shirt and a pair of trousers, I resolved to doff these garments at once, in order to preserve them in a suitable condition for wear should I again appear among civilized beings. I was consequently obliged to assume the Typee costume, a little altered, however, to suit my own views of propriety, and in which I have no doubt I appeared to as much advantage as a senator of Rome enveloped in the folds of his toga. A few folds of yellow tappa tucked about my waist, descended to my feet in the style of a lady's petticoat, only I did not have recourse to those voluminous paddings in the rear with which our gentle dames are in the habit of augmenting the sublime rotundity of their figures. This usually comprised my indoor dress: whenever I walked out, I superadded to it an ample robe of the same material, which completely enveloped my person, and screened it from the rays of the sun.

One morning I made a rent in this mantle; and to show the islanders with what facility it could be repaired, I lowered my bundle, and taking from it a needle and thread, proceeded to stitch up the opening. They regarded this wonderful application of science with intense admiration; and whilst I was stitching away, Marheyo, who was one of the lookers-on, suddenly clapped his hand to his forehead, and rushing to a corner of the house, drew forth a soiled and tattered strip of faded calico—which he must have procured some time or other in traffic on the beach—and besought me eagerly to exercise a little of my art upon it. I willingly complied, though certainly so stumpy a needle as mine never took such gigantic strides over calico before. The repairs completed, old Marheyo gave me a paternal hug; and divesting himself of his *maro* (girdle), swathed the calico about his loins, and slipping the beloved ornaments into his ears, grasped his spear and sallied out of the house, like a valiant Templar arrayed in a new and costly suit of armor.

I never used my razor during my stay in the island, but, although a very subordinate affair, it had been vastly admired by the Typees; and Narmonee, a great hero among them, who was exceedingly precise in the arrangements of his toilet and the general adjustment of his person, being the most accurately tattooed and laboriously horrified individual in all the valley, thought it would be a great advantage to have it applied to the already shaven crown of his head.

The implement they usually employ is a shark's tooth, which is about as well adapted to the purpose as a one-pronged fork for pitching hay. No wonder, then, that the acute Narmonee perceived the advantage my razor possessed over the usual implement. Accordingly, one day he requested as a personal favor that I would just run over his head with the razor. In reply, I gave him to understand that it was too dull, and could not be used to any purpose without being previously sharpened. To assist my meaning, I went through an imaginary honing process on the palm of my hand. Narmonee took my meaning in an instant, and running out of the house, returned the next moment with a huge rough mass of rock as big as a milestone, and indicated to me that that was exactly the thing I wanted. Of course there was nothing left for me but to proceed to business, and I began scraping away at a great rate. He writhed and wriggled under the infliction, but, fully convinced of my skill, endured the pain like a martyr.

Though I never saw Narmonee in battle, I will, from what I then observed, stake my life upon his courage and fortitude. Before commencing operations, his head had presented a surface of short bristling hairs, and by the time I had concluded my unskilful operation it resembled not a little a stubble field after being gone over with a harrow. However, as the chief expressed the liveliest satisfaction at the result, I was too wise to dissent from his opinion.

XVII

Improvement in health and spirits—felicity of the
Typees—their enjoyments compared with those of
more enlightened communities—comparative wickedness of civilized and unenlightened people—a
skirmish in the mountain with the
warriors of Happar.

DAY AFTER DAY wore on, and still there was no perceptible
change in the conduct of the islanders toward me. Gradually
I lost all knowledge of the regular occurrence of the days of
the week, and sunk insensibly into that kind of apathy which
ensues after some violent outbreak of despair. My limb suddenly healed, the swelling went down, the pain subsided,
and I had every reason to suppose I should soon completely
recover from the affliction that had so long tormented me.

As soon as I was enabled to ramble about the valley in
company with the natives, troops of whom followed me whenever I sallied out of the house, I began to experience an
elasticity of mind which placed me beyond the reach of those
dismal forebodings to which I had so lately been a prey.
Received wherever I went with the most deferential kindness;
regaled perpetually with the most delightful fruits; ministered
to by dark-eyed nymphs; and enjoying besides all the services
of the devoted Kory-Kory, I thought that for a sojourn among
cannibals, no man could have well made a more agreeable
one.

To be sure there were limits set to my wanderings. Toward
the sea my progress was barred by an express prohibition of
the savages; and after having made two or three ineffectual
attempts to reach it, as much to gratify my curiosity as anything else, I gave up the idea. It was in vain to think of
reaching it by stealth, since the natives escorted me in numbers

wherever I went, and not for one single moment that I can recall to mind was I ever permitted to be alone.

The green and precipitous elevations that stood ranged around the head of the vale where Marheyo's habitation was situated effectually precluded all hope of escape in that quarter, even if I could have stolen away from the thousand eyes of the savages.

But these reflections now seldom obtruded upon me; I gave myself up to the passing hour, and if ever disagreeable thoughts arose in my mind, I drove them away. When I looked around the verdant recess in which I was buried, and gazed up to the summits of the lofty eminence that hemmed me in, I was well disposed to think that I was in the Happy Valley, and that beyond those heights there was naught but a world of care and anxiety.

As I extended my wanderings in the valley and grew more familiar with the habits of its inmates, I was fain to confess that, despite the disadvantages of his condition, the Polynesian savage, surrounded by all the luxurious provisions of nature, enjoyed an infinitely happier, though certainly a less intellectual existence, than the self-complacent European.

The naked wretch who shivers beneath the bleak skies, and starves among the inhospitable wilds of Tierra del Fuego, might indeed be made happier by civilization, for it would alleviate his physical wants. But the voluptuous Indian, with every desire supplied, whom Providence has bountifully provided with all the sources of pure and natural enjoyment, and from whom are removed so many of the ills and pains of life—what has he to desire at the hands of Civilization? She may 'cultivate his mind,' may 'elevate his thoughts'—these I believe are the established phrases—but will he be the happier? Let the once smiling and populous Hawaiian Islands, with their now diseased, starving, and dying natives, answer the question. The missionaries may seek to disguise the matter as they will, but the facts are incontrovertible; and the devoutest Christian who visits that group with an unbiased mind, must go away mournfully asking—'Are these, alas! the fruits of twenty-five years of enlightening?'

In a primitive state of society, the enjoyments of life, though few and simple, are spread over a great extent, and are unalloyed; but Civilization, for every advantage she imparts, holds a hundred evils in reserve—the heart burnings, the jealousies, the social rivalries, the family dissensions, and the thousand self-inflicted discomforts of refined life, which make up in units the swelling aggregate of human misery, are unknown among these unsophisticated people.

But it will be urged that these shocking unprincipled wretches are cannibals. Very true; and a rather bad trait in their character it must be allowed. But they are such only when they seek to gratify the passion of revenge upon their enemies; and I ask whether the mere eating of human flesh so very far exceeds in barbarity that custom which only a few years since was practised in enlightened England—a convicted traitor, perhaps a man found guilty of honesty, patriotism, and suchlike heinous crimes, had his head lopped off with a huge axe, his bowels dragged out and thrown into a fire; while his body, carved into four quarters, was with his head exposed upon pikes, and permitted to rot and fester among the public haunts of men!

The fiendlike skill we display in the invention of all manner of death-dealing engines, the vindictiveness with which we carry on our wars, and the misery and desolation that follow in their train, are enough of themselves to distinguish the white civilized man as the most ferocious animal on the face of the earth.

His remorseless cruelty is seen in many of the institutions of our own favored land. There is one in particular lately adopted in one of the States of the Union, which purports to have been dictated by the most merciful considerations. To destroy our malefactors piecemeal, drying up in their veins, drop by drop, the blood we are too chickenhearted to shed by a single blow which would at once put a period to their sufferings, is deemed to be infinitely preferable to the old-fashioned punishment of gibbeting—much less annoying to the victim, and more in accordance with the refined spirit of the age; and yet how feeble is all language to describe the horrors we inflict upon these wretches, whom we mason up in the cells of our prisons, and condemn to perpetual solitude in the very heart of our population!

But it is needless to multiply the examples of civilized barbarity; they far exceed in the amount of misery they cause the crimes which we regard with such abhorrence in our less enlightened fellow creatures.

The term 'Savage' is, I conceive, often misapplied, and indeed when I consider the vices, cruelties, and enormities of every kind that spring up in the tainted atmosphere of a feverish civilization, I am inclined to think that so far as the relative wickedness of the parties is concerned, four or five Marquesan islanders sent to the United States as missionaries might be quite as useful as an equal number of Americans dispatched to the Islands in a similar capacity.

I once heard it given as an instance of the frightful depravity of a certain tribe in the Pacific, that they had no word in their language to express the idea of virtue. The assertion was unfounded; but were it otherwise, it might be met by stating that their language is almost entirely destitute of terms to express the delightful ideas conveyed by our endless catalogue of civilized crimes.

In the altered frame of mind to which I have referred, every object that presented itself to my notice in the valley struck me in a new light, and the opportunities I now enjoyed of observing the manners of its inmates, tended to strengthen my favorable impressions. One peculiarity that fixed my admiration was the perpetual hilarity reigning through the whole extent of the vale. There seemed to be no cares, griefs, troubles, or vexations in all Typee. The hours tripped along as gaily as the laughing couples down a country dance.

There were none of those thousand sources of irritation that the ingenuity of civilized man has created to mar his own felicity. There were no foreclosures of mortgages, no protested notes, no bills payable, no debts of honor in Typee; no unreasonable tailors and shoemakers, perversely bent on being paid; no duns of any description; no assault and battery attorneys, to foment discord, backing their clients up to a quarrel, and then knocking their heads together; no poor relations, everlastingly occupying the spare bedchamber, and diminishing the elbow room at the family table; no destitute widows with their children starving on the cold charities of the world; no beggars; no debtors' prisons; no proud and hardhearted nabobs in Typee; or to sum up all in one word —no Money! That root of all evil was not to be found in the valley.

In this secluded abode of happiness there were no cross old women, no cruel stepdames, no withered spinsters, no love-sick maidens, no sour old bachelors, no inattentive husbands, no melancholy young men, no blubbering youngsters, and no squalling brats. All was mirth, fun, and high good humor. Blue devils, hypochondria, and doleful dumps, went and hid themselves among the nooks and crannies of the rocks.

Here you would see a parcel of children frolicking together the livelong day, and no quarreling, no contention, among them. The same number in our own land could not have played together for the space of an hour without biting or scratching one another. There you might have seen a throng of young females, not filled with envyings of each other's charms, nor displaying the ridiculous affectations of gentility, nor yet moving in whalebone corsets, like so many automatons, but free, inartificially happy, and unconstrained.

There were some spots in that sunny vale where they would frequently resort to decorate themselves with garlands of flowers. To have seen them reclining beneath the shadows of one of the beautiful groves; the ground about them strewn with freshly gathered buds and blossoms, employed in weaving chaplets and necklaces, one would have thought that all the train of Flora had gathered together to keep a festival in honor of their mistress.

With the young men there seemed almost always some matter of diversion or business on hand that afforded a constant variety of enjoyment. But whether fishing, or carving canoes, or polishing their ornaments, never was there exhibited the least sign of strife or contention among them.

As for the warriors, they maintained a tranquil dignity of demeanor, journeying occasionally from house to house, where they were always sure to be received with the attention bestowed upon distinguished guests. The old men, of whom there were many in the vale, seldom stirred from their mats, where they would recline for hours and hours, smoking and talking to one another with all the garrulity of age.

But the continual happiness, which so far as I was able to judge appeared to prevail in the valley, sprung principally from that all-pervading sensation which Rousseau has told us he at one time experienced, the mere buoyant sense of a healthful physical existence. And indeed in this particular the Typees had ample reason to felicitate themselves, for sickness was almost unknown. During the whole period of my stay I saw but one invalid among them; and on their smooth clear skins you observed no blemish or mark of disease.

The general repose, however, upon which I have just been descanting, was broken in upon about this time by an event which proved that the islanders were not entirely exempt from those occurrences which disturb the quiet of more civilized communities.

Having now been a considerable time in the valley I began to feel surprised that the violent hostility, subsisting between its inhabitants, and those of the adjoining bay of Happar, should never have manifested itself in any warlike encounter. Although the valiant Typees would often by gesticulations declare their undying hatred against their enemies, and the disgust they felt at their cannibal propensities; although they dilated upon the manifold injuries they had received at their hands, yet with a forbearance truly commendable, they appeared patiently to sit down under their grievances, and to refrain from making any reprisals. The Happars, entrenched behind their mountains, and never even showing themselves on their summits, did not appear to me to furnish adequate cause for that excess of animosity evinced toward them by the heroic tenants of our vale, and I was inclined to believe that the deeds of blood attributed to them had been greatly exaggerated.

On the other hand, as the clamors of war had not up to this period disturbed the serenity of the tribe, I began to distrust the truth of those reports which ascribed so fierce and belligerent a character to the Typee nation. Sure', thought I, all these terrible stories I have heard about the inveteracy with which they carried on the feud, their deadly intensity of hatred, and the diabolical malice with which they glutted their revenge upon the inanimate forms of the slain, are nothing more than fables, and I must confess that I experienced something like a sense of regret at having my hideous anticipations thus disappointed. I felt in some sort like a 'prentice-boy who, going to the play in the expectation of being delighted with a cut-and-thrust tragedy, is almost moved to tears of disappointment at the exhibition of a genteel comedy.

I could not avoid thinking that I had fallen in with a greatly traduced people, and I moralized not a little upon the disadvantage of having a bad name, which in this instance had given a tribe of savages, who were as pacific as so many lambkins, the reputation of a confederacy of giant-killers.

But subsequent events proved that I had been a little too premature in coming to this conclusion. One day about noon, happening to be at the Ti, I had lain down on the mats with several of the chiefs, and had gradually sunk into a most luxurious siesta, when I was awakened by a tremendous outcry, and starting up beheld the natives seizing their spears and hurrying out, while the most puissant of the chiefs, grasping the six muskets which were ranged against the bamboos, followed after, and soon disappeared in the groves. These movements were accompanied by wild shouts, in which 'Happar, Happar,' greatly predominated. The islanders were now to be seen running past the Ti, and striking across the valley to the Happar side. Presently I heard the sharp report of a musket from the adjoining hills, and then a burst of voices in the same direction. At this the women, who had congregated in the groves, set up the most violent clamors, as they invariably do here as elsewhere on every occasion of excitement and alarm, with a view of tranquilizing their own minds and disturbing other people. On this particular occasion they made such an outrageous noise, and continued it with such perseverance, that for awhile, had entire volleys of musketry been fired off in the neighboring mountains, I should not have been able to have heard them.

When this female commotion had a little subsided I listened eagerly for further information. At last bang went another shot, and then a second volley of yells from the hills. Again all was quiet, and continued so for such a length of time that I began to think the contending armies had agreed upon a suspension of hostilities; when pop went a third gun, followed as before with a yell. After this, for nearly two hours nothing occurred worthy of comment, save some straggling shouts from the hillside, sounding like the halloos of a parcel of truant boys who had lost themselves in the woods.

During this interval I had remained standing on the piazza of the Ti, which directly fronted the Happar mountain, and with no one near me but Kory-Kory and the old superannuated savages I have before described. These latter never stirred from their mats, and seemed altogether unconscious that anything unusual was going on.

As for Kory-Kory, he appeared to think that we were in the midst of great events, and sought most zealously to impress me with a due sense of their importance. Every sound that reached us conveyed some momentous item of intelligence to him. At such times, as if he were gifted with second sight, he would go through a variety of pantomimic illustrations, showing me the precise manner in which the redoubtable Typees were at that very moment chastising the insolence of the enemy. *'Mehevi hanna pippee nuee Happar,'* he exclaimed every five minutes, giving me to understand that under that distinguished captain the warriors of his nation were performing prodigies of valor.

Having heard only four reports from the muskets I was led to believe that they were worked by the islanders in the same manner as the Sultan Solyman's ponderous artillery at the siege of Byzantium, one of them taking an hour or two to load and train. At last, no sound whatever proceeding from the mountains, I concluded that the contest had been determined one way or the other. Such appeared, indeed, to be the case, for in a little while a courier arrived at the Ti, almost breathless with his exertions, and communicated the news of a great victory having been achieved by his country-men: *'Happar poo arva!—Happar poo arva!'* (the cowards had fled). Kory-Kory was in ecstasies, and commenced a vehement harangue, which, so far as I understood it, implied that the result exactly agreed with his expectations, and which, moreover, was intended to convince me that it would be a perfectly useless undertaking, even for an army of fire-eaters, to offer battle to the irresistible heroes of our valley. In all this I of course acquiesced, and looked forward with no little interest to the return of the conquerors, whose victory I feared might not have been purchased without cost to themselves.

But here I was again mistaken; for Mehevi, in conducting his warlike operations, rather inclined to the Fabian than to the Bonapartean tactics, husbanding his resources and expos-ing his troops to no unnecessary hazards. The total loss of the victors in this obstinately contested affair was, in killed, wounded, and missing—one forefinger and part of a thumb-nail (which the late proprietor brought along with him in his hand), a severely contused arm, and a considerable effu-sion of blood flowing from the thigh of a chief, who had re-ceived an ugly thrust from a Happar spear. What the enemy had suffered I could not discover, but I presume they had succeeded in taking off with them the bodies of their slain.

Such was the issue of the battle, as far as its results came under my observation; and as it appeared to be considered an event of prodigious importance, I reasonably concluded that the wars of the natives were marked by no very sangui-nary traits. I afterward learned how the skirmish had origin-ated. A number of the Happars had been discovered prowling for no good purpose on the Typee side of the mountain; the alarm was sounded, and the invaders, after a protracted resistance, had been chased over the frontier. But why had not the intrepid Mehevi carried the war into Happar? Why had he not made a descent into the hostile vale, and brought away some trophy of his victory—some materials for the cannibal entertainment which I had heard usually terminated every engagement? After all, I was much inclined to believe that such shocking festivals must occur very rarely among the islanders, if, indeed, they ever take place.

For two or three days the late event was the theme of general comment; after which the excitement gradually wore away, and the valley resumed its accustomed tranquility.

XVIII

Swimming in company with the girls of the valley—
a canoe—effects on the taboo—a pleasure excursion
on the pond—beautiful freak of Fayaway—mantua-
making—a stranger arrives in the valley—his mysterious conduct—native oratory—the interview—
its results—departure of the stranger.

RETURNING HEALTH and peace of mind gave a new interest to everything around me. I sought to diversify my time by as many enjoyments as lay within reach. Bathing in company with troops of girls formed one of my chief amusements. We sometimes enjoyed the recreation in the waters of a miniature lake, into which the central stream of the valley expanded. This lovely sheet of water was almost circular in figure, and about three hundred yards across. Its beauty was indescribable. All around its banks waved luxuriant masses of tropical foliage, soaring high above which were to be seen here and there, the symmetrical shaft of the coconut tree, sur- mounted by its tuft of graceful branches, drooping in the air like so many waving ostrich plumes.

The ease and grace with which the maidens of the valley propelled themselves through the water, and their familiarity with the element, were truly astonishing. Sometimes they might be seen gliding along just under the surface, without apparently moving hand or foot—then throwing themselves on their sides, they darted through the water, revealing glimpses of their forms, as, in the course of their rapid progress, they shot for an instant partly into the air—at one moment they dived deep down into the water and the next they rose bounding to the surface.

I remember upon one occasion plunging in among a parcel of these river nymphs, and counting vainly upon my superior strength, sought to drag some of them under the water, but I quickly repented my temerity. The amphibious young creatures swarmed about me like a shoal of dolphins, and seizing hold of my devoted limbs, tumbled me about and ducked me under the surface, until from the strange noises which rang in my ears, and the supernatural visions dancing before my eyes, I thought I was in the land of spirits. I stood indeed as little chance among them as a cumbrous whale attacked on all sides by a legion of swordfish. When at length they relinquished their hold of me, they swam away in every direction, laughing at my clumsy endeavors to reach them.

There was no boat on the lake; but at my solicitation and for my special use, some of the young men attached to Marheyo's household, under the direction of the indefatigable Kory-Kory, brought up a light and tastefully carved canoe from the sea. It was launched upon the sheet of water, and floated there as gracefully as a swan. But, melancholy to relate, it produced an effect I had not anticipated. The sweet nymphs, who had sported with me before in the lake, now all fled its vicinity. The prohibited craft, guarded by the edicts of the taboo, extended the prohibition to the waters in which it lay.

For a few days, Kory-Kory, with one or two other youths, accompanied me in my excursions to the lake, and while I paddled about in my light canoe, would swim after me shouting and gamboling in pursuit. But I was ever partial to what is termed in the *Young Men's Own Book*—'the society of virtuous and intelligent young ladies;' and in the absence of the mermaids, the amusement became dull and insipid. One morning I expressed to my faithful servitor my desire for the return of the nymphs. The honest fellow looked at me bewildered for a moment, and then shook his head solemnly, and murmured 'Taboo! taboo!' giving me to understand that unless the canoe was removed, I could not expect to have the young ladies back again. But to this procedure I was averse; I not only wanted the canoe to stay where it was, but I wanted the beauteous Fayaway to get into it, and paddle with me about the lake. This latter proposition completely horrified Kory-Kory's notions of propriety. He inveighed against it, as something too monstrous to be thought of. It not only shocked their established notions of propriety, but was at variance with all their religious ordinances.

However, although the taboo was a ticklish thing to meddle with, I determined to test its capabilities of resisting an attack. I consulted the chief Mehevi, who endeavored to dissuade me from my object: but I was not to be repulsed; and accordingly increased the warmth of my solicitations. At last he entered into a long, and I have no doubt a very learned and eloquent, exposition of the history and nature of the taboo as affecting this particular case; employing a variety of most extraordinary words, which, from their amazing length and sonorousness, I have every reason to believe were of a theological nature. But all that he said failed to convince me: partly, perhaps, because I could not comprehend a word that he uttered; but chiefly, that for the life of me I could not understand why a woman should not have as much right to enter a canoe as a man. At last he became a little more rational, and intimated that, out of the abundant love he bore me, he would consult with the priests and see what could be done.

How it was that the priesthood of Typee satisfied the affair with their consciences, I know not; but so it was, and Fayaway's dispensation from this portion of the taboo was at length procured. Such an event I believe never before had occurred in the valley; but it was high time the islanders should be taught a little gallantry, and I trust that the example I set them may produce beneficial effects. Ridiculous, indeed, that the lovely creatures should be obliged to paddle about in the water, like so many ducks, while a parcel of great strapping fellows skimmed over its surface in their canoes.

The first day after Fayaway's emancipation I had a delightful little party on the lake—the damsel, Kory-Kory, and myself. My zealous body servant brought from the house a calabash of *poee-poee,* half a dozen young coconuts—stripped of their husks—three pipes, as many yams, and me on his back a part of the way. Something of a load; but Kory-Kory was a very strong man for his size, and by no means brittle in the spine. We had a very pleasant day; my trusty valet plied the paddle and swept us gently along the margin of the water, beneath the shades of the overhanging thickets. Fayaway and I reclined in the stern of the canoe, on the very best terms possible with one another; the gentle nymph occasionally placing her pipe to her lip, and exhaling the mild fumes of the tobacco, to which her rosy breath added a fresh perfume. Strange as it may seem, there is nothing in which a young and beautiful female appears to more advantage than in the act of smoking. How captivating is a Peruvian lady, swinging in her gaily woven hammock of grass, extended between two orange trees, and inhaling the fragrance of a choice cigarro! But Fayaway, holding in her delicately formed olive hand the long yellow reed of her pipe, with its quaintly carved bowl, and every few moments languishingly giving forth light wreaths of vapor from her mouth and nostrils, looked still more engaging.

We floated about thus for several hours, when I looked up to the warm, glowing, tropical sky, and then down into the transparent depths below; and when my eye, wandering from the bewitching scenery around, fell upon the grotesquely tattooed form of Kory-Kory, and finally encountered the pensive gaze of Fayaway, I thought I had been transported to some fairy region, so unreal did everything appear.

This lovely piece of water was the coolest spot in all the valley, and I now made it a place of continual resort during the hottest period of the day. One side of it lay near the termination of a long, gradually expanding gorge, which mounted to the heights that environed the vale. The strong trade wind, met in its course by these elevations, circled and eddied about their summits, and was sometimes driven down the steep ravine and swept across the valley, ruffling in its passage the otherwise tranquil surface of the lake.

One day, after we had been paddling about for some time, I disembarked Kory-Kory, and paddled the canoe to the windward side of the lake. As I turned the canoe, Fayaway, who was with me, seemed all at once to be struck with some happy idea. With a wild exclamation of delight, she disengaged from her person the ample robe of tappa which was knotted over her shoulder (for the purpose of shielding her from the sun), and spreading it out like a sail, stood erect with upraised arms in the head of the canoe. We American sailors pride ourselves upon our straight clean spars, but a prettier little mast than Fayaway made was never shipped aboard of any craft.

In a moment the tappa was distended by the breeze— the long brown tresses of Fayaway streamed in the air—and the canoe glided rapidly through the water, and shot toward the shore. Seated in the stern, I directed its course with my paddle until it dashed up the soft sloping bank, and Fayaway, with a light spring, alighted on the ground; whilst Kory-Kory, who had watched our maneuvers with admiration, now clapped his hands in transport, and shouted like a madman. Many a time afterward was this feat repeated.

If the reader have not observed ere this that I was the declared admirer of Miss Fayaway, all I can say is that he is little conversant with affairs of the heart, and I certainly shall not trouble myself to enlighten him any farther. Out of the calico I had brought from the ship I made a dress for this lovely girl. In it she looked, I must confess, something like an opera dancer. The drapery of the latter damsel generally commences a little above the elbows, but my island beauty's began at the waist, and terminated sufficiently far above the ground to reveal the most bewitching ankle in the universe.

The day that Fayaway first wore this robe was rendered memorable by a new acquaintance being introduced to me. In the afternoon I was lying in the house, when I heard a great uproar outside; but being by this time pretty well accustomed

to the wild halloos which were almost continually ringing
through the valley, I paid little attention to it, until old Marheyo, under the influence of some strange excitement, rushed
into my presence and communicated the astounding tidings,
'*Marnoo pemi!*' which being interpreted, implied than an individual by the name of Marnoo was approaching. My worthy
old friend evidently expected that this intelligence would produce a great effect upon me, and for a time he stood earnestly
regarding me, as if curious to see how I should conduct myself, but as I remained perfectly unmoved, the old gentleman
darted out of the house again, in as great a hurry as he had
entered it.

'Marnoo, Marnoo,' cogitated I, 'I have never heard that
name before. Some distinguished character, I presume, from
the prodigious riot the natives are making'; the tumultuous
noise drawing nearer and nearer every moment, while 'Marnoo!—Marnoo!' was shouted by every tongue.

I made up my mind that some savage warrior of consequence, who had not yet enjoyed the honor of an audience,
was desirous of paying his respects on the present occasion.
So vain had I become by the lavish attention to which I had
been accustomed that I felt half inclined, as a punishment
for such neglect, to give this Marnoo a cold reception, when
the excited throng came within view, convoying one of the
most striking specimens of humanity that I ever beheld.

The stranger could not have been more than twenty-five
years of age, and was a little above the ordinary height; had
he been a single hair's-breadth taller, the matchless symmetry
of his form would have been destroyed. His unclad limbs were
beautifully formed; whilst the elegant outline of his figure,
together with his beardless cheeks, might have entitled him
to the distinction of standing for the statue of the Polynesian
Apollo; and indeed the oval of his countenance and the reg-
ularity of every feature reminded me of an antique bust. But
the marble repose of art was supplied by a warmth and live-
liness of expression only to be seen in the South Sea islander
under the most favorable developments of nature. The hair
of Marnoo was a rich curling brown, and twined about his

temples and neck in little close curling ringlets, which danced up and down continually when he was animated in conversation. His cheek was of a feminine softness, and his face was free from the least blemish of tattooing, although the rest of his body was drawn all over with fanciful figures, which—unlike the unconnected sketching usual among these natives—appeared to have been executed in conformity with some general design.

The tattooing on his back in particular attracted my attention. The artist employed must indeed have excelled in his profession. Traced along the course of the spine was accurately delineated the slender, tapering, and diamond-checkered shaft of the beautiful *artu* tree. Branching from the stem on either side, and disposed alternately, were the graceful branches drooping with leaves all correctly drawn, and elaborately finished. Indeed, this piece of tattooing was the best specimen of the Fine Arts I had yet seen in Typee. A rear view of the stranger might have suggested the idea of a spreading vine tacked against a garden wall. Upon his breast, arms, and legs, were exhibited an infinite variety of figures; every one of which, however, appeared to have reference to the general effect sought to be produced. The tattooing I have described was of the brightest blue, and when contrasted with the light olive color of the skin, produced an unique and even elegant effect. A slight girdle of white tappa, scarcely two inches in width, but hanging before and behind in spreading tassels, composed the entire costume of the stranger.

He advanced surrounded by the islanders, carrying under one arm a small roll of the native cloth, and grasping in his other hand a long and richly decorated spear. His manner was that of a traveler conscious that he is approaching a comfortable stage in his journey. Every moment he turned good-humoredly to the throng around him, and gave some dashing sort of reply to their incessant queries, which appeared to convulse them with uncontrollable mirth.

Struck by his demeanor, and the peculiarity of his appearance, so unlike that of the shaven-crowned and face-tattooed natives in general, I involuntarily rose as he entered the house, and proffered him a seat on the mats beside me. But without deigning to notice the civility, or even the more incontrovertible fact of my existence, the stranger passed on, utterly regardless of me, and flung himself upon the further end of the long couch that traversed the sole apartment of Marheyo's habitation.

Had the belle of the season, in the pride of her beauty and power, been cut in a place of public resort by some supercilious exquisite, she could not have felt greater indignation than I did at this unexpected slight.

I was thrown into utter astonishment. The conduct of the savages had prepared me to anticipate from every newcomer the same extravagant expressions of curiosity and regard. The singularity of his conduct, however, only roused my desire to discover who this remarkable personage might be, who now engrossed the attention of every one.

Tinor placed before him a calabash of *poee-poee*, from which the stranger regaled himself, alternating every mouthful with some rapid exclamation which was eagerly caught up and echoed by the crowd that completely filled the house. When I observed the striking devotion of the natives to him, and their temporary withdrawal of all attention from myself I felt not a little piqued. The glory of Tommo is departed, thought I, and the sooner he removes from the valley the better. These were my feelings at the moment, and they were prompted by that glorious principle inherent in all heroic natures—the strong-rooted determination to have the biggest share of the pudding or go without any of it.

Marnoo, this all-attractive personage, having satisfied his hunger, and inhaled a few whiffs from a pipe which was handed to him, launched out into an harangue which completely enchained the attention of his auditors.

Little as I understood of the language, yet from his animated gestures and the varying expression of his features—reflected as from so many mirrors in the countenances around him—I could easily discover the nature of those passions which he sought to arouse. From the frequent recurrence of the words 'Nukuheva' and 'Franee' (French), and some others with the meaning of which I was acquainted, he appeared to be rehearsing to his auditors events which had recently occurred in the neighboring bays. But how he had gained the knowledge of these matters I could not understand, unless it were that he had just come from Nukuheva—a supposition which his travel-stained appearance not a little supported. But, if a native of that region, I could not account for his friendly reception at the hands of the Typees.

Never, certainly, had I beheld so powerful an exhibition of natural eloquence as Marnoo displayed during the course of his oration. The grace of the attitudes into which he threw his flexible figure, the striking gestures of his naked arms, and above all, the fire which shot from his brilliant eyes, imparted an effect to the continually changing accents of his voice, of which the most accomplished orator might have been proud. At one moment reclining sideways upon the mat, and leaning calmly upon his bended arm, he related circumstantially the aggressions of the French—their hostile visits to the surrounding bays, enumerating each one in succession—Happar, Puerka, Nukuheva, Tior—and then, starting to his feet and precipitating himself forward with clenched hands and a countenance distorted with passion, he poured out a tide of invectives. Falling back into an attitude of lofty command, he exhorted the Typees to resist these encroachments; reminding them, with a fierce glance of exultation, that as yet the terror of their name had preserved them from attack, and with a scornful sneer he sketched in ironical terms the wondrous intrepidity of the French, who, with five war canoes and hundreds of men, had not dared to assail the naked warriors of their valley.

The effect he produced upon his audience was electric; one and all they stood regarding him with sparkling eyes and trembling limbs, as though they were listening to the inspired voice of a prophet.

But it soon appeared that Marnoo's powers were as versatile as they were extraordinary. As soon as he had finished this vehement harangue, he threw himself again upon the mats, and, singling out individuals in the crowd, addressed them by name, in a sort of bantering style, the humor of which, though nearly hidden from me, filled the whole assembly with uproarious delight.

He had a word for everybody; and, turning rapidly from one to another, gave utterance to some hasty witticism, which was sure to be followed by peals of laughter. To the females, as well as to the men, he addressed his discourse. Heaven only knows what he said to them, but he caused smiles and blushes to mantle their ingenuous faces. I am, indeed, very much inclined to believe that Marnoo, with his handsome person and captivating manners, was a sad deceiver among the simple maidens of the island.

During all this time he had never, for one moment, deigned to regard me. He appeared, indeed, to be altogether unconscious of my presence. I was utterly at a loss how to account for this extraordinary conduct. I easily perceived that he was a man of no little consequence among the islanders; that he possessed uncommon talents; and was gifted with a higher degree of knowledge than the inmates of the valley. For these reasons, I therefore greatly feared lest having, from some cause or other, unfriendly feelings toward me, he might exert his powerful influence to do me mischief.

It seemed evident that he was not a permanent resident of the vale, and yet, whence could he have come? On all sides the Typees were girt in by hostile tribes, and how could he possibly, if belonging to any of these, be received with so much cordiality?

The personal appearance of the enigmatical stranger suggested additional perplexities. The face, free from tattooing, and the unshaven crown, were peculiarities I had never before remarked in my part of the island, and I had always heard that the contrary were considered the indispensable distinctions of a Marquesan warrior. Altogether the matter was perfectly incomprehensible to me, and I awaited its solution with no small degree of anxiety.

At length, from certain indications, I suspected that he was making me the subject of his remarks, although he appeared cautiously to avoid either pronouncing my name, or looking in the direction where I lay. All at once he rose from the mats where he had been reclining, and, still conversing, moved toward me, his eye purposely evading mine, and seated himself within less than a yard of me. I had hardly recovered from my surprise, when he suddenly turned round, and, with a most benignant countenance, extended his right hand gracefully toward me. Of course I accepted the courteous challenge, and as soon as our palms met, he bent toward me, and murmured in musical accents,—'How you do?' 'How long you been in this bay?' 'You like this bay?'

Had I been pierced simultaneously by three Happar spears, I could not have started more than I did at hearing these simple questions! For a moment I was overwhelmed with astonishment, and then answered something I know not what; but as soon as I regained my self-possession, the thought darted through my mind that from this individual I might obtain that information regarding Toby which I suspected the natives had purposely withheld from me. Accordingly I questioned him concerning the disappearance of my companion, but he denied all knowledge of the matter. I then inquired from whence he had come? He replied, from Nukuheva. When I expressed my surprise, he looked at me for a moment, as if enjoying my perplexity, and then, with his strange vivacity, exclaimed—'Ah! me taboo—me go Nukuheva—me go Tior—me go Typee—me go everywhere—nobody harm me—me taboo.'

This explanation would have been altogether unintelligible to me, had it not recalled to my mind something I had previously heard concerning a singular custom among these islanders. Though the country is possessed by various tribes, whose mutual hostilities almost wholly preclude any intercourse between them; yet there are instances where a person having ratified friendly relations with some individual belonging to the valley, whose inmates are at war with his own, may, under particular restrictions, venture with impunity into the country of his friend, where, under other circumstances, he would have been treated as an enemy. In this light are personal friendships regarded among them, and the individual so protected is said to be taboo, and his person, to a certain extent, is held as sacred. Thus the stranger informed me he had access to all the valleys in the island.

Curious to know how he had acquired his knowledge of English, I questioned him on the subject. At first, for some reason or other, he evaded the inquiry, but afterward told me that, when a boy, he had been carried to sea by the captain of a trading vessel, with whom he had stayed three years, living part of the time with him at Sydney, in Australia, and that, at a subsequent visit to the island, the captain had, at his own request, permitted him to remain among his countrymen. The natural quickness of the savage had been wonderfully improved by his intercourse with the white men, and his partial knowledge of a foreign language gave him a great ascendancy over his less accomplished countrymen.

When I asked the now affable Marnoo why it was that he had not previously spoken to me, he eagerly inquired what I had been led to think of him from his conduct in that respect. I replied, that I had supposed him to be some great chief or warrior, who had seen plenty of white men before, and did not think it worth while to notice a poor sailor. At this declaration of the exalted opinion I had formed of him, he appeared vastly gratified, and gave me to understand that he had purposely behaved in that manner, in order to increase my astonishment, as soon as he should see proper to address me.

Marnoo now sought to learn my version of the story as to how I came to be an inmate of the Typee valley. When I related to him the circumstances under which Toby and I had entered it, he listened with evident interest; but as soon as I alluded to the absence, yet unaccounted for, of my comrade, he endeavored to change the subject, as if it were something he desired not to agitate. It seemed, indeed, as if everything connected with Toby was destined to beget distrust and anxiety in my bosom. Notwithstanding Marnoo's denial of any knowledge of his fate, I could not avoid suspecting that he was deceiving me; and this suspicion revived those frightful apprehensions with regard to my own fate, which, for a short time past, had subsided in my breast.

Influenced by these feelings, I now felt a strong desire to avail myself of the stranger's protection, and under his safeguard to return to Nukuheva. But as soon as I hinted at this, he unhesitatingly pronounced it to be entirely impracticable; assuring me that the Typees would never consent to my leaving the valley. Although what he said merely confirmed the impression which I had before entertained, still it increased my anxiety to escape from a captivity which, however endurable, nay, delightful it might be in some respects, involved in its issues a fate marked by the most frightful contingencies.

I could not conceal from my mind that Toby had been treated in the same friendly manner as I had been, and yet all their kindness had terminated in his mysterious disappearance. Might not the same fate await me?—a fate too dreadful to think of. Stimulated by these considerations, I urged anew my request to Marnoo; but he only set forth in stronger colors the impossibility of my escape and repeated his previous declaration that the Typees would never be brought to consent to my departure.

When I endeavored to learn from him the motives which prompted them to hold me a prisoner, Marnoo again assumed that mysterious tone which had tormented me with apprehensions when I had questioned him with regard to the fate of my companion.

Thus repulsed, in a manner which only served, by arousing the most dreadful forebodings, to excite me to renewed attempts, I conjured him to intercede for me with the natives, and endeavor to procure their consent to my leaving them. To this he appeared strongly averse; but, yielding at last to my importunities, he addressed several of the chiefs, who with the rest had been eying us intently during the whole of our conversation. His petition, however, was at once met with the most violent disapprobation, manifesting itself in angry glances and gestures, and a perfect torrent of passionate words, directed to both him and myself. Marnoo, evidently repenting the step he had taken, earnestly deprecated the resentment of the crowd, and in a few moments succeeded in pacifying to some extent the clamors which had broken out as soon as his proposition had been understood.

With the most intense interest had I watched the reception his intercession might receive; and a bitter pang shot through my heart at the additional evidence, now furnished, of the unchangeable determination of the islanders. Marnoo told me, with evident alarm in his countenance, that although admitted into the bay on a friendly footing with its inhabitants, he could not presume to meddle with their concerns, as such a procedure, if persisted in, would at once absolve the Typees from the restraints of the taboo, although so long as he refrained from any such conduct, it screened him effectually from the consequences of the enmity they bore his tribe.

At this moment, Mehevi, who was present, angrily interrupted him; and the words which he uttered, in a commanding tone, evidently meant that he must at once cease talking to me, and withdraw to the other part of the house. Marnoo immediately started up, hurriedly enjoining me not to address him again, and, as I valued my safety, to refrain from all further allusion to the subject of my departure; and then, in compliance with the order of the determined chief, but not before it had again been angrily repeated, he withdrew to a distance.

I now perceived, with no small degree of apprehension, the same savage expression in the countenance of the natives which had startled me during the scene at the Ti. They glanced their eyes suspiciously from Marnoo to me, as if distrusting the nature of an intercourse carried on, as it was, in a language they could not understand, and they seemed to harbor the belief that already we had concerted measures calculated to elude their vigilance.

The lively countenances of these people are wonderfully indicative of the emotions of the soul, and the imperfections of their oral language are more than compensated for by the nervous eloquence of their looks and gestures. I could plainly trace, in every varying expression of their faces, all those passions which had been thus unexpectedly aroused in their bosoms.

It required no reflection to convince me, from what was going on, that the injunction of Marnoo was not to be rashly slighted; and accordingly, great as was the effort to suppress my feelings, I accosted Mehevi in a good-humored tone, with a view of dissipating any ill impression he might have received. But the ireful, angry chief was not so easily mollified. He rejected my advances with that peculiarly stern expression I have before described, and took care by the whole of his behavior toward me to show the displeasure and resentment which he felt.

Marnoo, at the other extremity of the house, apparently desirous of making a diversion in my favor, exerted himself to amuse with his pleasantries the crowd about him; but his lively attempts were not so successful as they had previously been, and, foiled in his efforts, he rose gravely to depart. No one expressed any regret at this movement, so seizing his roll of tappa, and grasping his spear, he advanced to the front of the *pi-pi,* and waving his hand in adieu to the now silent throng, cast upon me a glance of mingled pity and reproach, and flung himself into the path which led from the house. I watched his receding figure until it was lost in the obscurity of the grove and then gave myself up to the most desponding reflections.

XIX

Reflections after Marnoo's departure—battle of the
popguns—strange conceit of Marheyo—
process of making tappa.

THE KNOWLEDGE I HAD now obtained as to the intention of the savages deeply affected me.

Marnoo, I perceived, was a man who, by reason of his superior acquirements, and the knowledge he possessed of the events which were taking place in the different bays of the island, was held in no little estimation by the inhabitants of the valley. He had been received with the most cordial welcome and respect. The natives had hung upon the accents of his voice, and had manifested the highest gratification at being individually noticed by him. And yet, despite all this, a few words urged in my behalf, with the intent of obtaining my release from captivity, had sufficed not only to banish all harmony and goodwill; but, if I could believe what he told me, had gone nigh to endanger his own personal safety.

How strongly rooted, then, must be the determination of the Typees with regard to me, and how suddenly could they display the strangest passions! The mere suggestion of my departure had estranged from me, for the time at least, Mehevi, who was the most influential of all the chiefs, and who had previously exhibited so many instances of his friendly sentiments. The rest of the natives had likewise evinced their strong repugnance to my wishes, and even Kory-Kory himself seemed to share in the general disapprobation bestowed upon me.

In vain I racked my invention to find out some motive for the strange desire these people manifested to retain me among them; but I could discover none.

But however this might be, the scene which had just occurred admonished me of the danger of trifling with the wayward and passionate spirits against whom it was vain to struggle, and might even be fatal to do so. My only hope was to induce the natives to believe that I was reconciled to my detention in the valley, and, by assuming a tranquil and cheerful demeanor, to allay the suspicions which I had so unfortunately aroused. Their confidence revived, they might in a short time remit in some degree their watchfulness over my movements, and I should then be the better enabled to avail myself of any opportunity which presented itself for escape. I determined, therefore, to make the best of a bad bargain, and to bear up manfully against whatever might betide. In this endeavor I succeeded beyond my own expectations. At the period of Marnoo's visit, I had been in the valley, as nearly as I could conjecture, some two months. Although not completely recovered from my strange illness which still lingered about me, I was free from pain and able to take exercise. In short, I had every reason to anticipate a perfect recovery. Freed from apprehensions on this point, and resolved to regard the future without flinching, I flung myself anew into all the social pleasures of the valley, and sought to bury all regrets, and all remembrances of my previous existence, in the wild enjoyments it afforded.

In my various wanderings through the vale, and as I became better acquainted with the character of its inhabitants, I was more and more struck with the lighthearted joyousness that everywhere prevailed. The minds of these simple savages, unoccupied by matters of graver moment, were capable of deriving the utmost delight from circumstances which would have passed unnoticed in more intelligent communities. All their enjoyment, indeed, seemed to be made up of the little trifling incidents of the passing hour; but these diminutive items swelled altogether to an amount of happiness seldom experienced by more enlightened individuals, whose pleasures are drawn from more elevated but rarer sources.

What community, for instance, of refined and intellectual mortals would derive the least satisfaction from shooting popguns? The mere supposition of such a thing being possible would excite their indignation, and yet the whole population of Typee did little else for ten days but occupy themselves with that childish amusement, fairly screaming, too, with the delight it afforded them.

One day I was frolicking with a little spirited urchin, some six years old, who chased me with a piece of bamboo about three feet long, with which he occasionally belabored me. Seizing the stick from him, the idea happened to suggest itself, that I might make for the youngster, out of the slender tube, one of those nursery muskets with which I had sometimes seen children playing. Accordingly, with my knife I made two parallel slits in the cane several inches in length, and cutting loose at one end the elastic strip between them, bent it back and slipped the point into a little notch made for the purpose. Any small substance placed against this would be projected with considerable force through the tube, by merely springing the bent strip out of the notch.

Had I possessed the remotest idea of the sensation this piece of ordnance was destined to produce, I should certainly have taken out a patent for the invention. The boy scampered away with it, half delirious with ecstasy, and in twenty minutes afterward I might have been seen surrounded by a noisy crowd—venerable old greybeards—responsible fathers of families—valiant warriors—matrons—young men—girls and children, all holding in their hands bits of bamboo, and each clamoring to be served first.

For three or four hours I was engaged in manufacturing popguns, but at last made over my goodwill and interest in the concern to a lad of remarkable quick parts, whom I soon initiated into the art and mystery.

Pop, Pop, Pop, Pop, now resounded all over the valley. Duels, skirmishes, pitched battles, and general engagements were to be seen on every side. Here, as you walked along a path which led through a thicket, you fell into a cunningly laid ambush, and became a target for a body of musketeers whose tattooed limbs you could just see peeping into view through the foliage. There, you were assailed by the intrepid garrison of a house, who levelled their bamboo rifles at you from between the upright canes which composed its sides. Farther on you were fired upon by a detachment of sharpshooters, mounted upon the top of a *pi-pi*.

Pop, Pop, Pop, Pop! green guavas, seeds, and berries were flying about in every direction, and during this dangerous state of affairs I was half afraid that, like the man and his brazen bull, I should fall a victim to my own ingenuity. Like everything else, however, the excitement gradually wore away, though ever after occasional popguns might be heard at all hours of the day.

It was toward the close of the popgun war, that I was infinitely diverted with a strange freak of Marheyo's.

I had worn, when I quitted the ship, a pair of thick pumps, which, from the rough usage they had received in scaling precipices and sliding down gorges, were so dilapidated as to be altogether unfit for use—so, at least, would have thought the generality of people, and so they most certainly were, when considered in the light of shoes. But things unserviceable in one way, may with advantage be applied in another, that is, if one have genius enough for the purpose. This genius Marheyo possessed in a superlative degree, as he abundantly evinced by the use to which he put these sorely bruised and battered old shoes.

Every article, however trivial, which belonged to me, the natives appeared to regard as sacred; and I observed that for several days after becoming an inmate of the house, my pumps were suffered to remain, untouched, where I had first happened to throw them. I remembered, however, that after awhile I had missed them from their accustomed place; but the matter gave me no concern, supposing that Tinor—like any other tidy housewife, having come across them in some of her domestic occupations—had pitched the useless things out of the house. But I was soon undeceived.

One day I observed old Marheyo bustling about me with unusual activity, and to such a degree as almost to supersede Kory-Kory in the functions of his office. One moment he volunteered to trot off with me on his back to the stream; and when I refused, noways daunted by the repulse, he continued to frisk about me like a superannuated house dog. I could not for the life of me conjecture what possessed the old gentleman, until all at once, availing himself of the temporary absence of the household, he went through a variety of uncouth gestures, pointing eagerly down to my feet, and then up to a little bundle which swung from the ridgepole overhead. At last I caught a faint idea of his meaning, and motioned him to lower the package. He executed the order in the twinkling of an eye, and unrolling a piece of tappa displayed to my astonished gaze the identical pumps which I thought had been destroyed long before.

I immediately comprehended his desires, and very generously gave him the shoes, which had become quite moldy, wondering for what earthly purpose he could want them.

The same afternoon I descried the venerable warrior approaching the house, with a slow, stately gait, earrings in ears, and spear in hand, with this highly ornamental pair of shoes suspended from his neck by a strip of bark, and swinging backward and forward on his capacious chest. In the gala costume of the tasteful Marheyo, these calfskin pendants ever after formed the most striking feature.

But to turn to something a little more important. Although the whole existence of the inhabitants of the valley seemed to pass away exempt from toil, yet there were some light employments which, although amusing rather than laborious as occupations, contributed to their comfort and luxury. Among these, the most important was the manufacture of the native cloth—tappa—so well known, under various modifications, throughout the whole Polynesian Archipelago. As is generally understood, this useful and sometimes elegant article is fabricated from the bark of different trees. But, as I believe that no description of its manufacture has ever been given, I shall state what I know regarding it.

In the manufacture of the beautiful white tappa generally worn on the Marquesan Islands, the preliminary operation consists in gathering a certain quantity of the young branches of the cloth tree. The exterior green bark being pulled off as worthless, there remains a slender fibrous substance, which is carefully stripped from the stick, to which it closely adheres. When a sufficient quantity of it has been collected, the various strips are enveloped in a covering of large leaves, which the natives use precisely as we do wrapping paper, and which are secured by a few turns of a line passed round them. The package is then laid in the bed of some running stream, with a heavy stone placed over it, to prevent its being swept away. After it has remained for two or three days in this state, it is drawn out, and exposed, for a short time, to the action of the air, every distinct piece being attentively inspected, with a view of ascertaining whether it has yet been sufficiently affected by the operation. This is repeated again and again, until the desired result is obtained.

When the substance is in a proper state for the next process, it betrays evidences of incipient decomposition; the fibres are relaxed and softened, and rendered perfectly malleable. The different strips are now extended, one by one, in successive layers, upon some smooth surface—generally the prostrate trunk of a coconut tree—and the heap thus formed is subjected, at every new increase, to a moderate beating, with a sort of wooden mallet, leisurely applied. The mallet is made of a hard heavy wood resembling ebony, is about twelve inches in length, and perhaps two in breadth, with a rounded handle at one end, and in shape is the exact counterpart of one of our four-sided razor strops. The flat surfaces of the implement are marked with shallow parallel indentations, varying in depth on the different sides, so as to be adapted to the several stages of the operation. These marks produce the corduroy sort of stripes discernible in the tappa in its finished state. After being beaten in the manner I have described, the material soon becomes blended in one mass, which, moistened occasionally with water, is at intervals hammered out, by a kind of goldbeating process, to any degree of thinness required. In this way the cloth is easily made to vary in strength and thickness, so as to suit the numerous purposes to which it is applied.

When the operation last described has been concluded the newmade tappa is spread out on the grass to bleach and dry, and soon becomes of a dazzling whiteness. Sometimes, in the first stages of the manufacture, the substance is impregnated with a vegetable juice, which gives it a permanent color. A rich brown and a bright yellow are occasionally seen, but the simple taste of the Typee people inclines them to prefer the natural tint.

The notable wife of Kammahammaha, the renowned conqueror and king of the Sandwich Islands, used to pride herself in the skill she displayed in dyeing her tappa with contrasting colors disposed in regular figures; and, in the midst of the innovations of the times, was regarded, toward the decline of her life, as a lady of the old school, clinging as she did to the national cloth, in preference to the frippery of the

European calicoes. But the art of printing the tappa is unknown upon the Marquesan Islands.

In passing along the valley, I was often attracted by the noise of the mallet, which, when employed in the manufacture of the cloth, produces at every stroke of its hard, heavy wood, a clear, ringing, and musical sound, capable of being heard at a great distance. When several of these implements happen to be in operation at the same time, and near one another, the effect upon the ear of a person, at a little distance, is really charming.

XX

History of a day as usually spent in the Typee valley
—dances of the Marquesan girls.

NOTHING CAN BE more uniform and undiversified than the life of the Typees; one tranquil day of ease and happiness follows another in quiet succession; and with these unsophisticated savages the history of a day is the history of a life. I will, therefore, as briefly as I can, describe one of our days in the valley.

To begin with the morning. We were not very early risers—the sun would be shooting his golden spikes above the Happar mountain, ere I threw aside my tappa robe, and girding my long tunic about my waist, sallied out with Fayaway and Kory-Kory and the rest of the household, and bent my steps toward the stream. Here we found congregated all those who dwelt in our section of the valley; and here we bathed with them. The fresh morning air and the cool flowing waters put both soul and body in a glow, and after a half-hour employed in this recreation, we sauntered back to the house—Tinor and Marheyo gathering dry sticks by the way for firewood; some of the young men laying the coconut trees under contribution as they passed beneath them; while Kory-Kory played his outlandish pranks for my particular diversion, and Fayaway and I, not arm in arm to be sure, but sometimes hand in hand, strolled along, with feelings of perfect charity for all the world, and especial goodwill toward each other.

Our morning meal was soon prepared. The islanders are somewhat abstemious at this repast; reserving the more powerful efforts of their appetite to a later period of the day. For my own part, with the assistance of my valet, who, as I have before stated, always officiated as spoon on these occasions, I ate sparingly from one of Tinor's trenches of *poee-poee,* which was devoted exclusively for my own use, being mixed with the milky meat of ripe coconut. A section of a roasted breadfruit, a small cake of *almar,* or a mess of *kokoo,* two or three bananas, or a *mammee* apple; an *annuee,* or some other agreeable and nutritious fruit served from day to day to diversify the meal, which was finished by tossing off the liquid contents of a young coconut or two.

While partaking of this simple repast, the inmates of Marheyo's house, after the style of the indolent Romans, reclined in sociable groups upon the divan of mats, and digestion was promoted by cheerful conversation.

After the morning meal was concluded, pipes were lighted; and among them my own especial pipe, a present from the noble Mehevi. The islanders, who only smoke a whiff or two at a time, and at long intervals, and who keep their pipes going from hand to hand continually, regarded my systematic smoking of four or five pipefuls of tobacco in succession, as something quite wonderful. When two or three pipes had circulated freely, the company gradually broke up. Marheyo went to the little hut he was for ever building. Tinor began to inspect her rolls of tappa, or employed her busy fingers in plaiting grass mats. The girls anointed themselves with their fragrant oils, dressed their hair, or looked over their curious finery, and compared together their ivory trinkets, fashioned out of boars' tusks or whales' teeth. The young men and warriors produced their spears, paddles, canoe gear, battle clubs, and war conchs, and occupied themselves in carving all sorts of figures upon them with pointed bits of shell or flint, and adorning them, especially the war conchs, with tassels of braided bark and tufts of human hair. Some, immediately after eating, threw themselves once more upon the inviting mats, and resumed the employment of the previous night, sleeping as soundly as if they had not closed their eyes for a week. Others sallied out into the groves, for the purpose of gathering fruit or fibres of bark and leaves; the last two being in constant requisition, and applied to a hundred uses. A few, perhaps, among the girls, would slip into the woods after flowers, or repair to the stream with small calabashes and coconut shells, in order to polish them by friction with a smooth stone in the water. In truth these innocent people seemed to be at no loss for something to occupy their time; and it would be no light task to enumerate all their employments, or rather pleasures.

My own mornings I spent in a variety of ways. Sometimes I rambled about from house to house, sure of receiving a cordial welcome wherever I went; or from grove to grove, and from one shady place to another, in company with Kory-Kory and Fayaway, and a rabble rout of merry young idlers. Sometimes I was too indolent for exercise, and accepting one of the many invitations I was continually receiving, stretched myself out on the mats of some hospitable dwelling, and occupied myself pleasantly either in watching the proceedings of those around me or taking part in them myself. Whenever I chose to do the latter, the delight of the islanders was boundless; and there was always a throng of competitors for the honor of instructing me in any particular craft. I soon became quite an accomplished hand at making tappa—could braid a grass sling as well as the best of them—and once, with my knife, carved the handle of a javelin so exquisitely, that I have no doubt, to this day, Karnoonoo, its owner, preserves it as a surprising specimen of my skill. As noon approached, all those who had wandered forth from our habitation, began to return; and when midday was fairly come scarcely a sound was to be heard in the valley: a deep sleep fell upon all. The luxurious siesta was hardly ever omitted, except by old Marheyo, who was so eccentric a character, that he seemed to be governed by no fixed principles whatever; but, acting just according to the humor of the moment, slept, ate, or tinkered away at his little hut, without regard to the proprieties of time or place. Frequently he might have been seen taking a nap in the sun at noonday, or a bath in the stream at midnight. Once I beheld him perched eighty feet from the ground, in the tuft of a coconut tree, smoking; and often I saw him standing up to the waist in water, engaged in plucking out the stray hairs of his beard, using a piece of mussel shell for tweezers.

The noontide slumber lasted generally an hour and a half; very often longer; and after the sleepers had arisen from their mats they again had recourse to their pipes, and then made preparations for the most important meal of the day.

I, however, like those gentlemen of leisure who breakfast at home and dine at their club, almost invariably, during my intervals of health, enjoyed the afternoon repast with the bachelor chiefs of the Ti, who were always rejoiced to see me, and lavishly spread before me all the good things which their larder afforded. Mehevi generally produced among other dainties a baked pig, an article which I have every reason to suppose was provided for my sole gratification.

The Ti was a right jovial place. It did my heart, as well as my body, good to visit it. Secure from female intrusion, there was no restraint upon the hilarity of the warriors, who, like the gentlemen of Europe after the cloth is drawn and the ladies retire, freely indulged their mirth.

After spending a considerable portion of the afternoon at the Ti, I usually found myself, as the cool of the evening came on, either sailing on the little lake with Fayaway, or bathing in the waters of the stream with a number of the savages, who, at this hour, always repaired thither. As the shadows of night approached, Marheyo's household were once more assembled under his roof: tapers were lit, long and curious chants were raised, interminable stories were told (for which one present was little the wiser), and all sorts of social festivities served to while away the time.

The young girls very often danced by moonlight in front

of their dwellings. There are a great variety of these dances, in which, however, I never saw the men take part. They all consist of active, romping, mischievous evolutions, in which every limb is brought into requisition. Indeed, the Marquesan girls dance all over, as it were; not only do their feet dance, but their arms, hands, fingers, ay, their very eyes, seem to dance in their heads. In good sooth, they so sway their floating forms, arch their necks, toss aloft their naked arms, and glide, and swim, and whirl, that it was almost too much for a quiet, sober-minded, modest young man like myself.

The damsels wear nothing but flowers and their compendious gala tunics; and when they plume themselves for the dance, they look like a band of olive-colored Sylphides on the point of taking wing.

Unless some particular festivity was going forward, the inmates of Marheyo's house retired to their mats rather early in the evening; but not for the night, since, after slumbering lightly for a while, they rose again, relit their tapers, partook of the third and last meal of the day, at which *poee-poee* alone was eaten, and then, after inhaling a narcotic whiff from a pipe of tobacco, disposed themselves for the great business of night, sleep. With the Marquesans it might almost be styled the great business of life, for they pass a large portion of their time in the arms of Somnus. The native strength of their constitutions is no way shown more emphatically than in the quantity of sleep they can endure. To many of them, indeed, life is little else than an often interrupted and luxurious nap.

XXI

The spring of Arva Wai—remarkable monumental
remains—some ideas with regard to the history of
the *pi-pis* found in the valley.

ALMOST EVERY COUNTRY has its medicinal springs famed for
their healing virtues. The Cheltenham of Typee is embosomed
in the deepest solitude, and but seldom receives a visitor. It
is situated remote from any dwelling, a little way up the
mountain, near the head of the valley; and you approach it
by a pathway shaded by the most beautiful foliage and
adorned with a thousand fragrant plants.

The mineral waters of Arva Wai[2] ooze forth from the
crevices of a rock, and gliding down its mossy side, fall at
last, in many clustering drops, into a natural basin of stone
fringed round with grass and dewy-looking little violet-col-
ored flowers, as fresh and beautiful as the perpetual moisture
they enjoy can make them.

The water is held in high estimation by the islanders, some
of whom consider it an agreeable as well as a medicinal
beverage; they bring it from the mountain in their calabashes,
and store it away beneath heaps of leaves in some shady nook
near the house. Old Marheyo had a great love for the waters
of the spring. Every now and then he lugged off to the mountain a great round demijohn of a calabash, and, panting with
his exertions, brought it back filled with his darling fluid.

The water tasted like a solution of a dozen disagreeable
things, and was sufficiently nauseous to have made the fortune
of the proprietor, had the spa been situated in the midst of
any civilized community.

As I am no chemist, I cannot give a scientific analysis of

---

2 I presume this might be translated into 'Strong Waters.' *Arva* is the name
bestowed upon a root the properties of which are both inebriating and medicinal. *Wai* is the Marquesan word for water.

the water. All I know about the matter is, that one day Marheyo in my presence poured out the last drop from his huge calabash, and I observed at the bottom of the vessel a small quantity of gravelly sediment very much resembling our common sand. Whether this is always found in the water, and gives it its peculiar flavor and virtues, or whether its presence was merely incidental, I was not able to ascertain.

One day in returning from this spring by a circuitous path, I came upon a scene which reminded me of Stonehenge and the architectural labors of the Druid.

At the base of one of the mountains, and surrounded on all sides by dense groves, a series of vast terraces of stone rises, step by step, for a considerable distance up the hillside. These terraces cannot be less that one hundred yards in length and twenty in width. Their magnitude, however, is less striking than the immense size of the blocks composing them. Some of the stones, of an oblong shape, are from ten to fifteen feet in length, and five or six feet thick. Their sides are quite smooth, but though square, and of pretty regular formation, they bear no mark of the chisel. They are laid together without cement, and here and there show gaps between. The topmost terrace and the lower one are somewhat peculiar in their construction. They have both a quadrangular depression in the center, leaving the rest of the terrace elevated several feet above it. In the intervals of the stones immense trees have taken root, and their broad boughs stretching far over, and interlacing together, support a canopy almost impenetrable to the sun. Overgrowing the greater part of them, and climbing from one to another, is a wilderness of vines, in whose sinewy embrace many of the stones lie half hidden, while in some places a thick growth of bushes entirely covers them. There is a wild pathway which obliquely crosses two of these terraces; and so profound is the shade, so dense the vegetation, that a stranger to the place might pass along it without being aware of their existence.

These structures bear every indication of a very high antiquity, and Kory-Kory, who was my authority in all matters of scientific research, gave me to understand that they were coeval with the creation of the world; that the great gods themselves were the builders; and that they would endure until time shall be no more. Kory-Kory's prompt explanation, and his attributing the work to a divine origin, at once convinced me that neither he nor the rest of his countrymen knew anything about them.

As I gazed upon this monument, doubtless the work of an extinct and forgotten race, thus buried in the green nook of an island at the ends of the earth, the existence of which was yesterday unknown, a stronger feeling of awe came over me than if I had stood musing at the mighty base of the Pyramid of Cheops. There are no inscriptions, no sculpture, no clue, by which to conjecture its history: nothing but the dumb stones. How many generations of those majestic trees which overshadow them have grown and flourished and decayed since first they were erected!

These remains naturally suggest many interesting reflections. They establish the great age of the island, an opinion which the builders of theories concerning the creation of the various groups in the South Seas are not always inclined to admit. For my own part, I think it just as probable that human beings were living in the valleys of the Marquesas three thousand years ago as that they were inhabiting the land of Egypt. The origin of the island of Nukuheva cannot be imputed to the coral insect; for indefatigable as the wonderful creature is, it would be hardly muscular enough to pile rocks one upon the other more than three thousand feet above the level of the sea. That the land may have been thrown up by a submarine volcano is as possible as anything else. No one can make an affidavit to the contrary, and therefore I will say nothing against the supposition: indeed, were geologists to assert that the whole continent of America had in like manner been formed by the simultaneous explosion of a train of Etnas laid under the water all the way from the North Pole to the parallel of Cape Horn, I am the last man in the world to contradict them.

I have already mentioned that the dwellings of the islanders were almost invariably built upon massive stone foundations, which they call *pi-pis*. The dimensions of these, however, as well as of the stones composing them, are comparatively small: but there are other and larger erections of a similar description comprising the *morais,* or burying grounds, and festival places, in nearly all the valleys of the island. Some of these piles are so extensive, and so great a degree of labor and skill must have been requisite in constructing them, that I can scarcely believe they were built by the ancestors of the present inhabitants. If indeed they were, the race has sadly deteriorated in their knowledge of the mechanic arts. To say nothing of their habitual indolence, by what contrivance within the reach of so simple a people could such enormous masses have been moved or fixed in their places? and how could they with their rude implements have chiseled and hammered them into shape?

All of these larger *pi-pis*—like that of the Hoolah Hoolah ground in the Typee valley—bore incontestable marks of great age; and I am disposed to believe that their erection may be ascribed to the same race of men who were the builders of the still more ancient remains I have just described.

According to Kory-Kory's account, the *pi-pi* upon which stands the Hoolah-Hoolah ground was built a great many moons ago, under the direction of Monoo, a great chief and warrior, and, as it would appear, master mason among the Typees. It was erected for the express purpose to which it is at present devoted in the incredibly short period of one sun; and was dedicated to the immortal wooden idols by a grand festival, which lasted ten days and nights.

Among the smaller *pi-pis,* upon which stand the dwelling houses of the natives, I never observed any which intimated a recent erection. There are in every part of the valley a great many of these massive stone foundations which have no houses upon them. This is vastly convenient, for whenever an enterprising islander chooses to emigrate a few hundred yards from the place where he was born, all he has to do in order to establish himself in some new locality, is to select one of the many unappropriated *pi-pis,* and without further ceremony pitch his bamboo tent upon it.

XXII

Preparations for a grand festival in the valley—
strange doings in the Taboo Groves—monument of
calabashes—gala costume of the Typee damsels—
departure for the festival.

FROM THE TIME that my lameness had decreased, I had made
a daily practice of visiting Mehevi at the Ti, who invariably
gave me a most cordial reception. I was always accompanied
in these excursions by Fayaway and the ever-present Kory-
Kory. The former, as soon as we reached the vicinity of the
Ti—which was rigorously tabooed to the whole female sex—
withdrew to a neighboring hut, as if her feminine delicacy
restrained her from approaching a habitation which might be
regarded as a sort of Bachelors' Hall.

And in good truth it might well have been so considered.
Although it was the permanent residence of several distinguished chiefs, and of the noble Mehevi in particular, it was
still at certain seasons the favorite haunt of all the jolly,
talkative, and elderly savages of the vale, who resorted thither
in the same way that similar characters frequent a tavern in
civilized countries. There they would remain hour after hour,
chatting, smoking, eating *poee-poee*, or busily engaged in
sleeping for the good of their constitutions.

This building appeared to be the headquarters of the valley,
where all flying rumors concentrated; and to have seen it
filled with a crowd of the natives, all males, conversing in
animated clusters, while multitudes were continually coming
and going, one would have thought it a kind of savage Exchange, where the rise and fall of Polynesian Stock was dis-
cussed.

Mehevi acted as supreme lord over the place, spending
the greater portion of his time there: and often when, at

particular hours of the day, it was deserted by nearly every one else except the verde-antique-looking centenarians, who were fixtures in the building, the chief himself was sure to be found enjoying his *otium cum dignitate,* upon the luxurious mats which covered the floor. Whenever I made my appearance he invariably rose, and, like a gentleman doing the honors of his mansion, invited me to repose myself wherever I pleased, and calling out *'tammaree!'* (boy), a little fellow would appear, and then retiring for an instant, return with some savory mess, from which the chief would press me to regale myself. To tell the truth, Mehevi was indebted to the excellence of his viands for the honor of my repeated visits— a matter which cannot appear singular when it is borne in mind that bachelors, all the world over, are famous for serving up unexceptionable repasts.

One day, on drawing near to the Ti, I observed that extensive preparations were going forward, plainly betokening some approaching festival. Some of the symptoms reminded me of the stir produced among the scullions of a large hotel where a grand jubilee dinner is about to be given. The natives were hurrying about hither and thither, engaged in various duties; some lugging off to the stream enormous hollow bamboos, for the purpose of filling them with water; others chasing furious-looking hogs through the bushes, in their endeavors to capture them; and numbers employed in kneading great mountains of *poee-poee* heaped up in huge wooden vessels.

After observing these lively indications for a while, I was attracted to a neighboring grove by a prodigious squeaking which I heard there. On reaching the spot I found it proceeded from a large hog which a number of natives were forcibly holding to the earth, while a muscular fellow, armed with a bludgeon, was ineffectually aiming murderous blows at the skull of the unfortunate porker. Again and again he missed his writhing and struggling victim, but though puffing and panting with his exertions, he still continued them; and after striking a sufficient number of blows to have demolished an entire drove of oxen, with one crashing stroke he laid him dead at his feet.

Without letting any blood from the body, it was immediately carried to a fire which had been kindled near at hand, and four savages taking hold of the carcass by its legs, passed it rapidly to and fro in the flames. In a moment the smell of burning bristles betrayed the object of this procedure. Having got thus far in the matter, the body was removed to a little distance; and, being disemboweled, the entrails were laid aside as choice parts, and the whole carcass thoroughly washed with water. An ample thick green cloth, composed of the long thick leaves of a species of palm tree, ingeniously tacked together with little pins of bamboo, was now spread upon the ground, in which the body being carefully rolled, it was borne to an oven previously prepared to receive it. Here it was at once laid upon the heated stones at the bottom, and covered with thick layers of leaves, the whole being quickly hidden from sight by a mound of earth raised over it.

Such is the summary style in which the Typees convert perverse-minded and rebellious hogs into the most docile and amiable pork; a morsel of which placed on the tongue melts like a soft smile from the lips of Beauty.

I commend their peculiar mode of proceeding to the consideration of all butchers, cooks, and housewives. The hapless porker whose fate I have just rehearsed, was not the only one who suffered on that memorable day. Many a dismal grunt, many an imploring squeak, proclaimed what was going on throughout the whole extent of the valley; and I verily believe the firstborn of every litter perished before the setting of the fatal sun.

The scene around the Ti was now most animated. Hogs and *poee-poee* were baking in numerous ovens, which, heaped up with fresh earth into slight elevations, looked like so many anthills. Scores of the savages were vigorously plying their stone pestles in preparing masses of *poee-poee*, and numbers were gathering green breadfruit and young coconuts in the surrounding groves; while an exceeding great multitude, with a view of encouraging the rest in their labors, stood still, and kept shouting most lustily without intermission.

It is a peculiarity among these people, that when engaged in any employment they always make a prodigious fuss about it. So seldom do they ever exert themselves, that when they do work they seem determined that so meritorious an action shall not escape the observation of those around. If, for example, they have occasion to remove a stone to a little distance, which perhaps might be carried by two able-bodied men, a whole swarm gather about it, and, after a vast deal of palavering, lift it up among them, every one struggling to get hold of it, and bear it off yelling and panting as if accomplishing some mighty achievement. Seeing them on these occasions, one is reminded of an infinity of black ants clustering about and dragging away to some hole the leg of a deceased fly.

Having for some time attentively observed these demonstrations of good cheer, I entered the Ti, where Mehevi sat complacently looking out upon the busy scene, and occasionally issuing his orders. The chief appeared to be in an extraordinary flow of spirits, and gave me to understand that on the morrow there would be grand doings in the Groves generally, and at the Ti in particular; and urged me by no means to absent myself. In commemoration of what event, however, or in honor of what distinguished personage, the feast was to be given, altogether passed my comprehension. Mehevi sought to enlighten my ignorance, but he failed as signally as when he had endeavored to initiate me into the perplexing arcana of the taboo.

On leaving the Ti, Kory-Kory, who had as a matter of course accompanied me, observing that my curiosity remained unabated, resolved to make everything plain and satisfactory. With this intent, he escorted me through the Taboo Groves, pointing out to my notice a variety of objects, and endeavored to explain them in such an indescribable jargon of words, that it almost put me in bodily pain to listen to him. In particular, he led me to a remarkable pyramidical structure some three yards square at the base, and perhaps ten feet in height, which had lately been thrown up, and occupied a very conspicuous position. It was composed principally of large empty calabashes, with a few polished coconut shells, and looked not unlike a cenotaph of skulls. My cicerone perceived the astonishment with which I gazed at this monument of savage crockery, and immediately addressed himself to the task of enlightening me: but all in vain; and to this hour the nature of the monument remains a complete mystery to me. As, however, it formed so prominent a feature in the approaching revels, I bestowed upon the latter, in my own mind, the title of the 'Feast of Calabashes.'

The following morning, awakening rather late, I perceived the whole of Marheyo's family busily engaged in preparing for the festival. The old warrior himself was arranging in round balls the two grey locks of hair that were suffered to grow from the crown of his head; his earrings and spear, both well polished, lay beside him, while the highly decorative pair of shoes hung suspended from a projecting cane against the side of the house. The young men were similarly employed; and the fair damsels, including Fayaway, were anointing themselves with *aka*, arranging their long tresses, and performing other matters connected with the duties of the toilet.

Having completed their preparations, the girls now exhibited themselves in gala costume; the most conspicuous feature of which was a necklace of beautiful white flowers, with the stems removed, and strung closely together upon a single fibre of tappa. Corresponding ornaments were inserted in their ears, and woven garlands upon their heads. About their waist they wore a short tunic of spotless white tappa, and some of them superadded to this a mantle of the same material, tied in an elaborate bow upon the left shoulder, and falling about the figure in picturesque folds.

Thus arrayed, I would have matched the charming Fayaway against any beauty in the world.

People may say what they will about the taste evinced by our fashionable ladies in dress. Their jewels, their feathers, their silks, and their furbelows would have sunk into utter insignificance beside the exquisite simplicity of attire adopted by the nymphs of the vale on this festive occasion. I should like to have seen a gallery of coronation beauties, at Westminster Abbey, confronted for a moment by this band of Island girls; their stiffness, formality, and affectation contrasted with the artless vivacity and unconcealed natural graces of these savage maidens. It would be the Venus de' Medici placed beside a milliner's doll.

It was not long before Kory-Kory and myself were left alone in the house, the rest of its inmates having departed for the Taboo Groves. My valet was all impatience to follow them; and was as fidgety about my dilatory movements as a diner-out waiting hat in hand at the bottom of the stairs for some lagging companion. At last, yielding to his importunities, I set out for the Ti. As we passed the houses peeping out from the groves through which our route lay, I noticed that they were entirely deserted by their inhabitants.

When we reached the rock that abruptly terminated the path, and concealed from us the festive scene, wild shouts and a confused blending of voices assured me that the occasion, whatever it might be, had drawn together a great multitude. Kory-Kory, previous to mounting the elevation, paused for a moment, like a dandy at a ballroom door, to put a hasty finish to his toilet. During this short interval, the thought struck me that I ought myself perhaps to be taking some little pains with my appearance. But as I had no holiday raiment, I was not a little puzzled to devise some means of decorating myself. However, as I felt desirous to create a sensation, I determined to do all that lay in my power; and knowing that I could not delight the savages more than by conforming to their style of dress, I removed from my person the large robe of tappa which I was accustomed to wear over my shoulders whenever I sallied into the open air, and remained merely girt about with a short tunic descending from my waist to my knees.

My quick-witted attendant fully appreciated the compliment I was paying to the costume of his race, and began more sedulously to arrange the folds of the one only garment which remained to me. Whilst he was doing this, I caught sight of a knot of young lasses, who were sitting near us on the

grass surrounded by heaps of flowers which they were forming into garlands. I motioned to them to bring some of their
handiwork to me; and in an instant a dozen wreaths were at
my disposal. One of them I put round the apology of a hat
which I had been forced to construct for myself out of palmetto leaves, and some of the others I converted into a
splendid girdle. These operations finished, with the slow and
dignified step of a full-dressed beau I ascended the rock.

XXIII

The 'Feast of Calabashes.'

THE WHOLE POPULATION of the valley seemed to be gathered
within the precincts of the grove. In the distance could be
seen the long front of the Ti, its immense piazza swarming
with men, arrayed in every variety of fantastic costume, and
all vociferating with animated gestures; while the whole interval between it and the place where I stood was enlivened
by groups of females fancifully decorated, dancing, capering,
and uttering wild exclamations. As soon as they descried me
they set up a shout of welcome; and a band of them came
dancing toward me chanting as they approached some wild
recitative. The change in my garb seemed to transport them
with delight, and clustering about me on all sides, they accompanied me toward the Ti. When, however, we drew near
it these joyous nymphs paused in their career, and parting on
either side, permitted me to pass on to the now densely
thronged building.

So soon as I mounted to the *pi-pi* I saw at a glance that
the revels were fairly under way.

What lavish plenty reigned around!—Warwick feasting his
retainers with beef and ale was a niggard to the noble Mehevi!—All along the piazza of the Ti were arranged elabo-

rately carved canoe-shaped vessels, some twenty feet in length, filled with newly made *poee-poee,* and sheltered from the sun by the broad leaves of the banana. At intervals were heaps of green breadfruit, raised in pyramidical stacks, resembling the regular piles of heavy shot to be seen in the yard of an arsenal. Inserted into the interstices of the huge stones which formed the *pi-pi* were large boughs of trees; hanging from the branches of which, and screened from the sun by their foliage, were innumerable little packages with leafy coverings, containing the meat of the numerous hogs which had been slain, done up in this manner to make it more accessible to the crowd. Leaning against the railing of the piazza were an immense number of long, heavy bamboos, plugged at the lower end, and with their projecting muzzles stuffed with a wad of leaves. These were filled with water from the stream, and each of them might hold from four to five gallons.

The banquet being thus spread, nought remained but for everyone to help himself at his pleasure. Accordingly not a moment passed but the transplanted boughs I have mentioned were rifled by the throng of the fruit they certainly had never borne before. Calabashes of *poee-poee* were continually being replenished from the extensive receptacle in which that article was stored, and multitudes of little fires were kindled about the Ti for the purpose of roasting the breadfruit.

Within the building itself was presented a most extraordinary scene. The immense lounge of mats lying between the parallel rows of the trunks of coconut trees, and extending the entire length of the house, at least two hundred feet, was covered by the reclining forms of a host of chiefs and warriors, who were eating at a great rate, or soothing the cares of Polynesian life in the sedative fumes of tobacco. The smoke was inhaled from large pipes, the bowls of which, made out of small coconut shells, were curiously carved in strange heathenish devices. These were passed from mouth to mouth by the recumbent smokers, who, taking two or three prodigious whiffs, handed the pipe to his neighbor; sometimes for that purpose stretching indolently across the body of some dozing individual whose exertions at the dinner table had already induced sleep.

The tobacco used among the Typees was of a very mild and pleasing flavor, and as I always saw it in leaves, and the natives appeared pretty well supplied with it, I was led to believe that it must have been the growth of the valley. Indeed Kory-Kory gave me to understand that this was the case; but I never saw a single plant growing on the island. At Nukuheva, and, I believe, in all the other valleys, the weed is very scarce, being only obtained in small quantities from foreigners, and smoking is consequently with the inhabitants of these places a very great luxury. How it was that the Typees were so well furnished with it I cannot divine. I should think them too indolent to devote any attention to its culture; and, indeed, as far as my observation extended, not a single atom of the soil was under any other cultivation than that of shower and sunshine. The tobacco plant, however, like the sugar cane, may grow wild in some remote part of the vale.

There were many in the Ti for whom the tobacco did not furnish a sufficient stimulus, and who accordingly had recourse to *arva,* as a more powerful agent in producing the desired effect.

Arva is a root very generally dispersed over the South Seas, and from it is extracted a juice, the effects of which upon the system are at first stimulating in a moderate degree; but it soon relaxes the muscles, and exerting a narcotic influence produces a luxurious sleep. In the valley this beverage was universally prepared in the following way:—Some half-dozen young boys seated themselves in a circle around an empty wooden vessel, each one of them being supplied with a certain quantity of the roots of the *arva,* broken into small bits and laid by his side. A coconut goblet of water was passed around the juvenile company, who, rinsing their mouths with its contents, proceeded to the business before them. This merely consisted in thoroughly masticating the *arva,* and throwing it mouthful after mouthful into the receptacle provided. When a sufficient quantity had been thus obtained water was poured upon the mass, and being stirred about with the forefinger of the right hand, the preparation was soon in readiness for us. The *arva* has medicinal qualities.

Upon the Sandwich Islands it has been employed with no small success in the treatment of scrofulous affections, and in combating the ravages of a disease for whose frightful inroads the ill-starred inhabitants of that group are indebted to their foreign benefactors. But the tenants of the Typee valley, as yet exempt from these inflictions, generally employ the *arva* as a minister to social enjoyment, and a calabash of the liquid circulates among them as the bottle with us.

Mehevi, who was greatly delighted with the change in my costume, gave me a cordial welcome. He had reserved for me a most delectable mess of *kokoo*, well knowing my partiality for that dish; and had likewise selected three or four young coconuts, several roasted breadfruit, and a magnificent bunch of bananas, for my especial comfort and gratification. These various matters were at once placed before me; but Kory-Kory deemed the banquet entirely insufficient for my wants until he had supplied me with one of the leafy packages of pork, which, notwithstanding the somewhat hasty manner in which it had been prepared, possessed a most excellent flavor, and was surprisingly sweet and tender.

Pork is not a staple article of food among the people of the Marquesas, consequently they pay little attention to the *breeding* of the swine. The hogs are permitted to roam at large in the groves, where they obtain no small part of their nourishment from the coconuts which continually fall from the trees. But it is only after infinite labor and difficulty, that the hungry animal can pierce the husk and shell so as to get at the meat. I have frequently been amused at seeing one of them, after crunching the obstinate nut with his teeth for a long time unsuccessfully, get into a violent passion with it. He would then root furiously under the coconut, and, with a fling of his snout, toss it before him on the ground. Following it up he would crunch at it again savagely for a moment, and the next knock it on one side, pausing immediately after, as if wondering how it could so suddenly have disappeared. In this way the persecuted coconuts were often chased half across the valley.

The second day of the 'Feast of Calabashes' was ushered in by still more uproarious noises than the first. The skins of innumerable sheep seemed to be resounding to the blows of an army of drummers. Startled from my slumbers by the din, I leaped up, and found the whole household engaged in making preparations for immediate departure. Curious to discover of what strange events these novel sounds might be the precursors, and not a little desirous to catch a sight of the instruments which produced the terrific noise, I accompanied the natives as soon as they were in readiness to depart for the Taboo Groves.

The comparatively open space that extended from the Ti toward the rock, to which I have before alluded as forming the ascent to the place, was, with the building itself, now altogether deserted by the men, the whole distance being filled by bands of females, shouting and dancing under the influence of some strange excitement.

I was amused at the appearance of four or five old women who, in a state of utter nudity, with their arms extended flatly down their sides, and holding themselves perfectly erect, were leaping stiffly into the air, like so many sticks bobbing to the surface after being pressed perpendicularly into the water. They preserved the utmost gravity of countenance, and continued their extraordinary movements without a single moment's cessation. They did not appear to attract the observation of the crowd around them, but I must candidly confess that, for my own part, I stared at them most pertinaciously.

Desirous of being enlightened with regard to the meaning of this peculiar diversion, I turned inquiringly to Kory-Kory; that learned Typee immediately proceeded to explain the whole matter thoroughly. But all that I could comprehend from what he said was, that the leaping figures before me were bereaved widows, whose partners had been slain in battle many moons previously; and who, at every festival, gave public evidence in this manner of their calamities. It was evident that Kory-Kory considered this an all-sufficient reason for so indecorous a custom; but I must say that it did not satisfy me as to its propriety.

Leaving these afflicted females, we passed on to the Hoolah-Hoolah ground. Within the spacious quadrangle, the whole population of the valley seemed to be assembled, and the sight presented was truly remarkable. Beneath the sheds of bamboo which opened toward the interior of the square, reclined the principal chiefs and warriors, while a miscellaneous throng lay at their ease under the enormous trees which spread a majestic canopy overhead. Upon the terraces of the gigantic altars, at either end, were deposited green breadfruit in baskets of coconut leaves, large rolls of tappa, bunches of ripe bananas, clusters of *mammee* apples, the golden-hued fruit of the *artu* tree, and baked hogs, laid out in large wooden trenchers, fancifully decorated with freshly plucked leaves, whilst a variety of rude implements of war were piled in confused heaps before the ranks of hideous idols. Fruits of various kinds were likewise suspended in leafen baskets, from the tops of poles planted uprightly, and at regular intervals, along the lower terraces of both altars. At their base were arranged two parallel rows of cumbersome drums, standing at least fifteen feet in height, and formed from the hollow trunks of large trees. Their heads were covered with sharkskins, and their barrels were elaborately carved with various quaint figures and devices. At regular intervals they were bound round by a species of sinnate of various colors, and strips of native cloth flattened upon them here and there. Behind these instruments were built slight platforms, upon which stood a number of young men who, beating violently with the palms of their hands upon the drum heads, produced those outrageous sounds which had awakened me in the morning. Every few minutes these musical performers hopped down from their elevation into the crowd below, and their places were immediately supplied by fresh recruits. Thus an incessant din was kept up that might have startled Pandemonium.

Precisely in the middle of the quadrangle were placed perpendicularly in the ground, a hundred or more slender, fresh-cut poles, stripped of their bark, and decorated at the end with a floating pennon of white tappa, the whole being fenced about with a little picket of canes. For what purpose these singular ornaments were intended I in vain endeavored to discover.

Another most striking feature of the performance was exhibited by a score of old men, who sat cross-legged in the little pulpits, which encircled the trunks of the immense trees growing in the middle of the enclosure. These venerable gentlemen, who I presume were the priests, kept up an uninterrupted monotonous chant, which was nearly drowned in the roar of drums. In the right hand they held a finely woven grass fan, with a heavy black wooden handle curiously chased: these fans they kept in continual motion.

But no attention whatever seemed to be paid to the drummers or to the old priests; the individuals who composed the vast crowd present being entirely taken up in chatting and laughing with one another, smoking, drinking *arva*, and eating. For all the observation it attracted, or the good it achieved, the whole savage orchestra might, with great advantage to its own members and the company in general, have ceased the prodigious uproar they were making.

In vain I questioned Kory-Kory and others of the natives, as to the meaning of the strange things that were going on; all their explanations were conveyed in such a mass of outlandish gibberish and gesticulation that I gave up the attempt in despair. All that day the drums resounded, the priests chanted, and the multitude feasted and roared till sunset, when the throng dispersed, and the Taboo Groves were again abandoned to quiet and repose. The next day the same scene was repeated until night, when this singular festival terminated.

XXIV

Ideas suggested by the 'Feast of Calabashes'—inaccuracy of certain published accounts of the islands—a reason—neglected state of heathenism in the valley—effigy of a dead warrior—a singular superstition—the priest Kolory and the god Moa Artua—amazing religious observance—a dilapidated shrine—Kory-Kory and the idol—an inference.

ALTHOUGH I HAD BEEN baffled in my attempts to learn the origin of the 'Feast of Calabashes,' yet it seemed very plain to me that it was principally, if not wholly, of a religious character. As a religious solemnity, however, it had not at all corresponded with the horrible descriptions of Polynesian worship which we have received in some published narratives, and especially in those accounts of the evangelized islands with which the missionaries have favored us. Did not the sacred character of these persons render the purity of their intentions unquestionable, I should certainly be led to suppose that they had exaggerated the evils of Paganism, in order to enhance the merit of their own disinterested labors.

In a certain work incidentally treating of the Washington, or Northern Marquesas Islands, I have seen the frequent immolation of human victims upon the altars of their gods, positively and repeatedly charged upon the inhabitants. The same work gives also a rather minute account of their religion—enumerates a great many of their superstitions—and makes known the particular designations of numerous orders of the priesthood. One would almost imagine from the long list that is given of cannibal primates, bishops, archdeacons, prebendaries, and other inferior ecclesiastics, that the sacerdotal order far outnumbered the rest of the population, and that the poor natives were more severely priest-ridden than even the inhabitants of the papal states. These accounts are likewise calculated to leave upon the reader's mind an impression that human victims are daily cooked and served up upon the altars; that heathenish cruelties of every description are continually practised; and that these ignorant Pagans are in a state of the extremest wretchedness in consequence of the grossness of their superstitions. Be it observed, however, that all this information is given by a man who, according to his own statement, was only at one of the islands, and remained there but two weeks, sleeping every night on board his ship, and taking little kid-glove excursions ashore in the daytime, attended by an armed party.

Now, all I can say is, that in all my excursions through the valley of Typee, I never saw any of these alleged enormities. If any of them are practiced upon the Marquesas Islands they must certainly have come to my knowledge while living for months with a tribe of savages, wholly unchanged from their original primitive condition, and reputed the most ferocious in the South Seas.

The fact is, that there is a vast deal of unintentional humbuggery in some of the accounts we have from scientific men concerning the religious institutions of Polynesia. These learned tourists generally obtain the greater part of their information from the retired old South Sea rovers, who have domesticated themselves among the barbarous tribes of the Pacific. Jack, who has long been accustomed to the longbow, and to spin tough yarns on a ship's forecastle, invariably officiates as showman of the island on which he has settled, and having mastered a few dozen words of the language, is supposed to know all about the people who speak it. A natural desire to make himself of consequence in the eyes of the strangers, prompts him to lay claims to a much greater knowledge of such matters than he actually possesses. In reply to incessant queries, he communicates not only all he knows but a good deal more, and if there be any information deficient still he is at no loss to supply it. The avidity with which his anecdotes are noted down tickles his vanity, and his powers of invention increase with the credulity of his auditors. He knows just the sort of information wanted, and furnishes it to any extent.

This is not a supposed case; I have met with several individuals like the one described, and I have been present at two or three of their interviews with strangers.

Now when the scientific voyager arrives at home with his collection of wonders, he attempts, perhaps, to give a description of some of the strange people he has been visiting. Instead of representing them as a community of lusty savages, who are leading a merry, idle, innocent life, he enters into a very circumstantial and learned narrative of certain unaccountable superstitions and practices, about which he knows as little as the islanders do themselves. Having had little time, and scarcely any opportunity, to become acquainted with the customs he pretends to describe, he writes them down one after another in an offhand, haphazard style; and were the book thus produced to be translated into the tongue of the people of whom it purports to give the history, it would appear quite as wonderful to them as it does to the American public, and much more improbable.

For my own part, I am free to confess my almost entire inability to gratify any curiosity that may be felt with regard to the theology of the valley. I doubt whether the inhabitants themselves could do so. They are either too lazy or too sensible to worry themselves about abstract points of religious belief. While I was among them they never held any synods or councils to settle the principles of their faith by agitating them. An unbounded liberty of conscience seemed to prevail. Those who pleased to do so were allowed to repose implicit faith in an ill-favored god with a large bottle nose and fat shapeless arms crossed upon his breast; whilst others worshipped an image which, having no likeness either in heaven or on earth, could hardly be called an idol. As the islanders always maintained a discreet reserve with regard to my own peculiar views on religion, I thought it would be excessively ill-bred in me to pry into theirs.

But, although my knowledge of the religious faith of the Typees was unavoidably limited, one of their superstitious observances with which I became acquainted interested me greatly.

In one of the most secluded portions of the valley, within a stone's cast of Fayaway's Lake—for so I christened the scene of our island yachting—and hard by a growth of palms, which stood ranged in order along both banks of the stream, waving their green arms as if to do honor to its passage, was the mausoleum of a deceased warrior-chief. Like all the other edifices of any note, it was raised upon a small *pi-pi* of stones, which, being of unusual height, was a conspicuous object from a distance. A light thatching of bleached palmetto leaves hung over it like a self-supported canopy; for it was not until you came very near that you saw it was supported by four slender columns of bamboo rising at each corner to a little more than the height of a man. A clear area of a few yards surrounded the *pi-pi,* and was enclosed by four trunks of coconut trees resting at the angles on massive blocks of stone. The place was sacred. The sign of the inscrutable taboo was seen in the shape of a mystic roll of white tappa, suspended by a twisted cord of the same material from the top of a slight pole planted within the enclosure.³ The sanctity of the spot appeared never to have been violated. The stillness of the grave was there, and the calm solitude around was beautiful and touching. The soft shadows of those lofty palm trees!—I can see them now—hanging over the little temple, as if to keep out the intrusive sun.

On all sides as you approached this silent spot you caught sight of the dead chief's effigy, seated in the stern of a canoe, which was raised on a light frame a few inches above the level of the *pi-pi*. The canoe was about seven feet in length; of a rich, dark-colored wood, handsomely carved and adorned in many places with variegated bindings of stained sinnate, into which were ingeniously wrought a number of sparkling sea shells, and a belt of the same shells ran all round it. The body of the figure—of whatever material it might have been made—was effectually concealed in a heavy robe of brown

---

3 White appears to be the sacred color among the Marquesans.

tappa, revealing only the hands and head; the latter skillfully carved in wood, and surmounted by a superb arch of plumes. These plumes, in the subdued and gentle gales which found access to this sequestered spot, were never for one moment at rest, but kept nodding and waving over the chief's brow. The long leaves of the palmetto dropped over the eaves, and through them you saw the warrior holding his paddle with both hands in the act of rowing, leaning forward and inclining his head, as if eager to hurry on his voyage. Glaring at him for ever, and face to face, was a polished human skull, which crowned the prow of the canoe. The spectral figurehead, reversed in its position, glancing backward, seemed to mock the impatient attitude of the warrior.

When I first visited this singular place with Kory-Kory, he told me—or at least I so understood him—that the chief was paddling his way to the realms of bliss, and breadfruit—the Polynesian heaven—where every moment the breadfruit trees dropped their ripened spheres to the ground, and where there was no end to the coconuts and bananas; there they reposed through the livelong eternity upon mats much finer than those of Typee; and every day bathed their glowing limbs in rivers of coconut oil. In that happy land there were plenty of plumes and feathers, and boars' tusks and sperm-whale teeth, far preferable to all the shining trinkets and gay tappa of the white men; and, best of all, women far lovelier than the daughters of earth were there in abundance. A very pleasant place, Kory-Kory said it was; but after all, not much pleasanter, he thought, than Typee. Did he not then, I asked him, wish to accompany the warrior? Oh, no: he was very happy where he was; but supposed that some time or other he would go in his own canoe.

Thus far, I think, I clearly comprehended Kory-Kory. But there was a singular expression he made use of at the time, enforced by as singular a gesture, the meaning of which I would have given much to penetrate. I am inclined to believe it must have been a proverb he uttered; for I afterward heard him repeat the same words several times and in what appeared to me to be a somewhat similar sense. Indeed, Kory-Kory had a great variety of short, smart-sounding sentences, with which he frequently enlivened his discourse; and he introduced them with an air which plainly intimated, that in his opinion, they settled the matter in question, whatever it might be.

Could it have been then, that when I asked him whether he desired to go to his heaven of breadfruit, coconuts, and young ladies, which he had been describing, he answered by saying something equivalent to our old adage—'A bird in the hand is worth two in the bush?'—if he did, Kory-Kory was a discreet and sensible fellow, and I cannot sufficiently admire his shrewdness.

Whenever in the course of my rambles through the valley I happened to be near the chief's mausoleum, I always turned aside to visit it. The place had a peculiar charm for me; I hardly know why; but so it was. As I leaned over the railing and gazed upon the strange effigy and watched the play of the feathery headdress, stirred by the same breeze which in low tones breathed amidst the lofty palm trees, I loved to yield myself up to the fanciful superstition of the islanders, and could almost believe that the grim warrior was bound heavenward. In this mood when I turned to depart, I bade him 'God speed, and a pleasant voyage.' Aye, paddle away, brave chieftain, to the land of spirits! To the material eye thou makest but little progress; but with the eye of faith, I see thy canoe cleaving the bright waves, which die away on those dimly looming shores of Paradise.

This strange superstition affords another evidence of the fact, that however ignorant man may be, he still feels within him his immortal spirit yearning after the unknown future.

Although the religious theories of the islands were a complete mystery to me, their practical everyday operation could not be concealed. I frequently passed the little temples reposing in the shadows of the Taboo Groves and beheld the offerings—moldy fruit spread out upon a rude altar, or hanging in half-decayed baskets around some uncouth jolly-looking image; I was present during the continuance of the festival; I daily beheld the grinning idols marshaled rank and file in the Hoolah-Hoolah ground, and was often in the habit of meeting those whom I supposed to be the priests. But the temples seemed abandoned to solitude; the festival had been nothing more than a jovial mingling of the tribe; the idols were quite as harmless as any other logs of wood; and the priests were the merriest dogs in the valley.

In fact religious affairs in Typee were at a very low ebb: all such matters sat very lightly upon the thoughtless inhabitants; and, in the celebration of many of their strange rites, they appeared merely to seek a sort of childish amusement.

A curious evidence of this was given in a remarkable ceremony in which I frequently saw Mehevi and several other chiefs and warriors of note take part; but never a single female.

Among those whom I looked upon as forming the priesthood of the valley, there was one in particular who often attracted my notice, and whom I could not help regarding as the head of the order. He was a noble-looking man, in the prime of his life, and of a most benignant aspect. The authority this man, whose name was Kolory, seemed to exercise over the rest, the episcopal part he took in the 'Feast of Calabashes,' his sleek and complacent appearance, the mystic characters which were tattooed upon his chest, and above all the mitre he frequently wore, in the shape of a towering headdress, consisting of part of a coconut branch, the stalk planted uprightly on his brow, and the leaflets gathered together and passed round the temples and behind the ears, all these pointed him out as Lord Primate of Typee. Kolory was a sort of Knight Templar—a soldier-priest; for he often wore the dress of a Marquesan warrior, and always carried a long spear, which, instead of terminating in a paddle at the lower end, after the general fashion of these weapons, was curved into a heathenish-looking little image. This instrument, however, might perhaps have been emblematic of his double functions. With one end in carnal combat he transfixed the enemies of his tribe; and with the other as a pastoral crook he kept in order his spiritual flock. But this is not all I have to say about Kolory. His Martial Grace very often carried about with him what seemed to me the half of a broken war club. It was swathed round with ragged bits of white tappa, and the upper part, which was intended to represent a human head, was embellished with a strip of scarlet cloth of European manufacture. It required little observation to discover that this strange object was revered as a god. By the side of the big and lusty images standing sentinel over the altars of the Hoolah-Hoolah ground, it seemed a mere pigmy in tatters. But appearances all the world over are deceptive. Little men are sometimes very potent, and rags sometimes cover very extensive pretensions. In fact, this funny little image was the 'crack' god of the island; lording it over all the wooden lubbers who looked so grim and dreadful; its name was Moa Artua.[4] And it was in honor of Moa Artua, and for the entertainment of those who believe in him, that the curious ceremony I am about to describe was observed.

Mehevi and the chieftains of the Ti have just risen from their noontide slumbers. There are no affairs of state to dispose of; and having eaten two or three breakfasts in the course of the morning, the magnates of the valley feel no appetite as yet for dinner. How are their leisure moments to be occupied? They smoke, they chat, and at last one of their number makes a proposition to the rest, who joyfully acquiescing, he darts out of the house, leaps from the *pi-pi,* and disappears in the grove. Soon you see him returning with Kolory, who bears the god Moa Artua in his arms, and carries in one hand a small trough, hollowed out in the likeness of a canoe. The priest comes along dandling his charge as if it were a lachrymose infant he was endeavoring to put into a good humor. Presently, entering the Ti, he seats himself on the mats as composedly as a juggler about to perform his sleight-of-hand tricks; and with the chiefs disposed in a circle around him, commences his ceremony.

In the first place he gives Moa Artua an affectionate hug, then caressingly lays him to his breast, and, finally, whispers something in his ear; the rest of the company listening eagerly for a reply. But the baby god is deaf or dumb—perhaps both,

---

4 The word 'Artua,' although having some other significations, is in nearly all the Polynesian dialects used as the general designation of the gods.

for never a word does he utter. At last Kolory speaks a little
louder, and soon growing angry, comes boldly out with what
he has to say and bawls to him. He put me in mind of a
choleric fellow, who, after trying in vain to communicate
a secret to a deaf man, all at once flies into a passion and
screams it out so that everyone may hear. Still Moa Artua
remains as quiet as ever; and Kolory, seemingly losing his
temper, fetches him a box over the head, strips him of his
tappa and red cloth, and laying him in a state of nudity in
the little trough, covers him from sight. At this proceeding
all present loudly applaud and signify their approval by uttering the adjective *mortarkee* with violent emphasis. Kolory,
however, is so desirous his conduct should meet with unqualified approbation, that he inquires of each individual
separately whether, under existing circumstances, he has not
done perfectly right in shutting up Moa Artua. The invariable
response is '*Aa, Aa*' (yes, yes), repeated over again and again
in a manner which ought to quiet the scruples of the most
conscientious. After a few moments Kolory brings forth his
doll again, and while arraying it very carefully in the tappa
and red cloth, alternately fondles and chides it. The toilet
being completed, he once more speaks to it aloud. The whole
company hereupon show the greatest interest; while the priest
holding Moa Artua to his ear interprets to them what he
pretends the god is confidentially communicating to him. Some
items of intelligence appear to tickle all present amazingly;
for one claps his hands in a rapture; another shouts with
merriment; and a third leaps to his feet and capers about like
a madman.

What under the sun Moa Artua on these occasions had to
say to Kolory I never could find out: but I could not help
thinking that the former showed a sad want of spirit in being
disciplined into making those disclosures, which at first he
seemed bent on withholding. Whether the priest honestly interpreted what he believed the divinity said to him or whether
he was not all the while guilty of a vile humbug, I shall not
presume to decide. At any rate whatever as coming from the
god was imparted to those present seemed to be generally

of a complimentary nature: a fact which illustrates the sagacity of Kolory, or else the time-serving disposition of this hardly used deity.

Moa Artua having nothing more to say, his bearer goes to nursing him again, in which occupation, however, he is soon interrupted by a question put by one of the warriors to the god. Kolory hereupon snatches it up to his ear again, and after listening attentively, once more officiates as the organ of communication. A multitude of questions and answers having passed between the parties, much to the satisfaction of those who propose them, the god is put tenderly to bed in the trough, and the whole company unite in a long chant, led off by Kolory. This ended, the ceremony is over; the chiefs rise to their feet in high good humor, and my Lord Archbishop, after chatting awhile, and regaling himself with a whiff or two from a pipe of tobacco, tucks the canoe under his arm and marches off with it.

The whole of these proceedings were like those of a parcel of children playing with dolls and baby houses.

For a youngster scarcely ten inches high, and with so few early advantages as he doubtless had had, Moa Artua was certainly a precocious little fellow if he really said all that was imputed to him; but for what reason this poor devil of a deity, thus cuffed about, cajoled and shut up in a box, was held in greater estimation than the full-grown and dignified personages of the Taboo Groves, I cannot divine. And yet Mehevi, and other chiefs of unquestionable veracity—to say nothing of the Primate himself—assured me over and over again that Moa Artua was the tutelary deity of Typee, and was more to be held in honor than a whole battalion of the clumsy idols in the Hoolah-Hoolah grounds. Kory-Kory—who seemed to have devoted considerable attention to the study of theology, as he knew the names of all the graven images in the valley, and often repeated them over to me—likewise entertained some rather enlarged ideas with regard to the character and pretensions of Moa Artua. He once gave me to understand, with a gesture there was no misconceiving, that if he (Moa Artua) were so minded, he could cause a coconut tree to sprout out of his (Kory-Kory's) head; and that it would be the easiest thing in life for him (Moa Artua) to take the whole island of Nukuheva in his mouth and dive down to the bottom of the sea with it.

But in sober seriousness, I hardly knew what to make of the religion of the valley. There was nothing that so much perplexed the illustrious Cook, in his intercourse with the South Sea islanders, as their sacred rites. Although this prince of navigators was in many instances assisted by interpreters in the prosecution of his researches, he still frankly acknowledges that he was at a loss to obtain anything like a clear insight into the puzzling arcana of their faith. A similar admission has been made by other eminent voyagers: by Carteret, Byron, Kotzebue, and Vancouver.

For my own part, although hardly a day passed while I remained upon the island that I did not witness some religious ceremony or other, it was very much like seeing a parcel of Freemasons making secret signs to each other; I saw everything, but could comprehend nothing.

On the whole, I am inclined to believe that the islanders in the Pacific have no fixed and definite ideas whatever on the subject of religion. I am persuaded that Kolory himself would be effectually posed were he called upon to draw up the articles of his faith and pronounce the creed by which he hoped to be saved. In truth, the Typees, so far as their actions evince, submitted to no laws, human or divine—always excepting the thrice mysterious taboo. The 'independent electors' of the valley were not to be browbeaten by chiefs, priests, idols, or devils. As for the luckless idols, they received more hard knocks than supplications. I do not wonder that some of them looked so grim, and stood so bolt upright, as if fearful of looking to the right or the left lest they should give any one offence. The fact is, they had to carry themselves pretty straight, or suffer the consequences. Their worshipers were such a precious set of fickle-minded and irreverent heathens, that there was no telling when they might topple one of them over, break it to pieces, and making a fire with it on the very altar itself, fall to roasting the offerings of breadfruit, and eat them in spite of its teeth.

In how little reverence these unfortunate deities were held by the natives was on one occasion most convincingly proved to me. Walking with Kory-Kory through the deepest recesses of the groves, I perceived a curious-looking image, about six feet in height, which originally had been placed upright against a low *pi-pi*, surmounted by a ruinous bamboo temple, but having become fatigued and weak in the knees, was now carelessly leaning against it. The idol was partly concealed by the foliage of a tree which stood near, and whose leafy boughs drooped over the pile of stones, as if to protect the rude fane from the decay to which it was rapidly hastening. The image itself was nothing more than a grotesquely shaped log, carved in the likeness of a portly, naked man with the arms clasped over the head, the jaws thrown wide apart, and its thick, shapeless legs bowed into an arch. It was much decayed. The lower part was overgrown with a bright silky moss. Thin spears of grass sprouted from the distended mouth and fringed the outline of the head and arms. His Godship had literally attained a green old age. All its prominent points were bruised and battered, or entirely rotted away. The nose had taken its departure, and from the general appearance of the head it might have been supposed that the wooden divinity, in despair at the neglect of its worshippers, had been trying to beat its own brains out against the surrounding trees.

I drew near to inspect more closely this strange object of idolatry; but halted reverently at the distance of two or three paces, out of regard to the religious prejudices of my valet. As soon, however, as Kory-Kory perceived that I was in one of my inquiring, scientific moods, to my astonishment, he sprang to the side of the idol, and pushing it away from the stones against which it rested, endeavored to make it stand upon its legs. But the divinity had lost the use of them altogether; and while Kory-Kory was trying to prop it up, by placing a stick between it and the *pi-pi*, the monster fell clumsily to the ground, and would infallibly have broken its neck had not Kory-Kory providentially broken its fall by receiving its whole weight on his own half-crushed back. I never saw the honest fellow in such a rage before. He leaped furiously to his feet, and seizing the stick, began beating the poor image: every moment or two pausing and talking to it in the most violent manner, as if upbraiding it for the accident. When his indignation had subsided a little he whirled the idol about most profanely, so as to give me an opportunity of examining it on all sides. I am quite sure I never should have presumed to have taken such liberties with the god myself, and I was not a little shocked at Kory-Kory's impiety.

This anecdote speaks for itself. When one of the inferior order of natives could show such contempt for a venerable and decrepit God of the Groves, what the state of religion must be among the people in general is easily to be imagined. In truth, I regard the Typees as a back-slidden generation. They are sunk in religious sloth, and require a spiritual revival. A long prosperity of breadfruit and coconuts has rendered them remiss in the performance of their higher obligations. The wood-rot malady is spreading among the idols —the fruit upon their altars is becoming offensive—the temples themselves need rethatching—the tattooed clergy are altogether too lighthearted and lazy—and their flocks are going astray.

XXV

General information gathered at the festival—personal beauty of the Typees—their superiority over the inhabitants of the other islands—diversity of complexion—a vegetable cosmetic and ointment—testimony of voyagers to the uncommon beauty of the Marquesans—few evidences of intercourse with civilized beings—dilapidated musket—primitive simplicity of government—regal dignity of Mehevi.

ALTHOUGH I HAD BEEN unable during the late festival to obtain information on many interesting subjects which had much excited my curiosity, still that important event had not passed by without adding materially to my general knowledge of the islanders.

I was especially struck by the physical strength and beauty which they displayed, by their great superiority in these respects over the inhabitants of the neighboring bay of Nuku-heva, and by the singular contrasts they presented among themselves in their various shades of complexion.

In beauty of form they surpassed anything I had ever seen. Not a single instance of natural deformity was observable in all the throng attending the revels. Occasionally I noticed among the men the scars of wounds they had received in battle; and sometimes, though very seldom, the loss of a finger, an eye, or an arm, attributable to the same cause. With these exceptions, every individual appeared free from those blemishes which sometimes mar the effect of an otherwise perfect form. But their physical excellence did not merely consist in an exemption from these evils; nearly every individual of their number might have been taken for a sculptor's model.

When I remembered that these islanders derived no advantage from dress, but appeared in all the naked simplicity of nature, I could not avoid comparing them with the fine gentlemen and dandies who promenade such unexceptionable figures in our frequented thoroughfares. Stripped of the cunning artifices of the tailor, and standing forth in the garb of Eden— what a sorry set of round-shouldered, spindle-shanked, crane-necked varlets would civilized men appear! Stuffed calves, padded breasts, and scientifically cut pantaloons would then avail them nothing, and the effect would be truly deplorable.

Nothing in the appearance of the islanders struck me more forcibly than the whiteness of their teeth. The novelist always compares the masticators of his heroine to ivory; but I boldly pronounce the teeth of the Typees to be far more beautiful than ivory itself. The jaws of the oldest graybeards among them were much better garnished than those of most of the youths of civilized countries; while the teeth of the young and middle-aged, in their purity and whiteness, were actually dazzling to the eye. This marvellous whiteness of the teeth is to be ascribed to the pure vegetable diet of these people, and the uninterrupted healthfulness of their natural mode of life.

The men, in almost every instance, are of lofty stature, scarcely ever less than six feet in height, while the other sex are uncommonly diminutive. The early period of life at which the human form arrives at maturity in this generous tropical climate, likewise deserves to be mentioned. A little creature, not more than thirteen years of age, and who in other particulars might be regarded as a mere child, is often seen nursing her own baby; whilst lads who, under less ripening skies, would be still at school, are here responsible fathers of families.

On first entering the Typee Valley, I had been struck with the marked contrast presented by its inhabitants with those of the bay I had previously left. In the latter place, I had not been favorably impressed with the personal appearance of the male portion of the population; although with the females, excepting in some truly melancholy instances, I had been wonderfully pleased. I had observed that even the little intercourse Europeans had carried on with the Nukuheva natives had not failed to leave its traces amongst them. One of the most dreadful curses under which humanity labors had commenced its havocs, and betrayed, as it ever does among the South Sea islanders, the most aggravated symptoms. From this, as from all other foreign inflictions, the yet uncontaminated tenants of the Typee Valley were wholly exempt; and long may they continue so. Better will it be for them for ever to remain the happy and innocent heathens and barbarians that they now are, than, like the wretched inhabitants of the Sandwich Islands, to enjoy the mere name of Christians without experiencing any of the vital operations of true religion, whilst, at the same time, they are made the victims of the worst vices and evils of civilized life.

Apart, however, from these considerations, I am inclined to believe that there exists a radical difference between the two tribes, if indeed they are not distinct races of men. To those who have merely touched at Nukuheva Bay, without visiting other portions of the island, it would hardly appear credible the diversities presented between the various small clans inhabiting so diminutive a spot. But the hereditary hostility which has existed between them for ages fully accounts for this.

Not so easy, however, is it to assign an adequate cause for the endless variety of complexions to be seen in the Typee Valley. During the festival, I had noticed several young females whose skins were almost as white as any Saxon damsels'; a slight dash of the mantling brown being all that marked the difference. This comparative fairness of complexion, though in a great degree perfectly natural, is partly the result of an artificial process, and of an entire exclusion from the sun. The juice of the *papa* root, found in great abundance at the head of the valley, is held in great esteem as a cosmetic, with which many of the females daily anoint their whole person. The habitual use of it whitens and beautifies the skin. Those of the young girls who resort to this method of heightening their charms, never expose themselves to the rays of the sun; an observance, however, that produces little or no inconvenience, since there are but few of the inhabited portions of the vale which are not shaded over with a spreading canopy of boughs, so that one may journey from house to house, scarcely deviating from the direct course, and yet never once see his shadow cast upon the ground.

The *papa*, when used, is suffered to remain upon the skin for several hours; being of a light green color, it consequently imparts for the time a similar hue to the complexion. Nothing, therefore, can be imagined more singular than the appearance of these nearly naked damsels immediately after the application of the cosmetic. To look at one of them you would almost suppose she was some vegetable in an unripe state; and that, instead of living in the shade for ever, she ought to be placed out in the sun to ripen.

All the islanders are more or less in the habit of anointing themselves; the women preferring the *aker* or *papa*, and the men using the oil of the coconut. Mehevi was remarkably fond of mollifying his entire cuticle with this ointment. Sometimes he might be seen, with his whole body fairly reeking with the perfumed oil of the nut, looking as if he had just emerged from a soap-boiler's vat, or had undergone the process of dipping in a tallow chandlery. To this cause perhaps, united to their frequent bathing and extreme cleanliness, is ascribable, in a great measure, the marvellous purity and smoothness of skin exhibited by the natives in general.

The prevailing tint among the women of the valley was a light olive, and of this style of complexion Fayaway afforded the most beautiful example. Others were still darker, while not a few were of a genuine golden color, and some of a swarthy hue.

As agreeing with much previously mentioned in this narrative, I may here observe, that Mendanna, their discoverer, in his account of the Marquesas, described the natives as wondrously beautiful to behold, and as nearly resembling the people of southern Europe. The first of these islands seen by Mendanna was La Madelena, which is not far distant from Nukuheva; and its inhabitants in every respect resemble those dwelling on that and the other islands of the group. Figueroa, the chronicler of Mendanna's voyage, says, that on the morn-

ing the land was descried, when the Spaniards drew near
the shore, there sallied forth, in rude procession, about sev-
enty canoes, and at the same time many of the inhabitants
(females, I presume) made toward the ship by swimming.
He adds, that 'in complexion they were nearly white; of good
stature, and finely formed; and on their faces and bodies were
delineated representations of fishes and other devices.' The
old Don then goes on to say, 'There came, among others, two
lads paddling their canoe, whose eyes were fixed on the ship;
they had beautiful faces and the most promising animation of
countenance; and were in all things so becoming, that the
pilot-mayor Quiros affirmed, nothing in his life ever caused
him so much regret as the leaving such fine creatures to be
lost in that country.'5 More than two hundred years have gone
by since the passage of which the above is a translation was
written; and it appears to me now, as I read it, as fresh and
true as if written but yesterday. The islanders are still the
same; and I have seen boys in the Typee Valley of whose
'beautiful faces' and 'promising animation of countenance' no
one who has not beheld them can form any adequate idea.
Cook, in the account of his voyages, pronounces the Marquesans as by far the most splendid islanders in the South
Seas. Stewart, the chaplain of the U.S. ship *Vincennes*, in his
Scenes in the South Seas, expresses, in more than one place,
his amazement at the surpassing loveliness of the women; and
says that many of the Nukuheva damsels reminded him forcibly of the most celebrated beauties in his own land. Fanning,
a Yankee mariner of some reputation, likewise records his
lively impressions of the physical appearance of these people;
and Commodore David Porter of the U.S. frigate *Essex*, is
said to have been vastly smitten by the beauty of the ladies.
Their great superiority over all other Polynesians cannot fail

---

5 This passage, which is cited as an almost literal translation from the
original, I found in a small volume entitled *Circumnavigation of the Globe*,
in which volume are several extracts from *Dalrymple's Historical Collections*.
The last-mentioned work I have never seen, but it is said to contain a very
correct English version of great part of the learned Doctor Christoval Suaverde
de Figueroa's *History of Mendanna's Voyage*, published at Madrid A.D. 1613.

to attract the notice of those who visit the principal groups in the Pacific. The voluptuous Tahitians are the only people who at all deserve to be compared with them; while the dark-hued Hawaiians and the woolly-headed Feegees are immeasurably inferior to them. The distinguishing characteristic of the Marquesan islanders, and that which at once strikes you, is the European cast of their features—a peculiarity seldom observable among other uncivilized people. Many of their faces present a profile classically beautiful, and in the valley of Typee, I saw several who, like the stranger Marnoo, were in every respect models of beauty.

Some of the natives present at the 'Feast of Calabashes' had displayed a few articles of European dress; disposed, however, about their persons after their own peculiar fashion. Among these I perceived the two pieces of cotton cloth which poor Toby and myself had bestowed upon our youthful guides the afternoon we entered the valley. They were evidently reserved for gala days; and during those of the festival they rendered the young islanders who wore them very distinguished characters. The small number who were similarly adorned, and the great value they appeared to place upon the most common and most trivial articles, furnished ample evidence of the very restricted intercourse they held with vessels touching at the island. A few cotton handkerchiefs, of a gay pattern, tied about the neck, and suffered to fall over the shoulders; strips of fanciful calico, swathed about the loins, were nearly all I saw.

Indeed, throughout the valley, there were few things of any kind to be seen of European origin. All I ever saw beside the articles just alluded to, were the six muskets preserved in the Ti, and three or four similar implements of warfare hung up in other houses; some small canvas bags, partly filled with bullets and powder, and half a dozen old hatchet heads, with the edges blunted and battered to such a degree as to render them utterly useless. These last seemed to be regarded as nearly worthless by the natives; and several times they held up one of them before me, and throwing it aside with a gesture of disgust, manifested their contempt for anything that could so soon become unserviceable.

But the muskets, the powder, and the bullets were held in most extravagant esteem. The former, from their great age and the peculiarities they exhibited, were well worthy a place in any antiquarian's armory. I remember in particular one that hung in the Ti, and which Mehevi—supposing as a matter of course that I was able to repair it—had put into my hands for that purpose. It was one of those clumsy, old-fashioned, English pieces known generally as Tower Hill muskets, and, for aught I know, might have been left on the island by Wallace, Carteret, Cook, or Vancouver. The stock was half-rotten and worm-eaten; the lock was as rusty and about as well adapted to its ostensible purpose as an old door hinge; the threading of the screws about the trigger was completely worn away; while the barrel shook in the wood. Such was the weapon the chief desired me to restore to its original condition. As I did not possess the accomplishments of a gunsmith, and was likewise destitute of the necessary tools, I was reluctantly obliged to signify my inability to perform the task. At this unexpected communication Mehevi regarded me, for a moment, as if he half suspected I was some inferior sort of white man, who after all did not know much more than a Typee. However, after a most labored explanation of the matter, I succeeded in making him understand the extreme difficulty of the task. Scarcely satisfied with my apologies, however, he marched off with the superannuated musket in something of a huff as if he would no longer expose it to the indignity of being manipulated by such unskilful fingers.

During the festival I had not failed to remark the simplicity of manner, the freedom from all restraint, and, to a certain degree, the quality of condition manifested by the natives in general. No one appeared to assume any arrogant pretensions. There was little more than a slight difference in costume to distinguish the chiefs from the other natives. All appeared to mix together freely, and without any reserve; although I noticed that the wishes of a chief, even when delivered in the mildest tone, received the same immediate obedience which elsewhere would have been only accorded to a peremptory command. What may be the extent of the authority of the chiefs over the rest of the tribe, I will not venture to assert; but from all I saw during my stay in the valley, I was induced to believe that in matters concerning the general welfare it was very limited. The required degree of deference toward them, however, was willingly and cheerfully yielded; and as all authority is transmitted from father to son, I have no doubt that one of the effects here, as elsewhere, of high birth, is to induce respect and obedience.

The civil institutions of the Marquesas Islands appear to be in this, as in other aspects, directly the reverse of those of the Tahitian and Hawaiian groups, where the original power of the king and chiefs was far more despotic than that of any tyrant in civilized countries. At Tahiti it used to be death for one of the inferior orders to approach, without permission, under the shadow of the King's house; or to fail in paying the customary reverence when food destined for the king was borne past them by his messengers. At the Sandwich Islands, Kaahumanu, the gigantic old dowager queen—a woman of nearly four hundred pounds weight, and who is said to be still living at Mowee—was accustomed, in some of her terrific gusts of temper, to snatch up an ordinary-sized man who had offended her, and snap his spine across her knee. Incredible as this may seem, it is a fact. While at Lahainaluna—the residence of this monstrous Jezebel—a humpbacked wretch was pointed out to me, who, some twenty-five years previously, had had the vertebrae of his backbone very seriously discomposed by his gentle mistress.

The particular grades of rank existing among the chiefs of Typee, I could not in all cases determine. Previous to the 'Feast of Calabashes' I had been puzzled what particular station to assign to Mehevi. But the important part he took upon that occasion convinced me that he had no superior among the inhabitants of the valley. I had invariably noticed a certain degree of deference paid to him by all with whom I had ever seen him brought in contact; but when I remembered that my wanderings had been confined to a limited portion

of the valley, and that toward the sea a number of distinguished chiefs resided, some of whom had separately visited
me at Marheyo's house, and whom, until the festival, I had
never seen in the company of Mehevi, I felt disposed to believe that his rank after all might not be particularly elevated.

The revels, however, had brought together all the warriors
whom I had seen individually and in groups at different times
and places. Among them Mehevi moved with an easy air of
superiority which was not to be mistaken; and he whom I
had only looked at as the hospitable host of the Ti, and one
of the military leaders of the tribe, now assumed in my eyes
the dignity of royal station. His striking costume, no less than
his naturally commanding figure, seemed indeed to give him
pre-eminence over the rest. The towering helmet of feathers
that he wore raised him in height above all who surrounded
him; and though some others were similarly adorned, the
length and luxuriance of their plumes were far inferior to his.

Mehevi was in fact the greatest of the chiefs—the head of
his clan—the sovereign of the valley; and the simplicity of
the social institutions of the people could not have been more
completely proved than by the fact, that after having been
several weeks in the valley, and almost in daily intercourse
with Mehevi, I should have remained until the time of the
festival ignorant of his regal character. But a new light had
now broken in upon me. The Ti was the palace—and Mehevi
the king. Both the one and the other of a most simple and
patriarchal nature it must be allowed, and wholly unattended
by the ceremonious pomp which usually surrounds the purple.

After having made this discovery I could not avoid congratulating myself that Mehevi had from the first taken me
as it were under his royal protection, and that he still continued to entertain for me the warmest regard, as far at least
as I was enabled to judge from appearances. For the future
I determined to pay most assiduous court to him, hoping that
eventually through his kindness I might obtain my liberty.

XXVI

King Mehevi—allusion to His Hawaiian Majesty—
conduct of Marheyo and Mehevi in certain delicate
matters—peculiar system of marriage—number of
population—uniformity—embalming—places of sepulcher—funeral obsequies at Nukuheva—number of
inhabitants in Typee—location of the dwellings—
happiness enjoyed in the valley—a warning—some
ideas with regard to the civilization of the islands—
reference to the present state of the Hawaiians—
story of a missionary's wife—fashionable equipages
at Oahu—reflections.

KING MEHEVI!—A goodly sounding title!—and why should
I not bestow it upon the foremost man in the valley of Typee?
The republican missionaries of Oahu cause to be gazetted in
the Court Journal, published at Honolulu, the most trivial
movements of 'His Gracious Majesty' King Kammahammaha
III, and 'Their Highnesses the Princes of the Blood Royal.'[6]—

---

[6] Accounts like these are sometimes copied into English and American journals.
They lead the reader to infer that the arts and customs of civilized life are
rapidly refining the natives of the Sandwich Islands. But let no one be deceived
by these accounts. The chiefs swagger about in gold lace and broadcloth, while
the great mass of the common people are nearly as primitive in their appearance as in the days of Cook. In the progress of events at these Islands, the
two classes are receding from each other; the chiefs are daily becoming more
luxurious and extravagant in their style of living, and the common people more
and more destitute of the necessaries and decencies of life. But the end to
which both will arrive at last will be the same: the one are fast destroying
themselves by sensual indulgences, and the other are fast *being* destroyed by a
complication of disorders, and the want of wholesome food. The resources of
the domineering chiefs are wrung from the starving serfs, and every additional
bauble with which they bedeck themselves is purchased by the sufferings of
their bondsmen; so that the measure of gew-gaw refinement attained by the
chiefs is only an index to the actual state of degradation in which the greater
portion of the population lie groveling.

And who is 'His Gracious Majesty,' and what the quality of this 'blood royal'?—'His Gracious Majesty' is a fat, lazy, Negro-looking blockhead, with as little character as power. He has lost the noble traits of the barbarian, without acquiring the redeeming graces of a civilized being; and, although a member of the Hawaiian Temperance Society, is a most inveterate dram-drinker.

The 'Blood Royal' is an extremely thick, depraved fluid; formed principally of raw fish, bad brandy, and European sweetmeats, and is charged with a variety of eruptive humors, which are developed in sundry blotches and pimples upon the august face of 'Majesty Itself,' and the angelic countenances of the 'Princes and Princesses of the Blood Royal'!

Now, if the farcical puppet of a chief magistrate in the Sandwich Islands be allowed the title of King, why should it be withheld from the noble savage Mehevi, who is a thousand times more worthy of the appellation? All hail, therefore, Mehevi, King of the Cannibal Valley, and long life and prosperity of His Typeean Majesty! May Heaven for many a year preserve him, the uncompromising foe of Nukuheva and the French, if a hostile attitude will secure his lovely domain from the remorseless inflictions of South Sea civilization.

Previously to seeing the Dancing Widows I had little idea that there were any matrimonial relations subsisting in Typee, and I should as soon have thought of a Platonic affection being cultivated between the sexes as of the solemn connection of man and wife. To be sure, there were old Marheyo and Tinor, who seemed to have a sort of nuptial understanding with one another; but for all that, I had sometimes observed a comical-looking old gentleman dressed in a suit of shabby tattooing, who had the audacity to take various liberties with the lady, and that too in the very presence of the old warrior her husband, who looked on, as good-naturedly as if nothing was happening. This behavior, until subsequent discoveries enlightened me, puzzled me more than anything else I witnessed in Typee.

As for Mehevi, I had supposed him a confirmed bachelor, as well as most of the principal chiefs. At any rate, if they had wives and families, they ought to have been ashamed of themselves; for sure I am, they never troubled themselves about any domestic affairs. In truth, Mehevi seemed to be the president of a club of hearty fellows, who kept 'Bachelors' Hall' in fine style at the Ti. I had no doubt but that they regarded children as odious encumbrances; and their ideas of domestic felicity were sufficiently shown in the fact, that they allowed no meddlesome housekeepers to turn topsy-turvy those snug little arrangements they had made in their comfortable dwelling. I strongly suspected, however, that some of these jolly bachelors were carrying on love intrigues with the maidens of the tribe; although they did not appear publicly to acknowledge them. I happened to pop upon Mehevi three or four times when he was romping—in a most undignified manner for a warrior-king—with one of the prettiest little witches in the valley. She lived with an old woman and a young man in a house near Marheyo's; and although in appearance a mere child herself, had a noble boy about a year old, who bore a marvelous resemblance to Mehevi, whom I should certainly have believed to have been the father, were it not that the little fellow had no triangle on his face—but on second thoughts, tattooing is not hereditary. Mehevi, however, was not the only person upon whom the damsel Moonoony smiled—the young fellow of fifteen, who permanently resided in the house with her, was decidedly in her good graces. I sometimes beheld both him and the chief making love at the same time. Is it possible, thought I, that the valiant warrior can consent to give up a corner in the thing he loves? This too was a mystery which, with others of the same kind, was afterward satisfactorily explained.

During the second day of the 'Feast of Calabashes,' Kory-Kory—being determined that I should have some understanding on these matters—had, in the course of his explanations, directed my attention to a peculiarity I had frequently remarked among many of the females;—principally those of a mature age and rather matronly appearance. This consisted in having the right hand and the left foot most elaborately tattooed; while the rest of the body was wholly free from the operation of the art, with the exception of the minutely dotted lips and slight marks on the shoulders, to which I have previously referred as comprising the sole tattooing exhibited by Fayaway, in common with other young girls of her age. The hand and foot thus embellished were, according to Kory-Kory, the distinguishing badge of wedlock, so far as that social and highly commendable institution is known among these people. It answers, indeed, the same purpose as the plain gold ring worn by our fairer spouses.

After Kory-Kory's explanation of the subject, I was for some time studiously respectful in the presence of all females thus distinguished, and never ventured to indulge in the slightest approach to flirtation with any of their number. Married women, to be sure!—I knew better than to offend them.

A further insight however into the peculiar domestic customs of the inmates of the valley did away in a measure with the severity of my scruples, and convinced me that I was deceived in some at least of my conclusions. A regular system of polygamy exists among the islanders; but of a most extraordinary nature—a plurality of husbands, instead of wives; and this solitary fact speaks volumes for the gentle disposition of the male population. Where else, indeed, could such a practice exist, even for a single day?—Imagine a revolution brought about in a Turkish seraglio, and the harem rendered the abode of bearded men; or conceive some beautiful woman in our own country running distracted at the sight of her numerous lovers murdering one another before her eyes, out of jealousy for the unequal distribution of her favors!—Heaven defend us from such a state of things!—We are scarce amiable and forbearing enough to submit to it.

I was not able to learn what particular ceremony was observed in forming the marriage contract, but am inclined to think that it must have been of a very simple nature. Perhaps the mere 'popping the question,' as it is termed with us, might have been followed by an immediate nuptial alliance. At any rate, I have more than one reason to believe that tedious courtships are unknown in the valley of Typee.

The males considerably outnumber the females. This holds true of many of the islands of Polynesia, although the reverse of what is the case in most civilized countries. The girls are first wooed and won, at a very tender age, by some stripling in the household in which they reside. This, however, is a mere frolic of the affections, and no formal engagement is contracted. By the time this first love has a little subsided a second suitor presents himself, of graver years, and carries both boy and girl away to his own habitation. This disinterested and generous-hearted fellow now weds the young couple—marrying damsel and lover at the same time—and all three thenceforth live together as harmoniously as so many turtles. I have heard of some men who in civilized countries rashly marry large families with their wives, but had no idea that there was any place where people married supplementary husbands with them. Infidelity on either side is very rare. No man has more than one wife, and no wife of mature years has less than two husbands—sometimes she has three, but such instances are not frequent. The marriage tie, whatever it may be, does not appear to be indissoluble; for separations occasionally happen. These, however, when they do take place, produce no unhappiness, and are preceded by no bickerings; for the simple reason, that an ill-used wife or a henpecked husband is not obliged to file a bill in Chancery to obtain a divorce. As nothing stands in the way of a separation, the matrimonial yoke sits easily and lightly, and a Typee wife lives on very pleasant and sociable terms with her husbands. On the whole, wedlock, as known among these Typees, seems to be of a more distinct and enduring nature than is usually the case with barbarous people. A baneful promiscuous intercourse of the sexes is hereby avoided, and virtue, without being clamorously invoked, is, as it were, unconsciously practiced.

The contrast exhibited between the Marquesas and other islanders of the Pacific in this respect, is worthy of being noticed. At Tahiti the marriage tie was altogether unknown; and the relation of husband and wife, father and son, could hardly be said to exist. The Arreory Society—one of the most singular institutions that ever existed in any part of the world

—spread universal licentiousness over the island. It was the voluptuous character of these people which rendered the disease introduced among them by De Bougainville's ships, in 1768, doubly destructive. It visited them like a plague, sweeping them off by hundreds.

Notwithstanding the existence of wedlock among the Typees, the Scriptural injunction to increase and multiply seems to be but indifferently attended to. I never saw any of those large families in arithmetical or stepladder progression which one often meets with at home. I never knew of more than two youngsters living together in the same home, and but seldom even that number. As for the women it was very plain that the anxieties of the nursery but seldom disturbed the serenity of their souls; and they were never to be seen going about the valley with half a score of little ones tagging at their apron-strings, or rather at the breadfruit leaf they usually wore in the rear.

The ratio of increase among all the Polynesian nations is very small; and in some places as yet uncorrupted by intercourse with Europeans, the births would appear but very little to outnumber the deaths; the population in such instances remaining nearly the same for several successive generations, even upon those islands seldom or never desolated by wars, and among people with whom the crime of infanticide is altogether unknown. This would seem expressly ordained by Providence to prevent the overstocking of the islands with a race too indolent to cultivate the ground, and who, for that reason alone, would by any considerable increase in their numbers, be exposed to the most deplorable misery. During the entire period of my stay in the valley of Typee, I never saw more than ten or twelve children under the age of six months, and only became aware of two births.

It is to the absence of the marriage tie that the late rapid decrease of the population of the Sandwich Islands and of Tahiti is in part to be ascribed. The vices and disease introduced among these unhappy people annually swell the ordinary mortality of the islands, while, from the same cause, the originally small number of births is proportionally decreased. Thus the progress of the Hawaiians and Tahitians to utter extinction is accelerated in a sort of compound ratio.

I have before had occasion to remark that I never saw any of the ordinary signs of a place of sepulcher in the village, a circumstance which I attributed, at the time, to my living in a particular part of it, and being forbidden to extend my rambles to any considerable distance toward the sea. I have since thought it probable, however, that the Typees, either desirous of removing from their sight the evidence of mortality, or prompted by a taste for rural beauty, may have some charming cemetery situated in the shadowy recesses along the base of the mountains. At Nukuheva, two or three large quadrangular *pi-pis,* heavily flagged, enclosed with regular stone walls and shaded over and almost hidden from view by the interlacing branches of enormous trees, were pointed out to me as burial places. The bodies, I understood, were deposited in rude vaults beneath the flagging, and were suffered to remain there without being disinterred. Although nothing could be more strange and gloomy than the aspect of these places where the lofty trees threw their dark shadows over rude blocks of stone, a stranger in looking at them would have discerned none of the ordinary evidences of a place of sepulture.

During my stay in the valley, as none of its inmates were so accommodating as to die and be buried in order to gratify my curiosity with regard to their funeral rites, I was reluctantly obliged to remain in ignorance of them. As I have reason to believe, however, that the observances of the Typees in these matters are the same with those of all the other tribes on the island, I will here relate a scene I chanced to witness at Nukuheva.

A young man had died, about daybreak, in a house near the beach. I had been sent ashore that morning, and saw a good deal of the preparations they were making for his obsequies. The body, neatly wrapped in new white tappa, was laid out in an open shed of coconut boughs, upon a bier constructed of elastic bamboos ingeniously twisted together. This was supported, about two feet from the ground, by large canes planted upright in the earth. Two females, of a dejected appearance, watched by its side, plaintively chanting and beating the air with large grass fans whitened with pipeclay. In the dwelling house adjoining a numerous company were assembled, and various articles of food were being prepared for consumption. Two or three individuals, distinguished by headdresses of beautiful tappa, and wearing a great number of ornaments, appeared to officiate as masters of the ceremonies. By noon the entertainment had fairly begun, and we were told that it would last during the whole of the two following days. With the exception of those who mourned by the corpse, every one seemed disposed to drown the sense of the late bereavement in convivial indulgence. The girls, decked out in their savage finery, danced; the old men chanted; the warriors smoked and chanted; and the young and lusty, of both sexes, feasted plentifully, and seemed to enjoy themselves as pleasantly as they could have done had it been a wedding.

The islanders understand the art of embalming, and practice it with such success, that the bodies of their great chiefs are frequently preserved for many years in the very houses where they died. I saw three of these in my visit to the Bay of Tior. One was enveloped in immense folds of tappa, with only the face exposed, and hung erect against the side of the dwelling. The others were stretched out upon biers of bamboo, in open, elevated temples, which seemed consecrated to their memory. The heads of enemies killed in battle are invariably preserved and hung up as trophies in the house of the conqueror. I am not acquainted with the process which is in use, but believe that fumigation is the principal agency employed. All the remains which I saw presented the appearance of a ham after being suspended for some time in a smoky chimney.

But to return from the dead to the living. The late festival had drawn together, as I had every reason to believe, the whole population of the vale, and consequently I was enabled to make some estimate with regard to its numbers. I should imagine that there were about two thousand inhabitants in Typee; and no number could have been better adapted to the extent of the valley. The valley is some nine miles in length, and may average one in breadth; the houses being distributed at wide intervals throughout its whole extent, principally, however, toward the head of the vale. There are no villages: the houses stand here and there in the shadow of the groves, or are scattered along the banks of the winding stream; their golden-hued bamboo sides and gleaming white thatch forming a beautiful contrast to the perpetual verdure in which they are embowered. There are no roads of any kind in the valley —nothing but a labyrinth of footpaths twisting and turning among the thickets without end.

The penalty of the Fall presses very lightly upon the valley of Typee; for, with the one solitary exception of striking a light, I scarcely saw any piece of work performed there which caused the sweat to stand upon a single brow. As for digging and dwelling for a livelihood, the thing is altogether unknown. Nature had planted the breadfruit and the banana, and in her own good time she brings them to maturity, when the idle savage stretches forth his hand, and satisfies his appetite.

Ill-fated people! I shudder when I think of the change a few years will produce in their paradisiacal abode; and probably when the most destructive vices, and the worst attendances on civilization, shall have driven all peace and happiness from the valley, the magnanimous French will proclaim to the world that the Marquesas Islands have been converted to Christianity! and this the Catholic world will doubtless consider as a glorious event. Heaven help the 'Isles of the Sea'!—The sympathy which Christendom feels for them has, alas! in too many instances proved their bane.

How little do some of these poor islanders comprehend when they look around them, that no inconsiderable part of their disasters originate in certain tea-party excitements, under the influence of which benevolent-looking gentlemen in white cravats solicit alms, and old ladies in spectacles, and young ladies in sober russet low gowns, contribute sixpences toward the creation of a fund, the object of which is to ameliorate the spiritual condition of the Polynesians, but whose end has almost invariably been to accomplish their temporal destruction!

Let the savages be civilized, but civilize them with benefits, and not with evils; and let heathenism be destroyed, but not by destroying the heathen. The Anglo-Saxon hive have extirpated Paganism from the greater part of the North American continent; but with it they have likewise extirpated the greater portion of the red race. Civilization is gradually sweeping from the earth the lingering vestiges of Paganism, and at the same time the shrinking forms of its unhappy worshippers.

Among the islands of Polynesia, no sooner are the images overturned, the temples demolished, and the idolaters converted into nominal Christians, than disease, vice, and premature death make their appearance. The depopulated land is then recruited from the rapacious hordes of enlightened individuals who settle themselves within its borders, and clamorously announce the progress of the Truth. Neat villas, trim gardens, shaven lawns, spires, and cupolas arise, while the poor savage soon finds himself an interloper in the country of his fathers, and that too on the very site of the hut where he was born. The spontaneous fruits of the earth, which God in His wisdom had ordained for the support of the indolent natives, remorselessly seized upon and appropriated by the stranger, are devoured before the eyes of the starving inhabitants, or sent on board the numerous vessels which now touch at their shores.

When the famished wretches are cut off in this manner from their natural supplies, they are told by their benefactors to work and earn their support by the sweat of their brows! But to no fine gentleman born to hereditary opulence does manual labor come more unkindly than to the luxurious Indian when thus robbed of the bounty of Heaven. Habituated to a life of indolence, he cannot and will not exert himself; and want, disease, and vice, all evils of foreign growth, soon terminate his miserable existence.

But what matters all this? Behold the glorious result!—The abominations of Paganism have given way to the pure rites of the Christian worship, the ignorant savage has been supplanted by the refined European! Look at Honolulu, the metropolis of the Sandwich Islands!—A community of disinterested merchants, and devoted self-exiled heralds of the Cross, located on the very spot that twenty years ago was defiled by the presence of idolatry. What a subject for an eloquent Bible-meeting orator! Nor has such an opportunity for a display of missionary rhetoric been allowed to pass by unimproved!— But when these philanthropists send us such glowing accounts of one half of their labors, why does their modesty restrain them from publishing the other half of the good they have wrought?—Not until I visited Honolulu was I aware of the fact that the small remnant of the natives had been civilized into draught horses, and evangelized into beasts of burden. But so it is. They have been literally broken into the traces, and are harnessed to the vehicles of their spiritual instructors like so many dumb brutes!

Among a multitude of similar exhibitions that I saw, I shall never forget a robust, red-faced, and very ladylike personage, a missionary's spouse, who day after day for months together took her regular airings in a little go-cart drawn by two of the islanders, one an old grey-headed man, and the other a roguish stripling, both being, with the exception of the fig leaf, as naked as when they were born. Over a level piece of ground this pair of draft bipeds would go with a shambling, unsightly trot, the youngster hanging back all the time like a knowing horse, while the old hack plodded on and did all the work.

Rattling along through the streets of the town in this stylish equipage, the lady looks about her as magnificently as any queen driven in state to her coronation. A sudden elevation, and a sandy road however, soon disturb her serenity. The small wheels become imbedded on the loose soil,—the old stager stands tugging and sweating, while the young one frisks about and does nothing; not an inch does the chariot budge. Will the tenderhearted lady, who has left friends and home for the good of the souls of the poor heathen, will she think a little about their bodies and get out, and ease the wretched old man until the ascent is mounted? Not she; she could not dream of it. To be sure, she used to think nothing of driving the cows to pasture on the old farm in New England; but times have changed since then. So she retains her seat and bawls out, *'Hookee! hookee!'* (Pull, pull.) The old gentleman, frightened at the sound, labors away harder than ever; and the younger one makes a great show of straining himself, but takes care to keep one eye on his mistress, in order to know when to dodge out of harm's way. At last the good lady loses all patience; *'Hookee! hookee!'* and rap goes the heavy handle of her huge fan over the naked skull of the old savage; while the young one shies to one side and keeps beyond its range. *'Hookee! hookee!'* again she cries—*'Hookee tata kannaka!'* (Pull strong, men,)—but all in vain, and she is obliged in the end to dismount and, sad necessity! actually to walk to the top of the hill.

At the town where this paragon of humility resides, is a spacious and elegant American chapel, where divine service is regularly performed. Twice every Sabbath toward the close of the exercises may be seen a score or two of little wagons ranged along the railing in front of the edifice, with two squalid native footmen in the livery of nakedness standing by each, and waiting for the dismission of the congregation to draw their superiors home.

Lest the slightest misconception should arise from anything thrown out in this chapter, or indeed in any other part of the volume, let me here observe, that against the cause of missions in the abstract no Christian can possibly be opposed: it is in truth a just and holy cause. But if the great end proposed by it be spiritual, the agency employed to accomplish that end is purely earthly; and, although the object in view be the achievement of much good, that agency may nevertheless be productive of evil. In short, missionary undertaking, however it may be blessed of Heaven, is in itself but human; and subject, like everything else, to errors and abuses. And have not errors and abuses crept into the most sacred places, and may there not be unworthy or incapable missionaries abroad, as well as ecclesiastics of a similar character at home? May not the unworthiness or incapacity of those who assume apostolic function upon the remote islands of the sea more easily escape detection by the world at large than if it were displayed in the heart of a city? An unwarranted confidence in the sanctity of its apostles—a proneness to regard them as incapable of guile—and an impatience of the least suspicion as to their rectitude as men or Christians, have ever been prevailing faults in the Church. Nor is this to be wondered at: for subject as Christianity is to the assaults of unprincipled foes, we are naturally disposed to regard everything like an exposure of ecclesiastical misconduct as the offspring of malevolence or irreligious feeling. Not even this last consideration, however, shall deter me from the honest expression of my sentiments.

There is something decidedly wrong in the practical operations of the Sandwich Island missions. Those who from pure religious motives contribute to the support of this enterprise, should take care to ascertain that their donations, flowing through many devious channels, at last effect their legitimate object, the conversion of the Hawaiians. I urge this not because I doubt the moral probity of those who disburse these funds, but because I know that they are not rightly applied. To read pathetic accounts of missionary hardships, and glowing descriptions of conversions, and baptisms taking place beneath palm trees, is one thing; and to go to the Sandwich Islands and see the missionaries dwelling in picturesque and prettily furnished coral-rock villas, whilst the miserable natives are committing all sorts of immoralities around them, is quite another.

In justice to the missionaries, however, I will willingly admit, that whatever evils may have resulted from their collective mismanagement of the business of the mission, and from the want of vital piety evinced by some of their number, still the present deplorable condition of the Sandwich Islands is by no means wholly chargeable against them. The demoralizing influence of a dissolute foreign population, and the frequent visits of all descriptions of vessels, have tended not a little to increase the evils alluded to. In a word, here, as in every case where Civilization has in any way been introduced among those whom we call savages, she has scattered her vices, and withheld her blessings.

As wise a man as Shakespeare has said, that the bearer of

evil tidings hath but a losing office; and so I suppose will it prove with me, in communicating to the trusting friends of the Hawaiian Mission what has been disclosed in various portions of this narrative. I am persuaded, however, that as these disclosures will by their very nature attract attention, so they will lead to something which will not be without ultimate benefit to the cause of Christianity in the Sandwich Islands.

I have but one thing more to add in connection with this subject—those things which I have stated as facts will remain facts, in spite of whatever the bigoted or incredulous may say or write against them. My reflections, however, on those facts may not be free from error. If such be the case, I claim no further indulgence than should be conceded to every man whose object is to do good.

XXVII

The social condition and general character of the Typees.

I HAVE ALREADY mentioned that the influence exerted over the people of the valley by their chiefs was mild in the extreme: and as to any general rule or standard of conduct by which the commonalty were governed in their intercourse with each other, so far as my observation extended, I should be almost tempted to say that none existed on the island, except, indeed, the mysterious 'taboo' be considered as such. During the time I lived among the Typees, no one was ever put upon his trial for any offence against the public. To all appearances there were no courts of law or equity. There was no municipal police for the purpose of apprehending vagrants and disorderly characters. In short, there were no legal provisions whatever for the well-being and conservation of society, the enlightened end of civilized legislation. And yet everything went on in the valley with a harmony and smoothness unparalleled, I will venture to assert, in the most select, refined, and pious associations of mortals in Christendom. How are we to explain this enigma? These islanders were heathens! savages! ay, cannibals! and how came they, without the aid of established law, to exhibit, in so eminent a degree, that social order which is the greatest blessing and highest pride of the social state?

It may reasonably be inquired, how were these people governed? How were their passions controlled in their everyday transactions? It must have been by an inherent principle of honesty and charity toward each other. They seemed to be governed by that sort of tacit common-sense law which, say what they will of the inborn lawlessness of the human race, has its precepts graven on every breast. The grand principles of virtue and honor, however they may be distorted by arbitrary codes, are the same all the world over: and where these principles are concerned, the right or wrong of any action appears the same to the uncultivated as to the enlightened mind. It is to this indwelling, this universally diffused perception of what is *just* and *noble,* that the integrity of the Marquesans in their intercourse with each other is to be attributed. In the darkest nights they slept securely, with all their worldly wealth around them, in houses the doors of which were never fastened. The disquieting ideas of theft or assassination never disturbed them. Each islander reposed beneath his own palmetto thatching, or sat under his own breadfruit tree, with none to molest or alarm him. There was not a padlock in the valley, nor anything that answered the purpose of one: still there was no community of goods. This long spear, so elegantly carved and highly polished, belongs to Wormoonoo: it is far handsomer than the one which old Marheyo so greatly prizes; it is the most valuable article belonging to its owner. And yet I have seen it leaning against a coconut tree in the grove, and there it was found when sought for. Here is a sperm-whale tooth, graven all over with cunning devices: it is the property of Karluna: it is the most precious of the damsel's ornaments. In her estimation its price is far above rubies—and yet there hangs the dental jewel by its cord of braided bark, in the girl's house, which is far back in the valley; the door is left open, and all the inmates have gone off to bathe in the stream.[7]

So much for the respect in which 'personal property' is held in Typee; how secure an investment of 'real property' may be, I cannot take upon me to say. Whether the land of the valley was the joint property of its inhabitants, or whether it was parcelled out among a certain number of landed proprietors who allowed everybody to 'squat' and 'poach' as much as he or she pleased, I never could ascertain. At any rate, musty parchments and title-deeds there were none on the island; and I am half inclined to believe that its inhabitants hold their broad valleys in fee simple from Nature herself; to have and to hold, so long as grass grows and water runs; or until their French visitors, by a summary mode of conveyancing, shall appropriate them to their own benefit and behoof.

Yesterday I saw Kory-Kory hie him away, armed with a long pole, with which, standing on the ground, he knocked down the fruit from the topmost boughs of the trees, and brought them home in his basket of coconut leaves. Today I see an islander, whom I know to reside in a distant part of the valley, doing the self-same thing. On the sloping bank of the stream are a number of banana trees. I have often seen a score or two of young people making a merry foray on the great golden clusters, and bearing them off, one after another, to different parts of the vale, shouting and tramping as they went. No churlish old curmudgeon could have been the owner of that grove of breadfruit trees, or of these gloriously yellow bunches of bananas.

---

7 The strict honesty which the inhabitants of nearly all the Polynesian Islands manifest toward each other, is in striking contrast with the thieving propensities some of them evince in their intercourse with foreigners. It would almost seem that, according to their peculiar code of morals, the pilfering of a hatchet or a wrought nail from a European is looked upon as a praiseworthy action. Or rather, it may be presumed, that bearing in mind the wholesale forays made upon them by their nautical visitors, they consider the property of the latter as a fair object of reprisal. This consideration, while it serves to reconcile an apparent contradiction in the moral character of the islanders, should in some measure alter that low opinion of it which the reader of South Sea voyages is too apt to form.

From what I have said it will be perceived that there is a vast difference between 'personal property' and 'real estate' in the valley of Typee. Some individuals, of course, are more wealthy than others. For example: the ridgepole of Marheyo's house bends under the weight of many a huge package of tappa; his long couch is laid with mats placed one upon the other seven deep. Outside, Tinor has ranged along in her bamboo cupboard—or whatever the place may be called—a goodly array of calabashes and wooden trenchers. Now, the house just beyond the grove, and next to Marheyo's, occupied by Ruaruga, is not quite so well furnished. There are only three moderate-sized packages swinging overhead: there are only two layers of mats beneath, and the calabashes and trenchers are not so numerous, nor so tastefully stained and carved. But then, Ruaruga has a house—not so pretty a one, to be sure—but just as commodious as Marheyo's; and, I suppose, if he wished to vie with his neighbor's establishment, he could do so with very little trouble. These, in short, constituted the chief differences perceivable in the relative wealth of the people in Typee.

Civilization does not engross all the virtues of humanity: she has not even her full share of them. They flourish in greater abundance and attain greater strength among many barbarous people. The hospitality of the wild Arab, the courage of the North American Indian and the faithful friendships of some of the Polynesian nations, far surpass any thing of a similar kind among the polished communities of Europe. If truth and justice, and the better principles of our nature, cannot exist unless enforced by the statute book, how are we to account for the social condition of the Typees? So pure and upright were they in all the relations of life, that entering their valley, as I did, under the most erroneous impressions of their character, I was soon led to exclaim in amazement: 'Are these the ferocious savages, the bloodthirsty cannibals of whom I have heard such frightful tales! They deal more kindly with each other, and are more humane, than many who study essays on virtue and benevolence, and who repeat every night that beautiful prayer breathed first by the lips of the divine and gentle Jesus.' I will frankly declare, that after passing a few weeks in this valley of the Marquesas, I formed a higher estimate of human nature than I had ever before entertained. But alas! since then I have been one of the crew of a man-of-war, and the pent-up wickedness of five hundred men has nearly overturned all my previous theories.

There was one admirable trait in the general character of the Typees which, more than any thing else secured my admiration: it was the unanimity of feeling they displayed on every occasion. With them there hardly appeared to be any difference of opinion upon any subject whatever. They all thought and acted alike. I do not conceive that they could support a debating society for a single night: there would be nothing to dispute about; and were they to call a convention to take into consideration the state of the tribe, its session would be a remarkably short one. They showed this spirit of unanimity in every action of life: everything was done in concert and good fellowship. I will give an instance of this fraternal feeling.

One day, in returning with Kory-Kory from my accustomed visit to the Ti, we passed by a little opening in the grove; on one side of which, my attendant informed me, was that afternoon to be built a dwelling of bamboo. At least a hundred of the natives were bringing materials to the ground, some carrying in their hands one or two of the canes which were to form the sides, others slender rods of the hibiscus, strung with palmetto leaves, for the roof. Every one contributed something to the work; and by the united, but easy, and even indolent, labors of all, the entire work was completed before sunset. The islanders, while employed in erecting this tenement, reminded me of a colony of beavers at work. To be sure, they were hardly as silent and demure as those wonderful creatures, nor were they by any means as diligent. To tell the truth, they were somewhat inclined to be lazy, but a perfect tumult of hilarity prevailed; and they worked together so unitedly, and seemed actuated by such an instinct of friendliness that it was truly beautiful to behold.

Not a single female took part in this employment: and if

the degree of consideration in which the ever-adorable sex is held by the men be—as the philosophers affirm—a just criterion of the degree of refinement among a people, then I may truly pronounce the Typees to be as polished a community as ever the sun shone upon. The religious restrictions of the taboo alone excepted, the women of the valley were allowed every possible indulgence. Nowhere are the ladies more assiduously courted; nowhere are they better appreciated as the contributors to our highest enjoyments; and nowhere are they more sensible of their power. Far different from their condition among many rude nations, where the women are made to perform all the work while their ungallant lords and masters lie buried in sloth, the gentle sex in the valley of Typee were exempt from toil, if toil it might be called that, even in that tropical climate, never distilled one drop of perspiration. Their light household occupations, together with the manufacture of tappa, the platting of mats, and the polishing of drinking vessels, were the only employments pertaining to the women. And even these resembled those pleasant avocations which fill up the elegant morning leisure of our fashionable ladies at home. But in these occupations, slight and agreeable though they were, the giddy young girls very seldom engaged. Indeed these wilful, care-killing damsels were averse to all useful employment. Like so many spoiled beauties, they ranged through the groves—bathed in the stream—danced—flirted—played all manner of mischievous pranks, and passed their days in one merry round of thoughtless happiness.

During my whole stay on the island I never witnessed a single quarrel, nor anything that in the slightest degree approached even to a dispute. The natives appeared to form one household, whose members were bound together by the ties of strong affection. The love of kindred I did not so much perceive, for it seemed blended in the general love; and where all were treated as brothers and sisters, it was hard to tell who were actually related to each other by blood.

Let it not be supposed that I have overdrawn this picture. I have not done so. Nor let it be urged, that the hostility of this tribe to foreigners, and the hereditary feuds they carry on against their fellow islanders beyond the mountains, are facts which contradict me. No so: these apparent discrepancies are easily reconciled. By many a legendary tale of violence and wrong, as well as by events which have passed before their eyes, these people have been taught to look upon white men with abhorrence. The cruel invasion of their country by Porter has alone furnished them with ample provocation; and I can sympathize in the spirit which prompts the Typee warrior to guard all the passes to his valley with the point of his leveled spear, and, standing upon the beach, with his back turned upon his green home, to hold at bay the intruding European.

As to the origin of the enmity of this particular clan toward the neighboring tribes, I cannot so confidently speak. I will not say that their foes are the aggressors, nor will I endeavor to palliate their conduct. But surely, if our evil passions must find vent, it is far better to expend them on strangers and aliens, than in the bosom of the community in which we dwell. In many polished countries civil contentions, as well as domestic enmities, are prevalent at the same time that the most atrocious foreign wars are waged. How much less guilty, then, are our islanders, who of these three sins are only chargeable with one, and that the least criminal!

The reader will erelong have reason to suspect that the Typees are not free from the guilt of cannibalism; and he will then, perhaps, charge me with admiring a people against whom so odious a crime is chargeable. But this only enormity in their character is not half so horrible as it is usually described. According to the popular fictions, the crews of vessels, shipwrecked on some barbarous coast, are eaten alive like so many dainty joints by the uncivil inhabitants; and unfortunate voyagers are lured into smiling and treacherous bays; knocked in the head with outlandish war clubs; and served up without any preliminary dressing. In truth, so horrific and improbable are these accounts, that many sensible and well-informed people will not believe that any cannibals exist; and place every book of voyages which purports to give any account of them, on the same shelf with Blue Beard and Jack the Giant-Killer; while others, implicitly crediting the most extravagant fictions, firmly believe that there are people in the world with tastes so depraved that they would infinitely prefer a single mouthful of material humanity to a good dinner of roast beef and plum pudding. But here Truth, who loves to be centrally located, is again found between the two extremes; for cannibalism to a certain moderate extent is practiced among several of the primitive tribes in the Pacific, but it is upon the bodies of slain enemies alone; and horrible and fearful as the custom is, immeasurably as it is to be abhorred and condemned, still I assert that those who indulge in it are in other respects humane and virtuous.

XXVIII

Fishing parties—mode of distributing the fish—midnight banquet—timekeeping tapers—unceremonious style of eating the fish.

THERE WAS NO INSTANCE in which the social and kindly dispositions of the Typees were more forcibly evinced than in the manner they conducted their great fishing parties. Four times during my stay in the valley the young men assembled near the full of the moon, and went together on these excursions. As they were generally absent about forty-eight hours, I was led to believe that they went out toward the open sea, some distance from the bay. The Polynesians seldom use a hook and line, almost always employing large well-made nets, most ingeniously fabricated from the twisted fibres of a certain bark. I examined several of them which had been spread to dry upon the beach at Nukuheva. They resemble very much our own seines, and I should think were very nearly as durable.

All the South Sea islanders are passionately fond of fish; but none of them can be more so than the inhabitants of

Typee. I could not comprehend, therefore, why they so seldom sought it in their waters, for it was only at stated times that the fishing parties were formed, and these occasions were always looked forward to with no small degree of interest.

During their absence the whole population of the place were in a ferment, and nothing was talked of but *'pehee, pehee'* (fish, fish). Toward the time when they were expected to return the vocal telegraph was put into operation—the inhabitants, who were scattered throughout the length of the valley, leaped upon rocks and into trees, shouting with delight at the thoughts of the anticipated treat. As soon as the approach of the party was announced, there was a general rush of the men toward the beach; some of them remaining, however, about the Ti, in order to get matters in readiness for the reception of the fish, which were brought to the Taboo Groves in immense packages of leaves, each one of them being suspended from a pole carried on the shoulders of two men.

I was present at the Ti on one of these occasions, and the sight was most interesting. After all the packages had arrived, they were laid in a row under the veranda of the building and opened. The fish were all quite small, generally about the size of a herring, and of every variety of color. About one-eighth of the whole being reserved for the use of the Ti itself, the remainder was divided into numerous smaller packages, which were immediately dispatched in every direction to the remotest parts of the valley. Arrived at their destination, these were in turn portioned out, and equally distributed among the various houses of each particular district. The fish were under a strict taboo, until the distribution was completed, which seemed to be effected in the most impartial manner. By the operation of this system every man, woman, and child in the vale were at one and the same time partaking of this favorite article of food.

Once I remember the party arrived at midnight; but the unseasonableness of the hour did not repress the impatience of the islanders. The carriers dispatched from the Ti were to be seen hurrying in all directions through the deep groves; each individual preceded by a boy bearing a flaming torch of dried coconut boughs, which from time to time was replenished from the materials scattered along the path. The wild glare of these enormous flambeaux, lighting up with a startling brilliancy the inrermost recesses of the vale, and seen moving rapidly along beneath the canopy of leaves, the savage shout of the excited messengers sounding the news of their approach, which was answered on all sides, and the strange appearance of their naked bodies, seen against the gloomy background, produced altogether an effect upon my mind that I shall long remember.

It was on this same occasion that Kory-Kory awakened me at the dead hour of night, and in a sort of transport communicated the intelligence contained in the words '*pehee perni*' (fish come). As I happened to have been in a remarkably sound and refreshing slumber, I could not imagine why the information had not been deferred until morning; indeed, I felt very much inclined to fly into a passion and box my valet's ears; but on second thoughts I got quietly up, and on going outside the house was not a little interested by the moving illumination which I beheld.

When old Marheyo received his share of the spoils, immediate preparations were made for a midnight banquet; calabashes of *poee-poee* were filled to the brim; green breadfruit were roasted; and a huge cake of *amar* was cut up with a sliver of bamboo and laid out on an immense banana leaf.

At this supper we were lighted by several of the native tapers, held in the hands of young girls. These tapers are most ingeniously made. There is a nut abounding in the valley, called by the Typees *armor,* closely resembling our common horse chestnut. The shell is broken, and the contents extracted whole. Any number of these are strung at pleasure upon the long elastic fibre that traverses the branches of the coconut tree. Some of these tapers are eight and ten feet in length; but being perfectly flexible, one end is held in a coil, while the other is lighted. The nut burns with a fitful bluish flame, and the oil that it contains is exhausted in about ten minutes. As one burns down, the next becomes ignited, and the ashes of the former are knocked into a coconut shell kept for the purpose. This primitive candle requires continual attention, and must be constantly held in the hand. The person so employed marks the lapse of time by the number of nuts consumed, which is easily learned by counting the bits of tappa distributed at regular intervals along the string.

I grieve to state so distressing a fact, but the inhabitants of Typee were in the habit of devouring fish much in the same way that a civilized being would eat a radish, and without any more previous preparation. They eat it raw; scales, bones, gills, and all the inside. The fish is held by the tail, and the head being introduced into the mouth, the animal disappears with a rapidity that would at first nearly lead one to imagine it had been launched bodily down the throat.

Raw fish! Shall I ever forget my sensations when I first saw my island beauty devour one? Oh, heavens! Fayaway, how could you ever have contracted so vile a habit? However, after the first shock had subsided, the custom grew less odious in my eyes, and I soon accustomed myself to the sight. Let no one imagine, however, that the lovely Fayaway was in the habit of swallowing great vulgar-looking fishes: oh, no; with her beautiful small hand she would clasp a delicate, little, golden-hued love of a fish, and eat it as elegantly and as innocently as though it were a Naples biscuit. But, alas! it was after all a raw fish; and all I can say is, that Fayaway ate it in a more ladylike manner than any other girl of the valley.

When at Rome do as the Romans do, I held to be so good a proverb, that being in Typee I made a point of doing as the Typees did. Thus I ate *poee-poee* as they did; I walked about in a garb striking for its simplicity; and I reposed on a community of couches; besides doing many other things in conformity with their peculiar habits; but the farthest I ever went in the way of conformity, was on several occasions to regale myself with raw fish. These being remarkably tender, and quite small, the undertaking was not so disagreeable in the main, and after a few trials I positively began to relish them; however, I subjected them to a slight operation with my knife previously to making my repast.

XXIX

Natural history of the valley—golden lizards—tameness of the birds—mosquitos—flies—dogs—a solitary cat—the climate—the coconut tree—singular modes of climbing it—an agile young chief—fearlessness of the children—Too-Too and the coconut tree—the birds of the valley.

I THINK I MUST enlighten the reader a little about the natural history of the valley.

Whence, in the name of Count Buffon and Baron Cuvier, came those dogs that I saw in Typee? Dogs!—Big hairless rats rather; all with smooth, shining, speckled hides—fat sides, and very disagreeable faces. Whence could they have come? That they were not the indigenous production of the region, I am firmly convinced. Indeed they seemed aware of their being interlopers, looking fairly ashamed, and always trying to hide themselves in some dark corner. It was plain enough they did not feel at home in the vale—that they wished themselves well out of it, and back to the ugly country from which they must have come.

Scurvy curs! they were my abhorrence; I should have liked nothing better than to have been the death of every one of them. In fact, on one occasion, I intimated the propriety of a canine crusade to Mehevi; but the benevolent king would not consent to it. He heard me very patiently; but when I had finished, shook his head, and told me, in confidence, that they were taboo.

As for the animal that made the fortune of the ex-lord-mayor Whittington: I shall never forget the day that I was lying in the house about noon, everybody else being fast asleep; and happening to raise my eyes, met those of a big black spectral cat, which sat erect in the doorway, looking at me with its frightful goggling green orbs, like one of those monstrous imps that torment some of Teniers' saints! I am one of those unfortunate persons to whom the sight of these animals is at any time an insufferable annoyance.

Thus constitutionally averse to cats in general, the unexpected apparition of this one in particular utterly confounded me. When I had a little recovered from the fascination of its glance, I started up; the cat fled, and emboldened by this, I rushed out of the house in pursuit; but it had disappeared. It was the only time I ever saw one in the valley, and how it got there I cannot imagine. It is just possible that it might have escaped from one of the ships at Nukuheva. It was in vain to seek information on the subject from the natives; since none of them had seen the animal, the appearance of which remains a mystery to me to this day.

Among the few animals which are to be met with in Typee, there were none which I looked upon with more interest than a beautiful golden-hued species of lizard. It measured perhaps five inches from head to tail, and was most gracefully proportioned. Numbers of these creatures were to be seen basking in the sunshine upon the thatching of the houses, and multitudes at all hours of the day showed their glittering sides as they ran frolicking between the spears of grass or raced in troops up and down the tall shafts of the coconut trees. But the remarkable beauty of these little animals and their lively ways were not their only claims upon my admiration. They were perfectly tame and insensible to fear. Frequently after seating myself upon the ground in some shady place during the heat of the day, I would be completely overrun with them. If I brushed one off my arm, it would leap perhaps into my hair: when I tried to frighten it away by gently pinching its leg, it would turn for protection to the very hand that attacked it.

The birds are also remarkably tame. If you happened to see one perched upon a branch within reach of your arm, and advanced toward it, it did not fly away immediately, but waited quietly looking at you, until you could almost touch it, and then took wing slowly, less alarmed at your presence, it would seem, than desirous of removing itself from your path. Had salt been less scarce in the valley than it was, this was the very place to have gone birding with it.

I remember that once, on an uninhabited island of the Gallipagos, a bird alighted on my outstretched arm, while its mate chirped from an adjoining tree. Its tameness, far from shocking me, as a similar occurrence did Selkirk, imparted to me the most exquisite thrill of delight I ever experienced; and with somewhat of the same pleasure did I afterward behold the birds and lizards of the valley show their confidence in the kindliness of man.

Among the numerous afflictions which the Europeans have entailed upon some of the natives of the South Seas, is the accidental introduction among them of that enemy of all repose and ruffler of even tempers—the mosquito. At the Sandwich Islands and at two or three of the Society group there are now thriving colonies of these insects, who promise ere long to supplant altogether the aboriginal sand flies. They sting, buzz, and torment, from one end of the year to the other, and by incessantly exasperating the natives materially obstruct the benevolent labors of the missionaries.

From this grievous visitation, however, the Typees are as yet wholly exempt; but its place is unfortunately in some degree supplied by the occasional presence of a minute species of fly, which, without stinging, is nevertheless productive of no little annoyance. The tameness of the birds and lizards is as nothing when compared to the fearless confidence of this insect. He will perch upon one of your eyelashes, and go to roost there, if you do not disturb him, or force his way through your hair, or along the cavity of the nostril, till you almost fancy he is resolved to explore the very brain itself. On one occasion I was so inconsiderate as to yawn while a number of them were hovering around me. I never repeated the act. Some half-dozen darted into the open apartment, and began walking about its ceiling; the sensation was dreadful. I involuntarily closed my mouth, and the poor creatures being enveloped in inner darkness, must in their consternation have stumbled over my palate, and been precipitated into the gulf beneath. At any rate, though I afterward charitably held my mouth open for at least five minutes, with a view of affording egress to the stragglers, none of them ever availed themselves of the opportunity.

There are no wild animals of any kind on the island, unless it be decided that the natives themselves are such. The mountains and the interior present to the eye nothing but silent solitudes, unbroken by the roar of beasts of prey, and enlivened by few tokens even of minute animated existence. There are no venomous reptiles, and no snakes of any description to be found in any of the valleys.

In a company of Marquesan natives the weather affords no topic of conversation. It can hardly be said to have any vicissitudes. The rainy season, it is true, brings frequent showers, but they are intermitting and refreshing. When an islander bound on some expedition rises from his couch in the morning, he is never solicitous to peep out and see how the sky looks, or ascertain from what quarter the wind blows. He is always sure of a 'fine day,' and the promise of a few genial showers he hails with pleasure. There is never any of that 'remarkable weather' on the island which from time immemorial has been experienced in America, and still continues to call forth the wondering conversational exclamations of its elderly citizens. Nor do there even occur any of those eccentric meteorological changes which elsewhere surprise us. In the valley of Typee ice creams would never be rendered less acceptable by sudden frosts, nor would picnic parties be deferred on account of inauspicious snowstorms: for there day follows day in one unvarying round of summer and sunshine, and the whole year is one long tropical month of June just melting into July.

It is this genial climate which causes the coconuts to flourish as they do. This invaluable fruit, brought to perfection by the rich soil of the Marquesas, and borne aloft on a stately column more than a hundred feet from the ground, would seem at first almost inaccessible to the simple natives. Indeed the slender, smooth, and soaring shaft, without a single limb or protuberance of any kind to assist one in mounting it, presents an obstacle only to be overcome by the surprising agility and ingenuity of the islanders. It might be supposed that their indolence would lead them patiently to await the period when the ripened nuts, slowly parting from their stems, fall one by one to the ground. This certainly would be the case, were it not that the young fruit, encased in a soft green husk, with the incipient meat adhering in a jellylike pellicle to its sides, and containing a bumper of the most delicious nectar, is what they chiefly prize. They have at least twenty different terms to express as many progressive stages in the growth of the nut. Many of them reject the fruit altogether except at a particular period of its growth, which, incredible as it may appear, they seemed to me to be able to ascertain within an hour or two. Others are still more capricious in their tastes; and after gathering together a heap of the nuts of all ages, and ingeniously tapping them, will sip first from one and then from another, as fastidiously as some delicate winebibber experimenting glass in hand among his dusty demijohns of different vintages.

Some of the young men, with more flexible frames than their comrades, and perhaps with more courageous souls, had a way of walking up the trunk of the coconut trees which to me seemed little less than miraculous; and when looking at them in the act, I experienced that curious perplexity a child feels when he beholds a fly moving feet uppermost along a ceiling.

I will endeavor to describe the way in which Narnee, a noble young chief, sometimes performed this feat for my peculiar gratification; but his preliminary performances must also be recorded. Upon my signifying my desire that he should pluck me the young fruit of some particular tree, the handsome savage, throwing himself into a sudden attitude of surprise, feigns astonishment at the apparent absurdity of the request. Maintaining this position for a moment, the strange emotions depicted on his countenance soften down into one of humorous resignation to my will, and then looking wistfully up to the tufted top of the tree, he stands on tiptoe, straining his neck and elevating his arm, as though endeavoring to reach the fruit from the ground where he stands. As if defeated in this childish attempt, he now sinks to the earth despondingly, beating his breast in well-acted despair; and then, starting to his feet all at once, and throwing back his head, raises both hands, like a schoolboy about to catch a falling ball. After continuing this for a moment or two, as if in expectation that the fruit was going to be tossed down to him by some good spirit in the treetop, he turns wildly round in another fit of despair, and scampers off to the distance of thirty or forty yards. Here he remains awhile, eyeing the tree, the very picture of misery; but the next moment, receiving, as it were, a flash of inspiration, he rushes again toward it, and clasping both arms about the trunk, with one elevated a little above the other, he presses the soles of his feet close together against the tree, extending his legs from it until they are nearly horizontal, and his body becomes doubled into an arch; then, hand over hand and foot after foot, he rises from the earth with steady rapidity, and almost before you are aware of it, has gained the cradled and embowered nest of nuts, and with boisterous glee flings the fruit to the ground.

This mode of walking the tree is only practicable where the trunk declines considerably from the perpendicular. This, however, is almost always the case; some of the perfectly straight shafts of the trees leaning at an angle of thirty degrees.

The less active among the men, and many of the children of the valley, have another method of climbing. They take a broad and stout piece of bark, and secure either end of it to their ankles; so that when the feet thus confined are extended apart, a space of little more than twelve inches is left between them. This contrivance greatly facilitates the act of climbing. The band pressed against the tree, and closely embracing it, yields a pretty firm support; while with the arms clasped about the trunk, and at regular intervals sustaining the body, the feet are drawn up nearly a yard at a time, and a corresponding elevation of the hands immediately succeeds. In this way I have seen little children, scarcely five years of age, fearlessly climbing the slender pole of a young coconut tree, and while hanging perhaps fifty feet from the ground, receive the plaudits of their parents beneath, who clapped their hands, and encouraged them to mount still higher.

What, thought I, on first witnessing one of these exhibitions, would the nervous mothers of America and England say to a similar display of hardihood in any of their children? The Lacedemonian nations might have approved of it, but most modern dames would have gone into hysterics at the sight.

At the top of the coconut tree the numerous branches, radiating on all sides from a common center form a sort of green and waving basket, between the leaflets of which you just discern the nuts thickly clustering together, and on the loftier trees looking no bigger from the ground than bunches of grapes. I remember one adventurous little fellow—Too-Too was the rascal's name—who had built himself a sort of aerial baby house in the picturesque tuft of a tree adjoining Marheyo's habitation. He used to spend hours there,—rustling among the branches, and shouting with delight every time the strong gusts of wind rushing down from the mountain's side swayed to and fro the tall and flexible column on which he was perched. Whenever I heard Too-Too's musical voice, sounding strangely to the ear from so great a height, and beheld him peeping down upon me from out his leafy covert, he always recalled to my mind Dibdin's lines—

> 'There's a sweet little cherub that sits up aloft,
> To look out for the life of poor Jack.'

Birds—bright and beautiful birds—fly over the valley of Typee. You see them perched aloft among the immovable boughs of the majestic breadfruit trees, or gently swaying on the elastic branches of the Omoo; skimming over the palmetto thatching of the bamboo huts; passing like spirits on the wing through the shadows of the grove, and sometimes descending into the bosom of the valley in gleaming flights from the mountains. Their plumage is purple and azure, crimson and white, black and gold; with bills of every tint:—

bright bloody red, jet black, and ivory white; and their eyes are bright and sparkling; they go sailing through the air in starry throngs; but alas! the spell of dumbness is upon them all—there is not a single warbler in the valley!

I know not why it was, but the sight of these birds, generally the ministers of gladness, always oppressed me with melancholy. As in their dumb beauty they hovered by me whilst I was walking, or looked down upon me with steady curious eyes from out the foliage, I was almost inclined to fancy that they knew they were gazing upon a stranger, and that they commiserated his fate.

XXX

A professor of the Fine Arts—his persecutions— something about tattooing and tabooing—two anecdotes in illustration of the latter—a few thoughts on the Typee dialect.

IN ONE OF MY strolls with Kory-Kory, in passing along the border of a thick growth of bushes, my attention was arrested by a singular noise. On entering the thicket I witnessed for the first time the operation of tattooing as performed by these islanders.

I beheld a man extended flat upon his back on the ground, and, despite the forced composure of his countenance, it was evident that he was suffering agony. His tormentor bent over him, working away for all the world like a stonecutter with mallet and chisel. In one hand he held a short slender stick, pointed with a shark's tooth, on the upright end of which he tapped with a small hammerlike piece of wood, thus puncturing the skin, and charging it with the coloring matter in which the instrument was dipped. A coconut shell containing this fluid was placed upon the ground. It is prepared by mixing with a vegetable juice the ashes of the *armor,* or candlenut, always preserved for the purpose. Beside the savage, and spread out upon a piece of soiled tappa, were a great number of curious black-looking little implements of bone and wood, used in the various divisions of his art. A few terminated in a single fine point, and, like very delicate pencils, were employed in giving the finishing touches, or in operating upon the more sensitive portions of the body, as was the case in the present instance. Others presented several points distributed in a line, somewhat resembling the teeth of a saw. These were employed in the coarser part of the work, and particularly in pricking in straight marks. Some presented their points disposed in small figures, and being placed upon the body, were, by a single blow of the hammer, made to leave their indelible impression. I observed a few the handles of which were mysteriously curved, as if intended to be introduced into the orifice of the ear, with a view perhaps of beating the tattoo upon the tympanum. Altogether, the sight of these strange instruments recalled to mind that display of cruel-looking mother-of-pearl-handled things which one sees in their velvet-lined cases at the elbow of a dentist.

The artist was not at this time engaged on an original sketch, his subject being a venerable savage, whose tattooing had become somewhat faded with age and needed a few repairs, and accordingly he was merely employed in touching up the works of some of the old masters of the Typee school, as delineated upon the human canvas before him. The parts operated upon were the eyelids, where a longitudinal streak, like the one which adorned Kory-Kory, crossed the countenance of the victim.

In spite of all the efforts of the poor old man, sundry twitchings and screwings of the muscles of the face denoted the exquisite sensibility of these shutters to the windows of his soul, which he was now having repainted. But the artist, with a heart as callous as that of an army surgeon, continued his performance, enlivening his labors with a wild chant, tapping away the while as merrily as a woodpecker.

So deeply engaged was he in his work, that he had not observed our approach, until, after having enjoyed an unmolested view of the operation, I chose to attract his attention. As soon as he perceived me, supposing that I sought him in his professional capacity, he seized hold of me in a paroxysm of delight, and was all eagerness to begin the work. When, however, I gave him to understand that he had altogether mistaken my views, nothing could exceed his grief and disappointment. But recovering from this, he seemed determined not to credit my assertion and grasping his implements, he flourished them about in fearful vicinity to my face, going through an imaginary performance of his art, and every moment bursting into some admiring exclamation at the beauty of his designs.

Horrified at the bare thought of being rendered hideous for life if the wretch were to execute his purpose upon me, I struggled to get away from him, while Kory-Kory, turning traitor, stood by, and besought me to comply with the outrageous request.

On my reiterated refusals, the excited artist got half beside himself, and was overwhelmed with sorrow at losing so noble an opportunity of distinguishing himself in his profession.

The idea of engrafting his tattooing upon my white skin filled him with all a painter's enthusiasm: again and again he gazed into my countenance, and every fresh glimpse seemed to add to the vehemence of his ambition. Not knowing to what extremities he might proceed, and shuddering at the ruin he might inflict upon my figurehead, I now endeavored to draw off his attention from it, and holding out my arm in a fit of desperation, signed to him to commence operations. But he rejected the compromise indignantly, and still continued his attack on my face, as though nothing short of that would satisfy him. When his forefinger swept across my features, in laying out the borders of those parallel bands which were to encircle my countenance, the flesh fairly crawled upon my bones. At last, half wild with terror and indignation, I succeeded in breaking away from the three savages, and fled toward old Marheyo's house, pursued by the indomitable artist, who ran after me, implements in hand.

Kory-Kory, however, at last interfered, and drew him off from the chase.

This incident opened my eyes to a new danger; and I now felt convinced that in some luckless hour I should be disfigured in such a manner as never more to have the *face* to return to my countrymen, even should an opportunity offer.

These apprehensions were greatly increased by the desire which King Mehevi and several of the inferior chiefs now manifested that I should be tattooed. The pleasure of the king was first signified to me some three days after my casual encounter with Karky the artist. Heavens! what imprecations I showered upon that Karky! Doubtless he had plotted a conspiracy against me and my countenance, and would never rest until his diabolical purpose was accomplished. Several times I met him in various parts of the valley, and, invariably, whenever he descried me, he came running after me with his mallet and chisel, flourishing them about my face as if he longed to begin. What an object he would have made of me!

When the king first expressed his wish to me, I made known to him my utter abhorrence of the measure, and worked myself into such a state of excitement, that he absolutely stared at me in amazement. It evidently surpassed His Majesty's comprehension how any sober-minded and sensible individual could entertain the least possible objection to so beautifying an operation.

Soon afterward he repeated his suggestion, and meeting with a like repulse, showed some symptoms of displeasure at my obduracy. On his a third time renewing his request, I plainly perceived that something must be done, or my visage was ruined for ever; I therefore screwed up my courage to the sticking point, and declared my willingness to have both arms tattooed from just above the wrist to the shoulder. His Majesty was greatly pleased at the proposition, and I was congratulating myself with having thus compromised the matter, when he intimated that as a thing of course my face was first to undergo the operation. I was fairly driven to despair; nothing but the utter ruin of my 'face divine,' as the poets call it, would, I perceived, satisfy the inexorable Mehevi and his chiefs, or rather, that infernal Karky, for he was at the bottom of it all.

The only consolation afforded me was a choice of patterns: I was at perfect liberty to have my face spanned by three horizontal bars, after the fashion of my serving man's; or to have as many oblique stripes slanting across it; or if, like a true courtier, I chose to model my style on that of royalty, I might wear a sort of freemason badge upon my countenance in the shape of a mystic triangle. However, I would have none of these, though the king most earnestly impressed upon my mind that my choice was wholly unrestricted. At last, seeing my unconquerable repugnance, he ceased to importune me.

But not so some other of the savages. Hardly a day passed but I was subjected to their annoying requests, until at last my existence became a burden to me; the pleasures I had previously enjoyed no longer afforded me delight, and all my former desire to escape from the valley now revived with additional force.

A fact which I soon afterward learned augmented my apprehension. The whole system of tattooing was, I found, connected with their religion; and it was evident, therefore, that they were resolved to make a convert of me.

In the decoration of the chiefs it seems to be necessary to exercise the most elaborate penciling; while some of the inferior natives looked as if they had been daubed over indiscriminately with a house painter's brush. I remember one fellow who prided himself hugely upon a great oblong patch, placed high upon his back, and who always reminded me of a man with a blister of Spanish flies stuck between his shoulders. Another whom I frequently met had the hollow of his eyes tattooed in two regular squares, and his visual organs being remarkably brilliant, they gleamed forth from out this setting like a couple of diamonds inserted in ebony.

Although convinced that tattooing was a religious observance, still the nature of the connection between it and the superstitious idolatry of the people was a point upon which

I could never obtain any information. Like the still more important system of the taboo, it always appeared inexplicable to me.

There is a marked similarity, almost an identity, between the religious institutions of most of the Polynesian islands, and in all exists the mysterious taboo, restricted in its uses to a greater or less extent. So strange and complex in its arrangements is this remarkable system, that I have in several cases met with individuals who, after residing for years among the islands in the Pacific, and acquiring a considerable knowledge of the language, have nevertheless been altogether unable to give any satisfactory account of its operations. Situated as I was in the Typee valley, I perceived every hour the effects of this all-controlling power, without in the least comprehending it. Those effects were, indeed, widespread and universal, pervading the most important as well as the minutest transactions of life. The savage, in short, lives in the continual observance of its dictates, which guide and control every action of his being.

For several days after entering the valley I had been saluted at least fifty times in the twenty-four hours with the talismanic word 'taboo' shrieked in my ears, at some gross violation of its provisions, of which I had unconsciously been guilty. The day after our arrival I happened to hand some tobacco to Toby over the head of a native who sat between us. He started up, as if stung by an adder; while the whole company, manifesting an equal degree of horror, simultaneously screamed out 'taboo!' I never again perpetrated a similar piece of ill manners, which, indeed, was forbidden by the canons of good breeding, as well as by the mandates of the taboo. But it was not always so easy to perceive wherein you had contravened the spirit of this institution. I was many times called to order, if I may use the phrase, when I could not for the life of me conjecture what particular offence I had committed.

One day I was strolling through a secluded portion of the valley, and hearing the musical sound of the cloth mallet at a little distance, I turned down a path that conducted me in a few moments to a house where there were some half-dozen girls employed in making tappa. This was an operation I had frequently witnessed, and had handled the bark in all the various stages of its preparation. On the present occasion the females were intent upon their occupation, and after looking up and talking gaily to me for a few moments, they resumed their employment. I regarded them for a while in silence, and then carelessly picking up a handful of the material that lay around, proceeded unconsciously to pick it apart. While thus engaged, I was suddenly startled by a scream, like that of a whole boarding school of young ladies just on the point of going into hysterics. Leaping up with the idea of seeing a score of Happar warriors about to perform anew the Sabine atrocity, I found myself confronted by the company of girls, who, having dropped their work, stood before me with starting eyes, swelling bosoms, and fingers pointed in horror toward me.

Thinking that some venomous reptile must be concealed in the bark which I held in my hand, I began cautiously to separate and examine it. Whilst I did so the horrified girls redoubled their shrieks. Their wild cries and frightened motions actually alarmed me, and throwing down the tappa, I was about to rush from the house, when in the same instant their clamors ceased, and one of them seizing me by the arm, pointed to the broken fibres that had just fallen from my grasp, and screamed in my ears the fatal word 'taboo'!

I subsequently found out that the fabric they were engaged in making was of a peculiar kind, destined to be worn on the heads of the females, and through every stage of its manufacture was guarded by a vigorous taboo, which interdicted the whole masculine gender from even so much as touching it.

Frequently in walking through the groves I observed breadfruit and coconut trees, with a wreath of leaves twined in a peculiar fashion about their trunks. This was the mark of the taboo. The trees themselves, their fruit, and even the shadows they cast upon the ground, were consecrated by its presence. In the same way a pipe, which the king had bestowed upon me, was rendered sacred in the eyes of the natives, none of whom could I ever prevail upon to smoke from it. The bowl was encircled by a woven band of grass, somewhat resembling those Turks' heads occasionally worked in the handles of our whipstalks.

A similar badge was once braided about my wrist by the royal hand of Mehevi himself, who, as soon as he had concluded the operation, pronounced me 'taboo.' This occurred shortly after Toby's disappearance; and were it not that from the first moment I had entered the valley the natives had treated me with uniform kindness, I should have supposed that their conduct afterward was to be ascribed to the fact that I had received this sacred investiture.

The capricious operations of the taboo is not its least remarkable feature: to enumerate them all would be impossible. Black hogs—infants to a certain age—women in an interesting situation—young men while the operation of tattooing their faces is going on—and certain parts of the valley during the continuance of a shower—are alike fenced about by the operation of the taboo.

I witnessed a striking instance of its effects in the bay of Tior, my visit to which place has been alluded to in a former part of this narrative. On that occasion our worthy captain formed one of the party. He was a most insatiable sportsman. Outward bound, and off the pitch of Cape Horn, he used to sit on the taffrail, and keep the steward loading three or four old fowling pieces, with which he would bring down albatrosses, Cape pigeons, jays, petrels, and divers other marine fowl, who followed chattering in our wake. The sailors were struck aghast at his impiety, and one and all attributed our forty days' beating about that horrid headland to his sacrilegious slaughter of these inoffensive birds.

At Tior he evinced the same disregard for the religious prejudices of the islanders, as he had previously shown for the superstitions of the sailors. Having heard that there were a considerable number of fowls in the valley—the progeny of some cocks and hens accidentally left there by an English vessel, and which being strictly tabooed flew about almost in a wild state—he determined to break through all restraints, and be the death of them. Accordingly, he provided himself with a most formidable looking gun, and announced his landing on the beach by shooting down a noble cock that was crowing what proved to be his own funeral dirge, on the limb of an adjoining tree. 'Taboo,' shrieked the affrighted savages. 'Oh, hang your taboo,' says the nautical sportsman; 'Talk taboo to the marines'; and bang went the piece again, and down came another victim. At this the natives ran scampering through the groves, horror-struck at the enormity of the act.

All that afternoon the rocky sides of the valley rang with successive reports, and the superb plumage of many a beautiful fowl was ruffled by the fatal bullet. Had it not been that the French admiral, with a large party, were then in the glen, I have no doubt that the natives, although their tribe was small and dispirited, would have inflicted summary vengeance upon the man who thus outraged their most sacred institutions; as it was, they contrived to annoy him not a little.

Thirsting with his exertions, the skipper directed his steps to a stream; but the savages, who had followed at a little distance, perceiving his object, rushed toward him and forced him away from its bank—his lips would have polluted it. Wearied at last, he sought to enter a house, that he might rest for a while on the mats; its inmates gathered tumultuously about the door and denied him admittance. He coaxed and blustered by turns, but in vain; the natives were neither to be intimidated nor appeased, and as a final resort he was obliged to call together his boat's crew, and pull away from what he termed the most infernal place he ever stepped upon.

Lucky was it for him and for us that we were not honored on our departure by a salute of stones from the hands of the exasperated Tiors. In this way, on the neighboring island of Ropo, were killed, but a few weeks previously, and for a nearly similar offence, the master and three of the crew of the *K*——.

I cannot determine with anything approaching to certainty, what power it is that imposes the taboo. When I consider the slight disparity of condition among the islanders—the very limited and inconsiderable prerogatives of the king and chiefs—and the loose and indefinite function of the priesthood, most of whom were hardly to be distinguished from the rest of their countrymen, I am wholly at a loss where to look for the authority which regulates this potent institution. It is imposed upon something today, and withdrawn tomorrow; while its operations in other cases are perpetual. Sometimes its restrictions only affect a single individual—sometimes a particular family—sometimes a whole tribe; and in a few instances they extend not merely over the various clans on a single island, but over all the inhabitants of an entire group. In illustration of this latter peculiarity I may cite the law which forbids a female to enter a canoe—a prohibition which prevails upon all the northern Marquesas Islands.

The word itself (taboo) is used in more than one signification. It is sometimes used by a parent to his child, when in the exercise of parental authority he forbids it to perform a particular action. Anything opposed to the ordinary customs of the islanders, although not expressly prohibited, is said to be taboo.

The Typee language is one very difficult to be acquired; it bears a close resemblance to the other Polynesian dialects, all of which show a common origin. The duplication of words, as *lumee lumee, poee poee, muee muee,* is one of their peculiar features. But another, and a more annoying one, is the different senses in which one and the same word is employed; its various meanings all have a certain connection, which only makes the matter more puzzling. So one brisk, lively little word is obliged, like a servant in a poor family, to perform all sorts of duties; for instance, one particular combination of syllables expresses the ideas of sleep, rest, reclining, sitting, leaning, and all other things anywise analogous thereto, the particular meaning being shown chiefly by a variety of gestures and the eloquent expression of the countenance.

The intricacy of these dialects is another peculiarity. In the Missionary College at Lahainaluna, or Mawee, one of the

Sandwich Islands, I saw a tabular exhibition of a Hawaiian verb, conjugated through all its moods and tenses. It covered the side of a considerable apartment, and I doubt whether Sir William Jones himself would have not despaired of mastering it.

XXXI

Strange custom of the islanders—their chanting and the peculiarity of their voice—rapture of the king at first hearing a song—a new dignity conferred on the author—musical instruments in the valley—admiration of the savages at beholding a pugilistic performance—swimming infant—beautiful tresses of the girls—ointment for the hair.

SADLY DISCURSIVE AS I have already been, I must still further entreat the reader's patience, as I am about to string together, without any attempt at order, a few odds and ends of things not hitherto mentioned, but which are either curious in themselves or peculiar to the Typees.

There was one singular custom, observed in old Marheyo's domestic establishment, which often excited my surprise. Every night, before retiring, the inmates of the house gathered together on the mats, and squatting upon their haunches, after the universal practice of these islanders, would commence a low, dismal, and monotonous chant, accompanying the voice with the instrumental melody produced by two small half-rotten sticks tapped slowly together, a pair of which were held in the hands of each person present. Thus would they employ themselves for an hour or two, sometimes longer. Lying in the gloom which wrapped the further end of the house, I could not avoid looking at them, although the spectacle suggested nothing but unpleasant reflections. The flickering rays of the *armor* nut just served to reveal their savage lineaments, without dispelling the darkness that hovered about them.

Sometimes when, after falling into a kind of doze, and awaking suddenly in the midst of these doleful chantings, my eye would fall upon the wild-looking group engaged in their strange occupation, with their naked tattooed limbs, and shaven heads disposed in a circle, I was almost tempted to believe that I gazed upon a set of evil beings in the act of working a frightful incantation.

What was the meaning or purpose of this custom, whether it was practiced merely as a diversion, or whether it was a religious exercise, a sort of family prayers, I never could discover.

The sounds produced by the natives on these occasions were of a most singular description; and had I not actually been present, I never would have believed that such curious noises could have been produced by human beings.

To savages generally is imputed a guttural articulation. This, however, is not always the case, especially among the inhabitants of the Polynesian Archipelago. The labial melody with which the Typee girls carry on an ordinary conversation, giving a musical prolongation to the final words with a liquid, birdlike accent, was singularly pleasing.

The men, however, are not quite so harmonious in their utterance, and when excited upon any subject, would work themselves up into a sort of wordy paroxysm, during which all descriptions of rough-sided sounds were projected from their mouths, with a force and rapidity which was absolutely astonishing.

Although these savages are remarkably fond of chanting, still they appear to have no idea whatever of singing, at least as that art is practiced among other nations.

I never shall forget the first time I happened to roar out a stave in the presence of the noble Mehevi. It was a stanza from the 'Bavarian Broomseller.' His Typean Majesty, with all his court, gazed upon me in amazement, as if I had displayed some preternatural faculty which Heaven had denied to them. The king was delighted with the verse; but the chorus fairly transported him. At his solicitation I sang it again and again, and nothing could be more ludicrous than his vain attempts to catch the air and the words. The royal savage seemed to think that by screwing all the features of his face into the end of his nose, he might possibly succeed in the undertaking, but it failed to answer the purpose, and in the end he gave up, and consoled himself by listening to my repetition of the sounds fifty times over.

Previous to Mehevi's making the discovery, I had never been aware that there was anything of the nightingale about me; but I was now promoted to the place of court minstrel, in which capacity I was afterward perpetually called upon to officiate.

Besides the sticks and the drums, there are no other musical instruments among the Typees, except one which might appropriately be denominated a nasal flute. It is somewhat longer than an ordinary fife; is made of a beautiful scarlet-colored reed; and has four or five stops, with a large hole near one end, which latter is held just beneath the left nostril. The other nostril being closed by a peculiar movement of the muscle about the nose, the breath is forced into the tube, and produces a soft dulcet sound, which is varied by the fingers running at random over the stops. This is a favorite recreation with the females, and one in which Fayaway greatly excelled. Awkward as such an instrument may appear, it was, in Fayaway's delicate little hands, one of the most graceful I have ever seen. A young lady, in the act of tormenting a guitar strung about her neck by a couple of yards of blue ribbon, is not half so engaging.

Singing was not the only means I possessed of diverting the royal Mehevi and his easygoing subjects. Nothing afforded them more pleasure than to see me go through the attitude of pugilistic encounter. As not one of the natives had soul enough in him to stand up like a man, and allow me to hammer away at him, for my own personal gratification and that of the king,

I was necessitated to fight with an imaginary enemy, whom I invariably made to knock under to my superior prowess. Sometimes when this sorely battered shadow retreated precipitately toward a group of the savages, and, following him up, I rushed among them, dealing my blows right and left, they would disperse in all directions, much to the enjoyment of Mehevi, the chiefs, and themselves.

The noble art of self-defense appeared to be regarded by them as the peculiar gift of the white man; and I make little doubt but that they supposed armies of Europeans were drawn up provided with nothing else but bony fists and stout hearts, with which they set to in column, and pummeled one another at the word of command.

One day, in company with Kory-Kory, I had repaired to the stream for the purpose of bathing, when I observed a woman sitting upon a rock in the midst of the current, and watching with the liveliest interest the gambols of something, which at first I took to be an uncommonly large species of frog that was sporting in the water near her. Attracted by the novelty of the sight, I waded toward the spot where she sat, and could hardly credit the evidence of my senses when I beheld a little infant, the period of whose birth could not have extended back many days, paddling about as if it had just risen to the surface, after being hatched into existence at the bottom. Occasionally the delighted parent reached out her hands toward it, when the little thing, uttering a faint cry, and striking out its tiny limbs, would sidle for the rock, and the next moment be clasped to its mother's bosom. This was repeated again and again, the baby remaining in the stream about a minute at a time. Once or twice it made wry faces at swallowing a mouthful of water, and choked and spluttered as if on the point of strangling. At such times, however, the mother snatched it up, and by a process scarcely to be mentioned obliged it to eject the fluid. For several weeks afterward I observed this woman bringing her child down to the stream regularly every day, in the cool of the morning and evening, and treating it to a bath. No wonder that the South

Sea islanders are so amphibious a race, when they are thus launched into the water as soon as they see the light. I am convinced that it is as natural for a human being to swim as it is for a duck. And yet in civilized communities how many able-bodied individuals die, like so many drowning kittens, from the occurrence of the most trivial accidents!

The long, luxuriant, and glossy tresses of the Typee damsels often attracted my admiration. A fine head of hair is the pride and joy of every woman's heart. Whether, against the express will of Providence, it is twisted up on the crown of the head and there coiled away like a rope on a ship's deck; whether it be stuck behind the ears and hangs down like the swag of a small window curtain; or whether it be permitted to flow over the shoulders in natural ringlets, it is always the pride of the owner, and the glory of the toilette.

The Typee girls devote much of their time to the dressing of their fair and redundant locks. After bathing, as they sometimes do five or six times every day, the hair is carefully dried, and if they have been in the sea, invariably washed in fresh water, and anointed with a highly scented oil extracted from the meat of the coconut. This oil is obtained in great abundance by the following very simple process:

A large vessel of wood, with holes perforated in the bottom, is filled with the pounded meat, and exposed to the rays of the sun. As the oleaginous matter exudes, it falls in drops through the apertures into a wide-mouthed calabash placed underneath. After a sufficient quantity has been thus collected, the oil undergoes a purifying process, and is then poured into the small spherical shells of the nuts of the moo tree, which are hollowed out to receive it. These nuts are then hermetically sealed with a resinous gum, and the vegetable fragrance of their green rind soon imparts to the oil a delightful odor. After the lapse of a few weeks the exterior shell of the nuts becomes quite dry and hard, and assumes a beautiful carnation tint; and when opened they are found to be about two-thirds full of an ointment of a light yellow color, and diffusing the sweetest perfume. This elegant little odorous globe would not be out of place even upon the toilette of a queen. Its merits as a preparation for the hair are undeniable—it imparts to it a superb gloss and a silky fineness.

XXXII

Apprehensions of evil—frightful discovery—some remarks on cannibalism—second battle with the Happars—savage spectacle—mysterious feast—subsequent disclosures.

FROM THE TIME of my casual encounter with Karky the artist, my life was one of absolute wretchedness. Not a day passed but I was prosecuted by the solicitations of some of the natives to subject myself to the odious operation of tattooing. Their importunities drove me half wild, for I felt how easily they might work their will upon me regarding this or anything else which they took into their heads. Still, however, the behavior of the islanders toward me was as kind as ever. Fayaway was quite as engaging; Kory-Kory was devoted; and Mehevi the King just as gracious and condescending as before. But I had now been three months in their valley, as nearly as I could estimate; I had grown familiar with the narrow limits to which my wanderings had been confined; and I began bitterly to feel the state of captivity in which I was held. There was no one with whom I could freely converse; no one to whom I could communicate my thoughts; no one who could sympathize with my sufferings. A thousand times I thought how much more endurable would have been my lot had Toby still been with me. But I was left alone, and the thought was terrible to me. Still, despite my griefs, I did all in my power to appear composed and cheerful, well knowing that by manifesting any uneasiness, or any desire to escape, I should only frustrate my object.

It was during the period I was in this unhappy frame of mind that the painful malady under which I had been laboring —after having almost completely subsided—began again to show itself, and with symptoms as violent as ever. This added calamity nearly unmanned me; the recurrence of the complaint proved that without powerful remedial applications all hope of cure was futile; and when I reflected that just beyond the elevations which bound me in, was the medical relief I needed, and that, although so near, it was impossible for me to avail myself of it, the thought was misery.

In this wretched situation, every circumstance which evinced the savage nature of the beings at whose mercy I was, augmented the fearful apprehensions that consumed me. An occurrence which happened about this time affected me most powerfully.

I have already mentioned that from the ridgepole of Marheyo's house were suspended a number of packages enveloped in tappa. Many of these I had often seen in the hands of the natives, and their contents had been examined in my presence. But there were three packages hanging very nearly over the place where I lay, which from their remarkable appearance had often excited my curiosity. Several times I had asked Kory-Kory to show me their contents; but my servitor, who in almost every other particular had acceded to my wishes, always refused to gratify me in this.

One day, returning unexpectedly from the Ti, my arrival seemed to throw the inmates of the house into the greatest confusion. They were seated together on the mats, and by the lines which extended from the roof to the floor I immediately perceived that the mysterious packages were for some purpose or other under inspection. The evident alarm the savages betrayed filled me with forebodings of evil, and with an uncontrollable desire to penetrate the secret so jealously guarded. Despite the efforts of Marheyo and Kory-Kory to restrain me, I forced my way into the midst of the circle, and just caught a glimpse of three human heads, which others of the party were hurriedly enveloping in the coverings from which they had been taken.

One of the three I distinctly saw. It was in a state of perfect preservation, and, from the slight glimpse I had of it, seemed to have been subjected to some smoking operation which had reduced it to the dry, hard, and mummylike appearance it presented. The two long scalp locks were twisted up into balls upon the crown of the head in the same way that the individual had worn them during life. The sunken cheeks were rendered yet more ghastly by the rows of glistening teeth which protruded from between the lips, while the sockets of the eyes—filled with oval bits of mother-of-pearl shell, with a black spot in the center—heightened the hideousness of its aspect.

Two of the three were heads of the islanders; but the third, to my horror, was that of a white man. Although it had been quickly removed from my sight, still the glimpse I had of it was enough to convince me that I could not be mistaken.

Gracious God! what dreadful thoughts entered my mind! In solving this mystery perhaps I had solved another, and the fate of my lost companion might be revealed in the shocking spectacle I had just witnessed. I longed to have torn off the folds of cloth, and satisfied the awful doubts under which I labored. But before I had recovered from the consternation into which I had been thrown, the fatal packages were hoisted aloft and once more swung over my head. The natives now gathered round me tumultuously, and labored to convince me that what I had just seen were the heads of three Happar warriors, who had been slain in battle. This glaring falsehood added to my alarm, and it was not until I reflected that I had observed the packages swinging from their elevation before Toby's disappearance, that I could at all recover my composure.

But although this horrible apprehension had been dispelled, I had discovered enough to fill me, in my present state of mind, with the most bitter reflections. It was plain that I had seen the last relic of some unfortunate wretch, who must have been massacred on the beach by the savages, in one of those perilous trading adventures which I have before described.

It was not, however, alone the murder of the stranger that

overcame me with gloom. I shuddered at the idea of the subsequent fate his inanimate body might have met with. Was the same doom reserved for me? Was I destined to perish like him—like him, perhaps, to be devoured, and my head to be preserved as a fearful memento of the event? My imagination ran riot in these horrid speculations, and I felt certain that the worst possible evils would befall me. But whatever were my misgivings, I studiously concealed them from the islanders, as well as the full extent of the discovery I had made.

Although the assurances which the Typees had often given me, that they never eat human flesh, had not convinced me that such was the case, yet, having been so long a time in the valley without witnessing anything which indicated the existence of the practice, I began to hope that it was an event of very rare occurrence, and that I should be spared the horror of witnessing it during my stay among them; but, alas! these hopes were soon destroyed.

It is a singular fact, that in all our accounts of cannibal tribes we have seldom received the testimony of an eyewitness to the revolting practice. The horrible conclusion has almost always been derived either from the secondhand evidence of Europeans, or else from the admissions of the savages themselves, after they have in some degree become civilized. The Polynesians are aware of the detestation in which Europeans hold this custom, and therefore invariably deny its existence, and, with the craft peculiar to savages, endeavor to conceal every trace of it.

The excessive unwillingness betrayed by the Sandwich Islanders, even at the present day, to allude to the unhappy fate of Cook, has been often remarked. And so well have they succeeded in covering that event with mystery, that to this very hour, despite all that has been said and written on the subject, it still remains doubtful whether they wreaked upon his murdered body the vengeance they sometimes inflicted upon their enemies.

At Karakikova, the scene of that tragedy, a strip of ship's copper nailed against an upright post in the ground used to inform the traveler that beneath reposed the 'remains' of the great circumnavigator. But I am strongly inclined to believe not only that the corpse was refused Christian burial, but that the heart which was brought to Vancouver some time after the event, and which the Hawaiians stoutly maintained was that of Captain Cook, was no such thing; and that the whole affair was a piece of imposture which was sought to be palmed off upon the credulous Englishman.

A few years since there was living on the island of Mowee (one of the Sandwich group) an old chief, who, actuated by a morbid desire for notoriety, gave himself out among the foreign residents of the place as the living tomb of Captain Cook's big toe!—affirming, that at the cannibal entertainment which ensued after the lamented Briton's death, that particular portion of his body had fallen to his share. His indignant countrymen actually caused him to be prosecuted in the native courts, on a charge nearly equivalent to what we term defamation of character; but the old fellow persisting in his assertion, and no invalidating proof being adduced, the plaintiffs were cast in the suit, and the cannibal reputation of the defendant fully established. This result was the making of his fortune; ever afterward he was in the habit of giving very profitable audiences to all curious travelers who were desirous of beholding the man who had eaten the great navigator's great toe.

About a week after my discovery of the contents of the mysterious packages, I happened to be at the Ti, when another war alarm was sounded, and the natives rushing to their arms, sallied out to resist a second incursion of the Happar invaders. The same scene was again repeated, only that on this occasion I heard at least fifteen reports of muskets from the mountains during the time that the skirmish lasted. An hour or two after its termination, loud paeans chanted through the valley announced the approach of the victors. I stood with Kory-Kory leaning against the railing of the *pi-pi* awaiting their advance, when a tumultuous crowd of islanders emerged with wild clamors from the neighboring groves. In the midst of them marched four men, one preceding the other at regular intervals of eight or ten feet, with poles of corresponding length, extended from shoulder to shoulder, to which were lashed with thongs of bark three long narrow bundles, carefully wrapped in ample covering of freshly plucked palm leaves, tacked together with slivers of bamboo. Here and there upon these green winding sheets might be seen stains of blood, while the warriors who carried the frightful burdens displayed upon their naked limbs similar sanguinary marks. The shaven head of the foremost had a deep gash upon it, and the clotted gore which had flowed from the wound remained in dry patches around it. This savage seemed to be sinking under the weight he bore. The bright tattooing upon his body was covered with blood and dust; his inflamed eyes rolled in their sockets, and his whole appearance denoted extraordinary suffering and exertion; yet, sustained by some powerful impulse, he continued to advance, while the throng around him with wild cheers sought to encourage him. The other three men were marked about the arms and breasts with several slight wounds, which they somewhat ostentatiously displayed.

These four individuals, having been the most active in the late encounter, claimed the honor of bearing the bodies of their slain enemies to the Ti. Such was the conclusion I drew from my own observations, and, as far as I could understand, from the explanation which Kory-Kory gave me.

The royal Mehevi walked by the side of these heroes. He carried in one hand a musket, from the barrel of which was suspended a small canvas pouch of powder, and in the other he grasped a short javelin, which he held before him and regarded with fierce exultation. This javelin he had wrested from a celebrated champion of the Happars, who had ignominiously fled, and was pursued by his foe beyond the summit of the mountain.

When within a short distance of the Ti, the warrior with the wounded head, who proved to be Narmonee, tottered forward two or three steps, and fell helplessly to the ground; but not before another had caught the end of the pole from his shoulder, and placed it upon his own.

The excited throng of islanders, who surrounded the person of the king and the dead bodies of the enemy, approached the spot where I stood, brandishing their rude implements of warfare, many of which were bruised and broken, and uttering continual shouts of triumph. When the crowd drew up opposite the Ti, I set myself to watch their proceedings most attentively; but scarcely had they halted when my servitor, who had left my side for an instant, touched my arm, and proposed our returning to Marheyo's house. To this I objected; but to my surprise, Kory-Kory reiterated his request, and with an unusual vehemence of manner. Still, however, I refused to comply, and was retreating before him, as in his importunity he pressed upon me, when I felt a heavy hand laid upon my shoulder, and turning round, encountered the bulky form of Mow-Mow, a one-eyed chief, who had just detached himself from the crowd below, and had mounted the rear of the *pi-pi* upon which we stood. His cheek had been pierced by the point of a spear, and the wound imparted a still more frightful expression to his hideously tattooed face, already deformed by the loss of an eye. The warrior, without uttering a syllable, pointed fiercely in the direction of Marheyo's house, while Kory-Kory, at the same time presenting his back, desired me to mount.

I declined this offer, but intimated my willingness to withdraw, and moved slowly along the piazza, wondering what could be the cause of this unusual treatment. A few minutes' consideration convinced me that the savages were about to celebrate some hideous rite in connection with their peculiar customs, and at which they were determined I should not be present. I descended from the *pi-pi*, and attended by Kory-Kory, who on this occasion did not show his usual commiseration for my lameness, but seemed only anxious to hurry me on, walked away from the place. As I passed through the noisy throng, which by this time completely environed the Ti, I looked with fearful curiosity at the three packages, which now were deposited upon the ground; but although I had no doubt as to their contents, still their thick coverings prevented my actually detecting the form of a human body.

The next morning, shortly after sunrise, the same thundering sounds which had awakened me from sleep on the second day of the 'Feast of Calabashes,' assured me that the savages were on the eve of celebrating another, and, as I fully believed, a horrible solemnity.

All the inmates of the house, with the exception of Marheyo, his son, and Tinor, after assuming their gala dresses, departed in the direction of the Taboo Groves.

Although I did not anticipate a compliance with my request, still, with a view of testing the truth of my suspicions, I proposed to Kory-Kory that, according to our usual custom in the morning, we should take a stroll to the Ti: he positively refused; and when I renewed the request, he evinced his determination to prevent my going there; and, to divert my mind from the subject, he offered to accompany me to the stream. We accordingly went, and bathed. On our coming back to the house, I was surprised to find that all its inmates had returned, and were lounging upon the mats as usual, although the drums still sounded from the groves.

The rest of the day I spent with Kory-Kory and Fayaway, wandering about a part of the valley situated in an opposite direction from the Ti; and whenever I so much as looked toward that building, although it was hidden from view by intervening trees, and the distance of more than a mile, my attendant would exclaim, 'Taboo! Taboo!'

At the various houses where we stopped, I found many of the inhabitants reclining at their ease, or pursuing some light occupation, as if nothing unusual were going forward; but amongst them all I did not perceive a single chief or warrior. When I asked several of the people why they were not at the *Hoolah Hoolah* (the feast), they uniformly answered the question in a manner which implied that it was not intended for them, but for Mehevi, Narmonee, Mow-Mow, Kolor, Womonoo, Kalow—running over, in their desire to make me comprehend their meaning, the names of all the principal chiefs.

Everything, in short, strengthened my suspicions with regard to the nature of the festival they were now celebrating; and which amounted almost to a certainty. While in Nukuheva I had frequently been informed that the whole tribe were never present at these cannibal banquets; but the chiefs and priests only, and everything I now observed agreed with the account.

The sound of the drums continued, without intermission, the whole day, and falling continually upon my ear, caused me a sensation of horror which I am unable to describe. On the following day, hearing none of those noisy indications of revelry, I concluded that the inhuman feast was terminated; and feeling a kind of morbid curiosity to discover whether the Ti might furnish any evidence of what had taken place there, I proposed to Kory-Kory to walk over there. To this proposition he replied by pointing with his finger to the newly risen sun, and then up to the zenith, intimating that our visit must be deferred until noon. Shortly after that hour we accordingly proceeded to the Taboo Groves, and as soon as we entered their precincts, I looked fearfully round in quest of some memorial of the scenes which had so lately been acted there; but everything appeared as usual. On reaching the Ti, we found Mehevi and a few chiefs reclining on the mats, who gave me as friendly a reception as ever. No allusions of any kind were made by them to the recent events; and I refrained, for obvious reasons, from referring to them myself.

After staying a short time I took my leave. In passing along the piazza, previously to descending from the *pi-pi*, I observed a curiously carved vessel of wood, of considerable size, with a cover placed over it, of the same material, and which resembled in shape a small canoe. It was surrounded by a low railing of bamboos the top of which was scarcely a foot from the ground. As the vessel had been placed in its present position since my last visit, I at once concluded that it must have some connection with the recent festival; and, prompted by a curiosity I could not repress, in passing it I raised one end of the cover; at the same moment the chiefs, perceiving my design, loudly ejaculated, 'Taboo! Taboo!' But the slight glimpse sufficed; my eyes fell upon the disordered members of a human skeleton, the bones still fresh with moisture, and with particles of flesh clinging to them here and there!

Kory-Kory, who had been a little in advance of me, attracted by the exclamations of the chiefs, turned round in time to witness the expression of horror on my countenance. He now hurried toward me, pointing at the same time to the canoe, and exclaiming rapidly, 'Puarkee! Puarkee!' (Pig, pig). I pretended to yield to the deception, and repeated the words after him several times, as though acquiescing in what he said. The other savages, either deceived by my conduct or unwilling to manifest their displeasure at what could not now be remedied, took no further notice of the occurrence, and I immediately left the Ti.

All that night I lay awake, revolving in my mind the fearful situation in which I was placed. The last horrid revelation had now been made, and the full sense of my condition rushed upon my mind with a force I had never before experienced.

Where, thought I, desponding, is there the slightest prospect of escape? The only person who seemed to possess the ability to assist me was the stranger Marnoo; but would he ever return to the valley? And if he did, should I be permitted to hold any communication with him? It seemed as if I were cut off from every source of hope, and that nothing remained but passively to await whatever fate was in store for me. A thousand times I endeavored to account for the mysterious conduct of the natives. For what conceivable purpose did they thus retain me a captive? What could be their object in treating me with such apparent kindness, and did it not cover some treacherous scheme? Or, if they had no other design than to hold me a prisoner, how should I be able to pass away my days in this narrow valley, deprived of all intercourse with civilized beings, and forever separated from friends and home?

One only hope remained to me. The French could not long defer a visit to the bay, and if they should permanently locate any of their troops in the valley, the savages could not for any length of time conceal my existence from them. But what reason had I to suppose that I should be spared until such an event occurred—an event which might be postponed by a hundred different contingencies?

XXXIII

The stranger again arrives in the valley—singular interview with him—attempt to escape—failure— melancholy situation—sympathy of Marheyo.

'Marnoo, Marnoo pemi!' Such were the welcome sounds which fell upon my ear some ten days after the events related in the preceding chapter. Once more the approach of the stranger was heralded, and the intelligence operated upon me like magic. Again I should be able to converse with him in my own language; and I resolved at all hazards to concert with him some scheme, however desperate, to rescue me from a condition that had now become insupportable.

As he drew near, I remembered with many misgivings, the inauspicious termination of our former interview; and when he entered the house, I watched with intense anxiety the reception he met with from its inmates. To my joy, his appearance was hailed with the liveliest pleasure; and accosting me kindly, he seated himself by my side, and entered into conversation with the natives around him. It soon appeared, however, that on this occasion he had not any intelligence of importance to communicate. I inquired of him from whence he had last come? He replied from Pueearka, his native valley, and that he intended to return to it the same day.

At once it struck me that, could I but reach the valley under his protection, I might easily from thence reach Nukuheva by water; and animated by the prospect which this plan held out, I disclosed it in a few brief words to the stranger, and asked him how it could be best accomplished. My heart sunk within me when in his broken English he answered me that it could never be effected. 'Kannaka no let you go no where,' he said; 'you taboo. Why you no like to stay? Plenty *moee-moee* (sleep)—plenty *kiki* (eat)—plenty *whihenee* (young girls)— Oh, very good place Typee! Suppose you no like this bay, why you come? You no hear about Typee. All white men afraid Typee, so no white men come.'

These words distressed me beyond belief; and when I again related to him the circumstances under which I had descended into the valley, and sought to enlist his sympathies in my behalf by appealing to the bodily misery I endured, he listened to me with impatience and cut me short by exclaiming passionately, 'Me no hear you talk any more; by by Kannaka get mad, kill you and me too. No you see he no want you to speak to me at all?—you see—ah! by by you no mind—you get well, he kill you, eat you, hang your head up there, like Happar Kannaka.—Now you listen—but no talk any more. By by I go;—you see why I go.—Ah! then some night Kannaka all *moee-moee* (sleep)—you run away, you come Pueearka. I speak Pueearka Kannaka—he no harm you—ah! then I take you my canoe Nukuheva—and you no run away ship no more.' With these words, enforced by a vehemence of gesture I cannot describe, Marnoo started from my side, and immediately engaged in conversation with some of the chiefs who had entered the house.

It would have been idle for me to have attempted resuming the interview so peremptorily terminated by Marnoo, who was evidently little disposed to compromise his own safety by any rash endeavors to ensure mine. But the plan he had suggested struck me as one which might possibly be accomplished, and I resolved to act upon it as speedily as possible.

Accordingly, when he rose to depart, I accompanied him with the natives outside of the house, with a view of carefully noting the path he would take in leaving the valley. Just before leaping from the *pi-pi* he clasped my hand, and looking significantly at me, exclaimed, 'Now you see—you do what I tell you—ah! then you do good;—you no do so—ah! then you die.' The next moment he waved his spear in adieu to the islanders, and following the route that conducted to a defile in the mountains lying opposite the Happar side, was soon out of sight.

A mode of escape was now presented to me, but how was I to avail myself of it? I was continually surrounded by the savages; I could not stir from one house to another without being attended by some of them; and even during the hours devoted to slumber the slightest movement which I made seemed to attract the notice of those who shared the mats with me. In spite of these obstacles, however, I determined forthwith to make the attempt. To do so with any prospect of success, it was necessary that I should have at least two hours' start before the islanders should discover my absence; for with such facility was any alarm spread through the valley, and so familiar, of course, were the inhabitants with the intricacies of the groves, that I could not hope, lame and feeble as I was, and ignorant of the route, to secure my escape unless I had this advantage. It was also by night alone that I could hope to accomplish my object, and then only by adopting the utmost precaution.

The entrance to Marheyo's habitation was through a low narrow opening in its wickerwork front. This passage, for no conceivable reason that I could devise, was always closed after the household had retired to rest, by drawing a heavy slide across it, composed of a dozen or more bits of wood, ingeniously fastened together by seizings of sinnate. When any of the inmates chose to go outside, the noise occasioned by the removing of this rude door awakened everybody else; and on more than one occasion I had remarked that the islanders were nearly as irritable as more civilized beings under similar circumstances.

The difficulty thus placed in my way I determined to obviate in the following manner. I would get up boldly in the course of the night, and drawing the slide, issue from the house, and pretend that my object was merely to procure a drink from the calabash, which always stood without the dwelling on the corner of the *pi-pi*. On re-entering I would purposely omit closing the passage after me, and trusting that the indolence of the savages would prevent them from repairing my neglect, would return to my mat, and waiting patiently until all were again asleep, I would then steal forth, and at once take the route to Pueearka.

The very night which followed Marnoo's departure, I proceeded to put this project into execution. About midnight, as I imagined, I rose and drew the slide. The natives, just as I had expected, started up, while some of them asked, *'Arware poo awa, Tommo?'* (Where are you going, Tommo?) *'Wai'* (water) I laconically answered, grasping the calabash. On hearing my reply they sank back again, and in a minute or two I returned to my mat, anxiously awaiting the result of the experiment.

One after another the savages turning restlessly, appeared to resume their slumbers, and rejoicing at the stillness which prevailed, I was about to rise again from my couch, when I heard a slight rustling—a dark form was intercepted between me and the doorway—the slide was drawn across it, and the individual, however he was, returned to his mat. This was a sad blow to me; but as it might have roused the suspicions of the islanders to have made another attempt that night, I was reluctantly obliged to defer it until the next. Several times after I repeated the same maneuver but with as little success as before. As my pretense for withdrawing from the house was to allay my thirst, Kory-Kory, either suspecting some design on my part, or else prompted by a desire to please me, regularly every evening placed a calabash of water by my side.

Even under these inauspicious circumstances I again and again renewed the attempt; but when I did so my valet always rose with me, as if determined I should not remove myself from his observation. For the present, therefore, I was obliged to abandon the attempt; but I endeavored to console myself with the idea that by this mode I might yet effect my escape.

Shortly after Marnoo's visit I was reduced to such a state, that it was with extreme difficulty I could walk, even with the assistance of a spear, and Kory-Kory, as formerly, was obliged to carry me daily to the stream.

For hours and hours during the warmest part of the day I lay upon my mat, and while those around me were nearly all dozing away in careless ease, I remained awake gloomily pondering over the fate which it appeared now idle for me to resist, when I thought of the loved friends who were thousands and thousands of miles from the savage island in which I was held a captive, when I reflected that my dreadful fate would for ever be concealed from them, and that with hope deferred they might continue to await my return long after my inanimate form had blended with the dust of the valley —I could not repress a shudder of anguish.

How vividly is impressed upon my mind every minute feature of the scene which met my view during those long days of suffering and sorrow! At my request my mats were always spread directly facing the door, opposite which, and at a little distance, was the hut of boughs Marheyo was building.

Whenever my gentle Fayaway and Kory-Kory, laying themselves down beside me, would leave me awhile to uninterrupted repose, I took a strange interest in the slightest movements of the eccentric old warrior. All alone during the stillness of the tropical midday, he would pursue his quiet work, sitting in the shade and weaving together the leaflets of his coconut branches, or rolling upon his knee the twisted fibres of bark to form the cords with which he tied together the thatching of his tiny house. Frequently suspending his employment, and noticing my melancholy eye fixed upon him, he would raise his hand with a gesture expressive of deep commiseration, and then moving toward me slowly would enter on tiptoes, fearful of disturbing the slumbering natives, and, taking the fan from my hand, would sit before me, swaying it gently to and fro, and gazing earnestly into my face.

Just beyond the *pi-pi*, and disposed in a triangle before the entrance of the house, were three magnificent breadfruit trees. At this moment I can recall to my mind their slender shafts, and the graceful inequalities of their bark, on which my eye was accustomed to dwell day after day in the midst of my solitary musings. It is strange how inanimate objects will twine themselves into our affections, especially in the hour of affliction. Even now, amidst all the bustle and stir of the proud and busy city in which I am dwelling, the image of those three trees seems to come as vividly before my eyes as if they were actually present, and I still feel the soothing quiet pleasure which I then had in watching hour after hour their topmost boughs waving gracefully in the breeze.

XXXIV

The escape.

NEARLY THREE WEEKS had elapsed since the second visit of Marnoo, and it must have been more than four months since I entered the valley, when one day about noon, and whilst everything was in profound silence, Mow-Mow, the one-eyed chief, suddenly appeared at the door, and leaning forward toward me as I lay directly facing him, said in a low tone, '*Toby pemi ena*' (Toby has arrived here). Gracious heaven! What a tumult of emotions rushed upon me at this startling intelligence! Insensible to the pain that had before distracted me, I leaped to my feet, and called wildly to Kory-Kory, who was reposing by my side. The startled islanders sprang from their mats; the news was quickly communicated to them; and the next moment I was making my way to the Ti on the back of Kory-Kory, and surrounded by the excited savages.

All that I could comprehend of the particulars which Mow-Mow rehearsed to his auditors as we proceeded, was that my long-lost companion had arrived in a boat which had just entered the bay. These tidings made me most anxious to be carried at once to the sea, lest some untoward circumstance should prevent our meeting; but to this they would not consent, and continued their course toward the royal abode. As we approached it, Mehevi and several chiefs showed themselves from the piazza, and called upon us loudly to come to them.

As soon as we had approached, I endeavored to make them understand that I was going down to the sea to meet Toby. To this the king objected and motioned Kory-Kory to bring me into the house. It was in vain to resist; and in a few moments I found myself within the Ti, surrounded by a noisy group engaged in discussing the recent intelligence. Toby's name was frequently repeated, coupled with violent exclamations of astonishment. It seemed as if they yet remained in doubt with regard to the fact of his arrival, and at every fresh report that was brought from the shore they betrayed the liveliest emotions.

Almost frenzied at being held in this state of suspense, I passionately besought Mehevi to permit me to proceed. Whether my companion had arrived or not, I felt a presentiment that my own fate was about to be decided. Again and again I renewed my petition to Mehevi. He regarded me with a fixed and serious eye, but at length yielding to my importunity, reluctantly granted my request.

Accompanied by some fifty of the natives, I now rapidly continued my journey; every few moments being transferred from the back of one to another, and urging my bearer forward all the while with earnest entreaties. As I thus hurried forward no doubt as to the truth of the information I had received ever crossed my mind. I was alive only to the one overwhelming idea, that a chance of deliverance was now afforded me, if the jealous opposition of the savages could be overcome.

Having been prohibited from approaching the sea during the whole of my stay in the valley, I had always associated with it the idea of escape. Toby too—if indeed he had ever voluntarily deserted me—must have effected his flight by the sea; and now that I was drawing near to it myself, I indulged in hopes which I had never felt before. It was evident that a boat had entered the bay, and I saw little reason to doubt the truth of the report that it had brought my companion. Every time therefore that we gained an elevation, I looked eagerly around, hoping to behold him.

In the midst of an excited throng, who by their violent gestures and wild cries appeared to be under the influence of some excitement as strong as my own, I was now borne along at a rapid trot, frequently stooping my head to avoid the branches which crossed their path, and never ceasing to implore those who carried me to accelerate their already swift pace.

In this manner we had proceeded about four or five miles, when we were met by a party of some twenty islanders, between whom and those who accompanied me ensued an animated conference. Impatient of the delay occasioned by this interruption, I was beseeching the man who carried me to proceed without his loitering companions, when Kory-Kory, running to my side, informed me, in three fatal words, that the news had all proved false—that Toby had not arrived— 'Toby owlee permi.' Heaven only knows how, in the state of mind and body I then was, I ever sustained the agony which this intelligence caused me: not that the news was altogether unexpected; but I had trusted that the fact might not have been made known until we should have arrived upon the beach. As it was, I at once foresaw the course the savages would pursue. They had only yielded thus far to my entreaties, that I might give a joyful welcome to my long-absent comrade; but now that it was known he had not arrived, they would at once oblige me to turn back.

My anticipations were but too correct. In spite of the resistance I made, they carried me into a house which was near the spot, and left me upon the mats. Shortly afterward several of those who had accompanied me from the Ti, detaching themselves from the others, proceeded in the direction of the sea. Those who remained—among whom were Marheyo, Mow-Mow, Kory-Kory, and Tinor—gathered about the dwelling and appeared to be awaiting their return.

This convinced me that strangers—perhaps some of my own countrymen—had for some cause or other entered the bay. Distracted at the idea of their vicinity, and reckless of the pain which I suffered, I heeded not the assurances of the islanders, that there were no boats at the beach, but starting to my feet endeavored to gain the door. Instantly the passage was blocked up by several men, who commanded me to resume my seat. The fierce looks of the irritated savages admonished me that I could gain nothing by force, and that it was by entreaty alone that I could hope to compass my object.

Guided by this consideration, I turned to Mow-Mow, the only chief present whom I had been much in the habit of seeing, and carefully concealing my real design, tried to make him comprehend that I still believed Toby to have arrived on the shore, and besought him to allow me to go forward to welcome him. To all his repeated assertions, that my companion had not been seen, I pretend to turn a deaf ear: while I urged my solicitations with an eloquence of gesture which the one-eyed chief appeared unable to resist. He seemed indeed to regard me as a froward child, to whose wishes he had not the heart to oppose force, and whom he must consequently humor. He spoke a few words to the natives, who at once retreated from the door, and immediately passed out of the house.

Here I looked earnestly round for Kory-Kory; but that hitherto faithful servitor was nowhere to be seen. Unwilling to linger even for a single instant when every moment might be so important, I motioned to a muscular fellow near me to take me upon his back: to my surprise he angrily refused. I turned to another, but with a like result. A third attempt was as unsuccessful and I immediately perceived what had induced Mow-Mow to grant my request and why the other natives conducted themselves in so strange a manner. It was evident that the chief had only given me liberty to continue my progress toward the sea because he supposed that I was deprived of the means of reaching it.

Convinced by this of their determination to retain me a captive, I became desperate; and almost insensible to the pain which I suffered I seized a spear which was leaning against the projecting eaves of the house, and supporting myself with it, resumed the path that swept by the dwelling. To my surprise I was suffered to proceed alone, all the natives remaining in front of the house, and engaging in earnest conversation which every moment became more loud and vehement; and to my unspeakable delight I perceived that some difference of opinion had arisen between them; that two parties, in short, were formed, and consequently that in their divided counsels there was some chance of my deliverance.

Before I had proceeded a hundred yards I was again surrounded by the savages, who were still in all the heat of argument, and appeared every moment as if they would come to blows. In the midst of this tumult old Marheyo came to my side, and I shall never forget the benevolent expression of his countenance. He placed his arm upon my shoulder, and emphatically pronounced the only two English words I had taught him—'Home' and 'Mother.' I at once understood what he meant, and eagerly expressed my thanks to him. Fayaway and Kory-Kory were by his side, both weeping violently; and it was not until the old man had twice repeated the command that his son could bring himself to obey him, and take me again upon his back. The one-eyed chief opposed his doing so, but he was overruled, and, as it seemed to me, by some of his own party.

We proceeded onward, and never shall I forget the ecstasy I felt when I first heard the roar of the surf breaking upon the beach. Before long I saw the flashing billows themselves through the opening between the trees. Oh, glorious sight and sound of ocean! with what rapture did I hail you as familiar friends! By this time the shouts of the crowd upon the beach were distinctly audible, and in the blended confusion of sounds I almost fancied I could distinguish the voices of my own countrymen.

When we reached the open space which lay between the groves and the sea, the first object that met my view was an English whaleboat, lying with her bow pointed from the shore, and only a few fathoms distant from it. It was manned by five islanders, dressed in short tunics of calico. My first impression was that they were in the very act of pulling out from the bay; and that, after all my exertions, I had come too late. My soul sunk within me: but a second glance convinced me that the boat was only hanging off to keep out of the surf; and the next moment I heard my own name shouted out by a voice from the midst of the crowd.

Looking in the direction of the sound, I perceived, to my indescribable joy, the tall figure of Karakoee, an Oahu Kannaka, who had often been aboard the *Dolly*, while she lay in

Nukuheva. He wore the green shooting jacket with gilt buttons, which had been given to him by an officer of the *Reine Blanche*—the French flag-ship—and in which I had always seen him dressed. I now remembered the Kannaka had frequently told me that his person was tabooed in all the valleys of the island, and the sight of him at such a moment as this filled my heart with a tumult of delight.

Karakoee stood near the edge of the water with a large roll of cotton cloth thrown over one arm, and holding two or three canvas bags of powder; while with the other hand he grasped a musket, which he appeared to be proffering to several of the chiefs around him. But they turned with disgust from his offers, and seemed to be impatient at his presence, with vehement gestures waving him off to his boat, and commanding him to depart.

The Kannaka, however, still maintained his ground, and I at once perceived that he was seeking to purchase my freedom. Animated by the idea, I called upon him loudly to come to me; but he replied, in broken English, that the islanders had threatened to pierce him with their spears, if he stirred a foot toward me. At this time I was still advancing, surrounded by a dense throng of the natives, several of whom had their hands upon me, and more than one javelin was threateningly pointed at me. Still I perceived clearly that many of those least friendly toward me looked irresolute and anxious.

I was still some thirty yards from Karakoee when my further progress was prevented by the natives, who compelled me to sit down upon the ground, while they still retained their hold upon my arms. The din and tumult now became tenfold, and I perceived that several of the priests were on the spot, all of whom were evidently urging Mow-Mow and the other chiefs to prevent my departure; and the detestable word '*Roo-ne! Roo-ne!*' which I had heard repeated a thousand times during the day, was now shouted out on every side of me. Still I saw that the Kannaka continued his exertions in my favor—that he was boldly debating the matter with the savages, and was striving to entice them by displaying his cloth and powder, and snapping the lock of his musket. But all he said or did appeared only to augment the clamors of those around him, who seemed bent upon driving him into the sea.

When I remembered the extravagant value placed by these people upon the articles which were offered to them in exchange for me, and which were so indignantly rejected, I saw a new proof of the same fixed determination of purpose they had all along manifested with regard to me, and in despair, and reckless of consequences, I exerted all my strength, and shaking myself free from the grasp of those who held me, I sprung upon my feet and rushed toward Karakoee.

The rash attempt nearly decided my fate; for, fearful that I might slip from them, several of the islanders now raised a simultaneous shout, and pressing upon Karakoee, they menaced him with furious gestures, and actually forced him into the sea. Appalled at their violence, the poor fellow, standing nearly to the waist in the surf, endeavored to pacify them; but at length, fearful that they would do him some fatal violence, he beckoned to his comrades to pull in at once, and take him into the boat.

It was at this agonizing moment, when I thought all hope was ended, that a new contest arose between the two parties who had accompanied me to the shore; blows were struck, wounds were given, and blood flowed. In the interest excited by the fray every one had left me except Marheyo, Kory-Kory, and poor dear Fayaway, who clung to me, sobbing indignantly. I saw that now or never was the moment. Clasping my hands together, I looked imploringly at Marheyo, and moved toward the now almost deserted beach. The tears were in the old man's eyes, but neither he nor Kory-Kory attempted to hold me, and I soon reached the Kannaka who had been anxiously watching my movements; the rowers pulled in as near as they dared to the edge of the surf; I gave one parting embrace to Fayaway, who seemed speechless with sorrow, and the next instant I found myself safe in the boat, and Karakoee by my side, who told the rowers at once to give way. Marheyo and Kory-Kory, and a great many of the women, followed me into the water, and I was determined, as the only mark of gratitude I could show, to give them the articles which had been brought as my ransom. I handed the musket to Kory-Kory, with a rapid gesture which was equivalent to a 'Deed of Gift'; threw the roll of cotton to old Marheyo, pointing as I did so to poor Fayaway, who had retired from the edge of the water and was sitting down disconsolate on the shingles; and tumbled the powder bags out to the nearest young ladies, all of whom were vastly willing to take them. This distribution did not occupy ten seconds, and before it was over the boat was under full way; the Kannaka all the while exclaiming loudly against what he considered a useless throwing away of valuable property.

Although it was clear that my movements had been noticed by several of the natives, still they had not suspended the conflict in which they were engaged, and it was not until the boat was above fifty yards from the shore that Mow-Mow and some six or seven other warriors rushed into the sea and hurled their javelins at us. Some of the weapons passed quite as close to us as was desirable, but no one was wounded, and the men pulled away gallantly. But although soon out of the reach of the spears, our progress was extremely slow; it blew strong upon the shore, and the tide was against us; and I saw Karakoee, who was steering the boat, give many a look toward a jutting point of the bay round which we had to pass.

For a minute or two after our departure, the savages, who had formed into different groups, remained perfectly motionless and silent. All at once the enraged chief showed by his gestures that he had resolved what course he would take. Shouting loudly to his companions, and pointing with his tomahawk toward the headland, he set off at full speed in that direction, and was followed by about thirty of the natives, among whom were several of the priests, all yelling out 'Roo-ne! Roo-ne!' at the very top of their voices. Their intention was evidently to swim off from the headland and intercept us in our course. The wind was freshening every minute, and was right in our teeth, and it was one of those chopping angry seas in which it is so difficult to row. Still the chances seemed in our favor, but when we came within a hundred yards of the point, the active savages were already dashing into the water, and we all feared that within five minutes' time we should have a score of the infuriated wretches around us. If so, our doom was sealed, for these savages, unlike the feeble swimmers of civilized countries, are, if anything, more formidable antagonists in the water than when on the land. It was all a trial of strength; our natives pulled till their oars bent again, and the crowd of swimmers shot through the water despite its roughness, with fearful rapidity.

By the time we had reached the headland, the savages were spread right across our course. Our rowers got out their knives and held them ready between their teeth, and I seized the boathook. We were well aware that if they succeeded in intercepting us they would practice upon us the maneuver which has proved so fatal to many a boat's crew in these seas. They would grapple the oars, and seizing hold of the gunwale, capsize the boat, and then we should be entirely at their mercy.

After a few breathless moments I discerned Mow-Mow. The athletic islander, with his tomahawk between his teeth, was dashing the water before him till it foamed again. He was the nearest to us, and in another instant he would have seized one of the oars. Even at the moment I felt horror at the act I was about to commit; but it was no time for pity or compunction, and with a true aim, and exerting all my strength, I dashed the boathook at him. It struck him just below the throat, and forced him downward. I had no time to repeat my blow, but I saw him rise to the surface in the wake of the boat, and never shall I forget the ferocious expression of his countenance.

Only one other of the savages reached the boat. He seized the gunwale, but the knives of our rowers so mauled his wrists, that he was forced to quit his hold, and the next minute we were past them all, and in safety. The strong excitement which had thus far kept me up, now left me, and I fell back fainting into the arms of Karakoee.

The circumstances connected with my most unexpected escape may be very briefly stated. The captain of an Australian vessel, being in distress for men in these remote seas, had put into Nukuheva in order to recruit his ship's company; but not a single man was to be obtained; and the barque was about to get under weigh, when she was boarded by Karakoee, who informed the disappointed Englishman that an American sailor was detained by the savages in the neighboring bay of Typee; and he offered, if supplied with suitable articles of traffic, to undertake his release. The Kannaka had gained his intelligence from Marnoo, to whom, after all, I was indebted for my escape. The proposition was acceded to; and Karakoee, taking with him five tabooed natives of Nukuheva, again repaired aboard the barque, which in a few hours sailed to that part of the island, and threw her main topsail aback right off the entrance to the Typee bay. The whaleboat, manned by the tabooed crew, pulled toward the head of the inlet, while the ship lay 'off and on' awaiting its return.

The events which ensued have already been detailed, and little more remains to be related. On reaching the *Julia* I was lifted over the side, and my strange appearance and remarkable adventure occasioned the liveliest interest. Every attention was bestowed upon me that humanity could suggest. But to such a state was I reduced, that three months elapsed before I recovered my health.

The mystery which hung over the fate of my friend and companion Toby has never been cleared up. I still remain ignorant whether he succeeded in leaving the valley, or perished at the hands of the islanders.

SEQUEL

THE AUTHOR WAS more than two years in the South Seas, after escaping from the valley, as recounted in the last chapter. Some time after returning home the foregoing narrative was published, though it was little thought at the time that this would be the means of revealing the existence of Toby, who had long been given up for lost. But so it proved.

The story of his escape supplies a natural sequel to the adventure, and as such it is now added to the volume. It was related to the author by Toby himself not ten days since.

NEW YORK,
    July 1846.

THE STORY OF TOBY

THE MORNING MY comrade left me, as related in the narrative, he was accompanied by a large party of the natives, some of them carrying fruit and hogs for the purposes of traffic, as the report had spread that boats had touched at the bay.

As they proceeded through the settled parts of the valley, numbers joined them from every side, running with animated cries from every pathway. So excited were the whole party, that eager as Toby was to gain the beach, it was almost as much as he could do to keep up with them. Making the valley ring with their shouts, they hurried along on a swift trot, those in advance pausing now and then, and flourishing their weapons to urge the rest forward.

Presently they came to a place where the path crossed a band of the main stream of the valley. Here a strange sound came through the grove beyond, and the islanders halted. It was Mow-Mow, the one-eyed chief, who had gone on before; he was striking his heavy lance against the hollow bough of a tree.

This was a signal of alarm;—for nothing was now heard but shouts of 'Happar! Happar!'—the warriors tilting with their spears and brandishing them in the air, and the women and boys shouting to each other, and picking up the stones in the bed of the stream. In a moment or two Mow-Mow and two or three other chiefs ran out from the grove, and the din increased tenfold.

Now, thought Toby, for a fray; and being unarmed, he besought one of the young men domiciled with Marheyo for the loan of his spear. But he was refused; the youth roguishly telling him that the weapon was very good for him (the

Typee), but that a white man could fight much better with his fists.

The merry humor of this young wag seemed to be shared by the rest, for in spite of their warlike cries and gestures, everybody was capering about and laughing, as if it was one of the funniest things in the world to be awaiting the flight of a score or two of Happar javelins from an ambush in the thickets.

While my comrade was in vain trying to make out the meaning of all this, a good number of the natives separated themselves from the rest and ran off into the grove on one side, the others now keeping perfectly still, as if awaiting the result. After a little while, however, Mow-Mow, who stood in advance, motioned them to come on stealthily, which they did, scarcely rustling a leaf. Thus they crept along for ten or fifteen minutes, every now and then pausing to listen.

Toby by no means relished this sort of skulking; if there was going to be a fight he wanted it to begin at once. But all in good time,—for just then, as they went prowling into the thickest of the wood, terrific howls burst upon them on all sides, and volleys of darts and stones flew across the path. Not an enemy was to be seen, and, what was still more surprising, not a single man dropped, though the pebbles fell among the leaves like hail.

There was a moment's pause, when the Typees, with wild shrieks, flung themselves into the covert, spear in hand; nor was Toby behindhand. Coming so near getting his skull broken by the stones, and animated by an old grudge he bore the Happars, he was among the first to dash at them. As he broke his way through the underbrush, trying, as he did so, to wrest a spear from a young chief, the shouts of battle all of a sudden ceased, and the wood was as still as death. The next moment, the party who had left them so mysteriously rushed out from behind every bush and tree, and united with the rest in long and merry peals of laughter.

It was all a sham, and Toby, who was quite out of breath with excitement, was much incensed at being made a fool of.

It afterward turned out that the whole affair had been

concerted for his particular benefit, though with what precise
view it would be hard to tell. My comrade was the more
enraged at this boys' play, since it had consumed so much
time, every moment of which might be precious. Perhaps,
however, it was partly intended for this very purpose; and he
was led to think so, because, when the natives started again,
he observed that they did not seem to be in so great a hurry
as before. At last, after they had gone some distance, Toby,
thinking all the while that they never would get to the sea,
two men came running toward them, and a regular halt
ensued, followed by a noisy discussion during which Toby's
name was often repeated. All this made him more and more
anxious to learn what was going on at the beach; but it was
in vain that he now tried to push forward; the natives held
him back.

In a few moments the conference ended, and many of them
ran down the path in the direction of the water, the rest
surrounding Toby, and entreating him to '*Moce,*' or sit down
and rest himself. As an additional inducement, several calabashes of food, which had been brought along, were now
placed on the ground, and opened, and pipes also were lighted.
Toby bridled his impatience a while, but at last sprang to his
feet and dashed forward again. He was soon overtaken nevertheless, and again surrounded, but without further detention
was then permitted to go down to the sea.

They came out upon a bright green space between the
groves and the water, and close under the shadow of the
Happar mountain, where a path was seen, winding out of
sight through a gorge.

No sign of a boat, however, was beheld; nothing but a
tumultuous crowd of men and women, and some one in their
midst, earnestly talking to them. As my comrade advanced,
this person came forward and proved to be no stranger. He
was an old grizzled sailor, whom Toby and myself had frequently seen in Nukuheva, where he lived an easy devil-may-
care life in the household of Mowanna the king, going by the
name of 'Jimmy.' In fact, he was the royal favorite, and had
a good deal to say in his master's councils. He wore a Manilla

hat and a sort of tappa morning gown, sufficiently loose and negligent to show the verse of a song tattooed upon his chest, and a variety of spirited cuts by native artists in other parts of his body. He sported a fishing rod in his hand, and carried a sooty old pipe slung about his neck.

This old rover having retired from active life, had resided in Nukuheva for some time, could speak the language, and for that reason was frequently employed by the French as an interpreter. He was an arrant old gossip too; for ever coming off in his canoe to the ships in the bay, and regaling their crews with choice little morsels of court scandal; such, for instance, as a shameful intrigue of His Majesty with a Happar damsel, a public dancer at the feasts, and otherwise relating some incredible tales about the Marquesas generally. I remember in particular his telling the *Dolly's* crew what proved to be literally a cock-and-bull story, about two natural prodigies which he said were then on the island. One was an old monster of a hermit, having a marvelous reputation for sanctity, and reputed a famous sorcerer, who lived away off in a den among the mountains, where he hid from the world a great pair of horns that grew out of his temples. Notwithstanding his reputation for piety, this horrid old fellow was the terror of all the island round, being reported to come out from his retreat, and go a-man-hunting every dark night. Some anonymous Paul Pry, too, coming down the mountain, once got a peep at his den and found it full of bones. In short, he was a most unheard-of monster.

The other prodigy Jimmy told us about was the younger son of a chief, who although but just turned of ten, had entered upon holy orders, because his superstitious countrymen thought him especially intended for the priesthood from the fact of his having a comb on his head like a rooster. But this was not all; for still more wonderful to relate, the boy prided himself upon this strange crest, being actually endowed with a cock's voice, and frequently crowing over his peculiarity.

But to return to Toby. The moment he saw the old rover

on the beach, he ran up to him, the natives following after, and forming a circle round them.

After welcoming him to the shore, Jimmy went on to tell him how that he knew all about our having run away from the ship, and being among the Typees. Indeed, he had been urged by Mowanna to come over to the valley, and after visiting his friends there, to bring us back with him, his royal master being exceedingly anxious to share with him the reward which had been held out for our capture. He, however, assured Toby that he had indignantly spurned the offer.

All this astonished my comrade not a little, as neither of us had entertained the least idea that any white man ever visited the Typees sociably. But Jimmy told him that such was the case nevertheless, although he seldom came into the bay, and scarcely ever went back from the beach. One of the priests of the valley, in some way or other connected with an old tattooed divine in Nukuheva, was a friend of his, and through him he was taboo.

He said, moreover, that he was sometimes employed to come round to the bay, and engage fruit for ships lying in Nukuheva. In fact, he was now on that very errand, according to his own account, having just come across the mountains by the way of Happar. By noon of the next day the fruit would be heaped up in stacks on the beach, in readiness for the boats which he then intended to bring into the bay.

Jimmy now asked Toby whether he wished to leave the island; if he did, there was a ship in want of men lying in the other harbor, and would be glad to take him over, and see him on board that very day.

'No,' said Toby, 'I cannot leave the island unless my comrade goes with me. I left him up the valley because they would not let him come down. Let us go now and fetch him.'

'But how is he to cross the mountain with us,' replied Jimmy, 'even if we get him down to the beach? Better let him stay till tomorrow, and I will bring him round to Nukuheva in the boats.'

'That will never do,' said Toby; 'but come along with me now, and let us get him down here at any rate;' and yielding to the impulse of the moment he started to hurry back into the valley. But hardly was his back turned, when a dozen hands were laid on him, and he learned that he could not go a step further.

It was in vain that he fought with them; they would not hear of his stirring from the beach. Cut to the heart at this unexpected repulse, Toby now conjured the sailor to go after me alone. But Jimmy replied, that in the mood the Typees then were they would not permit him so to do, though at the same time he was not afraid of their offering him any harm.

Little did Toby then think, as he afterward had good reason to suspect, that this very Jimmy was a heartless villain, who, by his arts, had just incited the natives to restrain him as he was in the act of going after me. Well must the old sailor have known, too, that the natives would never consent to our leaving together, and he therefore wanted to get Toby off alone, for a purpose which he afterward made plain. Of all this, however, my comrade now knew nothing.

He was still struggling with the islanders when Jimmy again came up to him, and warned him against irritating them, saying that he was only making matters worse for both of us, and if they became enraged, there was no telling what might happen. At last he made Toby sit down on a broken canoe by a pile of stones, upon which was a ruinous little shrine supported by four upright paddles, and in front partly screened by a net. The fishing parties met there when they came in from the sea, for their offerings were laid before an image, upon a smooth black stone within. This spot Jimmy said was strictly taboo, and no one would molest or come near him while he stayed by its shadow. The old sailor then went off, and began speaking very earnestly to Mow-Mow and some other chiefs, while all the rest formed a circle round the taboo place, looking intently at Toby, and talking to each other without ceasing.

Now, notwithstanding what Jimmy had just told him, there presently came up to my comrade an old woman, who seated herself beside him on the canoe.

'*Typee mortarkee?*' said she. '*Mortarkee nuee,*' said Toby.

She then asked him whether he was going to Nukuheva; he nodded yes; and with a plaintive wail and her eyes filling with tears she rose and left him.

This old woman, the sailor afterward said, was the wife of an aged king of a small inland valley, communicating by a deep pass with the country of the Typees. The inmates of the two valleys were related to each other by blood, and were known by the same name. The old woman had gone down into the Typee valley the day before, and was now with three chiefs, her sons, on a visit to her kinsmen.

As the old king's wife left him, Jimmy again came up to Toby, and told him that he had just talked the whole matter over with the natives, and there was only one course for him to follow. They would not allow him to go back into the valley, and harm would certainly come to both him and me, if he remained much longer on the beach. 'So,' said he, 'you and I had better go to Nukuheva now overland, and tomorrow I will bring Tommo, as they call him, by water; they have promised to carry him down to the sea for me early in the morning, so that there will be no delay.'

'No, no,' said Toby desperately, 'I will not leave him that way; we must escape together.'

'Then there is no hope for you,' exclaimed the sailor; 'for if I leave you here on the beach, as soon as I am gone you will be carried back into the valley, and then neither of you will ever look upon the sea again.' And with many oaths he swore that if he would only go to Nukuheva with him that day, he would be sure to have me there the very next morning.

'But how do you know they will bring him down to the beach tomorrow, when they will not do so today?' said Toby. But the sailor had many reasons, all of which were so mixed up with the mysterious customs of the islanders, that he was none the wiser. Indeed, their conduct, especially in preventing him from returning into the valley, was absolutely unaccountable to him; and added to every thing else, was the bitter reflection, that the old sailor, after all, mighty possibly be deceiving him. And then again he had to think of me, left alone with the natives, and by no means well. If he went with Jimmy, he might at least hope to procure some relief for me. But might not the savages who had acted so strangely, hurry me off somewhere before his return? Then, even if he remained, perhaps they would not let him go back into the valley where I was.

Thus perplexed was my poor comrade; he knew not what to do, and his courageous spirit was of no use to him now. There he was, all by himself, seated upon the broken canoe—the natives grouped around him at a distance, and eying him more and more fixedly.

'It is getting late,' said Jimmy, who was standing behind the rest. 'Nukuheva is far off, and I cannot cross the Happar country by night. You see how it is: if you come along with me, all will be well; if you do not, depend upon it, neither of you will ever escape.'

'There is no help for it,' said Toby, at last, with a heavy heart, 'I will have to trust you;' and he came out from the shadow of the little shrine, and cast a long look up the valley.

'Now keep close to my side,' said the sailor, 'and let us be moving quickly.' Tinor and Fayaway here appeared; the kindhearted old woman embracing Toby's knees, and giving way to a flood of tears; while Fayaway, hardly less moved, spoke some few words of English she had learned, and held up three fingers before him—in so many days he would return.

At last Jimmy pulled Toby out of the crowd, and after calling to a young Typee who was standing by with a young pig in his arms, all three started for the mountains.

'I have told them that you are coming back again,' said the old fellow, laughing, as they began the ascent, 'but they'll have to wait a long time.' Toby turned, and saw the natives all in motion—the girls waving their tappas in adieu, and the men their spears. As the last figure entered the grove with one arm raised, and the three fingers spread, his heart smote him.

As the natives had at last consented to his going, it might have been that some of them, at least, really counted upon his speedy return, probably supposing, as indeed he had told them when they were coming down the valley, that his only object in leaving them was to procure the medicines I needed. This Jimmy also must have told them. And as they had done before, when my comrade, to oblige me, started on his perilous journey to Nukuheva, they looked upon me, in his absence, as one of two inseparable friends who was a sure guaranty for the other's return. This is only my own supposition, however, for as to all their strange conduct, it is still a mystery.

'You see what sort of a taboo man I am,' said the sailor, after for some time silently following the path which led up the mountain. 'Mow-Mow made me a present of this pig here, and the man who carries it will go right through Happar, and down into Nukuheva with us. So long as he stays by me he is safe, and just so it will be with you, and tomorrow with Tommo. Cheer up, then, and rely upon me, you will see him in the morning.'

The ascent of the mountain was not very difficult owing to its being near to the sea, where the island ridges are comparatively low; the path, too, was a fine one, so that in a short time all three were standing on the summit with the two valleys at their feet. The white cascades marking the green head of the Typee valley first caught Toby's eye; Marheyo's house could easily be traced by them.

As Jimmy led the way along the ridge, Toby observed that the valley of the Happars did not extend near so far inland as that of the Typees. This accounted for our mistake in entering the latter valley as we had.

A path leading down as from the mountain was soon seen, and, following it, the party were in a short time fairly in the Happar valley.

'Now,' said Jimmy, as they hurried on, 'we taboo men have wives in all the bays, and I am going to show you the two I have here.'

So, when they came to the house where he said they lived, —which was close by the base of the mountain in a shady nook among the groves,—he went in, and was quite furious at finding it empty—the ladies had gone out. However, they soon made their appearance, and, to tell the truth, welcomed Jimmy quite cordially, as well as Toby, about whom they were very inquisitive. Nevertheless, as the report of their arrival spread, and the Happars began to assemble, it became evident that the appearance of a white stranger among them was not by any means deemed so wonderful an event as in the neighboring valley.

The old sailor now bade his wives prepare something to eat, as he must be in Nukuheva before dark. A meal of fish, breadfruit, and bananas was accordingly served up, the party regaling themselves on the mats, in the midst of a numerous company.

The Happars put many questions to Jimmy about Toby; and Toby himself looked sharply at them, anxious to recognize the fellow who gave him the wound from which he was still suffering. But this fiery gentleman, so handy with his spear, had the delicacy, it seemed, to keep out of view. Certainly the sight of him would not have been any added inducement to making a stay in the valley,—some of the afternoon loungers in Happar having politely urged Toby to spend a few days with them,—there was a feast coming on. He, however, declined.

All this while the young Typee stuck to Jimmy like his shadow, and though as lively a dog as any of his tribe, he was now as meek as a lamb, never opening his mouth except to eat. Although some of the Happars looked queerly at him, others were more civil, and seemed desirous of taking him abroad and showing him the valley. But the Typee was not to be cajoled in that way. How many yards he would have to remove from Jimmy before the taboo would be powerless, it would be hard to tell, but probably he himself knew to a fraction.

On the promise of a red cotton handkerchief, and something else which he kept secret, this poor fellow had undertaken a rather ticklish journey, though, as far as Toby could ascertain, it was something that had never happened before.

The island-punch—*arva*—was brought in at the conclusion of the repast and passed round in a shallow calabash.

Now my comrade, while seated in the Happar house, began to feel more troubled than ever at leaving me: indeed, so sad did he feel that he talked about going back to the valley, and wanted Jimmy to escort him as far as the mountains. But the sailor would not listen to him, and, by way of diverting his thoughts, pressed him to drink of the *arva*. Knowing its narcotic nature, he refused; but Jimmy said he would have something mixed with it, which would convert it into an innocent beverage that would inspirit them for the rest of their journey. So at last he was induced to drink of it, and its effects were just as the sailor had predicted; his spirits rose at once, and all his gloomy thoughts left him.

The old rover now began to reveal his true character, though he was hardly suspected at the time. 'If I get you off to a ship,' said he, 'you will surely give a poor fellow something for saving you.' In short before they left the house, he made Toby promise that he would give him five Spanish dollars if he succeeded in getting any part of his wages advanced from the vessel, aboard of which they were going; Toby, moreover, engaging to reward him still further, as soon as my deliverance was accomplished.

A little while after this they started again, accompanied by many of the natives, and going up the valley, took a steep path near its head, which led to Nukuheva. Here the Happars paused, and watched them as they ascended the mountain, one group of bandit-looking fellows, shaking their spears and casting threatening glances at the poor Typee, whose heart as well as heels seemed much the lighter when he came to look down upon them.

On gaining the heights once more, their way led for a time along several ridges covered with enormous ferns. At last they entered upon a wooded tract, and here they overtook a party of Nukuheva natives, well armed, and carrying bundles of long poles. Jimmy seemed to know them all very well, and stopped for a while, and had a talk about the *wee-wees,* as the people of Nukuheva call the monsieurs.

The party with the poles were King Mowanna's men, and by his orders they had been gathering them in the ravines for his allies the French.

Leaving these fellows to trudge on with their loads, Toby and his companions now pushed forward again, as the sun was already low in the west. They came upon the valleys of Nukuheva on one side of the bay, where the highlands slope off into the sea. The men-of-war were still lying in the harbor, and as Toby looked down upon them, the strange events which had happened so recently seemed all a dream.

They soon descended toward the beach, and found themselves in Jimmy's house before it was well dark. Here he received another welcome from his Nukuheva wives, and after some refreshments in the shape of coconut milk and *poee-poee*, they entered a canoe (the Typee, of course, going along) and paddled off to a whale ship which was anchored near the shore. This was the vessel in want of men. Our own had sailed some time before. The captain professed great pleasure at seeing Toby, but thought, from his exhausted appearance, that he must be unfit for duty. However, he agreed to ship him, as well as his comrade, as soon as he should arrive.

Toby begged hard for an armed boat, in which to go round to Typee and rescue me, notwithstanding the promises of Jimmy. But this the captain would not hear of, and told him to have patience, for the sailor would be faithful to his word. When, too, he demanded the five silver dollars for Jimmy, the captain was unwilling to give them. But Toby insisted upon it, as he now began to think that Jimmy might be a mere mercenary, who would be sure to prove faithless if not well paid. Accordingly he not only gave him the money, but took care to assure him, over and over again, that as soon as he brought me aboard he would receive a still larger sum.

Before sunrise the next day, Jimmy and the Typee started in two of the ship's boats, which were manned by tabooed natives. Toby, of course, was all eagerness to go along, but the sailor told him that if he did, it would spoil all; so, hard as it was, he was obliged to remain.

Toward evening he was on the watch, and descried the boats turning the headland and entering the bay. He strained his eyes, and thought he saw me; but I was not there. Descending from the mast almost distracted, he grappled Jimmy as he struck the deck, shouting in a voice that startled him, 'Where is Tommo?' The old fellow faltered, but soon recovering, did all he could to soothe him, assuring him that it had proved to be impossible to get me down to the shore that morning; assigning many plausible reasons, and adding that early on the morrow he was going to visit the bay again in a French boat, when, if he did not find me on the beach—as this time he certainly expected to—he would march right back into the valley, and carry me away at all hazards. He, however, again refused to allow Toby to accompany him.

Now, situated as Toby was, his sole dependence for the present was upon this Jimmy, and therefore he was fain to comfort himself as well as he could with what the old sailor had told him.

The next morning, however, he had the satisfaction of seeing the French boat start with Jimmy in it. Tonight, then, I will see him, thought Toby; but many a long day passed before he ever saw Tommo again. Hardly was the boat out of sight, when the captain came forward and ordered the anchor to be weighed; he was going to sea.

Vain were all Toby's ravings,—they were disregarded; and when he came to himself the sails were set, and the ship fast leaving the land.

. . . Oh! said he to me at our meeting, what sleepless nights were mine. Often I started from my hammock, dreaming you were before me, and upbraiding me for leaving you on the island.

There is little more to be related. Toby left this vessel at New Zealand, and after some further adventures, arrived home in less than two years after leaving the Marquesas. He always thought of me as dead—and I had every reason to suppose that he too was no more; but a strange meeting was in store for us, one which made Toby's heart all the lighter.

APPENDIX

THE AUTHOR OF this volume arrived at Tahiti the very day that the iniquitous designs of the French were consummated by inducing the subordinate chiefs, during the absence of their queen, to ratify an artfully drawn treaty, by which she was virtually deposed. Both menaces and caresses were employed on this occasion, and the 32-pounders which peeped out of the portholes of the frigate were the principal arguments adduced to quiet the scruples of the more conscientious islanders.

And yet this piratical seizure of Tahiti, with all the woe and desolation which resulted from it, created not half so great a sensation, at least in America, as was caused by the proceedings of the English at the Sandwich Islands. No transaction has ever been more grossly misrepresented than the events which occurred upon the arrival of Lord George Paulet at Oahu. During a residence of four months at Honolulu, the metropolis of the group, the author was in the confidence of an Englishman who was much employed by his lordship; and great was the author's astonishment on his arrival at Boston, in the autumn of 1844, to read the distorted accounts and fabrications which had produced in the United States so violent an outbreak of indignation against the English. He deems it, therefore, a mere act of justice toward a gallant officer briefly to state the leading circumstances connected with the event in question.

It is needless to rehearse all the abuse that for some time previous to the spring of 1843 had been heaped upon the British residents, especially upon Captain Charlton, Her Britannic Majesty's consul-general, by the native authorities of the Sandwich Islands. High in the favor of the imbecile king at this time was one Dr. Judd, a sanctimonious apothecary adventurer, who, with other kindred and influential spirits, was animated by an inveterate dislike to England. The ascendancy of a junto of ignorant and designing Methodist elders in the councils of a half-civilized king, ruling with absolute sway over a nation just poised between barbarism and civilization, and exposed by the peculiarities of its relations with foreign States to unusual difficulties, was not precisely calculated to impart a healthy tone to the policy of the government.

At last matters were brought to such an extremity, through the iniquitous maladministration of affairs, that the endurance of further insults and injuries on the part of the British consul was no longer to be borne. Captain Charlton, insultingly forbidden to leave the islands, clandestinely withdrew, and arriving at Valparaiso, conferred with Rear-Admiral Thomas, the English commander-in-chief on the Pacific station. In consequence of this communication, Lord George Paulet was dispatched by the Admiral in the *Carysfort* frigate, to inquire into and correct the alleged abuses. On arriving at his destination, he sent his first-lieutenant ashore with a letter to the king, couched in terms of the utmost courtesy, and soliciting the honor of an audience. The messenger was denied access to His Majesty, and Paulet was coolly referred to Doctor Judd, and informed that the apothecary was invested with plenary powers to treat with him. Rejecting this insolent proposition, His Lordship again addressed the King by letter, and renewed his previous request; but he encountered another repulse. Justly indignant at this treatment, he penned a third epistle, enumerating the grievances to be redressed, and demanding a compliance with his requisitions, under penalty of immediate hostilities.

The government was now obliged to act, and an artful stroke of policy was decided upon by the despicable counsellors of the King to entrap the sympathies and rouse the indignation of Christendom. His Majesty was made to intimate to the British captain that he could not, as the conscientious ruler of his beloved people, comply with the arbitrary demands of His Lordship, and in deprecation of the horrors of war, tendered to his acceptance the 'provisional cession' of the islands, subject to the result of the negotiations then pending in London. Paulet, a bluff and straightforward sailor, took the King at his word, and after some preliminary arrangements, entered upon the administration of Hawaiian affairs, in the same firm and benignant spirit which marked the discipline of his frigate, and which had rendered him the idol of his ship's company. He soon endeared himself to nearly all orders of the islanders; but the King and the chiefs, whose feudal sway over the common people is laboriously sought to be perpetuated by their missionary advisers, regarded all his proceedings with the most vigilant animosity. Jealous of his growing popularity, and unable to counteract it, they endeavored to assail his reputation abroad by ostentatiously protesting against his acts, and appealing in Oriental phrase to the *wide universe* to witness and compassionate their *unparalleled wrongs*.

Heedless of their idle clamors, Lord George Paulet addressed himself to the task of reconciling the differences among the foreign residents, remedying their grievances, promoting their mercantile interests, and ameliorating as far as lay in his power the condition of the degraded natives. The iniquities he brought to light and instantly suppressed are too numerous to be here recorded; but one instance may be mentioned that will give some idea of the lamentable misrule to which these poor islanders are subjected.

It is well known that the laws at the Sandwich Islands are subject to the most capricious alterations, which, by confounding all ideas of right and wrong in the minds of the natives produce the most pernicious effects. In no case is this mischief more plainly discernible than in the continually shifting regulations concerning licentiousness. At one time the most innocent freedoms between the sexes are punished with fine and imprisonment; at another the revocation of the statute is followed by the most open and undisguised profligacy.

It so happened that at the period of Paulet's arrival the Connecticut blue laws had been for at least three weeks steadily enforced. In consequence of this, the fort at Honolulu was filled with a great number of young girls, who were confined there doing penance for their slips from virtue. Paulet, although at first unwilling to interfere with regulations having reference solely to the natives themselves, was eventually, by the prevalence of certain reports, induced to institute a strict inquiry into the internal administration of General Kekuanoa, governor of the island of Oahu, one of the pillars of the Hawaiian Church, and captain of the fort. He soon ascertained that numbers of the young females employed during the day at work intended for the benefit of the King, were at night smuggled over the ramparts of the fort—which on one side directly overhangs the sea—and were conveyed by stealth on board such vessels as had contracted with the General to be supplied with them. Before daybreak they returned to their quarters, and their own silence with regard to these secret excursions was purchased by a small portion of those wages of iniquity which were placed in the hands of Kekuanoa.

The vigor with which the laws concerning licentiousness were at that period enforced, enabled the General to monopolize in a great measure the detestable trade in which he was engaged, and there consequently flowed into his coffers—and some say into those of the government also—considerable sums of money. It is indeed a lamentable fact, that the principal revenue of the Hawaiian government is derived from the fines levied upon, or rather the licences taken out by, Vice, the prosperity of which is linked with that of the government. Were the people to become virtuous the authorities would become poor; but from present indications there is little apprehension to be entertained on that score.

Some five months after the date of the cession, the *Dublin* frigate, carrying the flag of Rear-Admiral Thomas, entered the harbor of Honolulu. The excitement that her sudden appearance produced on shore was prodigious. Three days after her arrival an English sailor hauled down the red cross which had been flying from the heights of the fort, and the Hawaiian colors were again displayed upon the same staff.

At the same moment the long 42-pounders upon Punchbowl Hill opened their iron throats in triumphant reply to the thunders of the five men-of-war in the harbor; and King Kammahammaha III, surrounded by a splendid group of British and American officers, unfurled the royal standard to assembled thousands of his subjects, who, attracted by the imposing military display of the foreigners, had flocked to witness the formal restoration of the islands to their ancient rulers.

The Admiral, after sanctioning the proceedings of his subaltern, had brought the authorities to terms; and so removed the necessity of acting any longer under the provisional cession.

The event was made an occasion of riotous rejoicing by the king and the principal chiefs, who easily secured a display of enthusiasm from the inferior orders, by remitting for a time the accustomed severity of the laws. Royal proclamations in English and Hawaiian were placarded in the streets of Honolulu, and posted up in the more populous villages of the group, in which His Majesty announced to his loving subjects the re-establishment of his throne, and called upon them to celebrate it by breaking through all moral, legal, and religious restraint for ten consecutive days, during which time all the laws of the land were solemnly declared to be suspended.

Who that happened to be at Honolulu during those ten memorable days will ever forget them! The spectacle of universal broad-day debauchery, which was then exhibited, beggars description. The natives of the surrounding islands flocked to Honolulu by hundreds, and the crews of two frigates, opportunely let loose like so many demons to swell the heathenish uproar, gave the crowning flourish to the scene. It was a sort of Polynesian saturnalia. Deeds too atrocious to be mentioned were done at noonday in the open street, and some of the islanders caught in the very act of stealing from the foreigners, were, on being taken to the fort by the aggrieved party, suffered immediately to go at large and to retain the stolen property—Kekuanoa informing the white men, with a sardonic grin, that the laws were *hannapa* (tied up).

The history of these ten days reveals in their true colors the character of the Sandwich islanders, and furnishes an eloquent commentary on the results which have flowed from the labors of the missionaries. Freed from the restraints of severe penal laws, the natives almost to a man had plunged voluntarily into every species of wickedness and excess, and by their utter disregard of all decency plainly showed, that although they had been schooled into a seeming submission to the new order of things, they were in reality as depraved and vicious as ever.

Such were the events which produced in America so general an outbreak of indignation against the spirited and high-minded Paulet. He is not the first man who, in the fearless discharge of his duty, has awakened the senseless clamors of those whose narrow-minded suspicions blind them to a proper appreciation of measures which unusual exigencies may have rendered necessary.

It is almost needless to add that the British Cabinet never had any idea of appropriating the islands; and it furnishes a sufficient vindication of the acts of Lord George Paulet, that he not only received the unqualified approbation of his own government, but that to this hour the great body of the Hawaiian people invoke blessings on his head, and look back with gratitude to the time when his liberal and paternal sway diffused peace and happiness among them.